ONE HAND CLAPPING

BILL WILSON

For
Bill and Mary Jane

Foreword

This story begins in Russia in the early 1900's. As described in the first book, *MAJESTY*, the Milanov family is rich, powerful and well connected. However, when the Romanov dynasty is swept off the throne in 1917, the rest of the ruling class is doomed as well. The Bolsheviks snuff out the lives of the Baron and Baroness, but unlike the Tsar's family, the Milanov children survive.

The eldest, Joseph, avoids being killed by enemy fire in World War I, only to escape death by inches from a saber in the hand of his own corporal. His little sister, Catrina, witnesses their parent's brutal rape and murder, narrowly avoiding capture. She flees the family estate on her brother's horse, Majesty, and makes a daring trek across a perilous countryside to Latvia.

With the help of the American Ambassador in St. Petersburg, Catrina obtains passage to the United States to start a new life in the land of opportunity.

Meanwhile, hundreds of thousands of Russian soldiers, including Joseph, desert the army's ranks. Upon his return home, he finds that his former aristocratic lifestyle no longer exists. Joseph is forced to fend for himself in a hostile country besieged by civil war.

Catrina finds work in a tavern in St. Louis and rents a room on the second floor. She sets about getting acquainted with her new country and meets a black man named James, her future business partner.

In *ONE HAND CLAPPING*, the siblings tread diverse paths, encountering opportunity, struggle and heartache as the twentieth century plows forward.

Prologue

November, 1942
Stalingrad, USSR

Joseph had been hiding in the bitter cold behind a partly demolished wall for three hours, the light of dawn still half an hour away. Broken plaster and other debris covered the wooden floor. He heard muffled footsteps and indistinct sounds of someone moving cautiously in his direction. He had chosen this spot after days of watching, scrutinizing, fitting pieces together. His choice was only a prediction...the right one.

There is a moment when life is over. That moment was near for one of them. All the knowledge and wisdom accumulated over years, dreams that had been realized or discarded, each breath followed by another and another...soon would be irrelevant. Joseph gripped his rifle, though he hoped to be able to use his knife. A gunshot would bring other soldiers; the Germans in control of this sector as of yesterday.

The leg of the sniper that had shot his son was within an arm's reach as he passed. Joseph held his breath. *This is for Nikky,* he thought to himself as he rose up and plunged the eight inch blade into the man's back.

Chapter 1

June 15, 1920
Kansas City, Missouri

Kitty stood behind the counter with an apron on and her hair tied back. The windows were all open and the warm summer breeze was blowing the thin white curtains like flags on a ship. The screen door opened to the gentle tinkle of a bell. Kitty looked up to see who the customer was. Instead, she was rewarded with the smiling face of James Madison Monroe, proprietor.

James had sweat on his brow and a flower in his hand. "Happy anniversary! It's been six months since we opened the doors of this business, and I decided you need a break." He stepped up to the counter and handed her the long-stemmed yellow rose. She took the rose with a flour-covered hand and lifted it to her nose. "That was very kind of you, sir. What kind of break did you have in mind? Are you going to watch the counter this afternoon?"

"No! We're both going to take a break. I've made my deliveries for the day, so we're going on a picnic."

"But we can't just close up the store," Kitty protested. It's Thursday afternoon and we may have customers."

"We can do whatever we want. We're the owners."

Kitty pulled a stray wisp of hair back from her face and curled it behind her ear, knowing it would not be there for long. "OK, boss," she said with a smile. "It looks like a beautiful day. I could use a little sunshine."

It was three in the afternoon by the time they had gathered their things, loaded the buggy and ridden a couple of miles into the countryside. James turned into a pretty little meadow that had a stream running through the middle of it. Kitty spread out the blanket under a large oak tree and began to unpack their picnic basket while he unhitched the horse.

A pair of bluebirds frolicked in some nearby bushes. "I'm glad you talked me into this," said Kitty, as James sat down on the blanket and took his boots off. It's beautiful out here, but now I'm famished. You pour the tea. I've got a new dessert for you to try when you're done with your sandwich."

Kitty was gradually increasing the variety of pastries, cakes and pies they were selling. Still, their main products by far were the two types of Latvian cheesecake, which were called Sophina and Solina, named after Kitty's Latvian friends who had taught her how to make them. The recipes called for plenty of chocolate and nuts and were very popular.

They discussed how they could grow the business for about an hour and a half. It was decided that James would tack *HELP WANTED* signs on poles at nearby street corners, and put a sign in the store window. Kitty would take the buggy, laden with boxes of assorted samples and a price list, to the big downtown hotels. They worked out a rough discount scheme based on order volume.

By the time they were finished talking about how much money they were likely to make, it was five-thirty. James called Henrietta, who had been grazing nearby, and hitched her back up to the buggy.

Chapter 2

The ceiling of Union Station's main lobby was nearly eighty feet above his head. James had been in the station several times, but it still amazed him how they could have suspended such a beautiful, yet obviously heavy, roof so far above the ground. Not only was it high, he thought, but it must be three hundred feet across in both directions. It kind of gave him a funny feeling, like the whole thing could come crashing down on him.

He looked up at the big clock that read *two forty-five* and decided to go have a cup of coffee while he waited for the rain to stop. He approached the large double door to Fred Harvey's Restaurant. A sign read, *Wait To Be Seated*, so James stood behind a couple who were already in line. When it was his turn, he followed a short woman in a long black skirt to a table near the kitchen. He saw several tables in better locations, but let it pass.

He ordered, "Just coffee," and got it almost immediately. There were some advantages to being seated near the kitchen after all. He sat there day-dreaming for about twenty minutes.

In a booth to his left, two men were talking about the corn still being in the field and not being able to get it harvested with all the rain they'd been having up north. One of them pulled the napkin from where it was tucked into his shirt under his chin and placed it on his empty plate. "Let's see if we can get our check," he said. As he raised his arm to summon their waitress, the other man exclaimed, "Aren't you going to have dessert?"

James noticed that the second man was rather hefty and looked like he was used to having dessert to finish a meal.

His companion pulled his watch from a vest pocket and flipped it open. "Can't; I don't want to miss my train. I may get some in the diner car if I can get a table." He motioned for the waitress and pulled his wallet from his coat breast pocket.

This conversation had a profound effect on James. It hit him so fast and hard that his head was reeling with the implications; DESSERT.....DINER CAR, DESSERT....DINER CAR. What a market! He reached into his pocket, put a nickel on the table for his coffee and nearly ran for the door. He could hardly wait to tell Kitty about this.

Kitty's reaction could be described in many ways, elation not being one of them. She was pleased with her success in establishing several large clients to bolster their profit, but keeping up with the volume was now becoming a serious chore. They had already hired a second full-time employee, and any more major clients would push the capacity limits of the ovens. The baking was becoming a sixteen-hour-a-day endeavor.

Kitty wiped her flour-coated hands on her white apron. She tucked a loose lock of hair behind her ear and then wiped what was left of a stream of water off James's forehead. She smiled at her friend's crestfallen expression. "I'm sorry I threw cold water on your idea." Her smile broadened as she said this, moving her eyes over the dripping clothes covering his drenched body. "I'll sleep on it. We can talk tomorrow."

She turned to go back to the kitchen and the ovens but halted, mid-stride. "I'll tell you what. After your morning deliveries, let's go out to Lenexa and see if we can find Whispering Farms. It's been nearly a year since the American Royal. I want to see Majesty. We can talk about your idea on the way." Kitty had concentrated on the business every day, dreamed about Majesty every night. It was time. She wanted to see her horse.

❧

James and Kitty stood below the open sliding-door of an empty box car. They had taken the trolley down to the Argentine district in order to catch a train on the Santa Fe line. Up front, behind the locomotive, were three passenger cars, but James was advocating hitching a ride for free.

"We have enough money, James."

"Come on, Kitty; it's more fun this way. And we're only going about fifteen miles."

Kitty stuck the dollar that she had intended to use for their fare back into her pocket. "OK, but if somebody catches us, I'm going to tell them you kidnapped me."

Perched on the wooden planks of the floor, legs hanging out the door, they sat in silence as the train crawled forward. Soon, it was rolling down the tracks, whistle blowing at every dusty road-crossing. Argentine was the second and last stop after leaving Union Station, before breaking into open country. The next depot on the Santa Fe would be Lenexa, where the two planned to leap off just before the train stopped moving to avoid a confrontation about their free passage.

The stretch was all farmland and Kitty enjoyed just letting her hair blow in the wind. They were both a little disappointed when the train began to slow down, signaling the end of their ride.

Kitty jumped off first, landing on both feet but misjudging her momentum, causing her to tumble to the ground in a heap. James followed her, hit the ground running and kept his feet under him. He had planned to show Kitty this trick, but she jumped before he had the chance. When he turned, Kitty was bent over, slapping the dust off her shirt and pants. He trotted up to her, trying to keep a smile off his face. With as much concern as he could muster, he asked, "Are you all right?"

She stood up straight with a wince and looked him in the eye to detect any sign of the patronizing gaze she expected. James was an expert at disguising his emotions and expressions. In this case, her icy stare helped him bite back the wise crack he otherwise would have tossed her way.

As it was, a little discretion was the order of the day, so he turned her around by the shoulders and gently brushed the dirt and dust off her backside. When he was done, he casually pinched her rear and then ducked to avoid the backhand he knew to be coming. He retreated a couple of steps to a safer distance.

She shook her fist in a mock threat and said, "One more of those, buster, and your black ass is going to be draggin' the ground."

His eyes opened wide in feigned fright. His pinch had produced the desired result; the feisty frolicker he knew and loved was back. He bowed low in submission and offered his arm, which she took as they proceeded to stroll into town.

James was leaning against a sturdy fence post, chewing on a piece of grass. Kitty was sitting with her legs dangling over the middle rail, with her elbows and chin propped on the top rail. The fence running around the perimeter of Whispering Farms was the beautiful white variety that was typical of Kentucky horse country. Both were thinking it also looked impressive in Kansas. The lush green grass blew in the wind like waves on a large lake. The white fence sectioned off several pastures, presumably to either separate certain animals or to rotate the grazing.

Kitty's eyes were focused on a group of horses that were grazing in a pasture about a quarter of a mile in from the perimeter. There was another fence between her and the group, but she thought she could make out the golden sheen of Majesty's coat amongst them.

As Kitty started to slide through the rails, following her legs to the ground, she said, "Let's go see if that's Majesty or not." She began striding through the pasture before James could protest.

He called after her, "Maybe we should go up to the house and ask if we can do this. You're trespassing, you know." Kitty did not respond, which was no surprise to James. He shrugged his shoulders, "What the hell; you can't live forever."

He climbed through the rails and started out after her at a trot. They had covered about half of the quarter mile to the next fence when they heard the pounding of hooves behind them and to the left. James stopped to see who or what was coming. Kitty just kept walking.

The rider reined up his horse ten yards directly in front of Kitty, blocking her path. She had little recourse but to stop and look up at the young man who was in his early twenties, wearing jeans and a blue-and-white long-sleeved shirt. He wore a sweat-stained cowboy hat, mostly hiding what looked like sandy red hair. His face was well tanned and covered with freckles.

"This is private property. You need to turn around and go back where you came from." He added, "Miss" as an afterthought.

James, who had just reached Kitty's side, said amiably, "We're sorry, sir. We just wanted to see the horses." He nodded his head in the direction of the grazing animals.

"Like I said, this is private property. Mr. Wax does not allow people to roam around his farm, so you best be on your way."

Kitty nonchalantly took a couple of steps sideways so she had a line of sight to the horses. Surprising both James and the farm hand, she pursed her lips and let out two shrill whistles. Both were pitched high and then jumped to a low note. Her action was obviously directed toward the grazing horses, which caused the men to shift their attention from Kitty to the herd.

One of the horses was bearing down on the tall white fence as if he would run right through it. At precisely the right moment, the golden stallion went airborne with a graceful leap that cleared the fence by a good foot.

The farm hand took off his hat, stunned by what he saw. Aurum, his boss's prize stallion, was now heading directly for them. He'd heard tales of animals going crazy if they happened to eat enough *loco weed*, marijuana that grows wild all across Kansas.

The man shifted his gaze back to the young woman and was surprised to see her smiling in the face of imminent danger. The horse was charging directly at them, yet there was not the slightest hint of concern or fear in her expression. The man's own horse had its ears pricked up, nervously alert. Just as it looked as if the stallion couldn't help but run them down, he broke his stride and managed to halt his momentum.

Making the low, throaty sounds that horses use to communicate with each other, the stallion began nuzzling the young woman with his nose. She reached an arm around his neck, affectionately, and said something in a strange language the man could not understand. Then, grabbing a fistful of mane at the base of the stallion's neck with her left hand, she leaped and swung her right leg over his back into riding position.

It was a slick move on a tall horse, and the farm hand was more than a little impressed. Actually, by now he was somewhat dumbfounded. *Who is this girl? What are she and this colored guy doing, walking around out in the country? And how in the hell did she manage to get Aurum, who was about as friendly as a pissed-off bobcat, to jump a fence and come running up like the family dog?*

While these thoughts were running through the farm hand's mind, Kitty was patting Majesty on the neck and talking softly into his ear. His head kept coming around as if to confirm who was sitting on his back. Finally, Kitty rose up and said to the farm hand, "This is my horse, or, at least, he's my brother's horse, and I'm supposed to be taking care of him."

The farm hand just looked at her blankly, not able to think of a suitable reply at the moment.

Then Kitty said something in an unintelligible language, followed by a nearly imperceptible nudge with her heels. The golden stallion took off like he was shot from a cannon.

The farm hand turned to the colored man and said, "What did she say?"

James shrugged his shoulders and raised his eyebrows. "Who knows? She's Russian, and so is the horse."

They both watched as horse and rider flew across the open field. There was little doubt that this young woman, with her long black hair streaming behind her, had spent most of her life on the back of a horse. The pasture was an eighty-acre section. James was wondering if Kitty and Majesty would leap the fence at the far end. The farm hand was thinking exactly the same thing. There was no point following her. Nothing on this farm could catch that horse, not the way she was letting him run.

To both men's relief, Kitty veered to the right and began to follow the perimeter of the fence that would bring her back to where they stood. James looked up at the farm hand, shading his eyes from the sun with his hand, and said, "Kitty says his name is *Majesty*. Where did this *Aurum* come from?"

The farm hand looked down at James and smiled. "You know, I asked the same question myself when that horse came to Whispering Farms. Mr. Wax says it's Latin for *Gold*."

James just nodded his head thoughtfully. They watched as Kitty and Majesty worked their way back to them.

When the pair approached, the horse was barely breathing hard, and the rider had a smile on her face that couldn't be wiped off with a saddle blanket. The farm hand took off his hat with his left hand, holding the reins in the crook of his right arm. He asked, with a smile of his own, "Where did you learn how to ride? That horse is mighty particular about who rides him, and he treats you like you raised him from a colt."

Kitty, jubilant from the reunion and the ride, looked down at James with an expression that said, *Isn't that what I just told this guy?* She lifted her right leg over Majesty's neck and slid off his back in a dismount that was as smooth and natural as her earlier display. She patted Majesty on the neck once more and then turned to the farm hand. She walked over and reached up, offering her hand, "I'm Kitty Wixon and this really is...was my horse. I'm planning on buying him back from your boss."

The man hesitated, then put his hat back on and reached down to shake Kitty's right hand with his left. The unfamiliar gesture drew Kitty's glance to the man's pinned-up right sleeve. The smile left her face, and there was an awkward moment before he said, "My name is Billy O'Riley." He lifted the pinned sleeve and said, "Lost my hand in France two years ago." With a smile that revealed no embarrassment, he added, "But I've learned to use my left to do most everything." After another pause, he gave her a shy look, "Actually, shaking hands is the one thing that I haven't gotten used to yet."

Kitty found herself drawn to the kind, boyish face. His vulnerable demeanor and shy smile showed a touch of innocence. Still, if he'd been fighting in France, lost a hand and managed to come back and hold down a job like this, there must be a depth there that would be interesting to know.

She turned and grabbed James by the elbow with both hands, drawing him closer to them. "This is James Monroe. He's a friend of mine as well as my business partner."

James automatically extended his hand and said, "Pleased to meet you."

This time Billy did not hesitate to take it, but before he did, James shot his left hand out and retracted his right, saying, "Let's try it this way." He smiled as the hands clasped in the natural grip, and Billy smiled back.

Billy turned his attention back to Kitty. "Tell you what. If you want to come out and ride Aurum or Majesty or whatever you want to call him, I'll try to see that he's in a place that you can get to him without being seen. The only thing is; I'd need to know when you're coming."

Kitty's heart leapt at the thought of being able to ride Majesty again. She frowned for a second, considering the offer. Finally, she said, "How about if I try to come out on Sunday afternoons? That's really the only day I can get away, and if I can't make it I could call you. This farm has a telephone, doesn't it?"

"Sundays sound fine, but I don't know about the telephone. Of course, there's a telephone in the big house, but I'm not so sure calling me on it is such a good idea. Let's just say, if you come you come, and if you don't, you don't." He shrugged his shoulders.

Kitty said, "That's very kind of you, Mr. O'Riley." She tapped James on the arm with the back of her fist and said, "Let's go." As they turned to leave, Kitty stopped to put her hands on either side of Majesty's head and kissed his nose. In Russian she said, "See you next week, my friend."

As they started walking back across the field to the road, Majesty turned to fall in step. Kitty stopped and looked at Majesty and smiled sadly. Then she looked back at Billy, raising her eyebrows.

"Seems to like you," he said. He dismounted and unfastened the halter on his own horse. He walked over to Majesty, slipping the halter over his head and said, "I'll keep a hold of him till you two are out of sight."

Kitty was silent during the two-mile walk back to the train depot except for sporadic comments like, "Boy, I miss riding him." And, "He can still run as fast as ever." And, "At least they've been taking good care of him." They took the train back to Kansas City and, this time, rode in the dining car as paying customers.

As the train was pulling away from the Lenexa depot, Kitty looked at James sitting across the table from her and said, "OK, let's talk about your idea of targeting the railroad food business."

James was ready to lay out the plan for her and proceeded to do so in the twenty-five minutes they had before reaching Union Station. He had purchased tickets to the downtown station because he wanted Kitty to experience the hustle and bustle surrounding Fred Harvey's Restaurant.

As he talked, he used the menu as a prop to illustrate to Kitty how their desserts would be a natural fit with the elaborate offerings already there. The menu not only listed what could be ordered in the dining car, it also had a section for Harvey's Lunchroom and Dining room meals at the next stop. In this case, the next major stop was Kansas City Union Station.

James did all of the talking. Kitty sat there listening, but he could see her mind absorbing and expanding on what he said. He knew that if he could get her on board with this idea, its fruition was assured. *We make a great team,* he thought to himself.

Chapter 3

April 30, 1921
Kansas City, Missouri

James stood with one foot on the bumper of their 1919 Model-T Ford truck. He had his left hand on his hip and his right arm in a white cotton sling. One of the guys who normally worked in the bakery was trying to get the truck's engine to turn over with the hand crank. It had rained last night, and the truck was not acting like it was going anywhere this morning. The tricky part is if the engine does turn over, the hand crank is thrown back the other direction and can easily break a person's arm; which is exactly why James had his arm in a sling and a scowl on his face.

The delivery truck was black and had *KITTY'S KAKES* written in red script on both doors. The letters had a white pin stripe along the edge, and a large white cake was painted on the black tarp that covered the bed in case of rain.

Under his breath, James mumbled to himself, "I told her we needed a truck. I told her we could save money if we didn't buy a brand new one. I should have told her we ought to just get another horse and wagon.....come on, Wray, just one more turn." Wray was a blond, curly-headed kid with fair skin and a boyish, nineteen-year-old face. He was doing his best with the crank, because if he got the truck started it meant that he would get to drive the deliveries with the boss instead of working at the ovens. Handling the gears on a Model-T required one hand, and steering required the other. Therefore, if he didn't screw up, he might get to be outside for several weeks until James's arm healed.

The reason they bought the truck in the first place was that James's idea of selling to the Harvey House system along the Santa Fe line had blossomed

12

just as he had hoped.

Once Kitty warmed up to the idea, she worked out a plan to get an appointment with Byron Harvey. It was a matter of finding out when he was going to be coming through Kansas City. Then she called Governor Gardner and asked him for the favor he had offered a year and a half ago. The three of them met for lunch at the Coates Hotel, and Kitty had pre-arranged the dessert options. The Coates was already a Kitty Kakes customer, so she merely asked that a piece of Sophina, their signature cheesecake, be served when the plates had been cleared.

The plan had worked...sort of. Mr. Harvey was so taken with the rich, creamy dessert, that when he found out Kitty had made it, he asked her to come work for him. "We don't have any female bakers or chefs, but I'll pay you the same as I pay our men." This was a compliment of the highest sort from the very successful restaurateur.

The lunch had been set up as a chance to discuss a business opportunity. Kitty and Governor Gardner felt that giving Mr. Harvey an objective trial of the dessert was the best way to get him to play his hand first. Kitty and the governor were both taken aback by the job offer. He recovered first and said, "Byron, I know we're old friends, but I didn't ask you to meet with me to find this young lady a job."

Byron broke in, "I'm not doing anything out of charity. I think this Sophina, or whatever it is, is excellent. I'd love to serve it to my customers."

At this point, the governor turned to Kitty and gave her a significant nod as if to say *OK, you can take it from here.*

Kitty said, "Mr. Harvey, my partner and I own a bakery. We make desserts for restaurants around Kansas City." She smiled and continued, "I'll bet you thought I worked in the Coates Hotel kitchen, didn't you?"

Byron Harvey was a very sharp man and he was leaping ahead of Kitty. There was little mystery as to where this was leading now. He nodded dumbly to her question but said nothing. He was ready for her to play *her* hand.

"I...we would like to make our desserts for your Kansas City restaurant and..." she hesitated. She was going to say, *if you like, we could make them for your other restaurants and your diner car business.* But instead, she offered, "We are willing to sell them on a consignment basis."

She and James had talked about how far to go as a first step. They couldn't decide, so they agreed that she would play it by ear. When it came down to it, Kitty decided that getting a foot in the door was the most important thing. So she went the conservative route.

Mr. Harvey responded, "You mean, if my restaurant sells your desserts you get paid; but if we don't, you bake them, deliver them, and then get nothing?" He knew what consignment meant, but he wanted to make sure she knew.

The deal was made. It was a well-known fact that Harvey's pies were cut in four servings instead of the traditional six. However, Sophina and Solina were so rich that they would be served in eighths. Otherwise, no one would be able to finish both their dinner and dessert. Each piece would be sold for forty cents and Kitty's Kakes would get half, which came out to one dollar and sixty cents per tin.

Chapter 4

July 8, 1921
Tula, Russia

Joseph Milanov leaned against the wall of a building in the center of town talking with Felix and a couple of strangers. "How far did you come today?" one of the strangers asked.

"Thirty miles," said Joseph. "If the talk is true, we decided it was worth it. We haven't had a drop of rain in over two months."

"Our crops have withered to nothing," the man replied.

Tula was the largest town in the region. There had been rumors that government aid, in the form of flour and seed-grain, was going to be distributed today. The news had filled the streets with people, carts and horses. Families were beyond hungry. They were beginning to starve and violence had been reported across the land.

Joseph caught someone staring at him and turned away. The scar on his face never failed to draw unwanted attention. The wound caused his left eye to droop and pulled his upper lip into a sneer. During the last four years the skin had healed, his self consciousness had not.

A toddler was hanging on to Joseph's leg as they waited for the women to finish their errands. The boy's name was Nikky, named after the man Joseph referred to as Uncle Nicholas, the last Tsar of the three-hundred-year Romanov dynasty. Nikky was nearly one and a half, his tiny hands clutching the coarse fabric of his father's pant leg, more for security than for balance.

A commotion of some sort could suddenly be heard off in the distance. It drew everyone's attention, though it was too far away to determine its cause. Elbows and shoulders were being used to gain advantage as the crowd began to compress in the direction of the noise. Joseph stood on his toes to try to see over their heads. He moved closer to the moving mass to get a better angle.

Felix jerked on Joseph's arm, spinning him to his left. Nikky had spotted his mother crossing the street through an opening in the crowd and was stumbling toward her, arms outstretched. His attempt to run was an awkward, stiff-legged, stop and start, adventure. He was nearly to the corner of the building where the surging mob of people threatened to crush him beneath boots, wheels and hooves.

"Nikky, stop!" Joseph yelled to no avail. He took a step in pursuit, realized he couldn't get there in time and yelled again. "NIKKY, STOP!!" This time, the words cut through the clamor like the enraged growl of a bear. The boy's legs melted, frightened by the harshness in his father's voice. He curled up on the ground, crying, just inches from being trampled.

Joseph moved quickly, stooped over and lifted Nikky into his arms. "It's Ok now. There...there, don't cry. Papa's got you." He tenderly hugged his son, the child's tears slippery on their cheeks. Irina emerged through the edge of the crowd and saw her husband and son locked in the embrace. She hesitated, curious of what had happened, yet not wanting to spoil the moment. Angry and desperate men pushed and scuffled past them, unnoticed. She stepped to Joseph's side, set down her basket of goods, and wrapped her arms around her husband and their son.

Chapter 5

Billy O'Riley and Kitty were enjoying their regular Sunday ride together, even though the day was a hot, ninety-five degrees. The powerful, mid-summer Kansas sun couldn't find a cloud in the sky to hide behind. Billy was used to being baked by the sun and didn't think anything of it. Kitty, on the other hand, was used to the heat of the ovens, but her skin was not tanned to a golden brown as his was and she was feeling it on her bare arms. She had her hair pulled off her neck and stuck under a wide brimmed straw hat that shaded her face and neck, but she was getting hot and sticky.

Billy's boss, Martin Wax, who Kitty now called *Marty*, had long since been aware of, and formally consented to, these weekly rides. After the first few weeks, he had confronted Billy regarding the movement of his prize stallion from pasture to pasture on Sundays. Billy was reluctant to spoil the routine by admitting Kitty's visits, but he refused to lie to his boss or anyone else.

As it turned out, the boss didn't mind his stallion getting the exercise. And when Billy described the obvious relationship between horse and rider and the fact that the rider truly did intend to buy the stallion back at some point, the businessman side of him rose to the surface. He remembered the scene at the American Royal and the ten-thousand-dollar price tag he had quoted off the top of his head. He thought he had chosen a figure so far beyond the young girl's means that it would close the book. *If she was actually trying to raise the money, and would pay the price, so much the better.*

In any case, Marty liked the handsome young woman and he admired her riding skill. Not only had he blessed their riding rendezvous, he had agreed to let them range beyond the confines of Whispering Farms. The farm covered nearly a thousand acres, but Kitty and Billy often chose to venture out for a change in scenery and today was one of those days.

Kitty looked over and saw the sweat trailing down Billy's face. "How about heading over to the stream and getting a drink," she offered.

He replied with a smile, "Race ya," and spurred his horse into a canter before Kitty could react.

She didn't have to do anything. Majesty reacted for her. He was at a dead run in about four steps, and Kitty's years of experience were the only reason she wasn't left lying on the ground in his wake. Majesty made up the few-lengths head start that Billy had, and the horses were now running neck and neck. They galloped across the open field, riders trusting their mounts to avoid chuck holes and ditches. Billy's hat had slid off his head and was trailing behind, a string securing it to his neck. Kitty was able to grab her hat just as it was parting from her head, holding it in her right hand, her left hand clutching the reins. Long black hair was whipping in the breeze behind her.

Their minds and bodies were no longer aware of the heat. The intensity and thrill of the chase captivated them like a magical elixir. Majesty was beginning to pull ahead when they reached the grove of trees that lined both sides of the stream. The riders reined in their horses and came to a halt in a cloud of dust. They dismounted and Billy panted, "Why don't we give the horses a rest for a while. They deserve it."

Kitty started to remove the English riding saddle from Majesty's back. "Might as well let them cool down in the stream while we're at it. By the way, I beat you, you know."

Billy had his back turned to her, loosening the girth on his gelding. Over his shoulder he said, "You didn't beat me, Aurum... I mean, Majesty did. Before the boss bought that horse of yours, my *Traveler* here was the fastest thing in the stables for three hundred yards. That two-year-old that Mr. Wax traded for Majesty was fast, but this guy could still beat him in a sprint." He pulled the western work-saddle off Traveler's sweaty back and dropped it to the ground in the shade of a tree.

They could hear the water gurgling through the trees. An animal trail led through the brush, so they followed it down to the stream which was about twenty feet wide. The water was clear and tumbling over rocks at either end of a large pool. There was a flat, open space at the base of the path, so Billy sat down and began taking off his boots and socks. Kitty sat down next to him while the horses walked knee deep into the cool water, lowered their snouts and began drinking their fill.

Even with the missing hand, Billy quickly had his boots off and began unbuttoning his shirt. Kitty looked at him and said, "You going swimming?"

"I hadn't planned on it, but it's not a bad idea. I was just going to soak my shirt to help me cool off." He rolled his pant legs up to his knees and stood up. He waded in about three steps, reached down with a cupped hand for a drink. "This water feels great!"

As he stooped over for more water, a hefty shove from behind caught him by surprise. He came up splashing and sputtering. In water now above his waist, he turned around to address the guilty party.

Kitty, standing in the water only to her ankles, had a grin on her face. She had taken off her pants, her white cotton bloomers covering her legs to just below the knees. Her hands were casually moving from button to button. Her shirt began to separate.

Billy stood there with his tongue lying in the bottom of his mouth, immobile. Finally, at the top of his lungs he let out what sounded like an Indian war cry, "Eeeeyyaaahhoooo; let's go swimming!!!" He leapt backwards into the middle of the pool and disappeared under the surface of the water.

Kitty tossed her sleeveless shirt onto the grassy bank and waded deeper into the stream. The water had just reached her camisole when she felt her legs being lifted off the sandy bottom. She flew through the air, splashed and disappeared.

This time it was her turn to come up sputtering, her feet no longer touching the bottom. She treaded water while wiping her eyes, looking around for Billy. He was nowhere to be seen, which told her to get ready for another assault. Suddenly from behind, she felt a hand on her shoulder, and under she went. She wriggled free, swam underwater to where it was shallower, and stood up.

Billy was following her with a big smile on his face, so she splashed him in the eyes the way she used to do to her brother back at Lake Kaspl'a. He responded in kind and a battle ensued, both flailing wildly in the midst of the turbulent onslaught.

Finally, getting the worst of it because of his missing hand, Billy leapt at Kitty, wrapping his arms around her and causing them both to go under the surface. He managed to get his feet under him, and straightened up, with Kitty still firmly in his grasp. Her arms were pinned to her side, but she was no longer struggling.

As the water streamed down their faces, they looked into each other's eyes. After several seconds of being pressed together, Kitty raised up and kissed him briefly on his wet lips, followed immediately by a hard pinch on the back of his leg.

Billy's heart soared as he shrieked in pain. He automatically released his hold on her and grabbed the back of his leg. With her freedom, Kitty took off running, if it could be called that in the waist-high water. She gained speed as it got shallower. She could hear the splashing behind her. Just as she reached the shore, her wrist was grasped in his confident grip.

Billy's weight and strength ended her escape, as he spun her around and slid his handless right arm around the small of her back. His movements slowed and became deliberate. With his left hand, and a serious and attentive expression, he gently pulled her streaming black hair away from her face. He noted the exaggerated widow's peak outlining her forehead, and then focused on her brilliant blue eyes.

Their faces were only inches apart, and Kitty could feel her heart pounding. *Or was it his chest beating against her breast?* He stooped slightly and tilted his head as their lips met in a firm and mutual kiss. Her arms rose to his shoulders as the kiss became hungrier. She felt his tongue moving, and she parted her lips to let him inside. His hand began to slide up and down her back. He reached down farther, squeezing her firm body and pulling her hips into his.

Billy marveled at the sweetness he tasted in her mouth. It was like she was a fresh spring flower, but he could sense the fire that was warming up inside her. They waded ashore and he began to lower her to the grassy bank.

He lay beside Kitty, in awe of her beautiful, clear face. Water droplets on her skin shimmered in the sunlight. She held his gaze for a moment with her eyes, and then let it go. His interest was drawn by the sheer, soaked camisole and bloomers, which clung to her like a coat of wet paint. The image left little to the imagination.

He became aware of his hand, which had been unconsciously caressing Kitty's cheek, and laid it gently on her rising and falling breast. He knew the excitement inside him was shared as he felt her nipple harden under his touch. Her eyes were serenely closed. Instinctively, he took a deep breath to calm himself. Apparently, the next move was his. She seemed content to let him lead, but what to do? His desire and nervous energy were about to overwhelm him. He didn't want to mess up the miracle that was happening by being too bold. He kissed her closed eyelids and the end of her nose. He nibbled on her ear lobes, and then kissed her neck with a dozen tiny kisses, bringing a smile to her lips, though her eyes were still closed.

Billy ran his fingers along all the contours of her body, barely touching her. He squeezed her hips and massaged her thighs, afraid of committing himself, of risking it all. He ran his palm along her flat stomach, still undecided. Slowly and gently, he slid his fingers underneath the edge of her bloomers. His heart was banging against his chest, and he was afraid she could feel the trembling in his fingers. A glance at her face gave no indication of alarm or encouragement. She just lay there as if daydreaming of the summer fair. He took that as a positive sign and hesitated no more.

The next time Billy looked at Kitty's face he saw a pair of blue beacons, not angry or sad. Her eyes were filled with innocence and a single tear. She reached up and pulled his face down to hers, pleading for a kiss to match his caress.

With joyful relief, he pressed himself against the entire length of her body and kissed her with all the love he felt at that moment. Surely, he must have died and gone to heaven.

Billy's touch began to send shivers through Kitty's body, her nipples protruding into the clinging camisole. She lifted his head, raised her camisole and then pressed his face firmly into her soft, white flesh. Kitty groaned as he suckled on her breast like an infant.

The pleasure and wonder of what followed would stay with them for the rest of their lives; sharing that first time, learning, knowing what to do instinctively. As they lay side by side in the sand their chests swelled in unison, taking in the warm summer air. The moisture on Kitty's smooth skin glistened in the sunlight. She rolled halfway on top of him, resting her head on his shoulder. She closed her eyes and listened to the birds as her body melted into his. It was an incredible bond.

After a while Kitty's thoughts drifted to an evening long ago, when she and Anastasia had spied on Marie and Peter in the rose garden. How far away Russia seemed, but it didn't matter as much anymore. This would be her home now.

Chapter 6

December 17, 1922
Kansas City, Missouri

James stood in the doorway to the office with a wreath in one hand and a red ribbon tied in a bow in the other. He tapped lightly on the doorjamb with a knuckle to get Kitty's attention. She had her elbow on the desk, propping her head up with her fist. Through the window, big flakes of snow were drifting lazily to the ground. Kitty's thoughts appeared to be drifting along with them.

The rap on the door snapped her back to the present. She looked up to see who was intruding on her day-dream.

"Do you know where there is some wire so I can attach this ribbon to the wreath and then hang it in the front window?" James spoke softly, matching the calm serenity of the room and snow outside.

Kitty had been doing the books before floating off to an imaginary wonderland of snowballs and ice forts. *Her brother Joseph, as always, decided where the fort would be built and where the enemy would come from.* Snow always reminded her of those cold Russian winters when she and her brother would play till it got dark and then warm up by the stove in the kitchen, where Sophie would make them hot chocolate.

Kitty shook her head just perceptibly to clear it. "Wire, wire...let's see. Try the bottom drawer under the counter in the store. I think that's where we put it when you were fixing that lamp. And if it's not there, I'll bet Wray could tell you where to find some. He's always tinkering with something."

Kitty got up from the desk and followed James out the door, turning the light out behind her. Her office opened onto a catwalk above the bakery floor. They had expanded the bakery three times since landing the Fred Harvey restaurant and dining car account. They now ran two shifts with around thirty employees in each shift.

It was six in the evening, which put it mid-way into the break between the two shifts. James was the one who suggested the evening schedule, avoiding yet another expansion. Kitty agreed to the idea but insisted on a three-hour break between shifts. This allowed the ovens, and the bakery itself, time to cool down and rest, as well as providing some sanity time for management.

Kitty and James were the management, but they had promoted Wray Brady to oversee the night group. He had been with them two years, had shown his ability to think on his feet, and got along well with co-workers. The owners normally arrived at seven, an hour before the day shift began. They were usually in and out during the nine-hour shift, and left around six. That made for an eleven-hour day.

The bakery had become highly successful, breaking into the bread and dinner-roll business, although desserts remained their forte. In addition to the specialty desserts, the Harvey House chain used their bakery as a back-up for any of their multitude of locations that needed assistance. Sometimes it would be a problem with the local ovens, and other times, it would be their shortage in baking staff.

Byron Harvey was renowned, as was his father, Fred, for maintaining the strictest standards for employees. It was not unusual for someone to get walking papers for some minor infraction of the Harvey *code*. If it happened to be the head baker, Kitty's Kakes was available to load a train car with baked goods and have them delivered to the desired location on the Santa Fe line almost before the guy could clean out his locker.

It was more likely, however, for them to supplement a Harvey Hotel or lunchroom restaurant when a large group or special event was expected. Even though Kitty actually closed the deal, she always gave James complete credit for the Harvey contract and resulting boom in business. The two of them were becoming rich for their efforts.

Chapter 7

October, 1926
Russia, 150 miles southeast of Moscow

"Don't move," Joseph whispered. He carefully pushed a branch to the side so he and Nikky had a clear view of the deer as they approached the spring-fed waterhole. They had been hiding downwind, behind a fallen log and some brush, since an hour before sunrise for this moment. He wetted his finger with his tongue and touched the bead at the end of the barrel to diminish the glare from the early-morning sun. Nikky solemnly followed suit, his slender finger touching the end of his stick, a weapon every bit as lethal as his father's.

The rifle that Joseph was aiming had been the demise of many Hungarian and German soldiers during the War. Nikki's oak branch had been carved with care the night before and had not yet been tested in battle, or a hunting expedition such as this. "Look there," Joseph whispered, "the buck is coming out."

Nikky closed his left eye and tilted his head as he had been taught, sighting down the long straight stick with his right eye. His finger held steady on the protruding nub, his trigger. He waited for his father, his excitement gnawing at the patience he had been sworn to maintain. *"You can't come along if you're not able to be calm and wait for the right moment,"* his father had said.

The large buck carried an impressive rack of antlers. Wary of being exposed in the open, the animal held its head high, turning it back and forth, sniffing the air, searching for danger. Finding none, it dipped its head to drink.

"As soon as he raises up," whispered Joseph. "Aim right behind the front leg. Ready? ...One, two," ...BANG! The loud report from the rifle hurt the six-year-old's ears. He dropped his stick, squeezed his eyes shut and covered both ears with his small hands against the ringing in his head.

Joseph peered through the puff of smoke, watching as the leader of the herd half-leapt, half-staggered and fell. The other deer scattered in a blink, vanishing into the safety of the trees. Jumping to his feet, Joseph lifted Nikky by the elbow and pulled a long-bladed knife from the sheath on his belt. "Come on, we need to make sure he's dead. If he's only wounded he might run for miles."

Nikky picked up his stick and the coil of rope they had brought with them, and hurried after his dad, who was striding through the brush and tall grass of the meadow.

Joseph knelt down and slit the already-dead animal's throat, then took a hold of the two hind legs and dragged it several more feet away from the water's edge. "Don't want to foul their drinking hole."

"What a beauty," said Nikky, repeating a phrase he'd often heard his dad use.

"He's a big one all right." Joseph smiled and placed a hand on his son's shoulder. "Good, you brought the rope. You're the best hunting partner I've got."

Nikky beamed with pride from the kind words.

Joseph looked around for a tree with a strong branch at the right height. Spotting one about twenty feet away, he stripped off his shirt and said, "Let's get to work." The deer's blood was already draining out the cut he'd made in the neck. With the point of his sharp hunting knife, he punctured the abdomen below the rib cage and cut a deep gash all the way to the rear end. He handed the knife to Nikky and inserted his arms into the animals belly all the way to his elbows and began pulling out the entrails. "The liver is for us. The animals can have the rest." Joseph handed the dark red organ to his son. "Go wash this off and set it on that rock."

The deer was lighter with its insides removed but still a heavy load as Joseph struggled to drag it over to the tree he had chosen earlier. He looped the rope around the antlers and tossed the other end over the branch. "OK son, pull." Joseph lifted the animal's carcass six feet off the ground. Nikky tugged on the end of the rope, taking up the slack. "Now wrap your end around that tree three or four times," Joseph instructed, while his knuckles turned white, bearing the weight.

They washed off the blood in the ice cold spring water and Joseph put his shirt back on. "Let's go get the horses."

The road they followed along the edge of the forest had knee-high grass growing between the two ruts. It was not much more than a trail, and seldom used because there was no bridge at the point it met the river. Mouka carried both riders, with Nikky perched on their night-blankets and holding on to his father's belt with one hand. His other hand clutched a rope leading their second horse which had the deer-carcass tied over its back. A large set of antlers, the rifle, and Nikky's carved stick were strapped down along-side the headless carcass.

When they reached the river, Joseph could tell the water was lower than normal by the markings on the far bank. However, it was not as low as he'd hoped. "I think we can make it. What do you think, son?"

Nikky looked doubtfully at the water's steady current. "Let's wait until we get to the bridge."

Joseph looked up at the sun. "Maybe we should see how deep it is first. It's a long way to the main road where the bridge is. Hand me the lead rope and put both your arms around me. If it starts to get deep, we'll turn around."

Nikky was scared, but he trusted his father above everything else. He locked a death grip around Joseph's middle. His arms were too short for his fingers to touch.

Several hours later, the river and forests were well behind them. The rolling hills and grassland extended to the horizon. When the horses climbed out of a draw onto flat ground, they had reached the outer edge of their crops. Sasha's gleeful barks announced their arrival. The two older boys, Vasily and Fedor, were digging potatoes in the field. Both stood and waved, dropping their diggers and sacks to greet the hunters.

"Looks like they are ready for a break," Joseph said over his shoulder to Nikky.

Sasha escorted the riders, weaving perilously close to the horses' hooves and making a nuisance of himself. Joseph held out his forearm so his son could grab it and swing down to the ground. Sasha immediately started licking the boy's hands and face, tail wagging with excitement. Joseph dismounted and stamped his feet on the ground to loosen up his legs after the long ride.

"Look's like we're eatin' good tonight," said Vasily in his squawky voice as the two boys approached. Both boys had a rash of pimples on forehead and chin.

"That's a big buck. Did you shoot him, Nikky?" Fedor asked with a good-natured smile.

"We shot at the same time. Papa said I got him, but he had the real gun," the boy admitted.

"Looks like twelve points," said Vasily, admiring the impressive rack of antlers.

"Are they back from town yet? Joseph asked, referring to the group that had gone to the market the day before.

"Not when we left the house. They probably got a late start." Fedor leaned his head back and pretended to be chugging down a bottle of vodka. They all chuckled at his antics.

"You're probably right," Joseph agreed. "Well, we need to get going. If you two are about done out here, I'm going to need someone to take a couple of packages of venison over the hill once the butchering is done."

"We'd be happy to, Joseph," said Vasily. "We're almost to the end of a row." They had a longstanding arrangement with two neighboring farms, to share meat whenever one brought home more than enough for their own use. Vasily and Fedor much preferred the prospect of riding to one of the farms to deliver meat - over spending a couple more hours digging potatoes.

Joseph worked at a table near the open double doors where the light was better. The shed had many uses, including storage of farm equipment, stalls for sick livestock or those birthing offspring. Today, it served as the slaughterhouse. Irina stood at another table scraping meat and sinew from the deer hide that had just been removed from the carcass. When she was done they would stretch and dry the skin as part of the tanning process. Nikky was off playing with Levin, brandishing his *stick-gun* and bragging about his role in the hunt. They stalked their prey, a pile of hay with one antler. The boys were the same age and nearly inseparable.

Joseph slammed the meat cleaver down hard, splitting the hindquarters in two. The dogs were watching him intently, hoping a chunk of meat would fall from the table. The sound of an approaching wagon, announcing the return of the men, caused the dogs to start barking and depart. Before long, Felix on horseback along with the pair of oxen, followed by the large wagon, came into view past the corner of the grain bin. The dogs circled at a safe distance, barking incessantly.

Joseph snapped the deer-leg at the joint and chopped off the hoof with the cleaver. He whistled to the dogs and threw the foreleg into the barn yard for them to fight over to get them to shut up. Felix dismounted and looped the reins around a rail of the corral. Watching Sasha trot off with the deer leg in his mouth, he said, "Your luck keeps our bellies full, as usual, Joseph."

"If it were luck," answered Joseph, "we would only have vegetables to eat most of the time." He looked up from his butchering and noticed an odd glint in his friend's eye. "How was the market this time, prices any better?"

Felix loosened the girth and slid the saddle and blanket off the horse's back. "That is something we need to talk about my friend." The expression on Felix's face and the use of the term *my friend* gave Joseph further reason to suspect something important had happened in town, and it wasn't good.

Leon and Anatoly were unloading a new plow-share they had traded for, from the back of the wagon. Vladimir was leaning against one of the wagon-wheels, watching. Felix turned in that direction and yelled, "Come here, brother!"

"I'm busy, as you can see!" Vladimir yelled back.

"When you're done, then." Frustrated, Felix sighed audibly but said nothing more. He carried the saddle over to the stall and heaved it up to the top rail.

"Tell me what happened," said Joseph, chopping the other deer leg with his cleaver, *whump!* Vladimir was Felix's younger brother by fifteen years. He had been run off from the last two places he'd lived because of his loud mouth, laziness and sour disposition. Vladimir's current status was tenuous, at best; having caused problems from the day he arrived at this farm six months earlier.

"I'm sorry this has happened," Felix said, taking the bridle off the horse and hanging it from a peg on the wall. He stopped next to Irina and held the frame steady to make it easier for her to stretch the deerskin across it. "What are you going to make this time?" he asked her.

"I was thinking about making my son a hunting shirt."

"You'll have to make it big. He's growing faster than you can sew."

"You're stalling, Felix," accused Joseph, as he sliced a large piece off the shoulder to make a roast.

"I want my brother here before I start."

Joseph noticed Vasily and Fedor crossing the farmyard, one pulling and one pushing the cart loaded with potatoes. "I'll be done here by the time you get those potatoes put up and saddle the horses," he called out to the boys.

Vladimir approached the open doors of the shed where Joseph stood. He did not come inside. "What do you want?" he asked his brother. Joseph looked up, but Vladimir would not look at him.

"We need to tell Joseph what happened last night and I want you to be here," said Felix. He turned to address Joseph. "We were in the tavern when three officials from Tula started talking to us about joining the Party. They said we would get better prices for the things we bought if we'd sign. Then they started telling us we should bring our wheat to Tula so they can sell it in the state stores."

Joseph continued to cut and trim strips of meat while he listened. He looked up when Felix paused to let his brother finish the story.

Vladimir finally made eye contact with Joseph for the briefest of moments, and then reached down to pick up the deer's antler that was leaning against the shed. Joseph waited. Vladimir inspected the hard, bone-like points. He took a deep breath. "They left us alone for a while," he began, "talking to other people about joining the communists. We were drinking and having a good time with a couple of women..."

"Get to it, little brother," Felix interrupted. He stole a glance at Irina.

"Two of the men came back to our table with a bottle and sat down. They were pouring us drinks and wanted to put our names on a list. They started talking about what would happen if we didn't sign up."

"It was the same old story," Felix broke in. "You heard it, Joseph, when you were in Tula last year. *They had one hand out, welcoming us; the other was in a fist behind their backs.*"

Irina stood up and lifted the deerskin that was now stretched tightly on its frame. She carried it outside to set it in the sun.

Joseph knew she was listening and detected her impatience. "One of you, tell me what happened," he said with an edge in his voice.

Felix tugged at the collar of his shirt. "They said almost all the factory workers in Tula were members, but they needed the farmers too. They were looking for one farm; a person to take charge and get things started in our sector. Whoever got in early would have the best chance to be promoted in the Party. And his farm, his comrades, would get special treatment as the Party gained power."

Felix's face showed tension that Joseph had not seen for years. He set his knife down and turned to Vladimir, knowing they were getting to the point. "Well?"

Vladimir nearly grimaced before he said, "I signed. I'm a member of the Communist Party."

"Good for you," Joseph said with disdain. Just leave the rest of us out of it."

"I can't. We had to give them all the names...yours, Irina's. They wanted to know how much land we had, what we were growing. They are coming out here today. They could be here any time."

Irina spun around. Joseph's mouth hung open as he gazed at Vladimir, blood starting to redden his face. He turned to Felix. "Did you sign?"

Felix slowly shook his head, no. "We were all drunk... me, Leon, Anatoly...but none of us would sign."

Joseph walked toward Vladimir until his chest was pressing against the antler that Vladimir held in front of him like a shield.

"You joined the Bolsheviks. You are an idiot! You know what they did to my family. And now you have invited them out for a visit?" Joseph's stare bore into Vladimir's eyes, daring him to look away.

"That was ten years ago. Things have changed. We would be smart to join them, all of us. Anyway, I told them you would never sign," Vladimir said defensively. "I told them your family had been killed, all of your land near Smolensk, taken."Joseph's expression got even more menacing. "You told them that my family had land?" He grabbed two of the tines of the antler with his blood-stained hands. "Not even you are that stupid!"

Vladimir tightened his grip to match Joseph's. "We were drunk. Maybe I should not have said that."

"What else did you tell them?"

"I don't even remember what I said." Vladimir could feel himself getting in deeper. He vaguely remembered saying something about a connection between Joseph and the Tsar's family, but didn't think that the others had overheard it. "I did not invite them out here. I didn't know they were coming until they stopped us on our way out of town this morning." Vladimir's confidence faltered, shifting his eyes to Felix for support.

"Joseph," Felix said with sadness in his voice, "I cannot undo what has been done. Let us talk about what we can do now."

Joseph released his grip on the antler and turned to Irina, who was standing next to the stretched deerskin, her fingers covering her mouth. "Go find Nikky and bring him in the house," he commanded.

As Joseph started across the farmyard, Fedor and Vasily emerged from the corral, each leading a horse. "The meat for our neighbors is there," he said, pointing to the table. "Felix, put saddles on Mouka, and the other two horses."

Chapter 8

Sixteen people stood in the farmyard; all but Vladimir, who was conspicuously and thankfully absent. Three horses were waiting nearby. The saddles had large bundles tied behind them. Nikky and Levin were locked together, tears tracing down their faces. Every few seconds, one would punch the other in the ribs and they would giggle, a pathetic attempt to cope with life's unfairness.

The women were wiping their eyes and giving Irina hugs as she handed out the Christmas gifts she'd been making secretly for months. A shawl, with fancy lace stitched around the edges, was draped over each of the women's shoulders.

The men were trying on their new goat-skin gloves that were lined with rabbit fur. "They are nice and soft," said Anatoly, smiling at Irina. "Thank you."

"Where will you go?" asked Felix. He and Joseph were standing a few feet away from the rest, talking privately.

"I haven't decided. Anyway, it is better you not know so you won't have to lie."

Vladimir emerged from the house, clean shaven and wearing his best clothes. He walked directly into the middle of the group and stopped. "We have five horses, Milanov, and you are taking three of them?"

A collective gasp of breath preceded silence. Joseph went taught, knuckles turning white and red in clenched fists. Felix swung an arm in front of his friend's chest. "Wait!" It was more of an appeal than a command. Felix stared at his little brother in disbelief. "You are a disgrace," he growled. "Because of you, he is leaving his home to save his family. Joseph owns all five horses and is leaving us two. He has provided meat for our table for years. And what have you done? Nothing!"

Fedor trotted his horse into the farmyard, returning from his errand to the neighboring farm. "There are a couple of riders headed this way," he announced. "Looks like they're coming from town." To Joseph, he added, "They said thank you for the meat and gave me these." He leaned down from his horse and handed Joseph a sack that held two ripe melons. Joseph handed the sack to Felix and started gathering the reins of the three horses from where they were tied.

"Don't worry, I will speak to them!" Vladimir said. "They are only here to verify our crops, our livestock, and to ask you to join the Party. We need to cooperate with them."

Joseph ignored him and led the horses to where there was more room to mount them.

Irina stepped over to Nikky, bent down and put her arm around his shoulders. "Time to go," she said simply. She still held the pair of Christmas gloves, intended for Vladimir. She had been able to convince herself to forgive him, his youthful stupidity, his misguided judgment. She changed her mind and handed the gloves to Levin. "You'll be big enough to wear these in a few years. When that day comes, remember your friend, Nikky. Now say good bye."

The sound of a galloping horse turned eighteen pairs of eyes toward the trail leading over the hill, the opposite direction Fedor had just come from. Vasily was slapping the colt's rear as he bore down on the farmstead. He reined in his horse to an abrupt halt, hooves cutting into dirt, kicking up dust. "There are some men coming from the south," he hollered breathlessly. "I counted ten riders, and they've got rifles."

The group erupted into a clamor of excited voices, which started the youngest children crying and dogs barking. "It's a trap!" someone shouted. The three packed horses started prancing around nervously, reins tugging and stretching Joseph's arms in different directions.

Leon grabbed Vladimir by the arm and spun him around. "They need the militia to ask us to join the party?" he demanded.

Felix pushed Leon aside and grabbed Vladimir by the front of his shirt. "Listen to me," he said. "I want you to put your clothes and your other things in Joseph's room like you've been living there. *No Milanov family ever lived here.* You understand? *You were just drunk. The farm you lived at a couple of months ago outside of Kaluga. That's where the Milanov's are.* Got it?"

Vladimir pried himself free of his brother's grip and said, "If I do that they'll think I'm either a dullard or a liar. I'm not going to mess up my chances with the Party. The communists are going to end up in power and you need to accept it."

"If anything happens to Joseph and Irina because I brought you here, I'll kill you myself, brother or not." Felix shoved Vladimir toward the house. "Don't test me!"

Vladimir faced his older brother, defiantly. "This is my chance and you're not going to stop me."

Felix took a step forward, but hesitated when he saw Joseph grab a rope from Mouka's saddle and step up behind Vladimir. Felix locked an iron grip on one of his brother's arms and Leon took hold of the other. Vladimir struggled to free himself but was no match for the older, farm-toughened men. Joseph slipped a loop over Vladimir's head and pulled it tight around his neck. "We'll take him with us. He might say anything and if they find out who I am, who my parents were..." Joseph shook his head. He wound the rope around Vladimir's wrists, biting into the skin with a final yank.

"You can't do this to me!" protested Vladimir. "Where are you taking me? Felix, don't let him take me. He's going to kill me!" Fear was replacing defiance in the younger man's voice. "I can talk to them. I'll tell them anything you say. The Milanov's never lived here." He turned to Joseph to plead his case. "I'm sorry I told them those things. I can fix it, though. They'll believe me. I'll tell them I was drunk. Please, Joseph."

"Let's go Irina. Nikky, you first." Joseph handed the rope to Felix, grabbed his son at the waist and hoisted him into the saddle. "Irina, you ride Mouka," he said, giving her a leg-up. Joseph mounted Mouka's second born, a young stallion.

Felix reached up to hand the rope to Joseph. "If you follow the draw behind the barn, they won't be able to see you from either direction. But you better get going."

Joseph took the rope and nodded his agreement. He looked at Irina to see that she had heard, tilted his head to signal for her to get started, and said, "Nikky, you follow her. I'll be right behind you." He turned back to Felix. "What will you tell them?"

"I'll think of something." Felix turned to his brother. "If Joseph lets you live, do not come back here." To Joseph, he added, "If Vladimir doesn't keep up, drag him."

"Joseph," said Irina, "it would be better to let Vladimir ride. Nikky can ride with me and hold the rope."

Joseph looked at his wife and realized she was right. The switch was made quickly, though with some difficulty, because of Vladimir's hands being tied behind him.

Nikky, squeezed tightly between his mother and the pack tied behind them, held onto the rope, importantly. As they started out, the boy called, "Let's go, Sasha!"

"The dog stays," Joseph said flatly. Leon snatched the dog and held onto the loose skin behind his neck. Sasha and Nikky both started to whine and squirm at the prospect of being separated.

"Papa, he has to come!"

"Levin will take care of Sasha," said Joseph.

Levin stepped forward and tried to pet Sasha, however, the dog would not be comforted. Its whine started to turn into a mournful howl. Levin gave up and looked through tears at his friend.

Nikky dropped the rope to the ground and tried to work himself free. Irina wrapped an arm around her son's struggling body to keep him from jumping off the horse. She directed an imploring look at her husband.

"Sasha stays here!" Joseph said, putting an end to it. "Go Irina or it will be too late!"

As the small caravan started out across the farmyard, Nikky was crying, Sasha was whimpering, everyone else was silent. Mouka halted before disappearing beyond the edge of the barn, causing the other two horses to stop as well. Irina still had a firm hold on her son, but her head was turned backward, arguing with her husband.

Getting nervous, Felix glanced in each direction, expecting to see riders any moment. Joseph finally turned in his saddle and raised his arm in resignation, a signal. Leon and Levin let go of Sasha, who promptly sprinted across the farmyard, making little yips of joy. He leapt into the air to nip at Nikky's pant leg. Mouka staggered a step, caught her balance and the troupe moved on.

Felix looked at the sad faces around him. "Everyone inside; we only have a few minutes and there's work to do."

Chapter 9

Kansas City

Kitty's Kakes continued to grow and prosper. It was becoming a well-known name for high quality baked goods that few women would care to compare with their own home-made efforts. James and Kitty decided to extend the concept of delivering to Harvey Houses down the Santa Fe line by opening several retail bakery shops. Most towns of any size had what they called farmers' markets or city markets, where fresh produce was brought in every day from the local farmers. The markets were invariably right downtown near the railway station.

It was simply a matter of setting up a booth, hiring a local person to run it, and making sure deliveries were on the early morning rail cars when they left Kansas City. The night shift became eighty percent dedicated to this type of business. The shops were established in towns within three hours by train on the Santa Fe, Kansas City Southern and Burlington lines. The bread, pastries and other desserts were *same-day* fresh. Locals couldn't match the low overhead or the quality, so the concept mushroomed in a matter of months.

Unable to keep up with the demand, Kitty's Kakes built another bakery, and this time James and Kitty decided to build in the Bottoms near Union Station. So much of their business was now being delivered by rail that it only made sense to shorten the distance to the railroad loading docks.

At this point, James talked Kitty into the idea of having four managers run the day-to-day operations of the bakeries. They selected two night managers and a day manager from the best of the expanding staff of employees. Wray Brady was moved from night manager for the Westport bakery to manager of the day operations in the Bottoms. The day manager was responsible not only for his shift, but also for keeping the books and maintaining supply inventory.

With this new organization, the owners decided to move their offices out of the bakery buildings. A very swank area called *The Valentine District* was being developed between the Westport bakery and the one in the West Bottoms. Kitty negotiated the purchase of a quarter of a block of land at the corner of Thirty- sixth and Broadway. They hired an architect and started plans to build an office building with the intention of occupying the top floor themselves.

※

It was November 11, 1926. Dmitri Milanov O'Riley, wearing his new navy blue pants and shoes, ran ahead of his parents. He also wore a tiny, navy pea-coat, which Kitty had made out of a piece of dyed wool. He was finishing up his terrible *twos* and looking forward to making the best of his terrible *threes*. Kitty and Billy both adored the little terror, except when he was uncontrollable, as was the case at present.

"Come back here, young man!" Kitty's voice mingled into the multitude of sounds and noises created by the throngs of people walking down the big hill toward Union Station. They were all headed to the long-awaited dedication of the Liberty Memorial, which was across Pershing Avenue from the railway station. The memorial was a huge, stone monument built to commemorate the fighting men of the *Great War*. Bronze busts of the allied generals had been worked into the wall itself, and several fountains and statues made this shrine a remarkable sight. Eighty-three thousand Kansas Citians had donated over two million dollars to build the memorial. President Calvin Coolidge and a host of others were here for the ceremony.

Billy had donned his uniform proudly, as had many of the other young men in the crowd. Kitty thought he looked very handsome. The Purple Heart, and other medals on his chest, gave evidence to the grim reality of war where millions of lives had been lost in Europe. His pinned sleeve showed that he had been lucky not to have lost more in the bitter struggle that had ended eight years ago on this day. Kitty thought again, as she often did, about her brother Joseph, not knowing how much he ultimately had given in the same slaughter of boys and men. She shook her head to escape that train of thought, which inevitably led to melancholy and gloom.

"Dmi, come back here!" Billy's voice brought her back to the present.

He understood why Kitty wanted to name their son after her father, but he couldn't seem to bring himself to call an infant *Dmitri*.

Billy also agreed to *Milanov* for his middle name. Kitty was intent on not having her family name slip into oblivion. Kitty had used the last name, *Wixon*, from age sixteen, when she landed in America, until age twenty-one, when they were married in 1922. Now, "*O'Riley*" seemed natural, and kind-of rolled off the tongue. *Kitty O'Riley—a fine Irish girl to be sure.*

The crowd was growing as the masses descending the hill merged with those coming from downtown. Neither Kitty nor Billy had ever seen so many people in one place before. The newspapers had been playing up the event for weeks, and now the hundred and seventy-two acres surrounding the monument, as well as the streets and Union Station's parking lot, were jammed with people.

Billy held one of Dmitri's hands and Kitty the other as the speaker announced the names of twenty-five Medal of Honor awardees that were in attendance. Each name brought thunderous applause from the jubilant crowd. Since clapping was something Billy really couldn't do anyway, they maintained their grip on the boy's hands. Dmitri, however, was insistent on trying to join the crowd in applause and kept trying to wrench his hands free from first his mother and then his father. Not finding this to be possible, he lifted his feet off the ground to swing in the air between them, tugging on their arms and shoulders.

He alternated these routines for the first half of the ceremony, while whining either, "Let go, Mommy," or "Swing me, Daddy." Finally, Billy realized that his son might be still if he could see better, so he reached down and scooped up Dmitri, placing him on his shoulder where he could see over the wall of people. This did the trick, so Kitty and Billy were both able to listen to the President's speech in peace.

Chapter 10

February 20, 1933
Chicago, Illinois

Billy lifted a glass of champagne and said, "Happy birthday to the most beautiful woman in the world!"

Kitty lifted her glass and beamed. The candlelight dancing in her eyes matched the meticulously cut crystal of the chandelier above. Their fluted glasses *pinged* when they touched, and bubbles rose in a renewed flurry. Then, both swung their glasses over and repeated the ritual with Dmitri who had a glass of champagne as well. They all drank a little of the cold, sizzling liquid; and by the time the glasses reached the table, their waiter, wearing an immaculate tuxedo with black tie, was refilling them from the bottle that had been chilling in the ice bucket.

Kitty lifted her glass again and said, "To my two favorite men. No woman could have a better thirty-second birthday than having dinner at the Drake Hotel in Chicago with such a handsome pair." They gently *pinged* their glasses together again and had another sip.

Dmitri's smile was spread from ear to ear. He was only eight, although he would be nine in five days. The only time he had tasted wine before tonight was Christmas dinner at Uncle James's house just two months earlier. He wasn't that fond of the champagne, but being included as an adult was about the best thing that ever happened to him. He set his glass down and picked up the leather-backed menu. "Mom, I can't read this menu. I know it's French, but I've never seen these words before."

Kitty picked up and opened her own menu, nodding at Billy to do the same. "OK, I'll read it for both of you. Now follow along with me because I want you to order, yourself, and in French. She began with the hors d'oeuvres and slowly read through the entrees and finished with the

39

desserts. As she read, she continually looked up to see that Dmitri was grasping and memorizing the new words as she translated them to English one line at a time.

As they sipped their coffee and finished their French pastry dessert, Billy reached into his coat pocket and brought out a small box covered in deep red velvet. With a sly grin he handed it to Kitty and said, "Happy birthday, darling."

Kitty looked into his eyes and saw the affection that was always there when she looked for it. "The wonderful dinner was enough. You shouldn't have done this too."

Dmitri piped up, "I helped pick it out today when you were in your meeting. It's from both of us."

Kitty reached over and slid her hand under her son's chin and up the side of his cheek. "Thank you, dear. Am I going to like it?"

With a broad smile Dmitri said, "You bet your boots."

To that, Kitty smiled and looked at Billy saying, "You're starting to sound just like your dad." She took the box in one hand, extending it toward the candle, and with the other hand she slowly opened the top so the candlelight bathed the amethyst stone with flickering violet blue brilliance. She felt the tears gather in her eyes and the tightness welling up in her throat. She took the brooch made of silver leaves surrounding the stone and pinned it to the sheer material of her formal evening dress. This diversion helped her calm her voice, but when she looked up at her husband, the tears were still there. "Thank you so much. It's beautiful."

She turned to Dmitri, but before she could say it, he chirped, "It's a *namistis*. It's our birth-stone." He said this with pride, showing off his knowledge to his mother, whom he worshipped.

This was too much for her to bear. She brought her napkin to her face. Spontaneously, the male members of the O'Riley clan became tearful as well. The tender moment of shared feelings lasted long enough to be noticed by a couple of the neighboring tables discreetly situated several feet away. Finally, Kitty became self-conscious and cleared her throat. Regaining her composure, she looked at the wet cheeks of her husband and child. "OK, how come everyone's sitting around crying? I thought we were supposed to have fun tonight."

Billy dabbed the corner of his eyes with his napkin and smiled sheepishly. "So, how did your meeting with the city commissioners go today? You haven't said a word about your plans for the new bakery all evening."

"I think we're home free," Kitty said with a sniff. They have to run it by the mayor's office but think he will welcome the news."

Constructing the building would give a thousand men jobs, and about two hundred and fifty permanent jobs to work in the bakery after it was built. Kitty's Kakes was asking the city to put up one-third of the money on a ten-year note.

"And what about your charity bread idea?" asked Billy.

"They'll have to run that one by the governor. Either way, it'll take some time, my time, to develop the northern market before we make a profit."

"Sounds like something right down your alley. It's a good thing James takes care of the operations side."

Kitty smiled and said, "Yep. We complement each other pretty well."

Billy looked at his son and said, "Dmitri and I are going to the museum tomorrow. Are you still going to the bank, or do you have to wait to hear from the governor and mayor?"

Kitty looked at the sandy-headed boy, then back to her husband. "I'd love to go with you two, but I think I'd better go to the bank and lay the groundwork for our deal." Before continuing, Kitty fondled the large snifter of brandy that Billy had ordered for each of them, her thoughts drifting back to the earlier meeting with Ernie Mitts. Like all the bankers these days, he needed something positive to tell his board. "If Mr. Mitts can get some good press about a big three-way deal with the city backing it, he could raise the confidence level a couple of notches. That's what he really needs, and that's why we might have a chance to get some of his precious cash."

Billy raised his brandy glass in salute, "I'll say one thing. You were damn smart to stay out of debt in '29 and '30. And just as smart not to have all your money in a bank. Plus, people gotta eat, and as they say, *bread is the staff of life.*"

Kitty raised her brandy snifter. "That was four things," she said with a wink. "I saw my father do this just before the Bolsheviks took over." She leaned her head back and drained the entire glass of the fiery liquid. The air was drawn from her lungs as if consumed by flames. She gasped for breath, tears coming to her eyes. She choked and giggled, her face turning crimson. "I guess the Baron was a little more used to that sort of thing. I was going to say, hopefully, America will come out of this chaos better than

41

Russia did fifteen years ago."

"I hope so too, said Billy." He paused as he watched his wife push back her beautiful long black hair in an attempt to regain a semblance of calm. "You know, I heard that Congress introduced an amendment to repeal prohibition today. It's such a farce anyway." He gestured toward his brandy glass. "Look at us. We're sitting in one of the best restaurants in Chicago drinking champagne and brandy, and all we had to do was tip the maitre d' for a table in the private dining room. I mean, nobody's paid any attention to the law in years. The government might as well make it legal again so they can tax it."

He finished his brandy. Raising his empty glass in the direction of the waiter, he nodded his head toward it, and then Kitty. The message was instantly acknowledged with a slight bow, the waiter disappearing through a door leading to the bar.

Chapter 11

The O'Rileys needed a place to invest, as a result of making a lot of money in the baking business in the mid-twenties. Kitty didn't trust the stock market or the banks, so they started accumulating large chunks of land south of town on both sides of the state line. Breeding horses was a natural fit.

Kitty relaxed on the top fence rail of the corral out back of the main stable. She was wearing jeans and riding boots. She hooked her feet around the rail below her, her hands resting on either side for stability. She watched with intense scrutiny as Billy and Dmitri worked a yearling colt. The colt had the golden metallic dun coat of his grand sire. They had bred Majesty, selectively, for thirteen years. Uncle Marty had given the stallion to them as a wedding present in 1922 and the first offspring, a filly, had been the benefactor's return present, which was only fitting.

Majesty was now twenty-four years old and had not been used for stud for the last four years. The Akhal-Teke bloodline, however, had a foothold in America. The thoroughbred mares that were chosen to receive him were of the highest standards. And on three occasions, suitable, pure-bred Akhal-Teke mares had been located. Although railroad transportation was required, these efforts had benefited the gene pool to a great extent.

Only the elite inner-circles of horse breeding were even aware of the Kansas City Stables and its rare Akhal-Teke bloodline. Anyone interested in obtaining these genes from the last Russian Tsar's stables had to clear some pretty high bars.

Kansas City's stockyards made the city the very heart of the cattle industry. Developing heavier, disease resistant cattle became one of the O'Riley's challenges. Also, cattle meant *quarter horses*, and Billy decided *if you need them, why not breed them and have the best*. Soon, top-notch cutting horses were a hallmark of the O'Riley stables. Although Kitty was excellent with horses in every aspect, her huge time commitment to building the

Chicago and New Orleans markets for Kitty's Kakes meant Billy directed the lucrative ranching side of the family's enterprise.

Not surprisingly, the money was rolling in and piling up. The time on the road was taking a toll on Kitty so she decided to create a regional sales unit. James, too, was over-taxed, trying to manage the operations of multiple bakeries in distant locations. James developed his own structure, making their very first employee, Wray Brady, Vice President of Operations. This insulated the co-founder from the daily decisions. The O'Rileys and James Madison Monroe had become multi-millionaires before the crash of '29 and continued to increase their fortunes during the depression.

☙

Dmitri peered into his parent's bedroom and found no one. He had come home from school to find the house quiet and empty. The maid and the cook, who would normally still be there when he got home, were gone. He had gone from one room to another yelling, "Mom...Dad," but no one answered. Their bedroom was on the second floor of the large three-story house. He made his way around the canopied bed and stuck his head through an arched doorway to the sitting room, expecting to find it empty as well.

Instantly, the sight startled him. His mother was sitting in the rocking chair staring at the opposite wall. She was rocking gently back and forth and was oblivious to his presence. Sitting on the bright flowery cushions of the white wicker love-seat next to the windows was his dad. He looked up when Dmitri appeared in the archway and raised a finger to his lips for silence.

Billy eased himself out of the love seat and softly moved to the archway, extending his arm to usher his son out of the room. Dmitri had always loved that room because it was full of light from the large bay windows. Plus, he associated it with his mother because it was her favorite room as well. Today, however, the room felt like gloom and doom, and that feeling was making his skin crawl.

They sat down on the swing on the front porch before Billy spoke. "Majesty's dead," he said simply. "I found him this morning under a tree in the meadow by the lake. He was old and it looked like he died peacefully, which is the best way for any of us to go. I called your mother at work, and

44

she came home and has been sitting up there ever since." He gestured to the ceiling as he said it.

"Majesty meant a lot to her, as you well know. But I think she is thinking more about her brother and your grandparents than anything else. Majesty saved her life a couple of times. He was her last and only connection to her family and her childhood in Russia. It's no wonder she felt like he was part of her own flesh and blood." Tears began to stream down Billy's face as he continued. "We'll just have to give her some time and space while she gets over it. Hell, I loved that horse too!" He put his arm around his son's shoulders, pulling him tightly against him. Dmitri could hear his father weeping softly and he couldn't help but join him.

After about twenty minutes of shared solitude, Billy had regained his composure and was about to stand up when Kitty pushed the front screen door open and stepped outside. She said, "I've decided to do two things. I'm going to Russia to see if I can find my brother Joseph, and then I'm going to Kentucky to pay a visit to Morgan Shay." She turned and went back inside.

Kitty had said this in the matter-of-fact tone Billy had heard many times before. He knew she meant it and that was that. Now, it was just a matter of when she was leaving. He decided to let it lie till morning.

Chapter 12

September 1, 1937
Paris, France

Kitty sat thinking about all the unanswered letters, the ones returned undelivered, and finally the ones she had written but never sent. She had hoped David Francis would turn up something when he was still Ambassador to Russia in 1918 and '19. But he had come home with no news. Not only could he not find out anything about Joseph, fighting in the Russian army, he had no luck finding out about Sophie or Morso either. Kitty suspected they would have left the Milanov estate at the earliest opportunity and headed for Sophie's home in Riga. But the Germans had occupied Latvia just as she had escaped to the north, and David's inquiries resulted in stony silence.

Kitty's plan was to locate Yuri and Solina Vyikzonoskia as the first rung of the ladder. The memories of her weeks spent in their cozy home near the wharf still held a special place in her heart. It had been right after her parents were killed and her own desperate trek across western Russia to escape the Bolsheviks. She hoped that finding the Vyikzonoskia's would surely lead her to Sophie. And if anyone would have information about Joseph, it would be Sophie.

Sitting on the bench in the Paris airport, Kitty began to second guess herself, again. She was tired. Sailing across the Atlantic had given her too much time to think. *After twenty years, would Yuri and Solina still be in the same house, on the same street? Hell, they would be over seventy years old by now.*

Her mood was low, and being depressed was not her style. She began talking herself into the fact that this trip was hopeless and that she was being naive to think she could just waltz half way around the world and find her long-lost brother after all these years. *I might as well trade this ticket back...*

"Bon Soir, Madame. Do you have a ticket for the flight to Berlin?" (spoken in French)

Kitty flinched, startled by the airport official hovering over her. She noted his navy-blue uniform with a red stripe down the pant leg. On his head sat a small round cap with a short black bill and a red hat band. Her mind switched to French as she fumbled through her purse for the ticket. She replied in French, "Oui, Monsieur. I have it here someplace."

As she finally produced it, the official snatched it from her grasp and quickly scanned it for confirmation. He said, in not-too-polite French, "You must hurry or you will miss the plane. We have already announced *all aboard.*"

Kitty was shaken by the urgency in his voice and realized that her luggage must now already be on board. She allowed the official to drag her by the elbow to the gate leading to the runway where another blue-uniformed official stood, impatiently waiting to take the obviously confused woman's ticket.

With her purse slung over her shoulder and her stub in her hand, Kitty stepped into the warm September air. The breeze blew her hair as she walked to the passenger door at the rear of the plane and ascended the four stairs. The pilot began revving up the engine on the right wing and the door was closed behind her. There was a single row of seats on either side of the aisle, so everyone was next to a window. She took the final empty seat as the plane began to taxi down the runway.

Chapter 13

Riga, Latvia

Kitty knocked on the door of the house that had been her refuge for several weeks, exactly twenty years ago. She waited, but heard no feet approaching the door from the other side. She knocked again, harder. No answer. The house was obviously lived in, kept up with meticulous care. *Just the way Sophie would want it,* Kitty thought. She stepped back several paces, putting her virtually in the street, which was cobbled stone, just as she remembered it. The place looked the same. The memory of those days, the trauma, the stress; there was no question that she was at the right house. She returned to the door and rapped hard one more time.

Thankful that she had checked into the hotel first, so she didn't have to lug her bag around with her, Kitty turned to go. She had taken about two dozen steps when she noticed a middle-aged man, coming from the other direction, turn into the walk leading to the house she had just left. She hurried back to catch him before he could unlock the door and disappear behind it.

Her command of the Latvian language was quite rusty, but she had been brushing up on it with the help from a book she had bought in the Berlin airport. "Sir, could you wait a moment?" she asked as she trotted up the short, stone walk. "I'm looking for the Vyikzonoskias. Do you know them?"

The man, standing on the step with one hand on the open door, looked down at Kitty over the brim of his glasses. He hesitated, as if trying to comprehend the question or maybe just attempting to place the accent. "The name is not familiar to me. How would I know these people?"

The disappointment on Kitty's face was unmistakable as she started to consider her options. She had been cautiously optimistic, at best, about her plan. Her contingencies were thinner still. The man stared impatiently at her silent thoughtfulness and finally cleared his throat, anxious to go inside after a long day's work.

Kitty grappled for words. "Yuri and Solina Vyikzonoskia used to live here. They are friends of mine."

The man let go of the doorknob and turned to face Kitty. "Well, Miss, I have lived here for six years and the people we bought this house from were named Barushka. Good day."

He turned to go inside, but Kitty blurted, "Do you know the Chekovichs, two doors down?" She pointed to the house. "I can't remember the man's name, but his wife was named Marla and they had a daughter about my age named Anna."

The man took off his glasses before he spoke. "I don't know any Chekovichs, but I do know there is a woman living in that house, named Anna. Now, good day to you." He stepped inside and shut the door rather firmly, leaving no doubt that the conversation was over.

Before she turned to go, Kitty stuck out her tongue at the heavy wooden door. The childish gesture brought a smile to her face and lifted her spirits back off the doormat. *Well,* she thought to herself, *let's go see about this Anna whose name may or may not be Chekovich.*

The door opened almost immediately after Kitty's first knock, as if someone was waiting for her to arrive. The woman had blond hair tied up in a red handkerchief, an apron around her waist. She had a broom and dust pan in one hand, while the other still gripped the door handle. Kitty couldn't tell if she was the maid or what. The two looked at each other in silence. Something about the woman's face looked familiar, but it had been twenty years and Anna was a teenager when they had spent those few weeks together.

Finally, Kitty found her voice and said simply, "Anna Chekovich?

The woman's face turned from blank to a frown. "I am Anna, but my name has not been Chekovich for eighteen years. Do I know you?"

With a flood of relief Kitty took a step toward Anna, who reflexively closed the door somewhat, not yet comfortable with this stranger. Kitty checked herself in mid-step, not expecting the paranoid reaction from her old friend. A smile broke out on Kitty's face. "Don't you know who I am?"

Anna's expression was still blank. Kitty suddenly began to enjoy the game. She took a step backward, giving Anna her psychological space.

After a moment's thought, she said, "We went shopping together twenty years ago." Anna's frown deepened. The lines that were not on her face as a teenager were now pronounced.

Recognizing that such games are only fun for the one in-the-know, Kitty quickly decided to end this one. "I am *Catrina Milanov*. You showed me around Riga twenty years ago when I was staying with the Vyikzonoskias."

As the words came tumbling out, the look on Anna's face changed to amazement and then joy. She literally dropped the broom and dust pan, opened the door wide and stepped over the threshold. The two women hugged briefly before Anna stood back to scrutinize her old acquaintance.

"You know, I can see it now. You were so young back then, and your hair was much shorter." Anna reached up and pushed Kitty's black hair off her forehead, exposing the sharp widow's peak. "I remember that," she said with a smile. "I'll bet I look different too...God, what a surprise! ...Come in, come in. You have to tell me everything. You were going to America when you left here, right?" Anna's voice was getting excited as the memories began to drop back into place from a long-closed chamber of her mind.

Kitty followed her into the small living room, but before Anna had a chance to offer her a seat, Kitty said, "How about if we go out and have something to eat or drink, and we can talk. I'll buy."

A light flickered in Anna's eyes, which Kitty correctly interpreted to mean that *going out* was not a common occurrence with the times so hard. Anna registered the expensive clothes worn by Kitty, then reached up and placed a hand on the handkerchief covering her head. A frown crossed her face but she said, "Give me a minute to get fixed up a bit first. Here, sit down. I'll be right back." Anna disappeared in a whirl. Kitty descended to the lumpy sofa, covered with some type of old quilt that served as upholstery.

The tavern on the wharf was filled with smoke, raucous laughter, and shouting. Kitty and Anna sipped their ale in between attempts at being heard over the noise. They sat at a table for two against the wall while sailors and dockworkers carried on around them in what seemed to be the standard routine after a day's work. Finally, Kitty put her hand on Anna's and said, "Let's go outside." They both downed their ale and Kitty plopped some money down on the table.

Outside, they walked along the cobbled streets, no hurry to get anywhere. After a few minutes of silence, Kitty got to the point. "I am looking for my brother Joseph. It's been over twenty years, and I don't even know if he was killed in the war or not. I was hoping to ask Sophie and Morso if they had heard anything, but now I don't know how to find them either." Kitty looked at the troubled expression on her friend's face and knew she was about to get some painful news.

Anna had suspected this was the reason for Kitty's return. She stopped, took a deep breath, and reached for Kitty's hands. She held them tightly as she began. "That was a long time ago, and I'm not sure where to start or how to tell you." She hesitated a moment and then plunged in. "There hasn't been any word about your brother. But not long after you left, Sophie and her husband showed up. I'd forgotten his name was Morso. I didn't really know him," she muttered. "Anyway, it was just the next Sunday...I'm sure they had only been here a week." Anna closed her eyes. "Yuri and Solina Vyikzonoskia, along with Sophie and Morso, died in the bombardment that crushed this city before the Germans marched in. They were in church at the time, and a direct hit brought the rafters down on their heads."

The finality of Anna's statement brought the conversation to a halt. Kitty had lost four people she dearly loved, just like that. People who had been dead for twenty years and she didn't even know it.

Kitty walked over to a bench and sat down, keeping her thoughts to herself. Her spirits were on a downward slide. *Before, she had little reason for hope of finding her brother. Now, she had none. Penetrating the Soviet Union's interior, only to risk being captured by Stalin's thugs, with not even a wisp of trail to follow... It would be madness.*

Kitty shook her head and slowly stood up. Anna joined her. They looked into each other's eyes and both knew that the other one understood. Kitty was about to give up. Give up and go home.

They walked back to Anna's house, hand in hand. Kitty went in to use the bathroom and when it was Anna's turn, Kitty stuffed all but a couple of bills of her Latvian money under the quilt on the couch.

Chapter 14

October 8, 1937

Yesterday, Kitty had steamed into New York harbor, and then had dinner at the Waldorf with Oliver Curwood. She had wired ahead from London and he met her at the dock when the *Queen Mary* tied up. They had talked at length about her fruitless efforts to find Joseph. Having talked that out, which was good for her soul, the conversation switched to her current dilemma.

There were only a few people in the world familiar with the saga of Morgan Shay's thievery of Majesty, and Oliver was one of them. Kitty had pretty much pushed it to the back burner, a loose end to be dealt with in the future. In fact, many times during her contented moods she had decided to just forgive and forget. But Majesty's recent death had gotten the juices flowing again.

She decided to remove the thorn that kept pricking her peace of mind. She didn't know what she was going to do when she got there, but she would go to Kentucky and follow her instincts. The thing that pushed her in that direction was the fact that she had failed her other objective, to find her brother. She knew she could find Mr. Shay. Kitty went to the counter and bought a ticket to Louisville.

❧

During the summer, before departing for Latvia, Kitty had spent her time getting the business organized to run without her, which meant giving James authority to make all decisions alone. It also meant relying on the sales staff to work on their own and temporarily report directly to James. Not knowing how long she would be gone, the two owners decided that any major undertakings should be put off until her return, unless the opportunity was too good to pass up.

Billy continued to run the horse and cattle business, as well as fill both parenthood roles for their teenage son.

In addition to these considerations, Kitty had done a little legwork for the trip itself. She had to do all the normal things like a passport, visas, traveling wardrobe, ticket reservations, etc. Unfortunately, she had no way to do any up-front research on her objective in Latvia and Russia. She had decided to just go there and react to whatever presented itself.

Kitty did, however, do some investigation into what might be accomplished if she stopped in Kentucky upon her return to the States. The thirties had been a very difficult time for most individuals and the country in general. Not surprisingly, Kitty had heard through the breeding circles that the Shay operation in Kentucky was feeling the strain of the collapsed economy.

Kitty decided to call her old friend in Chicago, Ernie Mitts, to see what he knew or could find out about the financial status of WTF (Walkers, Trotters and Flats), which is what Morgan called his farm. Ernie had told her he would get back to her in a couple of days, which he did.

Apparently, Morgan had his farm mortgaged to the hilt in an effort to cover some bad luck and poor business decisions. Ernie happened to have some business connections with the Louisville Commerce Bank, which was holding a very large note on WTF at the present time. The Commerce Bank president, Ronald Andrew Goetz, was not too excited about hearing from his old friend from Chicago, because the business dealings the two had in common were actually a couple of instances Ernie had bailed Goetz's ass out of potentially catastrophic situations. The result was that Ron owed Ernie a big favor or two, and one never wants to get a call out of the blue from somebody like that.

Ernie knew enough about business and enough about Kitty to know that they had Morgan Shay by the balls if that was their intention. He simply told Mr. Goetz that he might be sending a friend out to visit in the next couple of months and left it at that.

When the situation was explained to Kitty, she asked the president of the Chicago First National Bank to send a letter of introduction to the Churchill Downs Jockeys Club. If Kitty decided to stop in Louisville on her way back from Europe, she could simply go by the club, pick up the letter, and then visit with Mr. Goetz about making arrangements for a real estate deal.

The door opened, and out came a man with a big warm smile on his face. He was in his fifties, hair more white than brown, wearing a dingy brown suit and shoes. He held an open letter as he approached Kitty, who was sitting on a love seat outside his office. He stuck out his right hand. "My name is Ronald Goetz. I'm very pleased to meet you, Mrs. O'Riley. Mr. Mitts has said a lot of nice things about you; won't you come into my office."

Rather than sitting across from each other at the desk, Mr. Goetz led her to two large, high-backed leather chairs. He held the back of one, unnecessarily but gallantly, as Kitty was seated, and then took the other himself. Kitty was wearing a bright red silk dress that was simple but very stylish. She had just bought it in New York, and it was much more provocative than her normal attire. As she crossed her legs, Mr. Goetz was treated to a tantalizing view of silk stockings that nearly made him gasp. For some unexplained reason, Kitty was feeling ornery, and teasing the banker scratched the itch.

He raised a hand to his mouth and pulled the edge of his mustache as he regained his composure. He looked past Kitty's shoulder at the fine dark woodwork, knowing that otherwise his eyes would be drawn to her low scooped neckline. He had inadvertently witnessed more than he should have a moment ago when he was holding the back of her chair.

Kitty was amused that she had so easily and successfully unsettled this man. She tucked that bit of knowledge away for later use. It always amazed her at how most, not all, men were mesmerized by a woman's breasts. She began, "I'll get straight to the point, Mr. Goetz. We both know Morgan Shay has gotten himself into a difficult situation, and it may be that we'll need to help him out of it, so to speak. Ernie tells me that you are anxious to work with me on this matter and, depending on how it turns out, it could be very profitable to your bank in the long run."

Kitty continued, "You see, I used to know Mr. Shay a long time ago. He was helping me with something and...well, it didn't turn out exactly the way I would have wanted. So, I can't decide if I should just let it go as a bad experience or give him a little taste of his own medicine. The fact is that the situation helped motivate me to start my company and, in a way, maybe I should be thanking Morgan for his part. But then again, thanks may not be what he has coming to him."

Mr. Goetz sat quietly and soaked in this beautiful woman's calm demeanor, thanking his lucky stars that he was not the object of her thinly veiled wrath.

"As I said, Mr. Goetz, I'm kind of *sitting on the fence*. Ah, that's something we say in Kansas. I imagine with all the fences you folks have out here, you know what I mean. Anyway, I'd like to go out to see the farm and would rather not have Mr. Shay know who I am, at least to start with. If he seems to have mended his ways, well, I might just go on home and get back to work on my own business. On the other hand, I think I'll write out a check to you right now for the entire mortgage on the farm and the unsecured note that Ernie tells me you're holding. You know, just in case I think Morgan needs to be relieved of all that responsibility."

By now, the banker was slowly shaking his head back and forth. His lips formed a careful smile as he thought about bringing Morgan to his knees. The WTF had always been the biggest and most prestigious horse-breeding operation in the area, and Morgan made sure that everyone knew it. Goetz inwardly congratulated himself on his sudden good fortune. He had only extended Shay's credit in the hopes of getting back his original investment. There were few buyers out there able to pay what the bank had invested in WTF. Morgan had put up the horseflesh and even the furniture in the massive house as collateral.

Now, not only did it look like he might get the bank's money out in one fell swoop, he could enjoy seeing the rug being pulled out from under Morgan Shay's feet, the asshole!! ...And on top of that, he was paying off a large chit to Ernie Mitts, which in itself was a valuable stroke of luck. Starting to get a little giddy, he took it one more step. The Louisville Commerce Bank might be acquiring a new client, obviously long in assets, not the least being long legs. He halted that train of thought, other than to mentally register the fact that this would be an account that he would manage personally.

The banker snapped back to the present and immediately felt the blood begin to rise to his face. During his brief reverie, while he was patting himself on the back, he realized he had unconsciously been staring directly at Kitty's cleavage. He flashed a glance at the cool blue eyes that were watching him, noncommittally. He stood up and tried to remember where they were in the conversation. As he walked to his desk he said somewhat lamely, "I'll just get my keys and we can drive out to *Walkers, Trotters and Flats* if that would suit you, Mrs. O'Riley."

Chapter 15

It was about a twenty-mile drive to the WTF farm. Ron (they were now on a first-name basis) pointed out the windows of his brand new '37 Cadillac at all the attractions the community of Louisville had to offer. In the back of his mind he kept coming back to Kitty's statement about still being on the fence. Ron was fairly confident that Kitty intended to go through with the deal, but the stakes were high and that made him nervous.

As they drove down a gravel road that bordered a full mile of white fence, Ron proclaimed that Kitty was now looking at her prospective purchase. He wanted her to be leaning in the direction of buying, so he had been talking along the way as if the transaction was all but completed. Sometimes people needed a little push to actually make a big decision. She didn't seem like the type to need much help in that regard, but it couldn't hurt.

If it weren't for the fact that the O'Rileys really didn't need property in Kentucky, Kitty probably would have bought the place sight unseen. She and Billy had more than enough to do now without overseeing an operation of this size, five hundred miles from their home. Kitty was almost hoping she would find a good excuse to let Shay keep his damned farm so she could go on home.

However, Kitty had a nagging feeling that she wanted to hurt someone or something. It started when she was forced to admit that the search for her long-lost brother was at a dead end. It was kind of a suppressed evil desire, like when one holds a cat and is nearly overcome by the urge to squeeze it real hard. The combination of orneriness and evil was alien to Kitty, and she knew that her current attitude spelled trouble. Something was going to happen, and the excitement started to well up inside her.

As they turned into the drive, which had a white rail fence on either side, Kitty turned to Ron and said, "Let's just lie low for a little while. You can just tell him I asked to see what a real horse operation looks like. You're sure he won't mind us just popping in on him like this?"

Ron pulled the car to a halt in front of the huge southern-plantation-style home. "There's nothing Morgan enjoys more than showing off his house and horses." He gave Kitty a conspiratorial wink that almost made her break out in laughter.

Ron got out and hurried around the back of the car to open Kitty's door. Stepping to the side, he admired the way she arched her back in a stretch; *this is a kitty-cat with claws.* She straightened her dress before they strolled up the walk together. The butler, a colored man in an elegant black suit, indicated the master of the house was presently in the stables and suggested they wait in the sitting room. Kitty almost choked on the word *master*, but stifled herself sufficiently to receive only the slightest glance from the stiff doorman.

Ron offered, "I know my way, Henry. We'll just mosey 'round back if you think that would be all right."

"Very good, Mr. Goetz. It's a pleasure to see you again, sir." He bowed his head slightly toward Kitty and said, "And you are, Miss...?"

"Wixon," Ron blurted a little too loudly. "Mrs. Wixon." Kitty had suggested they use her former name.

"Very well, Mrs. Wixon, it was nice to meet you."

While they were still a hundred yards from the nearest set of stables, they began to hear sounds of a horse in distress. It was a sound that made Kitty uncomfortable and she unconsciously quickened her pace. The horse's anguish intensified as they neared the large, open double-doors of the brilliant-white building.

When they rounded the corner, Kitty's focus was riveted to the scene in the third stall. A young horse with hobbled forelegs was rearing up to avoid the whip. There was a rope stretched tightly around his neck, tethered to the rail. Kitty could tell by his movement, or lack of it, that at least one of his hind legs was tied to a rail as well. The horse's eyes were wide with fear and rage. Its coat had a sheen of sweat, lather forming around the edges of the saddle it still bore.

The man with the whip, who was mercilessly striking the poor animal, looked to be in his late fifties. His gray, thinning hair was wet from exertion, wisps flying wildly with the violent motion. There was a young man in riding clothes, holding on to the rope around the horse's neck, trying to restrict him further.

They were so intent on the beating that Kitty walked up behind the man with the whip, unnoticed. The violence had progressed to where he was winding up with his arm stretched backward in order to get a full swing with the sturdy riding crop. At the point of his full backward extension, Kitty grabbed the crop firmly in her hand, just before it began its powerful forward arch. The unexpected hindrance not only prevented the ensuing blow, it nearly dislocated the wielding man's shoulder.

He turned upon the intruder, adrenaline pumping fiercely. Kitty could see in his blazing eyes that he enjoyed the sick power he was exerting over the defenseless beast. Without doubt, she knew this was the man she had come to see. There was no recognition in his eyes, only anger. He reached for his shoulder with his free hand, the pain stoking his anger; anger that was quickly being transferred from the horse to the woman who dared interfere.

Kitty said in a controlled, firm voice, "Let's settle down for a minute."

He jerked the crop out of Kitty's hand and made a threatening motion with it, saying, "Mind your own business or I'll use this on you next."

Ron had moved into the barn, and Kitty took a step backward so they were standing side by side. Morgan was still fired up as his attention swung to the banker, then back to Kitty, then to the banker again. "What do you want?" he said to Ron.

Ron knew all about Morgan's temper. It had to be allowed to simmer down, like taking a whistling tea kettle off the stove. He managed a practiced, professional smile and slowed the tempo down to break the tension. "Well," he gestured toward Kitty, "Mrs. Wixon here wanted to see your operation so she could see how a really fine..."

Kitty stuck up her hand to stop the charade. "Screw all that, Ron." She turned to Morgan. "My name is Kitty O'Riley. You knew me once as Catrina Vyikzonoskia, in Russia." The recognition was immediate, his eyes changing from anger to caution.

Kitty smiled. It was not a friendly smile and Morgan did not take it as one. She continued, "I'm not going to string this out any longer than necessary, so listen carefully. That's my horse you're beating and I don't like it. These are my stables you're in and I don't want you here. Your clothes are in my house and I want them out within the hour or I'll burn them."

Morgan's mouth was hanging open, not knowing where his protest should begin. He was acutely aware of his financial predicament, and the fact that the president of the Louisville Commerce Bank was here meant that this young bitch knew it too. He relaxed his arm holding the whip and stopped rubbing his shoulder, which he had been doing unconsciously. He began his negotiation with, "What's a pretty young filly like you want with a big...?

"You're a pig, Shay!" she growled, cutting him off. "Here's the deal. You no longer own this farm. If you want to get out from under your rather sizeable unsecured note, you will be gone within the hour. If you agree, you're free and clear. If you don't, you still owe the bank the entire note. Either way, you lose the WTF. Plus, there's one more thing."

Morgan's mind was now back-pedaling fast, trying to find a direction to turn, thoughts of horse whipping long gone. "What thing?"

Kitty relaxed. This was a negotiating position she wished she was always in. "You tell me what really happened between England and New York and how you stole my horse. You know, I've read stories about how they used to hang horse thieves in this country."

The scene flashed into Morgan's head as if it were yesterday. *He was standing in the bowels of the ship looking at a beautiful horse, one of the Tsar's best, struggling to stand on a broken leg. A sailor in charge of the livestock cargo said the ship had listed from a wave, causing the animal to get his leg wedged in the rails of the overcrowded stalls. The leg simply snapped. There was nothing Morgan could do except take the loss. But, there was another way. He still had the magnificent Akhal-Teke stallion. What was that young immigrant child going to do with a horse like that in a new country, anyway?*

Kitty watched Shay's face. His recollection took about ten seconds.

He raised his eyes to meet hers. They gazed steadily and stubbornly at each other. He realized that only the truth would suffice. "One of my horses broke his leg so we put him down. I paid the crew to throw him overboard at night and keep quiet. Then, I merely substituted yours when we reached New York harbor. Since Liverpool's records showed bulk cargo, no actual count was done, and no one was the wiser. I've always wondered if I'd hear from you again, but I knew you had nothing to prove the horse was yours. It was your word against mine, and you were a young Russian who could barely speak English. Plus, possession is nine tenths of the law, or haven't you heard?"

Kitty's eyes narrowed at the remark.

"I sold the golden stallion to some New York Jew who was playing cowboy or something out in Kansas City. I think I remember him selling your horse to some Irish guy named O'Mally...or something. I'll admit he was quite a horse. I got a very good deal for him." Morgan had warmed up to the subject. Thoughts of better times temporarily made him lose track of the situation he now faced.

His story had ended, and Morgan turned to face the banker. "Ronald, we've known each other a long time. Are you going to let this out-of-towner steal WTF away from me while I'm having a small stretch of bad luck?"

Ron had to admit that if it was anybody else, he would rather side with the local citizen trying to save his land. But under the circumstances, his path was clear and, the future attractively bright, he might add. "It's just business, Morgan. I have a responsibility to the Bank. Sorry."

"Sorry, my ass!" He flipped the riding crop in Kitty's face saying, "I guess this is yours too," and walked out of the barn.

This whole exchange took barely five minutes. Kitty pivoted, noticing the abused horse had settled down some but his hobbled legs were still stepping around nervously and he was pulling against the rope around his neck. Her attention shifted to the boy wearing the riding clothes. He was standing back several paces, trying to be as inconspicuous as possible. As Kitty's eyes focused on him he flinched, then seemed to shrink physically. He was not looking forward to being addressed by the woman who had dared stand up to the boss...and won.

She said, "I want you to tell me why Morgan was beating this horse, but first untie him." The boy was about eighteen, she judged, and had probably spent his entire life around horses. Still, he was not anxious to get into that stall with a wild-blooded horse that could easily kick him senseless or maybe kill him.

He leaned over the rail and loosened the noose around the horse's head, then slipped it gently off. He walked around to the gate, but as he cautiously began to release the latch, the horse reared on his hind legs threateningly. The boy snapped the gate shut. He stepped back from the stall and shrugged his shoulders at Kitty as if to say, *See, I can't go in there.* "Ma'am, the reason the boss was beating him is on account of we can't break him. Ebony here could be the fastest two-year-old on the farm, but he won't let anyone ride him."

Kitty responded, "Take your pants off."

The boy's head jerked up, and he hesitated a moment to see if his ears were playing tricks..."Ma'am?"

"I said, take your pants off. You'll have to take off your boots too, but I don't need them." The boy just stood there, agape. "Don't worry; I've got a son just a couple of years younger than you. You can go in there if you're shy." She pointed to the door of the tack room. "By the way, what's your name?"

The boy muttered, "Mark White...Ma'am."

"Well, Mark, I'm the new boss, and if you want to keep your job, you'll have to learn to do things a lot differently around here." Again, she pointed to the tack room. "Get movin'. I'm going to give you and Mr. Goetz a little lesson today about horses."

Finally realizing she was serious, Mark started to unbuckle his pants as he headed for the tack room.

Kitty turned to Ron and asked, "Do you know who the best horse trainers and riders are?"

Ron looked up at the rafters of the stable as he began to sift through Kentucky's *finest* with a fair amount of pride in the state's reputation.

Kitty correctly interpreted his train of thought and said, "Wrong. You can bet your bank they live in Russia, and bet anything you have left that they're Cossacks." She turned her back to him and added, "Now, help me undo the buttons on this dress, and then go get those pants from young Mark.

Ron did as he was told, although he was all thumbs as he tried to get the tiny white buttons through the button holes of the red silk dress.

Kitty kicked off her shoes and slid one long slender leg, and then the other, into the riding pants. She pulled them up under her dress, having to tug slightly to get them over her hips. She let the dress slip off her shoulders and handed the almost weightless garment to Ron. "Hold that, if you please."

The only thing covering Kitty's upper half was a lacy camisole, which she tucked into the pants. She drew the thick leather belt out of its loops and tossed it on the ground, walked over to a bin full of oats and grabbed a handful. Mark emerged from the tack room with a blanket wrapped around him. She smiled at his modesty and walked slowly toward the stall where Ebony stood watching.

Kitty extended her hand with the oats out in front of her so the skittish young horse could plainly see them. She steadied her gaze on Ebony as her voice took on a warm, soothing tone. "The secret here is to exude confidence and caring. Horses can read your feelings just like a dog. If you feel hostility or fear, they know it and you've already lost. You have to let them know you're in charge, but that you're going to be working together."

She unlatched the gate of the stall and stepped in, keeping her hands low where Ebony could see them. His eyes were still on alert, but his breathing was calmer and he made no attempt to rear up in defense. Kitty left the gate halfway open and moved up to the black sleek head offering the oats in one hand and rubbing the underside of Ebony's chin with the other.

After a brief sniff to confirm the contents, Ebony began to munch the dry grain, swishing his tail at a fly. Kitty began to stroke the horse's neck and then pat him with a little feeling. She wanted him to get used to her non-threatening but firm touch. When he had finished the oats, Kitty ran her hand down the base of his neck and chest. Then, not losing contact while stooping over, she ran her hands down his forelegs to the rope hobbling the young racer. She untied the knot; not rushing, but with steady movements, maintaining her contact by leaning into his legs with her shoulders.

Ron and Mark watched in awe as she placed her head and body in harm's way, trusting her skill with this volatile animal. She stood up, gently dropping the rope outside the stall and began stroking the horse's neck again. "Good boy. That's better, isn't it. Now we're going to do your hind leg. We'll have you loose in a few more minutes. That's a good boy." The cooing of her voice was like a mother rocking her baby to sleep.

With the hind leg released, Ebony began stepping around in the stall, testing his freedom of movement. Kitty returned to his head and patted him some more. Talking to him continually she said, "OK, let's get rid of this saddle. That's a boy."

Taking the saddle and blanket in both hands, Kitty swung them up and balanced them on the top rail of the stall. She gripped the bridle and led him through the gate. The young black horse followed her out as Mark and Ron stepped back, giving the two plenty of room. "Mark, without any quick movements, get me a grooming brush out of the tack room, would you please."

Holding the reins, Kitty brushed Ebony's drying coat from head to tail. They were gaining a rapport with each other that she was about to put to the test. She led the horse back into the stall, then back around so his head was facing outward. "OK, boy, here we go." Kitty looked up at Ron and said, "Would you two move off that way a bit so Ebony can see he has a free passage out of here."

Mark had a puzzled look on his face, not guessing her intentions but complying with the request anyway. Kitty placed a silk-stockinged foot on the second rail of the fence. Then, with one hand on the horse's withers, she swung a leg gently over his bare back and settled in for whatever came next.

Startled a little from the weight but no saddle, Ebony began to prance around as he moved out of the stall. Kitty's legs were softly but firmly hugging his sides. Ron couldn't help but envy the horse for his fortuitous position. Kitty coaxed the high-stepping colt out of the barn. Addressing Mark, she said, "Open the gate to the pasture, the race track will come later."

Mark was incredulous, as this same animal had thrown him three times already that day. He walked calmly past his new boss and then, gathering the blanket around his hips, trotted over to the nearest gate leading to open grassland.

Kitty walked Ebony through the gate, leaned forward to unbuckle the bridle and let it and the bit fall to the ground along with the reins. She patted the horse's strong black neck, slid the fingers of her left hand into his mane and grabbed hold. "Does that feel better?" The words were too soft for Mark and Ron to hear and Ebony didn't understand them, but it was the tone that mattered to him and the exhilaration of having both a rider and a free head.

Kitty began walking him down the fence line. She urged him into a trot for about twenty yards, then placed her free hand down along his neck and *thumped* him with her heels. Ebony broke into a run as Kitty clung to him like a tick on a dog's back, feeling his motion and becoming part of it. With her head positioned right behind his ears, her black wavy hair intermixed with Ebony's mane and whipped in the wind behind them.

Ron and Mark leaned their elbows on the white rail fence and watched Kitty in the distance as she worked the young horse. She kept him busy changing gaits from a gallop to a trot, back to a canter, then walk. She steered him with pressure from her legs and hands.

After about fifteen minutes, they rode back up to the gate that Mark was holding open, and walked into the yard. They stopped and Kitty patted Ebony several times aggressively on the neck. "Good boy! We're going to give you a little treat. I'll bet we can find some carrots or brown sugar around here somewhere." She swung her leg over his neck and slid off.

Mr. Goetz was biting his lip with a peculiar glint in his eyes, a mix of pleasure and pain. Mark was staring at the ground. Kitty looked down and discovered that somewhere along the way her ample, left breast had slipped out of the camisole and was gathering sunshine. The flush on her face from the ride reddened a bit as she tugged the lacy silk back into place. "Show's over, boys." She walked past them to see about a treat for her horse.

Chapter 16

October, 1942
Stalingrad, Russia

When war reached the city of Stalingrad, the first eight weeks could only be described as...annihilation. Overwhelming strength, organized for the purpose of ending a way of life, demolishing it, ruthlessly.

On August 23, 1942, German tanks attacked from the south. German artillery and Luftwaffe bombers had begun to reduce Stalingrad into an unrecognizable heap of debris. The vibrant city, hugging thirty miles of the west bank of the Volga River, perished. By mid-October, only 40,000 of its 500,000 inhabitants remained, most living like rats beneath the earth's surface in the wreckage. Many of them fought to repel Hitler's onslaught, street by street, building by building. Sixty-thousand Russian troops did the same. They were surrounded. Hope for survival had withered. Seeing the next sunrise after all-night bombardments was the only reward. At least in the daylight, they could fight back.

Joseph watched as part of the ceiling collapsed, the explosion ringing in his ears. He turned back to his task, wrench in one hand, oily rag in the other. "Try it now!" he yelled. The starter cranked, cranked, nothing. The tank's big diesel engine would not fire-up. Joseph made another adjustment. "Try it again!" Crank, crank, crank...nothing. Another shell exploded, blasting a hole in the wall at the far end of the enormous factory, rattling the structure and everything in that vicinity. Besides the one Joseph was working on, there were only two remaining, unfinished tanks.

In the 1930's the factory had been one of largest farm tractor operations in the Soviet Union. Joseph had been the plant manager for nearly a decade. But Stalin needed tanks, not agriculture. They had built thousands of them since the war began. Around-the-clock production of the T-34s had supplied the Red Army with the most versatile, and therefore the most effective, tank on either side of war. Even the Germans conceded that they were the best in the world.

For Joseph, the Luftwaffe bombers thundering overhead no longer alarmed him. Their bombs and the pounding of heavy artillery had been constant for the last two months. But the sound of Panzer tanks was different. The clanking of the metal tracts through the streets, their diesel engines, and the unique sound of their big guns, meant ground troops were close at hand. Another shell disintegrated a wall of concrete and plaster into rubble, leaving another fifteen-foot hole. Closer this time. The percussion wasn't heard so much as felt, through boots, clenched teeth and the worst of all – pummeling eardrums with pressure enough to burst them. With his ears stuffed with bits of cloth, Joseph adjusted another valve, desperate to get this last tank moving before the Germans swarmed the factory. The other two tanks were not going to make it.

"Try it again!" he shouted. The starter engaged, gears grinding, over and over and... Vvrooom – vrooommm! The powerful music of the heavy diesel, bursting into life. Joseph extracted himself from the bowels of the tank and slammed the armored plate shut that protected the guts of the engine. He waved at Gregor, the driver, and pointed toward the exit door at the back of the factory. There was no way his voice could be heard over the rumble of the diesel so he didn't even try.

Joseph retrieved several tools that were scattered on the floor, tossing them into the canvas bag with the rest. He lifted the strap over his shoulder and headed for the side door. He knew that by tomorrow the language spoken within these crumbling walls could very well be German. Pockets of Russian soldiers were dug in amongst the rubble near the walls. Machine gun nests, heavy guns, and men with rifles, waiting for the enemy. Each group would be a separate battle.

ↄ৴

Three weeks later, only two narrow strips of territory along the Volga's west bank were not occupied by German forces. From the beginning, Stalin's reinforcements and supplies had been pounded by airplane attacks as they crossed the river. Now they were halted completely by huge chunks of ice floating in the current.

The first bullet had missed, though fragments of stone had peppered Nikky's neck and upper chest. The second bullet had not missed and was lodged between his ribs and lungs. Last night, in their basement lair, they had removed the shards of stone imbedded in his skin and surface tissue but he had been too weak to attempt removing the bullet.

Irina carefully unwound the final strip of bandage, exposing the blood-soaked pad. Fortunately, his lungs had not been punctured, but Irina was afraid further delay might produce a fatal infection. It was going to be a delicate procedure, one she was not trained for. Still, it had to be done and there was no one else to do it.

She lifted the pad and placed it and the bandage into the pot of boiling water on their makeshift stove. In the dim light from the kerosene lamp, Joseph could see blood trickling from the open gash. He sat on an empty ammunition box next to Nikky's legs, prepared to hold him still when Irina was ready to start. There was no anesthetic. Vonna caressed Nikky's cheeks and forehead, in position to hold his head and shoulders.

Irina swabbed the open wound with a damp cloth to clear away the blood and nodded for Vonna to slip the leather belt between her son's teeth. Irina stabbed a cooking fork into the boiling, bloody water and lifted the forceps out. The hot metal steamed when it met the frigid air. She stole a glance toward her husband, the distance that had grown between them, temporarily eliminated. Joseph's eyes said it all; fear, resignation. Both parents knew they could be childless within the hour.

Irina's work as a nurse at the hospital for the last ten years had hardened her to sights such as this. And during the last two months, caring for the steady stream of wounded soldiers, she had been required to do a myriad of things she was not trained for; including the extraction of foreign objects from every conceivable part of the anatomy. Performing surgery on her own son was different.

An hour later, nothing stirred. Nikky's body lay beneath the blanket, still as death. In Stalingrad, death was everywhere. The tiniest beat of a twenty-two year old heart, and breath so faint it was undetectable, were all that kept death from this basement.

Joseph stood up and moved the ammunition box out of the way. He began to put on his white parka and pants, clothes that would make him nearly invisible against the heavy snow that had been falling all night.

Joseph's rifle leaned against the wall next to Nikky's. *That will have to wait until tomorrow.* He picked up the bag of tools instead, knowing he had no chance to get in position this late in the morning. During the last month he and Nikky had proven to be extremely effective snipers with 73 dead Germans between them, two of them, yesterday. "I'm going to work on that turret, he said to Irina. "We may need to use it before long." The disabled Russian tank, just across the street, had its tracts blown off, the burnt out shell looking like a decaying dinosaur carcass. It wasn't going anywhere but Joseph thought he might be able to get the heavy gun to function. If so, he could point it where it might do some damage in a last resort.

Joseph looked at Nikky's pallid face, drained of color from the loss of blood. "I can't do anything here," he said, meeting Irina's hollow stare.

"I will come get you if...if you are needed," she mumbled, looking down at her son. His next breath could be his last. For several years, Nikky had been the glue that held their marriage together. Joseph's hatred of Stalin, and everything government, had driven a wedge between them. Irina was more tolerant, accepting reality for what it was. She wanted to move on with life. Joseph was bitter, always.

The moon's glow off the blanket of snow created a sort of twilight. Joseph was already in place an hour before sunrise, as was his custom these last several weeks. Earlier, a knock on their door and a few quiet words had provided him with the most recent intelligence of the German's positions. The visit had lasted less than a minute.

Joseph had chosen the third floor of a bank building, in the corner where he had a vantage point of two streets. Of course, there was so much rubble and debris dumped in the streets that vehicles, other than tanks, could not use them. It had taken some time for Joseph to reach the third floor, requiring him to climb from the floor below because the stairwell had been blown to bits.

Ice was forming on the scarf Joseph had tied around his face. The wool tempered the biting cold and concealed the puffs of steam his breath would otherwise make. He curled his gloved hands inside his mittens to keep them from getting stiff. Grayish-pink light, over the Volga River behind him, was starting to replace the moon's reflection, giving objects their true identities rather than the ones imagined in his mind. His ears started to pick up muffled sounds of the enemy, agents of death, his death as likely as not. He waited, knowing his eyes would detect the slightest movement in the growing light.

As Joseph gazed down the length of both streets to acquaint himself with the *killing zone*, he noted every detail, every brick and stone, every quagmire of wire and pipe cluttering the streets. His mind kept returning to Nikky's comatose figure. He and his son had become a team, specifically targeting officers when they could, wielding as much damage as possible with a single shot. Two snipers giving the German invaders fits.

Normally, Nikky would be set up a block away where they were able to create a cross-fire, or have a line-of-sight to protect each other, in case the enemy got too close to locating one of their hiding spots.

Joseph thought about all the hunting trips they had taken together. It was where Nikky had learned to shoot, learned to stalk his prey, learned to wait for the prey to enter the trap. It is where they had both learned to be snipers. The prey no longer had fur, claws, or antlers. The prey had helmets, boots, pictures of family in breast pockets. And more significantly, the prey shot back. Joseph pulled the dirty-white piece of canvas over his shoulders against the freezing gusts that whipped through the glassless windows. The building's roof was scattered around him and on the sidewalk below.

Joseph's rifle was the same one he'd used when they lived on the farm over fifteen years ago. The same rifle Felix had brought home the last time Russia was at war with Germany. It was a Mosin-Nagant, bolt action. Millions of them had been made to kill Russia's enemies. Joseph could have brought Nikky's rifle this morning. It was the same kind only newer, especially made for snipers with a scope. *Nikky might not ever need it again.* Joseph didn't like the scope, didn't need it, didn't want to worry about the sun's reflection on the glass, revealing his position.

Yesterday, Joseph had eliminated the sniper who had shot his son; a man with a reputation of his own. Joseph had been studying him, his tactics, his tendencies. He had anticipated what his next move would be and was waiting for him; hours before the sun came up.

The Germans were making a relentless push to the chemical factory, about a mile away. Joseph's position in the bank building was in *no-man's-land*. A strip of city blocks where the Germans had tried to flush out nests of the Red Army the day before. Neither side could claim they controlled the territory. The crumpled buildings and streets were the battlefield. This day would bring blood and death...again.

"How is he?" Joseph asked, leaning his rifle against the wall and stripping off his white outer garments.

"I think he is a little stronger," Irina said hopefully.

"How can you tell?"

Nikky resembled a corpse beneath the blanket, his eyes closed. Joseph placed his hand on his son's forehead. The skin was quite cool, but not as cold as death.

Irina blinked her eyes sadly, trying to be strong, yet close to breaking down under the strain. The blanket quivered, the freezing temperatures in the basement penetrating to the bone. Nikky's shivering body fought for life while his mind waited somewhere else.

All that was left of the tailor's shop above their heads were parts of two walls. The other walls, ceiling and roof were now rubble, succumbed to the Luftwaffe's bombs. The broken furniture, and everything made of wood, had already been burnt as fuel. *Two-knocks-a-pause-a-third-knock* drew their eyes upward. The trap door opened, allowing light and a pair of boots to descend the rickety stairs. The heavy, uniform coat of a Red Army officer appeared, followed by a second pair of legs that turned out to be Vonna. The officer and young girl both carried a small burlap bag filled with coal. Vonna handed hers to the officer so she could close the trap door.

"Thank you, comrade," said Joseph, accepting the bags of coal and setting them down next to their small stove. Joseph had made the stove from bricks that lay in the street. He removed the iron plate that served as the stove's door. It was a piece of an armored truck, also from the streets. He put three pieces of coal on the grate and stood to face the officer.

The colonel studied Nikky's face before reaching into his coat pocket and pressing a small bottle of vodka into Joseph's hand. "You have done well, comrade. My sergeant tells me you killed four Germans today, two of them officers. Comrade Stalin congratulates you."

Joseph glanced at the vodka, and then met the colonel's gaze. With tight lips, he said, "I spit on Stalin, and the rest of his murderers in Moscow. I fight to protect my family, our home."

The army officer stiffened. His stern face twitched with a nervous tic caused by stress. "It has been a difficult time for all of us," he said, biting back a stronger rebuke. Despite himself, he examined Joseph's disfigured face, the ugly scar stretching from eye to lip. "Do you know what you two are called by the men?"

Joseph was in no mood to chat and said nothing.

"They call you, *the-scar-that-bites*. And him," he nodded toward Nikky. "They call him, *the-son*."

"Thank you for the coal," said Joseph, turning away, dismissing the high ranking officer. He knelt down by the stove and prepared to light the coal. After an awkward silence, he relented. "My son will die from the cold if not his wounds. Thank you for the coal, comrade."

As the colonel brushed by Irina, she placed her hand on his sleeve, a strained smiled was all she could manage. With his boot on the first step, he muttered something to her about the NKVD, ending with, "...his mouth will get him shot."

When the trap door closed with a thump, Vonna, who had been standing to the side, stepped forward, reached inside the folds of her coat and said, "Look what I found." She withdrew her gloved hand and presented a half-loaf of bread, wrapped in a piece of newspaper. Her face beamed; the bread, a treasure that would last them several days.

Even Joseph smiled as the tension in the room lost its grip. "For a Jewish girl," he said, "you're not bad to have around." Joseph used humor to ease Vonna out of her shell. However, her heritage was never mentioned except in the strict confines of the demolished ruins of this tailor shop's basement. Nikky had brought her home six months ago, like an abandoned kitten. She had escaped the German's executions in the Crimea and fled to Stalingrad.

Irina was glad to have the bread, but she was still focused on Joseph's exchange with the army colonel. With a scowl, she faced her husband. "Protect our home?" she shouted, spreading her arms to indicate the squalor of their man-made cave. "Protect your family?" She gestured toward Nikky's unmoving body. "Is spitting on Stalin going to protect us?"

Joseph ignored Irina's outburst. "Give me that newspaper so I can start the fire," he said to Vonna. After a couple of minutes, his task completed, Joseph slipped the bottle of vodka into the bag of tools and lifted the strap over his shoulder. "I'm going to work on the tank." As he passed by Irina, he said, "Yes, to protect my family. Why don't you tell Vonna how I saved your life when the Reds thought you were Anastasia Romanov. How I took care of you when you had no place to go, just like she is now! Or have you forgotten?"

Irina had no intention of backing down. "I have not forgotten. But the

Tsar is dead, your parents are dead, your sister is dead..."

Joseph slapped her with the back of his hand, hard enough to bring blood to her lip. "Trina is not dead! We don't know that!"

The violence was enough to stop her. With her fingers touching the skin of her face that was turning crimson, Irina bowed her head slightly. "You're right. We don't know about Catrina, but we have to go on with our lives." Irina reached out to him. He pulled away. "Joseph, this is our country, our son. We have to let the past go."

"Never! Not as long as I am alive. You're right about one thing. This is our country." Joseph began to climb the stairs toward the trap door. "It's not the Bolshevik's, but first, we must fight the Germans."

Chapter 17

May 28, 1944
Johnson County, Kansas

Billy and Kitty sat on the porch swing listening to President Roosevelt on the radio. It was a beautiful spring evening, and they were enjoying the rosy-colored clouds as the sun settled below the horizon. There was not a breath of wind, and the birds could be heard calling to each other as they gathered to roost. Kitty loved the sound of the birds in the mornings and evenings, but what she really found soothing was the sound of the crickets as they took over the chorus after the sun went down.

Harvard University had let out for the summer, but their son was not at home. Dmitri had not attended classes the spring semester. When he came home from school at Christmas, he had brought his trunk of clothes and belongings with him. Billy and Kitty had met his train at Union Station on a cold, snowy December evening. When their son said he had to get his trunk from the baggage car, they assumed it was full of Christmas presents, and they were pleased he was feeling the holiday spirit.

But on the ride home the truth of the matter popped out. "I joined the Army," he blurted from the back seat. Kitty and Billy whipped around in their seats, the car swerved a bit.

Dmitri was prepared for this reaction. "I would have been drafted anyway. I'm nineteen years old and they need guys like me." He said this with a measure of pride and the words of the recruiting officer still in his head. "The Japs attacked us two years ago and I'm surprised I haven't been called already."

Kitty and Billy looked at each other. Neither spoke. Kitty had pulled the appropriate strings to spare their son from duty. They were loyal Americans and her gut knew it was wrong...but she couldn't face losing her son like she'd lost her brother. Billy had suspected as much but had not confronted her.

They rode in silence, a pall shrouding the car. As they turned into the half-mile driveway up to the house, Billy said, "Well, let's not let this spoil our Christmas. And you're right, Dmitri, the country does need men like you. But remember, I was there and this is no game you're playing. You're putting your life on the line, and your mother and I are planning on having at least six grandchildren. So, keep your goddamned head down and don't try to be a hero."

That had been five months ago, and now the president was on the radio, talking about the American war effort at home, the boys overseas, and protecting freedom in the name of God. Kitty was snuggled up against Billy's side as the evening air began to turn cool. When the broadcast ended, she said, "Where do you think he is right now?"

Billy sighed heavily, his chest rising and falling with the breath. "Well, we know he went to England and that they've taught him how to jump out of an airplane with a parachute and a rifle. We haven't invaded the continent yet, so he must still be in England. What do you think?"

It was Kitty's turn to sigh. She knew all of that. And she knew that he knew she knew all of that. But she wanted to hear him say it. As long as Dmitri was on friendly soil, there was no reason to think any harm had come to their only son. "Maybe they'll just attack with ships and won't need to send the paratroopers...maybe."

Billy stood up, "Let's make some ice cream. We haven't done that in a long time. I'll get it started and you can put in the nuts and chocolate like Dmitri always did when he was little." He opened the screen door. "How does that sound?"

Kitty curled up on the swing in a near fetal position, "Fine," she murmured.

⁂

James was hard at work, trying to figure out how to squeeze more production out of all ten bakeries to meet the demands of
their new defense contract. Man does not live on bread alone...but soldiers seem to, he thought to himself. Kitty's Kakes had landed a huge deal with

74

the United States government. The contract was to supply the military with box-car loads of thin-sliced dried toast that could be packed with the K-rations and shipped overseas.

In '42 and '43, ninety percent of the toast had been shipped west to feed the men in the Pacific. Now they had to equal that amount again for the effort in Europe. They had built new bakeries at the rate of two per year for the last three years, and had expanded the capacity of the original four bakeries as well. James was good at what he knew, production and operations, but he was starting to get overwhelmed by the sheer volume of demands.

Sitting in his plush office on the top floor of Kitty's Kakes' headquarters in Kansas City midtown, James threw his pencil down on the desk and leaned back in his high-backed leather chair. "We only have one choice," he said aloud. It was nine o'clock, dark outside, and the place had been closed up for hours. "Until this war is over, we're going to have to cut back on the cakes and pastries. We just can't do it all." His voice sounded eerie in the otherwise silent building.

He stood up and turned off the lamp on his desk. The lights in the hallway guided him to the elevator. He pressed the button and heard the pulleys and cables creaking in the shaft below. He looked down the hall and noticed Kitty's office door was open, but the dark hid the ever-present mounds of paper and ledgers stacked high on her desk and credenza. She knew exactly where to find anything she wanted, without fail. Anyone else needing to find something in there had little-to-no chance. Her pet peeve was discovering something out of place because it had been moved while she was out. It was pretty much sacred ground and holy writ that no one mess with Kitty's mess.

Each had a very large corner office. Kitty's faced the Plaza. His had a view of downtown. The rest of the floor was taken up by smaller offices, occupied by various vice presidents, and a secretarial pool. He and Kitty were the only ones who had private secretaries, mainly to screen calls. It was more efficient for the rest of the management team to share clerical staff.

James and Kitty were *somewhat* affectionately known as the *he-boss* and the *she-boss*. They nourished a positive working relationship with all levels of employees, treating them as equals. They earned respect through their actions and were open to suggestions and criticism. However, when it came to the vision and direction of the company as a whole, there were only two votes. The enormous success of the company was attributed to the fact that the two voters consistently balanced and complemented each other on major decisions.

A bell *pinged* and James swung open the heavy, glazed glass door. The brass gate of the elevator opened *accordion style* before he stepped in. He turned the knob to *lobby*; the gate closed. With a small jolt and sound of grinding gears, the lift began its slow descent. James's decision to cut back the *fluffy* product lines, as he and Kitty called them, would be presented to the Board tomorrow. This meant he would go into Kitty's office, lay down the facts, and see if she agreed. But that was tomorrow. Tonight he was headed to Rachel's house, and the thought made him shiver with anticipation.

Chapter 18

The war was finally over. Roosevelt was dead along with countless others, but Dmitri wasn't. He had left two years ago, still a boy, but had returned a man. After several months of celebrating, relaxing and readjusting to civilian life in America, Dmitri came to another crossroad. He, his mother and his father sat in the living room to discuss his future.

Billy paced back and forth, his eyes glued to, but not seeing, the expensive Oriental rug beneath his feet. His hand clutched his sleeved wrist at the small of his back, his customary *thinking position*. "...so your mother and I think it's time for you to make a decision. You can help me run the cattle and land-development business, or you can work with your mother and learn the bakery business."

Kitty's eyes were shifting from her husband to her son then back to her husband. They had decided that Billy would pose the issue to Dmitri, but she could not stay out of the conversation any longer. "Or, dear, you could go back to Harvard and finish your degree." This is what she really wanted to happen, and Billy had promised to include it as an option.

Dmitri was in his lounging position, his right arm stretched out on the back of the sofa with his legs crossed at the ankles on the floor. "I want to be a pilot," he said, ignoring the alternatives already suggested.

Billy and Kitty looked at each other, inquiring with their eyes as to whether the other had heard of this before. Kitty shrugged, then looked at her son and said, "What made you decide you wanted to be a pilot?" There were times when Dmitri offered little-to-no information and it had to be dragged out of him with specific questions. This appeared to be one of those times.

"I decided when we were flying missions in Europe and all of us grunts had to jump out of the plane with our rifles and packs. The pilots just turned the plane around and flew back to the base. I mean, it was dangerous to fly with the *Jerry's* shooting at you, but we had to go tromping through the mud and snow for weeks and months, sometimes behind the German lines. Hell, the pilots were back at the base, going out with the English girls and sleeping in real beds. I said to myself, if I ever get out of this hell-hole alive, I'm going to learn how to fly. That thought kept me going." End of explanation.

Surprising parents is what kids do best. Billy and Kitty looked at each other again and smiled. Both recognized and accepted Dmitri's ambition as a deep-seated desire, and were relieved that he at least had some plan in mind.

Billy had stopped pacing. He leaned against the baby-grand piano, ready to push the conversation forward. "Flying sounds exciting, but what are you going to do once you learn? I've heard there are lots of pilots looking for work since the war ended."

Dmitri leaned forward, hands clasped, elbows on his knees. "Actually, I was going to talk to Mom about flying her and James around the country as their company pilot. We could build an airstrip right here on the farm. It would save them both a lot of time." He glanced at Kitty to see her reaction. "I could deliver emergency orders to places that aren't close to one of the bakeries. I could fly you and Mom to Louisville to check on the horses whenever you wanted. Plus, I could start flying other businessmen around...kind of a VIP airline."

The speech had been rehearsed...at least in his mind. The enthusiasm in his voice matched the sparkle in his eyes.

Kitty had been sitting with her feet tucked underneath her on the couch next to Dmitri. She threw the crocheted afghan off her lap and stretched out her long legs to get the stiffness out before she stood up. She walked over to Billy and wrapped her arms around him from behind. On her tip toes she kissed his neck seductively, while her eyes were locked on her son's. She whispered in his ear so Dmitri could not hear, *"I think we ought to go look at airplanes tomorrow. If he's going to fly, I want the safest thing with wings to be our new company plane."*

Billy turned around and faced his wife. He reached his arms around her and dipped her like they were on the dance floor, bending her over till she was almost parallel to the floor. Then he kissed her hard on the lips and said out loud, obviously addressing his son, "What kind of airplane do you think we should buy?"

Dmitri could never figure out his parents' strange antics. A minute ago they were talking about what he was going to do with his life, and now they were dancing around, kissing each other. He had heard his father's words, though. He realized that during that brief interlude, his petition had been weighed, discussed and granted.

He jumped up off the sofa and spread his long arms around both of them. "I think we ought to get a Beechcraft C-45 Expediter. It's a twin engine, low wing plane the army used to fly the brass around. It can go over two hundred miles an hour and up to seven hundred miles without stopping to refuel. It holds six or seven passengers, depending on other cargo, and would be perfect for what I have in mind."

Dmitri had clearly done his homework on the subject, and was geared up to give his folks the rest of the C-45's specs in rapid fire. Kitty broke free from both her men and held up her hand, claiming the floor. "I want to know if it's safe; how long have they been building them; and what's the track record. If I'm going to be taxied around in this thing I want to be sure it lands when we want it to and not when it wants to." It was a mother's concern that prompted the statement. Kitty knew the boy had no fear. The only way she could protect him was to shift the focus to her own safety.

"I know they started building them in '42 and they were safe enough to fly the generals around Europe, but we'll have to go down to Fairfax tomorrow to get all the information. What do you think about that, Mom?"

Kitty looked at the glow in her son's face. "I think you and your father should do just that. I've got to go to work tomorrow, so I'll see how James feels about the idea of having another O'Riley on the payroll." She looked at Billy, who nodded, understanding perfectly that his mission was to lend some mature judgment to the project of purchasing an airplane.

Chapter 19

July 1952
Chicago, Illinois

Kitty stood by the fence of Chicago's Midway Airport with Ernie Mitts. The *Windy City* was true to its name, as strong gusts blew Kitty's light blue dress, exposing a pair of truly outstanding legs. Kitty was holding the unruly garment down as best she could with one hand, and with the other she held her stylish new hat in place. Her hair was fixed on top of her head, mostly under the hat, so at least that wasn't flying around as well.

Ernie suggested they wait in his Lincoln, but Kitty declined, enjoying the fresh air. She was too polite to mention it, but she dreaded being cooped up in the car while he chained-smoked. Fortunately, she was not one of the multitude of women who had taken up smoking during the war effort.

"I thought the meeting went very well," he said as he tried to light his cigarette in the gale. His hands were cupped around the match, his hunched shoulders turned against the pesky wind.

With her eyes scanning the sky, Kitty said, "If we get approval to develop the shopping center on Slowbotski's farm, I don't see how we can miss."

The plan was to first get the *go-ahead* for commercial development, and then buy up surrounding farmland for developing residential. When the war ended, people could start buying cars and gasoline again. Cities were spreading out.

Having discussed these issues many times before, Kitty revealed what was really on her mind. "Do you think he can land in this wind?"

As if on cue, Ernie's sleek, brimmed hat caught a gust and nearly flew off over the fence toward the runway. He whipped a hand up to grab it, burning his forehead with his cigarette in the process. "Shit!" he said loudly, as the sparks flew away in the wind. He threw the mangled cigarette down to stamp out the remaining ember, but that flew off, too, before he could get his foot on it.

Ernie recovered from the interruption and formulated his answer before speaking. "You know that boy of yours almost lives in that plane. Based on the times I've flown with him in the last six years, I'd say he could land the thing in a hurricane."

Kitty recognized her friend's attempt to quell her apprehension, rewarding him with two rows of sparkling white teeth. "You know, fella, it's a good thing I agree with you or I'd have to think you were just trying to appease a feeble old mother's petty anxiety."

"Feeble old mother? That's rich," he said with a chuckle. "You've slowed down kind of like a runaway freight train goin' down a mountain. Plus, you look like you're still in your late twenties. How old are you, anyway?" He posed this last question with a sort of mock frown on his face, looking into the distance as if he were trying to calculate backwards.

At that moment, a familiar-looking plane approached the landing strip. It was still too far away to make out the Kitty's Kakes logo on the fuselage, but the twin-spiked tail identified it as a Beechcraft C-45. Ernie and Kitty watched as the plane lurched up, down, and sideways, buffeted by the erratic cross-wind. Kitty's heart jumped as a strong gust suddenly drove the plane downward, but it bobbed back up like a cork as it continued its gradual descent. Finally, with less than ten feet of air between the Beechcraft and the concrete runway, the pilot fought to set her down. Anyone who flies will tell you the last few feet are the toughest. The wheels hit the ground hard. The plane jumped and was airborne again. Touchdown once more, a small bounce, and at last it stuck as the pilot put the flaps up all the way to hold it there.

Relief flooded over Kitty like the tide. She realized she hadn't been breathing for the last thirty seconds and took a deep breath. She turned to Ernie and noticed the strain leaving his face.

"See, what'd I tell ya?" he crowed. "One hell of a pilot, that boy of yours."

Kitty reached for his arm and squeezed it as hard as she could. It helped release her tension, but it made him wince. "Sorry about that," she said with a sheepish grin.

The C-45 Beechcraft, with the Kitty's Kakes logo painted brightly on the side, taxied up to the area where private VIP planes park. Dmitri shut down the engines. The propellers began to wind down until the actual blades, rather than a circular whirl, could be seen. This was one part of having the plane that Kitty liked best. She didn't have to deal with airport crowds, ticket lines, baggage check-ins, and all the rest of the hassles in the terminal.

The door between the wing and the tail on the pilot's side swung inward, and two folding steps appeared as if by magic. To Kitty's surprise, the first thing she saw emerging from the door was not her son but a pair of shapely long legs followed by a swirling pink dress and finally, a mass of wildly flying blond hair...very, very blond hair.

As the pair of pink three-inch pumps hit the concrete, a second pair of legs appeared. This body was clothed in pressed khakis, accompanied by the smiling face of her beloved son. He waved his arm enthusiastically above his head, reached an arm around the blond woman's waist and started toward them with long, powerful strides. After about three steps, the heels caused the woman to nearly sprawl on her face. Dmitri lifted her into his arms and began walking again. One of the shoes slipped off her toes, so he swooped down and grabbed it without missing a step while she held on to his neck like a lifeline.

When Dmitri set the woman down, she immediately turned into the wind so that her dress and hair would blow behind her instead of in her face. Kitty couldn't help but notice the deep brown eyes, brows and lashes which contrasted with the platinum blond hair. Her overall appearance gave the impression of a Hollywood starlet, though maybe a little older than that. Her body and face were as perfect as could be created by a master sculptor or painter.

His mother's brief but thorough scrutiny was not lost on Dmitri. He was amused to see that Eden was engaging in precisely the same activity. He would have loved to have been able to read both women's thoughts. On the other hand, he was probably better off not knowing. *Ignorance is bliss*, he reminded himself.

He leaned over the waist-high, chicken-wire fence and hugged his mother as best he could. "Hi, Mom! What did you think of my expert landing? A little rocky, huh?" He turned to Eden and reached out his hand. He pulled her to his side and said, "I want you to meet Eden Doniere. We met in Denver and she wanted to come along. Eden, this is my mom and this is Mr. Mitts."

"Like the garden," she giggled, shaking both their hands. "Very pleased to meet you."

Ernie bowed, as if to a princess, which annoyed Kitty slightly. She already didn't like Eden. *Oh well*, she thought, *the woman is gorgeous and Ernie is just being polite.*

"Let's go into the terminal and have a drink at the bar," Dmitri said over his shoulder, ushering Eden to the gate in the fence. The sharp look on Kitty's face made Dmitri smile. "Don't worry. I'm going to have a coke. But first, I have to go see about getting fueled up and submit my flight plan. Why don't the three of you go on ahead and I'll catch up to you in Sutera's in a minute. Get me a large coke with a lime in it, will you?"

Kitty returned the gin and tonic to the cocktail napkin and stirred it idly as she listened to Ernie explain their plans for the shopping center to Eden. He finished up by saying, "Now, all we need is a little luck and we're on our way."

Kitty broke in before Eden could ask another question. "So, tell us what you do in Denver, Eden."

Eden lifted her martini glass and finished the last sip, then popped one of the two olives into her mouth. "The olives are the best part, don't you think?" She crinkled her nose and squinted her eyes toward Ernie, making a cutesy, little girl face. Turning to Kitty, she said, "Well, I'm not really doing anything right now. You see, my husband and I got divorced about six months ago and he gave me enough money to get by on for a while. And I just want to enjoy myself for a while. You know, he would never take me out when we were married and he wouldn't let me go out alone... So, now I'm just going out and having a good time...for a while. That's how I met Dmitri."

Dmitri was just crossing the floor to their table. "Did I miss anything, folks?" He pulled the chair out and sat down. "Thanks for ordering my coke. Do you want another one, Eden?" He nodded toward her empty glass as he raised his arm for the waiter.

"Eden was just telling us about how you two met and what she's doing *for a while*," Kitty said a little coldly. "Weren't you, dear?"

Eden related the story about meeting at a bar, going to dinner and then dancing. Dmitri had told her about being a pilot and asked if she wanted to fly to Chicago to pick up his mother and then the three of them would fly down to Kansas City. That was last night.

Eden was on her second double martini, and as she finished up her story, her words began to slur. She popped both olives into her mouth and giggled.

Ernie said, "So, how did you like the flight? I'll bet that wind made it pretty bumpy, particularly the landing."

"Oh that didn't bother me," she said. "We stopped in Omaha for gas, so I was already used to landing. Plus, D.O. - that's what I call him. He's the best pilot around. We did something he's never done before while he was flying, didn't we, Doe-Doe? A little taste of the forbidden fruit." She reached over and squeezed his hand that was resting in his lap.

Kitty looked at her son, and the crimson couldn't have been any brighter if he'd been standing on his head for an hour.

Ernie stood up and said, "Well, I'll bet you three need to be on your way. And I've got to get back to work." He shook Dmitri's hand. "It was good to see you again. And be careful with my partner here. We've got a shopping center to build. It was nice meeting you, Eden."

Eden rose and gave him a friendly kiss on the neck. She couldn't reach his cheek, but didn't think a hand shake was enough for her new friend. Particularly, since he was a rich banker.

Ernie turned to Kitty, who was reaching into her purse to pay for the drinks. "Don't worry about that," he said. "I'll take care of the check. Just get yourself home and be ready to sign the papers once we get approval to start construction. And thanks for coming up for the meeting. You were very convincing. Probably made the difference for a couple of the members on the committee."

Kitty stood up, went over to the banker and kissed him on the neck, obviously mimicking Eden's display. "This must be your lucky day," she said with a wink and a smile. Then, whispering, "Better do something about that pink lipstick on your collar before you go home to your wife."

Chapter 20

October 30, 1952
Kansas City, Missouri

Kitty sat at her desk going over the plans and contracts one last time before signing them. It had taken three months and another trip to Chicago to get final approval on their shopping center and apartment development project. A few changes had been made from the original, but nothing substantial. Kitty suspected the committee was in need of justifying their existence, thus they spilled a little ink but no blood.

Kitty looked at the small clock on her desk. It was eleven o'clock, and she just had time to sign the papers and get them in the mail before lunch. She was supposed to meet Dmitri at the Savoy Grill downtown at twelve. He said he wanted to have lunch downtown because he was going to fly into the Municipal Airport, across the river, at eleven ETA. She wasn't sure why he wanted to meet her for lunch in the first place. But it would give her a chance to drop off the papers at the main post office on the way.

Maybe her son just wanted to have lunch with his mother. No law against that, she thought to herself.

It took her longer than expected to get out of the office. The telephone is a mixed blessing, she thought. Having just left the post office, she made her way down Baltimore to Ninth Street. The restaurant was on the corner. She pulled her little MG-TD into a parking place and got out. She loved the little British green sports car. Unfortunately, it was about time to put it up for the winter. Billy had given it to her last Christmas, though she had had to wait till Easter before she could drive it much. Once it got warm, the top came down and she never put it back up. She only drove it on nice days. The rest of the time she drove the Cadillac.

She was met just inside the door by a man in an elegant tuxedo. He was holding several menus and looking as stiff as his starched shirt. "Will you be dining alone, Madam?" he asked with a slight bow.

Being a few minutes late, Kitty scanned the tables in view before answering. "I'm supposed to meet my son, but I don't see him. Our name is O'Riley. He was flying in from out of town and may not have arrived on time either."

"Yes, Madam. The gentleman and a lady were seated a few minutes ago in a private booth. Would you please follow me?"

As Kitty followed the man, whose tuxedo matched the black and white tiled floor, she puzzled over *the lady* comment. *What is that boy up to now? Sounds like I get to meet a new girl friend. Maybe this will be the one,* she hoped. As they approached a high-backed booth, Kitty could see one side of the table was still empty. *Naturally,* Dmitri and his girl were sitting together. She could hear the sounds but not the words of their private conversation just before the maître'd picked up her napkin and waved her into her place with another impeccable bow.

Before Kitty could slide in, Dmitri had risen to greet his mother with a smooch on the cheek. She gave him a radiant smile and began to sit as she turned to be introduced to *the lady*. Kitty's sparkling blue eyes were met by a pair of warm brown ones, artfully enhanced by expensive makeup. The woman's careful smile revealed the uneasiness that lay just beneath the surface.

"You remember Eden, Mom," said Dmitri as he reclaimed his seat.

Kitty controlled her expression, smiling sweetly, "It's nice to see you again, Eden." She met Eden's cold fingers and sweaty palm half way across the table. Eden's grip was feminine and mechanical.

Both women raised their water glasses at the same time as the maître'd handed Kitty her napkin and said, "Shall I ask the waiter to bring you a cocktail or something else to drink, Madam?"

Before Kitty could finish her sip of water and answer, her eyes were dazzled by a pin prick of light coming from Eden's hand. The diamond was big, and Kitty choked on the water she was swallowing. ...Coughing, she held one hand over her mouth and waved the man and tuxedo away with the other. Through watering eyes, she looked at her son, then back at the ring.

Dmitri picked up the thread without difficulty. "That's why we wanted to meet you for lunch." He grasped Eden's hand tenderly and held it up so

Kitty could clearly see the ring. "We got married in Las Vegas on Saturday."

Kitty nearly choked again but managed to keep it to a small gasp of breath. Indeed, there were two bands on Eden's finger. The stone was impressive, though Kitty preferred clusters of smaller diamonds rather than a large solitaire. The ring was startling, in more ways than one. Finally, she felt her feet on the floor again. "Congratulations, I...I don't know what to say. It's such a surprise."

Dmitri smiled broadly. "We wanted to tell you first. We thought you could help us spring it on Dad." His eyes met Eden's, and then, he turned back to his mother. "And since you took the first part so well, we might as well tell you the rest." He paused... "You're going to be a grandmother!"

This did not surprise Kitty nearly as much as the first revelation. In fact, she would have been surprised if that hadn't been part of the scenario. She reached over, and this time took both of Eden's hands in hers. They were still ice cold. Deciding to accept the fact that this woman was going to be the mother of her grandchild, Kitty gripped her hands warmly. "Congratulations again, and welcome to the family." She looked deeply into Eden's brown eyes and they both understood. Kitty's support derived from a mother's love for her son. Beyond that, Eden would have to earn a place in her heart.

The waiter, standing a few feet away just out of ear shot, recognized this to be a break in the conversation and moved in to take their order. Trained to remember the order without writing it down, he asked, "So, have the three of you made any decisions?"

The irony of the question caused mother, son, and now, daughter to burst into a fit of laughter. After a few seconds, Kitty turned to the bewildered waiter and said between convulsions, "These two have; that's for sure."

The rest of lunch was spent discussing where they were going to live and other domestic issues. Kitty was resigned to her son's fate and hoped, but doubted, it would all work out. She kept thinking to herself, *Hadn't they spent just that one weekend together?*

❧

Dmitri stubbed the Lucky Strike he had been smoking into the ashtray and stood up. He gave his mother a tired hug as she entered the waiting room of St. Luke's maternity ward. Dmitri automatically offered his left hand to his father. Billy, dressed in corduroys and a cardigan sweater, reached out and shook his son's hand warmly. "How's Eden doing? I can tell you've been up all night." The large double doors to the corridor of the delivery rooms swung open as a nurse hustled past them and down another hallway.

"She's OK, Pop, I think. She's been in labor now for twelve hours. I was with her until forty-five minutes ago when they took her to the delivery room. That's when I called you two and I haven't heard anything since. She was getting awfully tired of the pain and then it really started to get bad. I wish the baby would hurry up and come. Does it always take this long?"

The little house in Prairie Village hadn't been the same since mother and child came home. After a few months, the household had settled into a routine and, at any given moment, there were now three possible scenarios. In one, the house was silent, which meant little Joseph was sleeping and everyone else kept as quiet as possible. In the second, the house was filled with *oohs* and *ahhs* and laughter, which meant that little Joseph was playing with something or just being cute. In the third, the house was in turmoil, which meant little Joseph was crying and everyone worked at re-establishing either one of the other two choices.

As time went on, Eden began developing into a *fair weather* mother. She was fine when things were going well; normally taking credit for her wonderfully behaved child. She lost all of her postpartum weight and soon looked as if she was on the women's tennis circuit. The part she couldn't seem to deal with was when little Joseph showed that he had a mind of his own. He was beginning to wear on her nerves. By Thanksgiving the kid was becoming damned inconvenient.

Dmitri was very fond of his son. In fact, he adored him. He still had to fly for a living and be out of town, but when he was home he spent hours and hours playing with the boy. He had wanted to call his son Joseph from the very start, for his mother. Eden was hoping for a girl and didn't object. A father should name his son, she had said. So Dmitri named him Joseph Milanov O'Riley. He knew it would please both his parents. His mom still brooded over her brother once in a while. He had heard many stories about his uncle and felt like it would be a good way to honor him; or at least his memory.

The family decided to have their traditional February birthday celebration at Dmitri and Eden's house. The party was on the 22nd, which meant that little Joseph would also celebrate his ten months of life. Grandma had turned fifty-three two days earlier, and Daddy would be hitting the big *3-0* on the 25th. Uncle James and Billy enjoyed not being in the limelight and sat back on either end of the sofa as the presents were being opened after dinner.

Dinner itself had been somewhat of a strain. Eden was irritable because she was not a good cook and, therefore, was very defensive about every little thing. She snapped at Dmitri several times in the kitchen while he was trying to help. It could be plainly heard by the others in the small dining room. Kitty, Billy and James tried to ignore it and spent their energy trying to make little Joseph laugh in his high chair.

One of the ongoing frictions that had developed in the family was related to money. Specifically, Kitty and Billy did not share much of their fortune with their only son and his family. It didn't really bother Dmitri. He had everything he wanted and enjoyed life every day.

Eden, on the other hand, did not have a job to keep her mentally stimulated. She was not happy spending all day, every day, at the beck and call of someone who couldn't even talk. In Eden's mind, she should be spending her days at the country club, and have someone else do most of the babysitting and the other domestic chores. Then motherhood wouldn't be too bad. She loved to go shopping and that was something she could do with the kid and get out of the house for a while. But they didn't have enough money to go down to the Plaza and buy the kind of things she wanted. Joseph's grandparents had millions and millions. Why wouldn't they spend it on their own flesh and blood? Eden was frustrated.

❧

Kitty stuffed Billy's duffle bag with another flannel shirt. It was already nearly full with wool socks, warm pants, long underwear and everything else a man needs to go fishing in Canada. Kitty had always packed Billy's bags for him when he went on a trip. It wasn't that he couldn't do it himself. It made her feel like she was going with him in a way.

Fishing had become the father-son activity of choice. The only years they had missed their spring trip was when Dmitri had been overseas in World War II, plus last year when Joseph was only a few weeks old. Hunting ducks, pheasants and quail was right up there with fishing, but one didn't think about that until autumn. Occasionally, Kitty joined them on hunting outings if it was going to be a one-day trip. But fishing was a sacred male thing, and she was glad to see them spend a week together every year on the Canadian lakes drinking ale and telling stories.

For several years now, Dmitri had been flying them from Kansas City to International Falls, on the northern Minnesota border. After clearing customs, they hired a pontoon plane and pilot for the final leg into a remote fishing camp. This year was a little different because Kitty had to go to Washington D.C. for a couple of days. The men decided that Canada was a big place, and fish were fish. Why not go farther east this year and try out some new territory. After the fishing trip, they would pick up Kitty in Washington on their way back.

Kitty crammed one last pair of heavy woolen socks into the duffle and pulled the eye-loops closed with the knotted draw string. Billy was still in the basement finishing up some last-minute preparations of fishing tackle, hip boots, rain gear and other stuff they needed to take in the morning.

Kitty slipped out of her clothes and went into the bathroom to draw the bath water. One of the best things about these trips was that they always had really good sex the night before Billy left. It was like part of the tradition. Kitty had felt the warm glow growing in her loins as soon as she started to pack Billy's bag. As she stepped into the luxuriously steamy water, she thought to herself with growing excitement, *That man better hurry up and get up here or I might start without him.* A devilish grin creased her lips as she lay back and became one with the water.

Kitty had been invited to Washington by the senior senator from New York, Oliver Curwood, for two reasons. First, he chaired a committee that was debating the right to strike by the railway workers. He wanted her to give her version of how strikes affect American businesses that rely heavily on railroads for shipping. Passenger commuting and traveling bottleneck issues were on the table as well.

Secondly, there was a big gala at the White House, and Mrs. Curwood was not feeling up to it due to a recurring bout with pneumonia. Kitty would be the perfect stand-in for an ailing wife. Susan Curwood and Kitty were close friends and had been for years, so there would be no trouble with the home front. And the seventy-year-old senator would be the envy of most of the men, having a slim yet voluptuous woman on his arm. Kitty still looked like she was in her middle-to-late thirties and was basically an unknown, so the rumor mills would have plenty of fuel. Older men tended to enjoy that sort of attention.

Kitty's TWA non-stop flight to Washington's National Airport was scheduled to depart the next morning. She had a retirement dinner to attend tonight, so she began putting her things together for the trip early. Normally, she packed in a rush at the last moment. She decided that going to the White House and appearing before a senate committee called for a little forethought on her part. She was going through her jewelry box when the phone rang.

Kitty picked it up, "Hello?"

"Hi, this is Eden. I know you're leaving tomorrow, but I was wondering, if you're not busy tonight, could you watch Jo Jo for me? A girlfriend and I want to see the new movie with Zsa Zsa Gabor. You know, *Lili*. It's at the Uptown. Dmitri can't stand musicals and doesn't like Zsa Zsa, *my daaarling*, so I thought it would be a good time to see it, while he's gone. I could bring him out there and then pick him up in the morning before you have to leave." Eden was talking so fast it sounded like a script she had rehearsed.

Finally, she came up for air and Kitty broke in. "I'd love to, dear, but I've got to go out tonight myself. It's a retirement dinner for one of our vice presidents and it will probably be fun, but frankly, I'd much rather stay home with my grandson and rest before my trip tomorrow. I'm sorry; I really have to be there. You certainly deserve a break, though; can't you find a baby sitter in the neighborhood?"

"Well, I'll try. You know Dmitri, though. He doesn't want me to leave Jo Jo with just anyone. You tell him that I tried you first, OK?"

Kitty hung up thinking the name, Jo Jo, sounded like somebody's dog. *What's wrong with Joey or Joseph or just plain Joe?*

Chapter 21

Dmitri watched his father tie a fisherman's knot with one hand. He had always admired him for his ability to manage even intricate tasks with his left hand, and supporting right arm. It had been more than thirty-five years since Billy lost his dominant right hand. There must be things his father couldn't do, but Dmitri couldn't think of any.

This trip had turned out to be an all-time high in terms of fishing success. They had made their customary five-dollar bet on the biggest catch of each type of fish. They had netted lots of smaller and medium-size fish, but Dmitri started out the contest for *size* with a six-pound walleye pike. The normal size, and actually better eating, was about two-and-a-half to three pounds.

Billy picked up the gauntlet and threw it back to his son with an eighteen-pound northern. Father and son both realized that these two were pretty much ringers and since they weren't fishing for muskies, the tie breaker was going to be the winning lake trout.

The Wounded Moose Lodge was located on a point at the southern end of Raleigh Lake. The medium-sized lake in western Quebec province was not particularly deep as Canadian lakes go. The Wounded Moose was the only lodge on the lake and consisted of five rustic cabins and the lodge itself. The cabins had no running water but had wood-burning stoves for the morning coffee. The stoves doubled as the only means of heat.

Billy and Dmitri had been fishing for northerns and walleyes for the last three days on Raleigh Lake within about three miles of the lodge. Their luck had been phenomenal, but unfortunately, the lake was too shallow for lake trout, which required greater depths for the warm summer months.

The secret to catching lake trout is to have the line in the water during the first two weeks after the ice goes out of the lakes. During this brief period, the trout are hungry and still within ten to forty feet of the surface.

After that, the warming water drives them to the bottom and the chance for a catch is missed till the following year.

The advertisement in *Field and Stream* had said... *Walleye pike, northern pike and lake trout could be caught in abundance at Wounded Moose Lodge.* What it didn't say was that you had to fly in to another lake to get a chance at the lake trout. Normally, this wouldn't be a big deal. Billy and Dmitri had already flown into Raleigh Lake in a pontoon plane. Another hop to a second lake was a minor detail.

The problem was that they only had one more day of fishing, and the pontoon plane had not been available, due to season start-up chores. Paul Cox, the Wounded Moose Lodge proprietor, hadn't even had a chance to have his pilot do a fly-by to see if the ice was out of Lake Victoria or not.

The options were discussed over dinner in the lodge. Several of the other guests, having been to the fishing camp before, encouraged them to give Lake Victoria a shot. The lake trout fishing was worth it. And the rock cliffs and pine covered islands made the scenery a fisherman's fantasy. After a couple of scotch-and-waters plus a bottle of wine at dinner, the stories pretty much made it a clear decision. First thing in the morning, they would load a ten-horse outboard motor, some gas and their fishing gear on the plane and head for Lake Victoria.

☙

Kitty sat next to James at the head table. On her other side was the guest of honor, David Ward, and his wife, Dorris. David had been the first person hired at their Chicago bakery back in the early thirties. Wray Brady and James had gone up there to get the place on its feet, but once it was going they had turned the manager's job over to David. He had run a tight and profitable ship. He had a reputation for being hard but fair, and most of his employees had only good things to say about him.

Kitty and James had offered him a vice president's position in the home office in 1942. So David and Dorris had packed up their teenage kids and belongings and moved to Kansas City. His responsibilities included shipping and transportation. He reported directly to James on the operations side of the company and had loosely been considered Dmitri's boss. That was one part of his job he could have lived without. Having the boss's son work for you was not an ideal situation. The good news was that Dmitri was a good employee whose duties were outside the mainstream operation.

The retirement dinner was in a private room of the Muehlbach Hotel restaurant. There were about seventy-five people making toasts and telling stories. Two-thirds of them were from the home office, and the other third were old-time employees from Chicago who had come down on the train. James had made arrangements for an extra dining car to be coupled to the train for their trip down. It didn't hurt to have connections, and when the Burlington Northern found out it was for David Ward's retirement party, they contributed the car at their own cost.

"Mr. Ward has given us quite a bit of business over the years, both in Chicago and while he was in Kansas City. It would be a pleasure for the railroad to help celebrate his richly deserved retirement."

It was getting close to midnight, and it appeared the party would continue for some time. Many of the people were on their feet, mingling or moving from table to table, joining in this or that conversation. Kitty gave her warmest wishes to the Wards and got up to leave.

James had risen with her, holding her chair like a proper gentleman. "Can I give you a ride home?" he asked.

Kitty patted him on the cheek. "Don't be silly. It's way out of your way, and I've been drinking water for over an hour. I can drive myself without any trouble. It's just that I have that morning flight and it's going to be a long day tomorrow. Anyway, if we both leave, everyone will think the party's over and it looks like they're still having fun. I'll see you in a few days.

As Kitty was looking through her purse for her stub for the hat-check girl, she passed the entrance to the bar. She happened to glance up when a small group broke into laughter after an apparently hilarious punch-line to some joke. Kitty did a double-take at the group when she thought she had seen her daughter-in-law's face. *What would Eden be doing here?* She shook her head as if to clear it and continued on her way to claim her coat.

As she put one arm into a sleeve and then the other, she had a nagging feeling, a feeling she decided to satisfy so she wouldn't wonder about it all night long. She knew the mind plays tricks and in this case; a glimpse of blond hair, red lipstick and part of a pretty face suggested her daughter-in-law. Kitty returned to the entrance of the bar, but saw only the broad shoulders and backs of two men and the edges of a green dress. As the men swayed slightly, Kitty saw a brunette, wearing a red dress, seated on a bar stool with her legs crossed. A third man was hanging on her like wallpaper.

After Kitty took three or four steps in their direction, one of the men reached for his drink on the bar and Eden's profile came clearly into view. Kitty stopped dead in her tracks. It was none of her business if her daughter-in-law went out for a couple of drinks after a movie, and since she had not yet been discovered, Kitty was about to turn and slip out of the bar when something happened that made her catch her breath. The tall man standing nearest to Eden, slid his hand down, grabbed her rear and pulled her firmly against his thigh. Kitty gaped at them, preparing for the indignant slap that was sure to follow. But instead, Eden wrapped her black-stockinged leg and slender toes around his knee. Then, holding her drink in one hand, pulled his neck down with the other and started nibbling provocatively on his ear.

Kitty groaned inside her throat, reached for the bar for support. The movement caught Eden's eye and she surprised Kitty once more by shamelessly continuing her sensual games. If anything, the flirtation intensified as Eden began caressing the man's neck with teasing fingertips, her eyes locking onto Kitty's in defiance.

A fire began to burn inside Kitty as she recovered from the initial shock of what was happening. Standing up straight, she placed the strap of her small evening-purse over her shoulder and marched over to the group of revelers. Ignoring the three men and other woman, Kitty grabbed Eden's arm that was still draped around the tall man. She dug her nails into Eden's flesh and tore her free with one aggressive tug. Eden's drink splattered down the man's shirt. The jocularity on everyone's face swiftly changed to surprise and then confusion as the two women faced each other.

Kitty scowled at Eden's plunging neckline, then noticed her daughter-in-law's left hand was sporting a cluster of rubies instead of the diamond solitaire. This further confirmation infuriated Kitty, and she laid into the younger woman with a vengeance.

"How dare you dishonor my son, you sleazy little bitch! Is this your Zsa Zsa Gabor act?" The heat and ice in Kitty's voice seemed to bounce off Eden, though it had a profound effect on the rest of the group. They all stepped back a step as if making room for a couple of street fighters.

Eden's well-liquored voice shot back in kind. "Get off my back, Grandmaaa! What's wrong with me wanting to go out and have some fun once in a while? Dmitri hasn't taken me out since I had that little brat of his, so hit the road and leave me alone!" Eden turned back to her friends as if the episode was over, just an inconvenient interruption.

Kitty trembled with rage, coming within an eyelash of ripping Eden's face with a swipe of bared claws. The thought flashed into her mind that *cat fight* was an appropriate phrase as she felt the *animal* in her blood rise to the surface. Her body was taut, primed to release the fury pent up inside.

The onlookers watched Kitty expectantly, figuring a violent response was imminent. But to their relief, no assault occurred. Kitty's voice became calm, matter-of-fact. "I'd like to know where my grandson is right now. You're not fit to be his mother, nor wife to my son."

Without turning around to face Kitty, Eden spat, "Fine. I'm tired of taking care of the little *shit* anyway. He's at the next-door neighbors, the Pattersons. Hell, if I'd known you weren't going to share any of those millions with your own son, I never would have had the kid in the first place."

Kitty's mouth dropped open; she was speechless. The worthless gold-digger didn't have an ounce of maternal compassion in her. She burned a hole in the back of Eden's head with the fire in her eyes, saying nothing. After a couple of seconds, which seemed longer, Kitty pivoted and walked deliberately out of the bar and back to the party room.

James saw Kitty enter the still noisy room, having thought she was already on her way home. He excused himself from a conversation and walked over to intercept her. "Having car trouble?" he asked, before she had a chance to speak. One look in her eyes told him it was far more serious than that. He simply said, "I'll get my coat," and they walked out together.

Chapter 22

May 17, 1954
Quebec Province, Canada

Dmitri and Billy were up an hour before daylight, drinking coffee from the pot on the old stove. Billy had stuffed a bag with their rain gear and a dry set of clothes while Dmitri stoked the fire and got the coffee on. They had separated their fishing gear the night before so they could travel light, combining the two tackle boxes into one. They both decided to take casting rods and reels, figuring they would be either trolling or still fishing for the lake trout. Strangely enough, a spinning rod and reel were much more adept for casting than a casting rod.

Dmitri was spreading butter on some sweet rolls when they heard a rap on the door. Billy, leaning back in a rickety old wooden chair, pushed himself off the wall with the back of his head and crossed the small cabin to the door. He opened the door but the light from the oil lamps barely penetrated the darkness outside.

The owner of the fishing camp, Paul Cox, was standing back a few paces at the edge of illumination from the feeble light. He took a couple of steps forward so Billy could see him clearly and said, "Mind if I come in for a minute?"

"Sure," Billy said as he moved out of the way so the big red-bearded man could enter. He closed the door behind him and gestured to Paul to have a seat. Billy returned to his chair, leaned back again and said, "OK, what's up?"

After lighting his pipe with a kitchen match and puffing on it till there was a small cloud around him, Paul began. "We have a problem. I know you boys are set on catching lake trout and this is your last day with us. There's a lake about four miles from here that you can hike into and..."

Dmitri interrupted him, "What's wrong? No, don't tell me. I'll bet there's still ice on Lake Victoria. Or is there something wrong with the plane?"

Paul took the pipe out of his mouth and smiled at the youth's impatience. He had been like that himself when he was thirty. He had mellowed considerably after his second thirty years, half of them running this fishing camp during the warm months.

"There's nothing wrong with the plane and I still don't know about the ice. The problem is with the pilot. Old Louis Bouttell is drunk as a skunk. By the end of last season he was drinkin' pretty good and I told him he'd have to control it or I'd have to find a new pilot. Well, he said he'd work on it during the winter and be clean as a fourteen-year-old virgin by spring. And I thought he had done it too. This year his eyes are clear and you can really tell a difference. But last night Monsieur Bouttell got to passin' a bottle around with a couple of the guides and talkin' 'bout old times. Well, there was more than one bottle and there were a lot of old times."

Paul shook his head slowly back and forth. "I'm awful sorry, boys. But what I was going to say is, there's a lake that you can get to on foot that has some lakers, and I'll throw the guide in free to show you where it is and help carry your stuff."

The disappointment Billy felt was immediate. *Some lakers* didn't sound much like the fantastic fishing stories they had heard last night about Victoria. He looked over at his son and saw the wheels churning behind a blank stare. Billy quickly realized what Dmitri was thinking about, but decided to remain silent for the moment. When Dmitri looked up from the floor, he saw his father just sitting there, looking right back at him.

"Mr. Cox, I've never flown a pontoon plane before, but that de Havilland Beaver out there is just like the trainer my flight instructor had me cut my teeth on. I sat up front with Louis on the way in here, and I watched him take off and land, and we talked some about it. It doesn't seem much different than doing it on land. How about if I fly me and Dad into Lake Victoria this morning and be back before sundown?"

This is exactly what Billy thought his son was thinking about, but he hadn't realized Dmitri had been taught on the same type of plane. It was so noisy on their way into the fishing camp, Billy hadn't been able to hear anything the two up front were talking about. His eyes moved from Dmitri's hopeful expression to the camp owner's frowning face.

Paul, holding his pipe with one hand and rubbing his red-bearded chin with the other, considered the matter. After a few seconds of silence with the offer on the table, Billy made his first comment. "My son is an excellent pilot. He's been flying company executives, including my wife, all around the country for about eight years. And, Mr. Cox, I know it's your plane and risking that investment is a big decision, so I think it would only be reasonable for me to add a hundred dollars to our total bill to cover this accommodation if you choose to let us take her."

Planes and ships have always been called *her* as opposed to *him. Him* just didn't sound right, as in, I think I'll take *him* out for a spin. In the case of the Beaver, servicing the Wounded Moose Lodge, *she* looked as if she had an abusive husband, or maybe *she* played football for the Green Bay Packers. There were dents and bruises up and down the aluminum fuselage.

As Dmitri set his foot on the near pontoon to load their fishing gear, he noticed how the support bars looked as if they'd been welded and re-welded in place. The good news is that he had heard and felt the engine pull her through the air, and it sounded like an engine is supposed to sound. It didn't miss or cough or backfire like they do in Hollywood. A pilot is concerned about the engine, the wings and the steerage control. He was now satisfied that this plane was sound from those perspectives.

He had already checked the plane out as thoroughly as he could without taking her up, which was one of the conditions Paul had made before giving his approval. Billy's offer of an extra hundred dollars was not to be sneezed at, but Paul still had his conscience to think about. If something happened to two of his guests, he at least wanted to make sure they checked things out and made the final decision on their own. Paul had thought about getting them to sign a statement saying he was not responsible if something did happen, but decided that would be bad luck and even a little morbid.

As Billy strapped himself in, Dmitri and Paul stood shoulder-to-shoulder going over the map he had recently acquired from Quebec's transportation agency. The map had been drawn from a series of aerial photos taken the year before. There were almost no roads in this part of the province, and it was very difficult to determine spatial relationships from anywhere but the air. Raleigh Lake and the Wounded Moose Lodge were roughly in the center of the fifty-mile diameter map. Lake Victoria was near the top of the map and Paul was showing Dmitri landmarks that were visible from five hundred feet that would guide their way. Only one of the landmarks was man-made, and that was a ranger's station that would appear on their right about half way to their destination.

Confident that he now knew where he was going, Dmitri buckled himself in as Paul untied the ropes securing the plane to the dock. Paul and one of the guides were just preparing to cast them off when Dmitri pushed open the small pilot's window. "What frequency do you monitor?" he asked.

Paul's face broke into a smile as he held up both hands showing three fingers on each. "Three point three...just remember, *three's a charm*," he declared with a wink.

Billy had heard the exchange. "Three's my lucky number! Guess that means I'm 'bout to catch the biggest lake trout you've ever seen. Let's go driver!"

Dmitri turned back to Paul and said, "Push us out." When their nose was several feet out from the dock, Dmitri leaned down to his still-open pilot's window and yelled crisply, "Clear!" The engine erupted into the silent morning calm, the explosions of its powerful cylinders shutting out the peace of a new spring day.

Dmitri taxied out into the lake for take-off, checking the gauges and controls, getting comfortable with his surroundings. The Beaver had a steering column with two handles, called a *yoke* that resembled a steering wheel on a car. It did not have a *stick* that ran between the pilot's legs like the Piper Cubs and old bi-planes. But the jargon *pull back on the stick* still held on. He felt the nostalgia of his training days, and confidence flowed through his veins as he acknowledged the hours he had logged since that time. "OK, Dad, here's the map. You're the navigator. We'll take off into the wind heading west, then we'll turn north and you start looking for this island on Lake Obiwanee." Dmitri pointed to the spot on the map, and then continued with the other landmarks Paul had just given him.

When they were well into the lake, Dmitri looked at Billy and said, "All set?"

Billy looked in his lap at the map, checked his seat belt and then turned around in his seat, looking over his shoulder at their fishing gear. "Did they remember to put that ten-horse Evenrude and gas in?"

Dmitri gave him a thumbs up and smiled, "Did it myself. All we need now is a chance to drop our line in Lake Victoria's clear blue water." He reached over and pounded his dad's thigh good-naturedly, then pushed the throttle forward. As the plane started to gain speed across the dark water, Dmitri said, "I think we ought to raise the bet to ten dollars. You can afford it and I could use the money."

"You got it," said Billy. He sat back and watched his son concentrate on the business at hand as the pontoons broke free from their watery grasp. The plane soared above the trees as the sun burst into splendor behind them, and then out the side window as they banked to the north.

☙

Kitty handed little Joseph to James and picked up her cup of coffee for the drive to the airport. James had put her bags in the back of the Cadillac while she was making them all a breakfast of Cheerios and sliced bananas. "Be sure to check his diapers every hour and see that he takes his nap."

It was the third time she had reminded James of his duties, but he just nodded his head and bounced the boy gently in his arms. He leaned toward Joe's ear and whispered just loud enough for Kitty to hear, "It's OK, fella; she'll be gone in a minute and then we can go in the living room and play poker."

Kitty smiled at him and feigned a punch to his free shoulder. "I'll be back by tomorrow night. Will you be all right till then?"

James nodded confidently, "We'll hold down the fort." He knew she was under a strain after the episode with Eden the night before, and was worrying about how, if, or what she should say to her son. Kitty had described the confrontation to James as they drove to the neighbors to pick up her grandson. Then they had stayed up most of the night talking about what was to be done. James had acted mostly as a sounding board until Kitty was talked out. He got two-and-a-half hours sleep, sacked out in the guest room.

Chapter 23

Billy ticked off the landmarks as they appeared and were left behind. The fact that Dmitri had an accurate compass bearing to follow meant the landmarks merely served as confirmation and a measure of distance. The payoff came when they saw brilliant blue water exactly where Lake Victoria was supposed to be. The blue made a beautiful contrast to the evergreen forest with patches of white snow still holding on from winter.

Dmitri made a low fly-by run to be sure there were no big chunks of ice floating in the lake that could cause trouble when the pontoons cut into the water. Satisfied that it was all clear, he made a wide turn above the trees, pointed the nose of the plane into the wind and began his first attempt at landing on liquid. It turned out to be so simple he was almost disappointed. The water was calm, and his runway was almost three quarters of a mile wide. Pretty hard to mess that up.

By the time the plane had slowed down and stabilized in the water, Billy was scanning the hand-drawn map of the lake that one of the guides had made for them the night before. It showed where the boat was stored during the winter, under a large tree in a protected cove. The shorelines of several islands were also marked where they were guaranteed to catch their limit.

After peering out the plane's windows for a moment, Billy found what he was looking for. A huge set of rock cliffs marked on the map, *The Palisades*, became his reference point. "Here, look at this," he said to Dmitri as he handed the map over to his son. Pointing to the map with his finger and then out the window, across Dmitri's chest, with his handless arm, he said, "There's the cliffs, on your side. That means the boat should be straight behind us, just past that island we cleared on the way in. See there?"

Dmitri handed the map back to his dad and grabbed the throttle and steering column, "You're the navigator," he said. "I'll just turn this baby around and we'll be on our way."

They taxied along through the water, talking about having another bet on who catches the first fish and how easy it was to fly into the lake. "You know," said Dmitri, "if we didn't live in Kansas; I mean, if we lived in a place like Minnesota or Wisconsin, I think it would be neat to have a plane with pontoons on it. You and I could fly around to a different lake every weekend and go fishing. I wonder if you could tie a little boat to the bottom of the plane?"

Billy smiled at his son, reflecting on the thought of spending their weekends together and, in a couple of years, bringing little Joseph along too. All was right with the world. Part of him hoped his son would catch the first and biggest fish today, but only part of him. The competition was what made the betting fun. He'd show this young whippersnapper who the angler of the family is.

They passed the island and entered the little protected cove where the boat was supposed to be stored. Billy unstrapped himself and climbed between the seats back to where the gear was stowed in the tail-end of the plane. He took off his boots and began donning a pair of chest waders that were stuffed in a canvas bag along with a length of heavy rope. These items were considered part of the standard flight equipment, as there were many lakes that did not have a dock or pier to tie up to and the water was normally freezing cold; today being no exception.

Billy climbed out the door and stood on the pontoon, holding on to the struts that supported the wing above his head. Dmitri eased the plane forward and cut the engine as they neared shore. Billy could see the rocky bottom beneath him through the crystal-clear water. However, he'd been fooled many times in his life when the water turned out to be deeper than it looked. As he prepared to jump off his perch, he tied one end of the rope around a metal bar supporting the pontoon and hung the remaining coil over his shoulder. Dmitri had warned him not to tie it to a wing support. *Screwing with the wings is a good way to limit length-of-life.*

Billy took the plunge into thigh-deep water and waded to shore. He planted his feet and applied his powerful legs as if he were in a tug-of-war, pulling the plane until the pontoons hit bottom. By the time Billy had tied the loose end of the rope around a tree, Dmitri was stepping into the water, carrying the ten-horse-power motor.

Billy smiled and said, "Next time I drive, and you pull us to shore. I'll go check out the boat while you finish unloading." Billy sat down on a rock and began stripping off the rubber waders. "Now that I think of it," he said, "let's get the boat in the water and we can put the gear right into it. No point in lugging that stuff ashore."

Dmitri nodded. "You're always thinkin', Pop. Must come with age."

About fifty yards from where they had landed, they found a lean-to type shelter braced against a huge rock. It was made out of a dozen sturdy, shaved poles covered with a tarpaulin. There was still about six inches of snow covering most of the tarp where the shade from the rock and a huge white pine had prevented the sun from doing its work. Dmitri lifted an edge of the canvas cautiously, a little nervous about coming face-to-face with sharp teeth and claws, intent on defending its den.

As they peeled the tarp down, light penetrated the space. Billy noted the bones and animal droppings, signifying that indeed this had served as some creature's home the past winter. They started to dismantle the poles of the lean-to, lining them up as rollers to get the heavy wooden boat to the water. It took all their strength to turn the boat over, but when that was accomplished, it rolled down the hill on the logs like a toboggan. They towed it along the shoreline and nestled it up to the pontoon beneath the plane's open door. The aluminum ice chest was the last thing to be loaded. Dmitri turned to his father and said with a smile, "We'll have to lighten this a bit before we try to lift it back into the Beaver. Want a beer?"

Billy tilted his head before saying, "It's only eight-thirty in the morning, but if you're going to be flying this afternoon, I guess you better do your drinking early." He stuck out his hand and accepted the bottle of ice cold Labatts, a rich Canadian Ale. He set the bottle between his legs, pulled his fishing pliers from the leather sheath on his belt, and levered the metal top off. He offered the pliers to his son. "Smart of those fellas to put a bottle-opener on these things. Must of been beer drinkers. You know, we're going to have to make room in the ice chest for our limit of lake trout, too. How about stoppin' your lollygagging around and get that motor fired up so we can do some fishing."

They spent a couple of hours trolling around the areas marked on the little map, catching fish at almost every spot. Next, they decided to do some still fishing, underneath the huge palisades. The sky was solid blue, as was the water, with just enough breeze to drift leisurely along the cliffs.

They had their boat cushions, which doubled as life preservers, braced against the gunwales, supporting their backs as they stretched their legs out on the boat's bench seats. With ale in hand and rods leaning over the side, they talked and laughed between frequent strikes from below. The morning's catch was record-shattering, with a see-saw battle for the prize for biggest fish. Dmitri's fourteen-pounder had the edge when they finally broke for lunch.

Chapter 24

With his knees resting on a boat-seat cushion, Dmitri was bent over, blowing on tiny flames. There was a wisp of smoke rising from the birch bark and pine twigs that he was using to get the fire started. As the fire took hold, Dmitri fed it with larger and larger sticks.

Billy was at the water's edge, admiring two stringers full of lake trout. He could hear the fire popping and snapping as the flames licked at the dead, dried-out wood. He leaned down and untied one of the rope stringers from a low-lying pine branch near the water.

Most of the fish were still alive but a few of them had swallowed the hook and were floating belly up. He chose one of those for their lunch entre and returned to the fire. "Do you want to clean *Moby Dick* or take charge of starting the potatoes, onions and beans?"

Dmitri began to pull the utensils and frying pan from the lunchbox. "I'll do the cooking today. Maybe you could move down the road a piece to clean that fish, and take the flies with you."

As Billy turned to go, he said, "OK, boss, but this'll just take a minute for an old salt like me."

"Well, *Old Salt*, how about baitin' our hooks with a couple of chunks of meat and lettin' them sit on the bottom while we eat." On some trips, the biggest fish they caught all day had been while they were sitting around having a shore-lunch and drinking beer, rods propped up with stones. Two years ago Dmitri had forgotten to loosen the drag on his reel and a fish had taken the hook-line-and-sinker, not to mention the rod, into the lake, never to be seen again.

After lunch they flipped a coin to see who would have to clean up the mess kits, and Billy lost. With everything stacked into the greasy skillet, he grabbed the brillo pad and returned to where he had cleaned the fish. It was more level there and easier to get down to the water than the rocky shelf where they had built the fire.

Dmitri made himself comfortable for a little snooze with a seat cushion to prop his head and a straw fishing hat over his eyes. Getting up early, drinking ale all morning, and then having lunch had made him drowsy. And since he had won the coin toss, why not?

It seemed as if he had just closed his eyes when he heard some kind of commotion down by the boat. He lifted the brim of his hat, expecting to see his dad putting the lunchbox back in the boat, but what he saw woke him up with a start. A young bear cub was busy sloshing around in the water, creating havoc with the stringers of fish.

Dmitri jumped to his feet and ran toward the cub, shouting and picking up a rock as he went. He was about to hurl the stone to help make his point, when he heard a deep-chested growl coming from the bushes to his right. He froze, as a dark furry shape appeared from the brush and knocked him off his feet with a blow from a massive paw. He landed half-in and half-out of the water and the mother bear was on him in an instant. Dmitri was so stunned he couldn't think, pinned by the enormous weight of his attacker. Searing pain racked his body as he felt the claws and savage teeth rip into his flesh.

Billy had been gathering the cleaned mess kits and utensils when he heard his son shout at the cub. He started back to their lunch site to see what was going on. The unmistakable snarl of an angry bear turned him to ice. He dropped the plates with a clatter and sprinted over the rocks, branches whipping his face. As he reached the clearing, his mind nearly burst with the vision of bloodied legs writhing beneath the huge brown hind quarters of the bear.

Without a moment's thought for his own safety, Billy leapt to the fire and grabbed a large stick, blazing strongly at the other end. He nearly fell as he stumbled down the rocky incline to where his son was being mauled. He jammed the flaming wooden torch between the bear's hind legs, driving upward into her soft underbelly where the fur was sparse.

With a deafening roar and unimaginable quickness, a murderous sweep of the she-bear's right front paw raked Billy's wrist, flinging the fiery stick into the water with a hisssssss. Billy scrambled up the slope without risking a glance backward, afraid that one step might be the only thing between him and death, fire his only weapon.

In a single motion, Billy scooped up another flaming branch in his bloodied left hand and spun around in a crouch, ready for the beast to attack... Nothing. His eyes shifted to where his son lay silent, still. The bear was in the water about six feet off shore, slowly moving away. Billy's confusion disappeared as he digested the scene. The bear cub had escaped to the forest. The mother bear had simply been defending her young, exactly as he had protected his son. With the danger to the cub removed, the she-bear had no interest in continuing the attack, particularly with an adversary wielding red hot embers and flame. She was cooling her blistered skin and calling it a draw.

Relief flooded through Billy as he became conscious of his pounding heart. Carrying the fire stick with him just in case, he moved cautiously back down the rocky slope, careful not to appear threatening to the mother bear who was still only thirty feet away from his son. Kneeling, he set the stick down and lifted Dmitri's head to look into his bloody face for signs of life.

Dmitri's eyes opened and blinked as blood ran into them. He moaned with pain and began to speak in a weak voice. "Is it gone?" There was no fear, just a matter-of-fact question. "It hurts, Pop. How bad is it?"

Billy was no doctor, but he sized up the damage he could see, and said as calmly as he could, "You'll be all right. You're bleeding from about six wounds, but it doesn't look like any arteries are punctured." In his heart, he knew they would have to act fast in order to save Dmitri's life. "We need to get you back to the plane. There's a first-aid kit in there."

Billy reached beneath his son's shoulders and pulled him to a sitting position. Dmitri gasped in pain from the movement. Billy cradled him in his powerful left arm as they made their way awkwardly and painfully into the boat. He quickly untied the bow-rope and pushed them away from shore with an oar. The motor cranked up on the first pull and they were off, speeding away in a matter of seconds, a small victory but gratifying none the less. The wake of white water and waves strung out behind them, a flat surface and clear air ahead.

They were only about ten minutes from the plane with the motor at full tilt, but it gave Billy time to analyze their situation. The amount of blood staining Dmitri's pants around the inside of his thigh was alarming. They were going to have to get some help and that posed a big problem. He reached into his pocket, pulled out a neatly folded red bandanna and leaned forward, pressing it against the torn, bloody blue jeans. "I want you to hold that as firmly against your leg as you can."

Dmitri smiled wanly, moving his arm and shoulder carefully so that his hand would reach the spot. "Is this like sticking your finger in the dike?"

The attempt at humor was comforting but nearly broke a father's heart. Billy replied, "Those bandages will do the trick, and then you can use those hands to make like a pilot. Do you think you can fly the plane if I help you?"

Dmitri's smile broadened as his mind focused on his beloved flying. "I can fly a plane in my sleep. Did I ever tell you about my flight from Denver to Chicago and how little Joseph came to be?"

At any other time, Billy would have been appalled at the reference to his grandson's conception, but under the circumstances, he could see the topic gave his son strength. "Tell you what. I think I get the picture, but let's wait till we get that bird airborne and then you can fill me in."

Dmitri's eyes kind of glazed over as his mind drifted off to thoughts of a more pleasant day. Billy ran the boat hard till they were nearly up to the plane and then shut her down, causing the wake to overtake them and lift the boat and pontoons of the plane, up and down, as the waves cascaded against the shore.

Billy leapt from his boat seat to the pontoon and opened the door of the plane. He scrambled into the co-pilot's seat, flicked the radio on and turned the frequency dial to three. "Help! Can anyone hear me?"

...Static and silence...

Again, pressing the radio microphone to his lips and pushing the *talk* button Billy shouted desperately, "S.O.S....MAYDAY...Is there anyone there!?"

Clasping the wing's support strut in his left hand, he braced himself with one foot on the pontoon and the other planted on the gunwale of the boat. Straddling the water with most of his weight on the pontoon, he stretched down to his son, bending his handless right arm at the elbow. "OK, now; let go of your leg and grab on to my arm. I can pull, but you have to help." Dmitri bit his lips to keep his agony from torturing his father, and together they were able to get him into the plane.

Billy immediately produced his fishing pliers and quickly cut away the tattered jeans with the razor sharp blade. As he suspected, the blood was flowing freely. He twisted around, finding the kit with the red cross on it, exactly where it was supposed to be. Bandaging the leg as tightly as he could, he realized the other wounds would have to wait. Dmitri's eyes were beginning to flutter, and the only chance he had for life was to get this plane in the air, something Billy couldn't do on his own.

He grabbed a canteen, soaked a length of bandage, and proceeded to wipe the dried blood from Dmitri's face. He noticed a gash in his forehead that was still seeping blood, so he handed his son the canteen saying, "Drink some water. I'm going to wrap this last cut to keep the trickle of blood out of your eyes, and then we're going to have to get this show on the road." Billy quickly wrapped the white cloth around and around, taping it down with a strip of tape that crossed the top of his son's head. "OK, now; let's get you into the pilot's seat and I'll get us free of the land."

Billy helped his weak and listless pilot into position. Then he jumped out of the plane, untied the rope from the pontoon support, leaving it tied to the tree, and put his back into the job of launching the Beaver for take-off.

Although Dmitri was not in his own plane, he felt at home in the pilot's seat, as renewed life (you couldn't call it vigor) began to course through his body. He automatically began an abbreviated pre-flight check and start-up routine, as Billy clambered on board, soaking wet. Dmitri hit the starter and the propeller turned slowly, slowly...then life surged into the engine with the flow of fuel. The noise of power never sounded so good.

The wind was almost nonexistent below the tree line, so it didn't matter in which direction they took off. Dmitri looked at his dad with a slight smile and said, "I don't think I can work the pedals because I can't feel my legs except for the pain. You'll have to do it from your side, but I'll tell you what to do. For takeoff, just give me a little right rudder to make up for the torque of the engine. I may need you to help me pull back on the stick too, OK?"

Billy nodded, as Dmitri pushed the throttle all the way forward. It never occurred to Billy that he was risking his life in the attempt to save his son's life. This was the only possible course of action and he just went with it. The plane began to get light on the water as their speed reached the brink where man can cheat gravity. Billy's eyes shifted from the water ahead to his son's face, his hand clutching the steering column in front of him. They bounced free a couple of times before Dmitri judged the time was right. Finally, he nodded to his father, too weak to shout over the noise of the engine, and together they pulled back firmly on the yoke.

The plane lifted into the sky, and Billy felt the motion in his stomach that normally made him feel a little queasy. This time he felt exhilarating relief as they cleared the trees of the shoreline. He started to believe that this nightmare might not end in tragedy, causing a lump in his throat. He bit back his emotion and focused his attention on the co-pilot's pedals and stick while keeping a close eye on his son.

The Beaver was doing fine, but Dmitri's eyelids were beginning to look heavy as if he were fighting back sleep. "Are you all right, son?" Billy shouted. He opened the canteen and sprinkled Dmitri's face by flicking water from his fingers. Dmitri shook his head to clear it, but winced in pain with the effort. Billy looked out his window and saw the ranger's tower in the distance to their right. "We need to head more south," he yelled. "That fire look-out should be on our left."

Dmitri opened his mouth to say something, but the noise was too loud. They leaned toward each other until their shoulders met, and Billy heard the words, "Right hand means right pedal...gently." Dmitri took his right hand from the stick and made a motion like a hitchhiker with his thumb. Billy gradually pushed down on the right pedal, and Dmitri tilted the stick as the plane began a wide turn to the south and then west. Billy split his attention between judging the appropriate bearing and Dmitri's face. He decided to take charge of the navigation responsibilities, knowing his son was flying on instinct alone.

The plane's altered course took them directly over the ranger's station, but there was no place to land, as the tower was built high on a hill for the best vantage point. When they neared the point to turn back south toward the lodge, Billy gave the hitchhiker's thumb to the left. Dmitri banked her over while Billy pressed the left pedal till they reached the new heading.

As they straightened it out, Billy was alarmed to see that his cherished son, and pilot, was nearly unconscious. He reached over and pinched Dmitri's cheek. "Hold on for ten more minutes! Those two guests from Peoria are doctors, remember? All we have to do is land this baby and they'll take care of you. Hang in there, kid!"

Billy was looking out his window to see if he could spot Lake Obiwanee and the island that would confirm their course. Suddenly, the plane began to dive. Billy's guts turned to stone as he spun his head around to see his son slumping forward against the stick, white as a ghost. Unfortunately, the Beaver not only dove, it began to roll. The force of their descent pushed

Dmitri back against his seat so that Billy could pull the stick back, but the right pedal was jammed to the floor and the tailspin prevented him from righting the plane.

All Billy could see was a green whirl through the front windows. They had been flying at a low altitude and he knew there was very little time. Struggling frantically against the combined downward and centrifugal forces, Billy clamped his right arm around the co-pilots steering column. He gave Dmitri's leg a solid shove with his left hand, freeing the jammed pedal, and then pulled himself back into his seat. Billy pushed on the left pedal and steered away from the spin, hoping it would counter the death spiral.

Chapter 25

May 17 1954
Washington DC

James heard the telephone ring in the study. He and little Joseph were playing with blocks in the middle of the living room. "Now don't you go anywhere, my good man." He pointed his finger at the youngster like one would to a dog to get him to stay. "I'll be right back." He trotted into the other room to get the phone. James was creeping up on his sixtieth birthday, but he could still move his feet when he wanted to; usually when nobody was watching. He never wanted to look like he was in a hurry - wasn't dignified. Meant you weren't in control of what was going on. But since little Joe didn't count, he got to the phone before the third ring.

"O'Rileys" he announced. "Oh, hi, Kitty." .... "Yep, we're doin' just fine. The boy had his nap, we had lunch together and now we're buildin' a fort. How was your flight?" ...., ... "Nope, haven't heard from Eden. You better get started getting ready. I can take care of things here and it's not every day you get invited to a party at the White House." .... "You bet, see you tomorrow night." He hung up and returned to the living room. The fort, which had been ready for the flag to be placed on top, was scattered evenly across most of the thirty-by-twenty foot, 14th century, Persian carpet.

છ

Kitty was sipping a glass of champagne, enjoying the fact that she was in the house of a long list of America's leaders. She and Senator Curwood had arrived at half past seven, and she was now on her third glass of the bubbly French wine. She promised herself that this one would be her last, *although she might try whatever was served with dinner.*

Someone had captured Oliver by grabbing his elbow, explaining that it was an important matter but would only take a second. Kitty had taken the opportunity to visit the powder room and was now standing alone at the fringe of the activity, soaking in the elegant affair. It was black tie, and the ladies were all decked out in their finest attire.

Kitty was wearing a floor-length, ivory, lace gown she had bought in San Francisco two weeks earlier, specifically with this party in mind. Seeing a woman in a black dress with several strands of pearls caused her to wisp her fingers across the diamond necklace around her own neck. It was the one given to her by Mrs. Walstrom in St. Louis thirty-five years ago. The touch of it sparked a memory, and Kitty wondered how many of these parties David Francis had attended. She was also wearing her mother's blue sapphire earrings. She still thought of them as her mother's. Kitty had only worn them three times, that she could remember, since she was escorted to the Tsar's ball by Ambassador Francis when she was a child, bent on starting a new life in America.

Kitty took another sip of champagne. She had been restless all day, her thoughts returning to the previous evening's fray with her daughter-in-law. *How was she going to tell Dmitri, tomorrow when they picked her up at the airport? Maybe she should...*

"Hello, I was just admiring your earrings; they're beautiful." A woman had slid up to Kitty unnoticed, startling her.

"Oh, why, thank you," Kitty managed to say.

"My name is Betty Johnson. My husband, George, is the Senator from Minnesota. I don't believe I've seen you before at one of these things."

"No...no this is my first time at the White House. I'm filling in for Susan Curwood. She isn't feeling too well right now. My name is Kitty O'Riley. Oliver and I are old friends."

"Those are sapphires, aren't they?" Betty asked, reaching up and touching the stones dangling from Kitty's ears. "They certainly are a *cornflower* blue. And those diamonds. My word! May I ask where you got them?"

"They were my mother's," Kitty responded politely. Betty looked to be about sixty-five and was a full head shorter than Kitty. Her eyes remained riveted on the earrings. Kitty warmed up a bit and smiled. "Cornflower blue?" she asked, having never heard the term.

The woman's focus reluctantly switched to Kitty's eyes. A startled expression swept her face. "Wow! You know, dear, your eyes are a perfect match for those sapphires. My word... Um, cornflower blue is the rarest color of sapphires. Nearly all of them come from Ceylon. That's why I asked where you got them. George would never get me anything like those, you can bet on that. *Can't afford the stuff you buy now,* he would say."

Kitty's face lit up with the openness of this woman's personality. "Actually, they were a gift to my mother from her best friend. I was born in Russia and my mother's best friend was Xenia Romanov, who happened to be the sister of the Tsar, Nicholas Romanov." Kitty was not bragging or name dropping. The truth seemed to be the easiest way to explain how she came by the objects of this woman's fascination.

"Uh...hmmm."

Both women turned to the man who was so obviously trying to get their attention.

"Oh, George, I want you to meet Kitty O'..."

"O'Riley," Kitty offered.

Betty continued, "Kitty is here with Oliver Curwood, dear. Kitty, this is my husband, George."

The elderly senator from Minnesota gallantly kissed Kitty's hand as only an older man can do without looking silly.

"Now, what did you want, George?" Betty demanded, a little irritated that he had interrupted them.

"Actually, darling, I came to tell you they have asked us to sit at the head table with the President. Walter and Jane, I mean, the Secretary of State was not able to make it, so we are being asked to fill in. Do you mind, dear?"

Betty did not seem particularly thrilled by the honor. "That will be fine, George. Just let me know when you need me at your side." She reached up and squeezed the loose skin of the senator's jowl and smiled, dismissing him.

"Uh...hmmm. Yes, well, there is something else." He turned to Kitty. "Mrs. O'Riley... it is Mrs.?" he said, glancing down at the wedding band on her left hand.

"Please call me Kitty. May I call you George, Senator?"

"Yes, yes, by all means, please do. Uh...hmmm, Kitty, I happened to overhear a bit of your conversation with my wife a second ago, unintentionally of course, and if I may say so, this is really a remarkable coincidence. I happen to have the dubious honor of sitting on a panel charged with interviewing a woman claiming to be Anastasia Romanov, the late Tsar's youngest daughter. She is the latest of numerous petitioners over the years, professing to be heir to the Romanov fortune. Based on what I just heard about your mother's relationship with the family, I was wondering if you might be able to help us get to the bottom of this."

Kitty had read in the paper about others claiming to be Anastasia and always wrote it off as the efforts of another gold-digger. "I did know Anastasia when we were children. We played together quite often. If I actually thought this woman was my old friend, I would like nothing more than to see her. But I'm afraid she will turn out to be nothing more than another charlatan, and I'm supposed to appear before a committee tomorrow with Oliver. And then, my husband and son are going to pick me up on their way back from a fishing trip in Canada. We're all heading back to Kansas City."

Maybe before your hearing tomorrow you could pop in and see what you think about this woman's claim. It shouldn't take more than a few minutes to expose her, I would think."

Senator Johnson had one of those winning smiles that got him elected over and over. "I'll see what I can do," Kitty said.

A servant approached and asked if he could escort the Johnsons to the head table. Before the elderly couple had to awkwardly leave Kitty standing by herself, Oliver arrived with two fresh glasses of champagne and a broad smile. Handing one glass to Kitty and offering the other to Betty, he said, "Well, George, I see you and Betty have met this ravishing beauty. Did she tell you any wild stories about how I met her in New York, forty years ago when she had only been off the boat for an hour?"

"No, Senator, she didn't. But she did tell us that she knew Anastasia as a child and has agreed to help us sort out the truth about this latest claim to the Romanov fortune." George bowed slightly as he took his wife's arm. "Excuse us. We're sitting with the Big Cheese tonight."

Kitty had been answering questions for about an hour after her presentation to the subcommittee. The subject was railroad strikes, but she spent half the time explaining how she had turned a small bakery shop in Kansas City into a multimillion dollar operation called Kitty's Kakes. The men on the committee had all heard of the company and its products, but having this attractive woman named Kitty sitting in their midst brought the Kitty's Kakes story down to a personal level.

The fact that she was from Russia raised some eyebrows initially, but the telling of how her parents were killed by the Bolsheviks allayed any fears regarding the possibility of her being a communist sympathizer. Kitty had elaborated on her views about labor and what she thought of the Teamsters Union. Her view, of allowing the railway workers to strike, was basically to be sure the workers were getting a fair deal.

Kitty received a rousing round of applause as she was escorted from the hearing by one of the senate interns. She turned and waved to Oliver, who still occupied the subcommittee chairman's seat. Oliver returned the wave as Kitty departed through the wide double-doors.

Another intern was waiting in the hallway. "Senator Johnson has asked me to show you to the chamber where his panel is investigating the claim on the Romanov fortune...if you still have time, that is." The pretty, young intern smiled at Kitty.

Kitty nodded, "Lead the way young lady."

After winding their way through several corridors, the intern asked Kitty to wait, and entered the small chamber alone to announce her arrival. Kitty peeked through the partially open door and noted a table with four chairs on one side, three of which were occupied by men wearing dark business suits, including George Johnson. Sitting behind a smaller table, facing the panel of senators, was a woman about Kitty's age and an older gentleman, presumably her lawyer.

The three senators stood as Kitty entered the room. The elderly lawyer made the gesture by rising only halfway out of his seat without pulling his gaze from the papers scattered on the table in front of him. Senator Johnson led Kitty to the empty fourth chair next to the senators. "May I introduce Mrs. William O'Riley," he said to his colleagues. They all shook hands before settling into their seats. "Mrs. O'Riley is..."

"Please call me Kitty," she interrupted.

"Kitty," Senator Johnson continued, "is going to assist us with this inquiry." Kitty's attention had been drawn to the other woman's face since the moment she had entered the chamber. *At least,* Kitty thought, *the woman looked to be the proper age, if her childhood friend was somehow still alive.*

The woman stared back at Kitty as if searching for something. "Do I know you?" she asked in broken English.

Senator Johnson raised his hand, "We'll be asking the questions here." He nodded toward Kitty for her to begin.

Surprising everyone in the room, Kitty asked in perfectly fluent Russian, "My name is actually Xenia Catrina Milanov. Do you remember me?"

A profoundly confused expression fell upon the woman's face. A moment later, a broad smile appeared as the woman bolted out of her chair, approaching Kitty with open arms. "I can't believe it's you, but I can see it in your face!" she gushed in equally fluent Russian. The three senators and the lawyer all watched in amazement as the woman embraced Kitty. Senator Johnson quickly got out of his chair, pulled the woman off Kitty and returned her to her seat.

"What was that all about?" Senator Johnson whispered in Kitty's ear.

Kitty, who looked bewildered, whispered, "I told her my Russian name and asked if she remembered me. ...You saw the rest."

"Is this her? Anastasia, I mean. Do you think this could really be the Tsar's daughter?" Senator Johnson continued to whisper just loud enough so that the two other senators could hear him.

Kitty shook her head slightly and blinked, then squinted at the woman sitting across from her, trying again to detect something familiar. "It's been 37 years. I don't think it is my friend but let me ask her a few questions."

"Fine, but please speak in English so we can all understand what is being said. Are you all right?"

"Yes...a little startled; I'm fine."

Senator Johnson gave Kitty a paternal pat on the back and returned to his seat. Before Kitty could proceed, a clerk entered the room, walked crisply over to Senator Johnson, and handed him a slip of paper. It read:

Mrs. Kitty O'Riley, please call home. Urgent!

James

The senator immediately stood up, stepped over to where Kitty was sitting and gave her the piece of paper. "Here, let me help you up," he urged, lifting her by the arm and pulling back her chair at the same time. "Excuse us," Senator Johnson said as he began leading Kitty toward the door. "We'll take a fifteen minute break."

Kitty clutched the note in her hand as they quickly walked down the hall. Anxiety made her want to run. The turmoil she had felt about identifying Anastasia had vanished, pushed aside by dread, dread of what she was about to hear from her partner. She knew it wasn't business. She knew James almost as well as she knew herself. She started to run a few steps, walked, then, ran again. Senator Johnson threw dignity to the wind, keeping up with her as their heels clicked noisily on the marble floor. Congressmen and aides stepped aside to let them pass, gawked; tried to guess what was happening.

"The switchboard will connect you. Just give her the number." Senator Johnson stood with his arm extended across his desk, holding the telephone receiver toward Kitty. Kitty looked at the concerned expression on his face, then at the crumpled note in her hand:

Mrs. Kitty O'Riley, please call home. Urgent!

James

"It must be little Joseph," she babbled into the phone.

"Please repeat that," the switchboard operator responded.

"Sorry, will you connect me with....."

There was a pause before Kitty heard the familiar voice. "James, it's Kitty. Tell me." .... "What do you mean they haven't heard from them since yesterday morning?" .... "What was my son doing flying the pontoon plane?" Kitty's voice was rising in pitch and volume as the conversation progressed. .... "I know you're just telling me what they told you, but this is ridiculous." .... "I'm on my way to the airport right now. Do me a favor and arrange to have a plane waiting for me at the Montreal airport that can fly me into the fishing camp. What did you say it was called?" .... "OK. I'll be in Montreal this afternoon and you tell them I want to be at the Wounded Moose Lodge before dark." .... "Right. Take care of Joe. Is he all right?" .... "I'll be in touch."

Kitty replaced the receiver, turned and looked at Senator Johnson. Her worried expression conveyed how she felt, but her voice was now calm. "Billy and Dmi...my husband and son are missing. Dmitri flew the fishing camp's pontoon plane into God-knows-where, and they haven't been seen since. There was something about a ranger's station spotting a plane that seemed to be lost but they couldn't identify it."

The senator stepped around his desk and put his arm around Kitty's shoulders. "I'm sure they're all right. Come on; my driver will take us to the airport."

Chapter 26

May 17, 1954
Quebec Province, Canada

Billy opened his eyes. He was lying face down, half-buried in snow. A dense pine canopy loomed overhead. His view was that of a field mouse. His eye above the surface of the snow saw the mangled wreckage and twisted metal that was once a DeHavilland Beaver pontoon plane. He could smell the unmistakable scent of freshly cut pine. Lifting his head, he traced the ugly path of destruction where the plane had plowed through the branches, needles and trunks of the Canadian forest.

He pushed himself to his knees, then gradually to his feet. He straightened up, spreading his arms and looking to the sky, amazed that he had been thrown clear and somehow spared. In that moment of exuberance and vitality, he brought his arms down and clapped his hands together. Suddenly, his ears started ringing and lights flashed in his head. He looked down at his clasped hands and began to feel the top of his head expanding with a familiar yet unfamiliar tingling sensation.

Staring at his hands, he staggered through the snow to the wreckage. The dismembered fuselage had lost its wings to the mighty trunks of ancient pine trees. Climbing over severed struts and torn sheet metal, Billy peered into the cockpit and saw two bodies. One was his son, Dmitri, still strapped into the pilot's seat. Sprawled next to him was the body of a man with an empty sleeve. Both bodies looked vacant - absent of life. The gruesome scene was somehow peaceful. The carnage of metal and flesh seemed content at lying on the forest floor.

Billy turned away and began to walk amongst the trees, listening to the birds and watching the squirrels play in the branches. Gradually, his head began to feel feathery light, as if heavy, warm syrup was somehow slowly seeping away through his scalp. His awareness was merging with the sweet air of nature, and he was comfortable with that. He had always known that death would come some day, wondered what it would be like. He clapped his hands together again. It was time to be free.

Chapter 27

May 23, 1954
Denver, Colorado

Richard Schilling lifted the doorknocker and rapped it several times, making a sharp metallic sound that would draw the attention of anyone inside apartment 4C. It was a fairly new apartment complex, not fancy but not run-down either. He noticed before entering the building that each apartment had a small balcony, and 4C's happened to have a perfect view of the mountains. Too bad Kansas doesn't have any mountains, he thought to himself as he heard the clicking of the dead bolt lock. The door opened about four inches and then stopped as it reached the end of the safety chain on the night lock. A woman's face, bearing no make-up and surrounded by mussed hair, appeared in the gap.

"What do you want?" was the greeting he received.

Mr. Schilling took off his felt brimmed-hat and introduced himself. "Good morning. My name is Richard Schilling, and I am Mrs. O'Riley's attorney. I believe you were expecting me? You are Eden O'Riley?"

The door closed in his face. He heard the chain lock being slid over, and then the door opened about a foot. "Yeah, I expected you, but not at eight-thirty in the f——ing morning."

The door remained partially open but went no farther, so Richard Schilling pushed it the rest of the way open just in time to see the back of a woman's night gown disappear through a door in the hallway. He stepped inside, closing the door behind him. The apartment was void of furniture except for a cheap dinette set in the kitchen that still had the tags from the store attached to it. He walked over and set his briefcase down on the small table. Turning, he decided to check out the view. He crossed the empty living room and pulled the curtain back from the sliding-glass door to the

122

balcony, stepped outside and was rewarded with a brilliant blue sky against the majestic Rocky Mountains. The thin mountain air was exhilarating as he leaned his elbows on the black metal railing and waited.

He heard the toilet flush, and a minute later the shower come on, so he leaned back against the wall and thought about what he was about to go over with his boss's daughter-in-law. Well, sort of *former* daughter-in-law. Mrs. O'Riley had been very explicit about what he was to say. By the time he began to hear noises in the kitchen, he had drifted off to thoughts about baseball and whether the new team in Kansas City, *The Athletics*, would be worth a darn or not.

He walked into the apartment and found Eden going through his briefcase. *"Uh...hmmm."* He cleared his throat as he walked into the kitchen.

Eden looked up, unashamed at being caught. "Let's hear it," she said. "I don't want to have to read all this stuff." She dropped a handful of official looking documents back into the expensive leather case. She was wearing a t-shirt and a pair of very short shorts that looked like they were painted on. It was quite obvious there was nothing worn underneath the t-shirt, and her feet were bare.

Mr. Schilling, the man, was thinking *holy smokes*. Mr. Schilling, the lawyer, was thinking that Eden looked as little like a mourning widow as a woman possibly could. Her disrespect and poor manners quickly put a bad taste in his mouth and he began to warm to the subject for which he had been retained.

"May I sit down?" he asked.

"Of course, Richard. That's why I bought all this furniture. So I could have guests. Should I call you Rick?"

"Mr. Schilling, if you please. Let's get to the point." He sat down, opened his briefcase, took out the documents and straightened the mess she had just made of them. Kitty had told him about the incident in the bar so he would understand the situation. He decided it would be best to conclude matters as quickly as possible and head back to the airport.

"Mrs. O'Riley tells me that you two have already discussed the important points of this arrangement, so I intend to identify the legal documents and their purpose and obtain your signature. At which point, I will hand over the two-hundred-thousand-dollar check and be on my way. Is that the way you understand things to be?"

Eden stood up, flashed her rear in his face and said, "That's right. Do you want some coffee?"

"No, thank you." Richard shuddered at her brazen sexuality, but allowed his eyes to stare while she poured herself a cup. God made men without morals when it comes to their eyes. When she turned, he looked away, picking up his file and extracting the first form that needed to be signed.

"This states that you are entitled to all property and assets owned by your late husband, Dmitri Milanov O'Riley. It includes a list of said items and goes on to point out that your husband did not inherit anything from his father, the late William (NMI) O'Riley. Ownership of that entire estate resides in the person of Xenia Catrina Milanov O'Riley. If you would just sign right here by the *X* on both copies."

Mr. Schilling placed the signed documents in the file and handed Eden two more. "Please read this one carefully. It states that you grant guardianship responsibility of your son, Joseph Milanov O'Riley, to your mother-in-law, Xenia Catrina Milanov O'Riley. This arrangement is effective the day you sign it, which is today. It points out that Joseph is not currently a beneficiary of his grandmother's estate and won't be until the forms you are signing today are filed and registered. By signing this document, you waive all visitation rights to your son until his eighteenth birthday. It stipulates that upon satisfaction of this provision, you will receive the amount of three hundred thousand dollars on April 22, 1971. One contact with your son, either by phone, letter, or in person will void this provision, and you forfeit payment of the entire amount."

Thinking this concession would be nearly impossible for any mother to agree to, Mr. Schilling watched Eden's eyes for any sign of remorse or regret. When there was none, he decided this made it easier for both of them. She doesn't give a shit about the boy. He handed her the pen. "Please sign both copies by the *X.*"

He returned both signed copies to his briefcase and pulled out a cashier's check for two hundred thousand dollars, handing it to Eden. "I think this concludes our business. I will have these documents executed by Mrs. O'Riley, filed at Kansas City city hall, and send you a copy for your records. That cashier's check is made out in your name and is now endorsed. Don't lose it."

He stood up, put on his hat and said, "Good day, ma'am."

Chapter 28

July 21, 1954
Mission Hills, Kansas

Kitty sat on the living room floor playing little Joe's favorite game...blocks. They'd always build something, together. Joe always got to knock it down all by himself. Sometimes he waited until the fort or whatever it was, was completed before destroying it, but rarely.

It had been two months since Kitty had buried her husband and son. She still wore black, but was getting tired of it. The constant reminder was not doing her much good. She had spent those two months extricating herself from the day-to-day operations of Kitty's Kakes. She had made up her mind to devote her full attention to raising her grandson. James understood, and together they developed a plan that left him in charge of all facets of the baking business.

They still owned the company fifty-fifty and would share in the profits equally. They had introduced profit-sharing incentives for upper management when Kitty's Kakes diversified into several areas other than baking. Since Kitty had pretty much established the financial and real estate investment portion of the company, it was decided that she could continue to manage them from her home. So, as part of the plan, these activities fell into what they jokingly called the *grandmother operation.*

Besides being in charge of diapers and her scaled-down duties for Kitty's Kakes, the recently widowed tycoon had to deal with their cattle and horse-breeding businesses. Although Kitty had been involved in them to some extent, Billy had been the one spending the needed time to manage them. In need of a foreman, she began interviewing those already employed by *O'Riley's Cattle Company* and *His Majesty's Horses.*

She was pretty confident that Mark White, whom she had met the same day Morgan Shay had departed, could handle their Kentucky thoroughbred breeding stables.

At home, Kitty sat behind the desk in her office staring out the window. She picked up a lengthy letter in front of her and started through it for the third time. It was handwritten in Russian, the first she had received in her native language since immigrating to the United States in 1917.

Dear Catrina Milanov O'Riley;

I am embarrassed that we met under false pretenses, related to my attempt at claiming to be something I am not, a Romanov. Let me first say how sorry I am for the loss of your husband and son. Unfortunately, I have experienced the same loss and know the distress you are in. For that reason, I have not contacted you sooner. However, I feel it would be unfair to withhold information about your brother for even one more day.

Although we were never officially married, your brother Joseph and I lived as husband and wife for 28 years. We raised a son together, Nikky, though I have long since given up hope that he still breathes the air of this earth.

Joseph would never allow himself, or me, to assume such a fate for his sister. He was convinced you were alive. Without any hint of where you were or how you might have survived, he had faith in you. When I realized who was sitting before me at the table with the senators, I was amazed by miracle of actually seeing you.

Things were not good between me and your brother the last few years. Joseph was obsessed with how the Communists took his country. The bitterness ate at him, poisoned him with hatred. It wore us down, what we had together. The only thing that kept us together was Nikky. But after Stalingrad, where Nikky almost died from German bullets, our son left with the army to chase the Nazis back to Berlin. We never heard from him again.

With Nikky gone, there was nothing left between your brother and me. I tried to stay, tried to make it work, hoping our son would return. Finally, I left him. Six months later he was arrested. Joseph had been valuable at the factory, building tractors and then tanks. They left him alone. And he was a hero, fighting against the Germans, a sniper. To the people, he was a legend. When the war was over, nothing could save him from Stalin's fist. He was sent to Siberia, to the camps, to work, to die.

I waited three more years for news of Nikky. In 1949 I left Stalingrad, lived in Poland for two years, got married and then came to America with my new husband. He is the one that convinced me to say I was Anastasia, to try to take advantage of what I knew, what I used to be.

Something I didn't tell you is your brother saved my life. My mother was a servant for the Tsarina. We lived with the Romanovs when they were being held by the Bolsheviks. I was assigned to help the girls, help them dress, do different things. Anastasia and I looked a lot alike back then; we played together, talked to the soldiers. The night the family was killed, one of the guards had me switch places with Anastasia to save her life. Joseph saved me, thinking he was saving Anastasia. That is how it happened that your brother and I lived together. I owe him my life.

I do not know if Joseph is still alive. They say no one lives more than a few years in the camps of Siberia. I'm sorry. I do not know if Anastasia is alive either; the rumors in Europe that she had survived; more rumors in America. It was stupid of me to listen to my husband, to try to steal what is not mine. The Tsar and his family did not deserve to be shot like criminals. For me, it is over.

I am glad I met you, even for a moment. It is one part of my life that is finally settled. I am sorry Joseph will never see his sister. It would be the one thing that might soothe his tortured soul.

Sincerely,
Irina Kordovna

Chapter 29

January, 1953 (18 months earlier)
Gulag labor camp – Norilsk, Siberia

At midday, it was dark outside the coal mine where Joseph spent day after day without end. The sun had not risen above the Arctic horizon in two months. Kerosene lamps provided light within the shaft where he worked alongside 20 other filthy, starving men. There was one good thing about toiling in the dusty mine while choking for air. The temperature was 80 degrees warmer than it was outside on the tundra. The minus-30-degree air outside the shaft's mouth made the 50 degrees underground feel balmy. The mine he had worked in last year was less dusty because it was wet. Freezing water had dripped constantly from above, creating its own form of torment.

Joseph swung his pick into a crevice and stepped aside while Otabek pummeled the loosened hunks of coal with a sledge hammer. They shoveled the black rubble into a wooden cart. When full, they would push it to the mine's entrance, dump the coal, return with the empty cart and start over. This had been Joseph's life, twelve hours a day, seven days a week, for the last four years. Before that at another camp, he had spent two years mining nickel ore...same routine.

At the noon break, men huddled in groups, eating their ration of bread and dipping the metal cup they shared into a bucket of water to wash it down. Many of the men remained silent while others talked in low voices about release, going home.

"It won't be much longer," said Anton. "The word is he had another stroke last month."

"You've been saying that for two years. Where did you hear it this time?"

"Yesterday, Gavriil was part of the train detail. He heard it from a conductor. Uncle Joe is sick, you'll see."

"Otabek heard it too," Joseph said, "from Shahlo. You might be right this time." He glanced at his friend, who nodded. Otabek rarely spoke. When he did, it was only to Joseph or his sister, Shahlo.

It had been a common topic for years. Stalin, the ruthless dictator, was sure to die soon and they would all be set free. It was the only thing that kept many of the prisoners alive, one more day, one more week... Recently, it had been different. Joseph had noticed that the general attitude of the men had improved; not just wishing Stalin would die, but expecting it. Nearly every single prisoner held Stalin personally responsible for being sentenced to these frozen labor camps of hell. Their discussions were usually tempered by caution, fear of informers. Treason would lengthen your sentence, or worse.

"Otabek," Joseph whispered with a smile, "ask Shahlo how long men from Georgia are living these days." Joseph had emerged as a leader of the men years ago. The camp commanders needed leaders within the prisoner ranks for channels of communication to keep things calm. It was easier if the men worked out differences amongst themselves. And Joseph understood the value of hope. He clung to it just like the rest. Trying to convince others, helped convince himself.

Two months later, on March 5th, Joseph Stalin died. The tyrant that ruled the Soviet Union for thirty years, responsible for the death of forty million people within its borders, was gone. The long awaited event that was to trigger the end of their unspeakable existence had finally arrived. Many exiled families (kulaks) were free to go. Thousands of political prisoners were granted amnesty. Hundreds of thousands were not. Releasing the prisoners labeled as criminals was not even considered.

The flicker of hope was snuffed with a single gust for more than a million prisoners denied freedom. That's when the strikes began. They formed committees, produced leaflets - passed them among their own and smuggled them from camp to camp. With nothing to lose, the prisoners simply gave up worrying about consequences. The revolt caused many commanders of remote camps to flee, guards died, informers quaked in utter fear. Joseph was in the middle of it all, organizing the men, building their strength and resolve.

Joseph stood before Gleb Marchenko, Commandant of the Norillag system of Gulag labor camps. The system had thirty camps with over seventy thousand prisoners. Marchenko had come to the Gorlag camp to deal with the unrest. The commander's office was simple; wooden plank walls and floor, maps on the walls between the stark windows, papers strewn in piles on the lone table and, several unmatched wooden chairs. "We are prepared to die," said Joseph, "every prisoner in this camp...every camp." It was his opening statement.

The commandant, whose back was turned to Joseph, spun on his heel to face him. "What is to stop me from doing exactly that? Kill every prisoner that does not return to the mines." Their eyes met and locked.

Joseph knew the commandant was responsible for very aggressive levels of production. The Gulag work camps were how Stalin got things done. Removing his opposition from Russian society was only part of Stalin's motivation. In addition to working the mines, prisoners built roads, bridges and canals, logged forests, produced all sorts of goods. "If you kill us, your coal will remain in the ground."

Marchenko laughed. "Russia has many more who will take your place."

"If that were true, I would not be in this office," Joseph said defiantly.

"Why not just kill you, their leader?" Marchenko asked.

Joseph bit back his response, lowering his eyes to his hands tied in front of him. He knew his tongue could easily betray him. He glanced at the armed guards that stood nearby. Marchenko could deliver death with a single word. He did not hate this man, but hatred for what the man stood for blazed in Joseph's eyes. Malnutrition had taken its toll on his body but the muscle that remained, and his spirit, were tempered like steel. "I have prevented your informers from being killed," said Joseph. "I am your only chance to prevent many deaths on both sides. If you kill me the strikes will grow worse for you."

Marchenko looked at the list of demands he held in his hand. "Nine hour work-days. Less crowded barracks. More food. A day of rest on Sunday." He tossed the list on the table and looked back at Joseph. "I can help you with two of these by doing what has been done in other camps." He turned to the camp commander standing next to the guards. "Line up the prisoners and shoot every tenth man." Pointing at the list, he added. "That will help with the overcrowding and lack of food. To make up for it, the prisoners in this camp will work fourteen hours a day, not twelve... including Sunday."

The commandant walked out the door without looking at Joseph.

The strikes continued, on and off, for over a year. New arrivals from other camps spoke of how conditions had gradually gotten better after Stalin's death. Not in Joseph's camp. He leaned against the wall and sipped on a cigarette. A shallow puff was all his damaged lungs would allow. His body shook with a raspy cough, so deep and grotesque it was as if his guts were coming up. Wiping the spittle from his lips, he studied the specks of black coal-dust and blood on the back of his boney wrist. Before the war, Joseph Milanov had been a solid 195 pounds. During the siege of Stalingrad he had dropped to 165 pounds, though he had gained most of it back before his arrest in 1946. Now, after eight years in the labor camps, he weighed 150 pounds, before or after what was considered a meal.

"It's going to be tomorrow," said Joseph, apparently talking to himself. Closer inspection showed a crack in the crude wall made of posts, planks and plaster. It separated the men's and women's prison yards. The crack was big enough for words to drift through, nothing else.

"But no one has said anything to me, yet. And how can I leave my brother?"

"Do not start with that again. It has been agreed. The baby will not be born in this camp. They will not let your brother go, and he is still in isolation. It is tomorrow, be ready." Joseph looked up at the watchtower, a small hut built on stilts with a view of his side of the compound and beyond the barbed wire perimeter.

"What time did they say?" Shahlo's voice was resigned, despondent.

"After the trucks leave for the mine...to prove the strike is over. The guards think we're being sent to Vorkuta. They'll be told it is to get rid of me. And you...to punish your brother. Joseph pushed himself away from the wall, dropped his cigarette and ground it into the dirt with his leather boot. "Tomorrow." He meandered away from the wall, forcing himself not to look up at the guard house.

Chapter 30

August 9, 1954
Tundra, east of Norilsk, Siberia

Joseph and Shahlo had been walking across the marshy land for a week. No trees to break up the landscape, the ground frozen for most of a year. Hoards of mosquitoes, black flies and other insects were a constant nuisance. Though there was no actual darkness, above the Arctic Circle, the sun dipped below the horizon for a few hours each day, allowing dusk and dawn to touch each other. Joseph was wheezing, his tortured lungs desperately sucking the warm, humid air. He carried a canvas bag with the provisions they had been given; water, bread, some potatoes, two blankets and half a box of thin wooden matches. Shahlo carried only the dress she was wearing and her unborn child, about three months from her due date.

Joseph found a dry patch on slightly higher ground where they could sit down to rest. He set the bag down and reached for Shahlo's hands. "I'll help you," he said, struck once more by her eyes, which were the color of sand. Set against her tanned skin, high cheek bones and straight brown hair, it was a face that required a second look. He lowered her gently into a sitting position and sat down so they were back-to-back, supporting each other.

"I think we should have headed west to catch the train," she said. It was a statement Shahlo made three or four times a day, every day.

It was something Joseph had also been thinking about since their second long day in the bog. "Riding on a train is no good if your heart is not beating," he said. They were the same words he'd used each time in response. Neither of them bothered to come up with anything more original. The exchange had turned into sort of a game between them.

Joseph tried unsuccessfully to stifle a cough while digging into their bag. "Here, eat some bread, it will give you strength." He coughed a couple of more times; talking had its price. He shaded his eyes from the sun, which was straight south on its parallel path along the horizon. By tomorrow they would be in the foothills, he decided.

They had agreed to head east to the foothills of the mountains because they suspected treachery on the part of the camp commander. The arrangement had been that if Joseph would end the strike and the prisoners returned to the mines, he and Shahlo would gain their freedom. For the appearance of discipline, it would be done under the guise of a transfer to another camp in the notorious Vorkuta Gulag District. Getting out before the baby was born had pressed the negotiation. Joseph had demanded that Otabek and Shahlo be the ones released, which the commander flatly rejected.

Joseph had tested the commander's power frequently during the last year of strikes. A bullet to Joseph's head, the preferred solution, had been a breath away on several occasions. The commander had displayed considerable restraint in the matter.

However, the tension remained between the two men. Joseph felt the chances were good that once he was out of sight of the camp's other prisoners, a bullet would find its way through his skull. Shahlo's death would be a matter of cleaning up loose ends. They were not given papers, any sort or documentation of their release. So, they had decided to cross the tundra to the mountains rather than be betrayed as escaped prisoners and sent to another camp or executed. Where they were headed, there would be no people, no one to betray them. But it was not going to be easy.

Shahlo swatted at a fly, stinging her neck like a needle, one of dozens swarming them as they sat. "Auughh! These monsters are eating me alive," she shrieked. "Let's get moving."

They sat on a rocky bank of a stream, thankful to finally be out of the endless sludge of the marsh. The water gurgled down the gentle slope; cold, clear and refreshing. With his hands braced on a couple of half-submerged rocks like he was doing a push-up, Joseph dipped his head down for another drink. They had been climbing into the hills all morning and were resting before turning south.

"The trees make the air smell good, don't they?" Joseph coughed, hands on his knees, then sat down beneath the tree next to Shahlo. It was a larch tree; small, thin and about the only type of tree that could withstand the arctic winter months.

"Umhhmmm," she yawned, back against the tree, eyes closed, exhausted. "I think the baby needs to sleep." She rubbed her swollen belly and mumbled, "Just an hour or so."

Joseph patted her on the thigh. "Have a little bread first." Her breath had already changed to the deep, slow cadence of sleep. Joseph studied her tired face. Sleep brought peace to his pretty, twenty-four-year-old companion. He smoothed out the coarse dress to cover her bare legs, stretched out on the ground and closed his eyes, one step closer to freedom.

☙

They were able to cover about twenty miles a day, up and down hills, crossing small streams. The sparse grass and rocky terrain gradually changed to pine, spruce, and fir trees. Moss covered everything near the ground. Their days were spent walking and sleeping. They had both survived for years eating almost nothing in the labor camps, which allowed them to stretch their meager provisions further than others might have. Even so, by mid-September the food was gone.

They had journeyed about three hundred miles south of the Arctic Circle. Joseph was actually feeling stronger from the steady exercise and breathing the fresh, clean air. He coughed less, and his lungs allowed him to take deeper and deeper breaths as they showed signs of clearing.

On the other hand, Shahlo was getting less travel-worthy with her advancing pregnancy. Every day was a struggle. She wasn't gaining weight because of a lack of food, body sapped of energy. Her speed and stamina were slipping, down to fifteen miles a day, requiring frequent stops for rest.

With no supply of food, they fell into a routine where Joseph would go out ahead, collect nuts, berries, tuberous roots, anything he could find that they could eat. When Shahlo arrived they would sit down to share whatever he had found. He made a spear out of a stick by sharpening one end on the edge of a rock, reverting back to the hunting skills he'd developed over the years. A small animal or unwary fish pierced by the end of his spear provided protein when luck was going their way. Sometimes they would stop long enough to build a fire to cook it, but usually they ate the meat raw.

By early October, ten miles was all Shahlo could manage before she was completely played out for the day. She was eight months pregnant and they had already endured two light snowfalls, a warning. Joseph had promised to get Shahlo back to her home in Uzbekistan, but his immediate goal was to get as far south as possible before winter closed in on them.

Besides a couple of trails, they had seen no evidence of other people along the way, which was their intention to begin with. Now, he knew that they would need to find a settlement soon. Joseph was growing anxious.

"Do you want to see if there is a better place to cross downstream or keep going this way?" asked Joseph.

Shahlo was sitting on a rock, catching her breath. "I don't want to do either one. Let's just cross here."

Joseph looked doubtfully at the clear, swift moving water. "It looks pretty deep," he said. The water was coming down from the mountains and he knew it would be ice cold.

"We've already walked a half-mile out of our way." Shahlo bent down and started to untie her work-boots.

The stream was about twenty-five feet wide, nearly a river. Joseph had hoped to find a fallen tree on which to cross. "I'll try it first," he said, sitting down and taking off his boots. "If we get our clothes and blankets wet we're in trouble." The temperature had dropped from fifty to about forty degrees in the past hour, and it looked like a storm was moving in.

He left his clothes and the blankets next to Shahlo and climbed down the rocky bank. "Oohhh!" he cried, as he took his first step into the water. Shahlo smiled, watching Joseph's bare backside as he fought to keep his balance against the current. He tested the bottom with each step to avoid slipping. Near the middle of the stream, the water reached his groin. "Whoooa!" he called out in protest.

Shahlo couldn't help but giggle. "What happened, Joseph? Is it getting shorter? Turn around and let me see." Her giggles turned into full laughter, the first he'd heard in several weeks. It was sweet music to his ears. He scowled at her anyway. "You're next, bright eyes!" he shouted. It's the name he started using for her after she told him that *Shahlo*, loosely translated into Russian, means mesmerizing eyes.

Joseph made his way back up the bank, picked up his clothes, boots and blankets and said, "I'll lead. If you can hold your boots and lift your dress with one hand you can hold onto my shoulder with the other.

"Let's go," she said. Shahlo followed Joseph down the bank and into the water, determined not to cry out like he had.

At knee-deep he turned to see how she was doing. Her face cringed from the shock of the cold water, eyes barely slits, a mouth full of teeth. He looked down at her full, round belly and protruding navel. In back, the dress was drooping down to her rear. "I think you need to just take off your dress. The water is going to come up above your middle."

Without a word, Shahlo let go of his shoulder, returned to the bank and set her boots on a rock. She slid her arms out of the sleeves, pulled the dress over her head, wrapped her boots in it and waded back to where he stood. They both stood there naked and smiled at each other. "Maybe I should make two trips," Joseph suggested.

Shahlo put her free hand on his shoulder, pointed him toward the far bank with a little push and said, "Let's go, old man, I'm getting cold."

They both stumbled a couple of times but reached the other side without incident. "These rocks look slippery," Joseph said. "Let me put my stuff down on the bank and I'll come back to help you."

"I'm fine," she said, giving him another little push on the shoulder to get him moving.

Joseph stepped gingerly from stone to stone, making his way up the steep slant. *"AAiiyyahh!!"* The high-pitched screech was followed by a thud-snap and a splash. Joseph twisted around to see Shahlo's head and shoulders, face-down in the water, her legs pinned awkwardly between some rocks. He dropped his clothes and blankets and scooted back down the bank. His haste caused him to slip and fall headlong into the water himself. He came up sputtering and quickly lifted Shahlo above the surface.

"Aaugghh!" She cried out in pain as he tried to get her upright. He tried to lift her again. "Aaugghh!!" she screamed.

"I'm sorry, I'm sorry." Joseph was holding her clumsily by the shoulders, her face inches above the water. The broken leg was twisted unnaturally, toes and knee toward the sky, her hips and belly contorted sideways.

Shahlo was whimpering, coughing and crying, all at the same time. "It hurts! Aaugghh! ...Help me!!!"

Joseph's mind was about to explode, adrenaline pumping, revulsion from the grotesque image of her twisted leg. In about two seconds he knew what had to be done. Explaining it would not have helped. Joseph twisted her shoulders and torso so they were in line with her legs and lowered her into the water, face up.

The water cut off Shahlo's scream as her face plunged below the surface. Joseph heard it as; *gulp, choke, silence*. Drowning might be merciful under the circumstances. He tugged on one of the rocks to free her. It didn't move. He heaved with all his strength on another. It slid about an inch. Enough, he hoped. He grabbed her heel and calf, pulling upward. The ankle bone caught, too big. He was tempted to force it; checked himself. He leaned down to get more leverage on the rock, heard Shahlo flailing her arms in the water, splashing, choking and sputtering as she fought to get her face above water. He pushed with everything he had. The rock budged another inch, the one that counted.

Joseph slid one arm beneath her shoulders, the other below the top of her thighs. He whisked her out of the water and climbed the bank, trusting to fate that his feet would find their way on rocks he couldn't see, obscured by the hundred pounds of flesh in his arms. He set her bare bottom on the grass, pounding on her back to get her breathing. Shahlo, nearly unconscious from it all, coughed and choked for life, the body's survival instinct taking charge. After nearly a minute, she was lying on her back, breathing irregularly. Every few seconds she'd gasp and cough, and then calm down again.

Snowflakes started drifting down, melting when they touched Shahlo's bare, wet skin. Joseph slid one of the blankets beneath her a section at a time so he didn't have to move her. The slightest jostling of her leg caused an agonizing groan.

Shahlo's eyes began to flutter. He knew he had to find shelter and get her warm or she'd die from shock and exposure. He stood up and surveyed the immediate area. The forest was set back from the stream about twenty feet, due to times of high water. The pine trees were tall with some brush beneath, the ground mostly covered with moss and pine needles. He spotted a fallen tree farther upstream that looked like the wind had blown over because it had unearthed its root system on the way down.

Joseph pulled on his boots and carried her to the base of the tree. He ran back for the other blanket, his clothes and canvas bag. He noticed Shahlo's dress, still wrapped around her boots, lying at the edge of the water, and retrieved them too. It was already snowing harder, her eyes were closed and she looked like she was dead. He dumped everything and spread the second blanket over her, even her head.

He pulled his pants right over his untied boots, slid into his shirt and spent about fifteen seconds deciding what needed to be done. The base of the tree trunk and the uprooted ground formed a sort of elbow, blocking the wind. Joseph began to scoop up armloads of the spongy moss and pine needles that carpeted the forest floor. He built up a thick layer nearly a foot deep in the crux of what was to become their shelter. He lifted her, blankets and all, placing her on the soft bedding before sliding the blanket off her face to confirm she was still breathing. "Don't leave me yet, Bright Eyes."

Joseph grabbed the dress and shook her boots onto the ground. He found two sticks and shoved them into the sleeves, stuck the other ends into the ground and pinned the bottom of the dress against the top of the log with a large branch lying nearby. The log and makeshift lean-to would protect them from the ever increasing snow.

Now, to build a fire. Joseph had already cleared the ground of needles to make their bed so he headed back to the riverbank for rocks. It took him a dozen trips, one rock each, to get what he needed. With his heart pounding, panting for breath, he glanced at Shahlo's face, worried about how much time this was taking. The snowflakes were large and floating down at an alarming rate. He could no longer see the far bank of the stream in the blur of white. He quickly stacked the rocks into a semi-circle with the open end a few feet from their shelter.

The one thing they had in their favor was that there was dead firewood everywhere. He gathered two armloads within fifteen feet of the shelter, followed by dry needles and smaller twigs to get the fire started; reached for the canvas bag. Joseph was moving like a machine; fast, efficient, deliberate, everything being done in the proper order, working against the clock and the elements. He pulled out the box of matches; two left. He put them in his shirt pocket, built a little structure of twigs over the dry needles and struck one of the matches. A tiny flame burst forth and went out.

Joseph gasped, his jaw hung open in disbelief. He sat back on his heels and took a deep breath. He put the box with the final match back in his pocket and rubbed his face with his palms to calm himself. "You have to do this right," he said out loud. "Get control, think." Joseph forced himself to wait. Deadly serious, he rebuilt the dry needles and twigs closer to the rocks. To help block the wind or a stray snowflake, he crept up on his knees, back hunched over the twigs, forming a canopy. He reached in his shirt pocket for the match. Cupping his hands, he struck it; it broke in half, the end with the sulfur falling into the stack of twigs. Joseph scrambled to recover it, picking it out of the needles and putting it back in the box.

He sat back on his heels, took a deep breath and sighed. "This time, baby," he whispered. He got back into position, muscles taught. He opened the box, pinched the remaining half of the match in his fingertips and carefully struck it. Relief surged through him as a blue flame appeared. Ignoring the pain from being burned, Joseph slid the tiny flame into the needles and joyously watched as they ignited into bright yellow. The twigs caught fire. Joseph added more, flames rising, adding bigger sticks, the blaze nearly catching his beard on fire, pushing him back a little. That tiny flame from their final match was a life-altering event. He licked the blistered tips of his forefinger and thumb.

With the fire roaring, the satisfied grin on Joseph's face lasted a few more seconds before the stress was back. He turned, ready for the next challenge. He stripped off his clothes, maneuvered himself over Shahlo's corpse-still body to get behind her, and slid between the blankets. There was just enough room for him between her and the log at his back. His adrenaline and frantic activities had warmed him. Now he needed to transfer that warmth into her. Trying not to bump the injured leg, Joseph draped his body over her, attempting to press as much of his skin against her skin as possible. Her breath was shallow, her heartbeat faint. He rubbed her with his arm and hand - up, down and around - to create friction and stimulate blood flow. He gently laid his hand on her belly. His eyes blinked, blinked again as he waited - then a tiny movement.

Snow was falling steadily, but between the fire and their body contact, Joseph could feel her warming up. After about fifteen minutes, he untangled himself and slid out from beneath the blanket. He put his pants and boots back on, put some more wood on the fire and knelt down at Shahlo's feet. He lifted the blanket to inspect her leg. There was an abrasion several inches above the knee, the surrounding tissue turning blue, starting to swell. Her knee and foot were pointing in the wrong direction and the leg appeared to be an inch shorter than the other one.

Joseph closed his eyes, knowing full well what that meant. He also understood that they would never have a better time to set it than right now. He raised the blanket above her waist and slid his palm up her inner thigh into her crotch. He paused, glancing at her dark, curly pubic hair and bulging abdomen. *Within a month...maybe tomorrow,* he thought, *the baby would be trying to enter the world right through there.* Joseph wondered how that was going to happen with her leg like it was. He shuddered. "One thing at a time," he said, trying to focus on what he was about to do. He grabbed the underside of her knee, pinned her calf and ankle against his side with his elbow, and with steady firmness pulled in opposite directions. He knew she'd be sore where his hands were gripping flesh, no choice. He could actually see and feel the skin and muscles stretch. When he thought the broken ends of the bone were no longer overlapping he rotated her knee and ankle, guessing at the alignment. He gradually allowed the tissue and skin to contract to its natural state, hoping the ends of the bone would meet and mesh. It was a long shot, the only one they had.

Pounding heart, sweat on his face and slippery hands were evidence of Joseph's intense focus and exertion. He took a deep breath, coughed and wiped his forehead with the back of his hand. Shahlo mercifully hid in unconsciousness. Joseph reached for his threadbare shirt, tore it in half along the seam that ran down the back, and ripped the sleeves off at the shoulders. He wrapped one half of the shirt around her leg, from calf to upper thigh, to protect her skin. He selected four straight sticks out of the pile of firewood, arranged them on both sides of her leg and wrapped the other half of the shirt around the whole thing. He tied the sleeves around the makeshift splint below her knee and above the break, holding the sticks in place, her leg immobile.

He covered Shahlo back up with the blanket, put some bigger logs on the fire, took off his boots and pants, and slid in next to her. He wrapped himself around her and waited for her to wake up. As the tension left his body, exhaustion started to take hold. He fought to stay awake, afraid the fire might go out while he slept. He fell asleep anyway, their bodies warming each other, snow falling in silence.

Chapter 31

Joseph stared out at the white splendor, the morning sun sparkling off ice crystals, the air cold and crisp. He couldn't remember how many times he'd gotten up during the night to feed the fire with more wood, maybe six. He stroked Shahlo's cheek with his fingers.

Her eyes popped open, startling him. "I've been waiting for you to wake up," she said.

Tears filled Joseph's eyes as he kissed her cheek. He moved his arm when he realized it was lying across her bare breasts. "I was afraid..." He coughed, partly for his lungs, partly because emotion was tightening his throat. "I was afraid you might not make it through the night," he croaked.

"My leg hurts real bad and I've got something wrapped around it, but don't know why. The last thing I remember is watching you wade into the river, naked. That's it."

"You fell. Leg's broken pretty bad. I tried to fix it. What does it feel like?"

"In one way it's completely numb. I can't feel my toes at all. But there's a throbbing ache in my thigh. It throbs in my head, too. I tried to move just a little and the pain shot through my whole body. I'm not going to do that again, ever." *Shahlo saw sympathy in Joseph's eyes and tears on his cheeks. A mixture of strain and relief was there, too. She realized that his night hadn't been easy either.* "Tell me what happened."

Omitting a few of the details, like her almost drowning, Joseph relived the events for her. When he was finished, he added, "I'm going to put some wood on the fire and fill our water-skin."

When he came back, Shahlo asked, "What are we going to do now?"

Without answering, Joseph knelt down and gently helped her lift her head enough to drink some water without choking. He set the water-skin down where she could reach it. "I'm going to see if I can find something we can eat and then build our shelter up a little more. You should try to get some more sleep."

They spent the next three days staying alive but little else. Shahlo spent much of the time sleeping, or trying to. When she was awake, Joseph talked about how everything was going to work out. When she was asleep, he tried to come up with a plan that had any chance of ending with them both being alive. Whenever the plan included, *having a baby*, it collapsed.

The snow had continued, off and on. They talked about all sorts of things to pass the time and to keep from thinking about their desperate situation. On the third night, with the fire's light flickering on their faces, Shahlo traced the scar on Joseph's face with her finger. "Tell me how you got this," she said softly. It was a question she had been afraid to ask.

The deep scar that caused a droopy left eye and ran to his lip could not be hidden with whiskers. For the eight years he worked in the labor camp, he was only confronted by a mirror a few times. He pulled her hand from his face and said, "I'll tell you about it if you tell me who the father is."

Shahlo gasped a little. Nothing he could have said would cut as deep. Their eyes searched each other, her nearly certain death, and maybe his as well, changing the rules. Her eyes welled and twinkled in the firelight. "Otabek would have got himself killed, avenging my honor, if I had told him."

"I know. It was all I could do to make him think of something else."

"It was the camp commander," she mumbled.

Joseph's eyes widened at this revelation. "Did he force you?"

"It doesn't matter. He is married. My brother would have tried to kill him either way."

Joseph's mind started processing the implications. Negotiating with the commander, Joseph assumed that ending the strike and getting rid of him, preventing another one, had been the basis for their release. He wiped a tear off Shahlo's cheek.

She blinked at him, causing two more tears to run down her face. "It's not my baby's fault who her father is."

Joseph smiled at her. "So it's a girl, is it?"

Shahlo covered her eyes with her forearm, dealing with the knowledge that she would likely never get to know her own child. Joseph hugged her as they lay together, feeling her sobs, mad at himself for having asked the question.

When she was still, he began. "My sister Trina's horse was named Mouka. When I was sixteen I wanted to enlist in the cavalry. My dad was against it so he took my horse away from me, hoping it would stop me. My sister gave me hers. You have to understand, we were very attached to our horses and I promised to take care of Mouka. My corporal tried to give Mouka to our lieutenant but I wouldn't let him have her. So, he took a swipe with his saber, trying to kill me. I ducked, just not quite enough."

Shahlo said, "Thank you for telling me. I'll bet your sister was glad to see you and her horse after the war."

Joseph nibbled on his lip looking at her. This had been the first time in a long time he had spoken about his family to anyone. It was a painful subject, and because of Stalin, a dangerous one. "I never saw my sister again. The Bolsheviks killed my parents and when I got home, my sister was gone. That was thirty-five years ago, and I still don't know where she is or whether she is even alive."

"You said her name is Trina? Is she older or younger?"

"Catrina, actually. I called her Trina most of the time, and she is a year younger than me."

Shahlo became thoughtful, her eyes losing their focus. "I will probably never see Otabek again," she said matter-of-factly.

Joseph was still holding onto her hand from when he had pulled it from his face. He raised it to his lips and kissed it softly. "Let's talk about something else. If we don't get out of here, neither of us will ever see anybody again." Joseph paused for a minute. "I've changed my mind. I still don't like leaving you here, but I think you're right. I have to go get help. It's the only way."

"First, you have to promise. You walk until you find help. If you don't find anybody, you keep going. There's no reason to come back here to die too. That's the plan...promise me."

The next morning, Joseph was up early. He filled the water-skin for her and piled huge stacks of firewood, around and inside their shelter. He wore only his pants and boots. The temperature was about thirty degrees, same as it had been. Having used his shirt for Shahlo's splint, he intended to wrap the empty canvas bag around his shoulders for a little protection. He refused to take one of the blankets, although she tried to insist. He left her the little food he'd rummaged from the forest and a half-eaten rabbit that he had caught yesterday and roasted for them. When he had done all he could to prepare for his absence, he grabbed his walking stick with the sharpened end. Walking away would be about the hardest thing he had ever done.

Shahlo looked up at him, trying to be brave. Fear, the dread of being alone, was almost more than she could take. "Come here," she said, lifting an arm, her voice quavering. "I want to give you a kiss for luck."

Joseph set his spear and bag down, knelt down on his knees and said, "I'll be back in a few days. Everything is going to work out just like we said." When he lowered his cheek to receive her good-luck peck, she kissed him hard on the mouth, locking her lips against his, pressing her hand behind his neck. Joseph felt the desperation, her body trembling, a young girl afraid to die alone in the woods.

He couldn't do it. "I won't leave you," he said. "We'll take our chances right here. I'll build a better shelter, you'll have your baby and if we need to spend the winter here, we will."

Shahlo's smile nearly broke his heart. She started to cry, relief replacing the terror that had stripped her confidence. The rest of the morning she was cheerful, chatting about how her leg would be better in a week or so. Joseph speared a fish in a backwater pool he'd found upstream and they enjoyed a hot breakfast.

By late afternoon, Shahlo was brooding again. The baby was kicking. The hopeless anxiety of knowing winter, the real winter, was coming. The winter that was sure to kill them both. "I can do it," she said. "Tomorrow you go and you're taking one of the blankets. You're not going to do me any good if you freeze to death. Fill the bag with some dry needles and I'll use it to prop me up. I'm tired of lying on my back. And I've got the fire. Why do I need two blankets? Tomorrow, don't say goodbye, just leave."

At dusk they started to hear a muffled rumbling sound and noises like something was crashing through the brush on the other side of the river. It was mixed with grunts, and bellowing like animals calling to each other. "Is it bears?" Shahlo whispered. "Wolves?"

Joseph held up his hand, listening intently. "Not unless they're chasing down some other sort of animal, he said. "I'm going to have a look. He stood, hidden within the tree line, above the stream. Whatever it was, was obviously getting closer, the sounds louder and more distinct.

Joseph started to get nervous. He turned toward Shahlo and held up both hands, gesturing that he couldn't figure out what was happening.

He took several cautious steps toward the river, exposing himself to the open. That's when it happened. Half a dozen large animals burst into the clearing, a quarter of a mile beyond the other bank of the river. Behind them came hundreds more, pouring into the meadow. The huge racks of antlers left no doubt; reindeer.

Joseph watched in awe as they kept coming, more and more and more. He started to get concerned that they might cross the river and trample their campsite, with them in it. There was no way to move Shahlo in time. Some motion to his right caught his attention. Three animals had already made it across the river and were moving steadily in his direction. As he began to return to the cover of the trees, he noticed something odd. It was like the animals had two heads, or were carrying something on their back.

They were riders. The three reindeer were being ridden like horses. Astounded at this sight, but still worried about the stampede, Joseph looked back at the moving mass of brown legs, heads and antlers filling the meadow. The lead animals plowed through the snow. Joseph saw two men on foot break into the open. They were waving their arms. Shrill whistles could be heard above the din. Joseph realized they were herding these animals, at least trying to. When he looked back up-river, the three riders were much closer. They were just boys and they were waving small blankets as the first animals started to enter the water. The boys were apparently positioned to keep the herd from coming across.

Joseph shouted to Shahlo. "They're reindeer, lots of them!" Joseph turned around and watched as the herd swarmed into the cold water to drink. He guessed there were more than a thousand beasts, ranging in size and color, including this year's calves. When Joseph searched out the two men on foot he saw that ten more men were fanned out around the perimeter. The meadow was full of animals but they were no longer pouring out of the trees.

Joseph was anxious to reassure Shahlo, knowing she might be scared and frustrated, not being able see for herself. Just as he was about to turn away he saw four more reindeer come out of the trees, pulling a sled. Skins covered whatever was loaded on the sled, and on top of the skins, hanging onto leather straps, were two toddlers.

Chapter 32

April 21, 1965
Mission Hills, Kansas

Joe was sitting on the floor in front of the television with his legs crossed, a bowl of popcorn on his lap going fast. He was watching his favorite show, Bonanza. A few years ago he would have been wearing his holster with a six-gun strapped to his leg. He had also insisted on being called, *Little Joe*. He was too old for that now. His twelfth birthday was tomorrow.

The next morning the sun was shining brightly so Kitty decided to drive her MG. The 1952 British-green sports car was her prize, a gift from her late husband, Billy. Joe had helped her pull down the cream-colored canvas top, snapping the cover in place. It was springtime, trees moving from buds to leaves, crab apples and magnolias in full bloom. They stopped at McGonigle's, a neighborhood grocery store with an excellent meat counter, and picked up two slabs of smoked ribs, piping hot. Kitty wrapped them in a blanket she kept behind the driver's seat.

Joe spent most of the twenty-five minute drive to their country home with his arm outside the car, pointing his hand into the wind and slicing it in a roller coaster motion. As they drove up to the house and parked, Joe jumped out of the low-riding car without opening the door and ran up the walk to where Uncle James was dozing on the porch swing.

The gentle, old black man was seventy-four years old. Wearing blue jeans and a sweatshirt, most people would not have guessed he ran a hugely successful corporation like Kitty's Kakes. His short, curly hair was now snow white, but his mind was still as sharp as ever. Few businessmen got the best of him, even now.

Joe slipped around behind the swing and began pushing it back and forth, waking James from his peace. Without looking, he sneaked a hand across his chest and snagged Joe's wrist. "I'll bet this hand belongs to somebody I know who happens to be twelve years old today!"

He smiled at his long-time best friend and partner, strolling up the walk. Kitty was wearing a pink spring dress that was light and cheery. She loosened the pink scarf she'd worn for the ride, allowing her black, wavy hair to fall to her shoulders. So far, she had decided not to cover the wisps of gray that were beginning to appear.

Joe laughed boyishly and tried to pull his hand free. Not until he stopped struggling did the black gnarly hand release its prey.

"What are you doing out here, Uncle James?" Joe asked, as he slid in beside the old man on the swing. "It's Monday. How come you're not at work?"

James patted the boy on the knee and produced a colorfully- wrapped package from under his elbow. "Well, I needed a day off, and since I found this package lying around, decided to bring it out here and give it to you for your birthday."

Kitty got comfortable in an outdoor lounge-chair as Joe began opening his present, tearing the paper ferociously. The box was taped shut, so James reached into his left front pocket and pulled out a small knife, handing it to the eager boy. Joe got the blade open with his thumbnail and slid the sharp edge along the seam. His eyes lit up as his fingers felt the smooth leather. He held onto the box with one hand and pulled with the other. Out came a major-league size baseball glove. He plunged his face into the mitt, engulfing himself with the smell of new leather. Jumping off the swing, he stuck his right hand into the glove and pounded the pocket with his left. "Look, Grandma, Jackie signed it." He handed the glove to Kitty. *"To Little Joe, -Jackie Robinson-"* she read. Joe scampered around to the back of the swing and gave James an enthusiastic hug around the neck. "Thanks, Uncle James. It's *zackly* what I wanted. Does Jackie remember me?"

"He sure does. Last week in New York, he said to tell you to keep your eye on the ball and maybe you'll make the majors some day."

"Let's go out and play catch to try it out, want to?"

James chuckled, warmed by the youth's open affection. "I tell you what, Lefty. If you can find me a bat and a ball, I'll hit you some grounders."

"Yes sir!" Joe charged into the house, slamming the door on his way. Kitty got up, moved over to the swing and sat down next to James.

"It was fun watchin' Jackie play that year in Kansas City, wasn't it? ...Before he got famous playin' with the white boys."

"That's true," James said, recalling all the Monarch games he had watched back in the forties. "But Jackie did a great thing, bein' the first Negro in the majors. It's too bad everybody was so hard on him in the beginning."

"Well, thank you for the glove. Jackie is still Joe's hero, even though he's only seen him play in the old film clips."

"And your backyard," James reminded her.

"So, how are things with you? Are we still going to the ball game this evening?"

James reached into his pocket, pulled out three tickets to the Athletics/Yankees game, and said with a smile, "Right behind home plate. You gotta see Mickey Mantle hit."

He lowered his voice to a whisper. "When are you going to show him his...?" He pointed in the direction of the stables around back.

Kitty looked toward the door for a second. "Let's wait for a little while. He's thinking about baseball right now. I'll put these ribs in the oven to keep them warm while you're out playing with the next Jackie Robinson. And then there's cake and ice cream."

The door burst open, crashing on its hinges against the wall. Joe ran out with a bat, an old grass stained baseball, and a pair of black high-top tennis shoes. He flopped down on the floor and began pulling off his new cowboy boots.

Kitty spoke to her grandson in Russian as if she had never left the old country. "I know it's your birthday, but would you mind not breaking the door down whenever you go in or out."

"Sure, Grandma. Sorry." Joe's response was also in perfect Russian. He had been speaking it, as well as French, for as long as he could remember.

Chapter 33

November 23, 1971
San Francisco, California

They picked up their menus and, with a straight face, Kitty began ordering her meal in Russian. The confusion on their waiter's face made them laugh. Enjoying the ruse, Joe switched to French and started ordering his dinner. However, this time the waiter began making notes with his pencil, then turning back to Kitty, he said, "*Madame?*"

Kitty giggled softly and ordered her dinner in French, ending with "*merci*" and a wink to the waiter for playing along with them.

Joe looked fondly at his grandmother. Kitty noticed the affectionate expression, searched into his eyes for an answer, and then said, "OK, I give up. What are you thinking about?"

Joe took a swig of beer and replied, "This just reminded me of the French and Russian vacations we used to take. My favorite was the one to the Grand Canyon when we spoke Russian the whole two weeks. I was only ten, and everyone thought you were my mother."

Kitty got a far-away look on her face as she recalled the trip. Suddenly, a big grin spread across her face. "Do you remember the guy at the gas station on the way down, when you couldn't get him to understand what you wanted? Finally you broke down and said in English, *Where in the hell is the key to the bathroom?* I think that was the first time I'd ever heard you use a cuss word. I couldn't help but laugh even though I knew I shouldn't."

Joe was smiling, remembering the episode as if it had been yesterday. "Yeah, it was in Oklahoma. It's been a while since I've thought about that one. I almost didn't make it on time. ...You know, the hardest part was pretending we didn't quite understand what people were saying in English. I think they thought we were a couple of *commies* or something."

Kitty finished her drink, set it on the table and said, "I think I liked the trip to New Orleans the best, when we spoke French all week. They could understand us pretty well there. It would be fun to go to France so you can really get a feel for the accent."

Joe nodded. "I'd like to go to Moscow, too, and to the Milanov estate to see where you grew up. It's too bad those *commy-pinko-fags* have locked all their people in and, everyone else out."

With a look that waffled between resignation and determination, Kitty mumbled, "Someday, Joe; maybe someday."

Joe woke to a sharp rap on the door. The effects of the nightcap he'd had at the Fairmont Hotel with his grandmother caused him to wince. He rolled over, putting the pillow over his head, hoping that whoever was at the door would think he wasn't there and go away. This time the knock on the door was more demanding, as if he was being summoned. He slipped on some boxers. "Who in the hell?"

He opened the door, and to his amazement, Kitty was standing there with her arm outstretched ready to knock on the door again. "Rise and shine, buster." She walked past him into his room. It was a typical college dorm room. Clothes were strewn all over the desk, floor and chair. The doorknobs to the closet and bathroom had shirts and pants hanging from them. Kitty walked into the bathroom and brought out two bras and some panties. "Yours?" she asked.

Pulling on some jeans that had been lying on the floor, Joe looked up to see his grandmother holding the lingerie and said, "Those are Jann's next door. We share the bathroom, but she washes her things in the sink, so I call it the laundry room."

"There's a woman living on the other side of that door?" Kitty pointed through the bathroom to a door on the far side. "I knew this was a coed dorm, but I thought men lived on one floor and the women on the next."

"Nope, this is California. We all love each other out here. Doesn't matter if you got boobs or not. Sharin' with a woman's not so bad, though. At least she doesn't pee on the floor."

Kitty returned the underwear to the *laundry room*. "I didn't think they wore bras these days."

Joe slipped a sweatshirt over his head. "She doesn't most of the time, but she plays tennis, and the way she's built..."

Kitty and Joe spent the day in Napa Valley. They visited several wineries, took two tours and tasted a wide range of whites and reds. They had an impromptu picnic high on a hillside overlooking the vineyards, sharing two more bottles of wine with bread and cheese. They had a terrific time but, returning over the Golden Gate Bridge, Kitty was glad Joe was driving.

It was barely dawn when Kitty walked past the doorman of the Fairmont Hotel and crossed the street to the little park. She was still on Kansas City time, had awakened at four-thirty, and waited for the sun to arrive. She strolled around the gardens, enjoying the relative peace and quiet of the big city on the day after Thanksgiving. Kitty sat down on a bench beneath a trellis that was covered by a thick growth of flowering vines. She closed her eyes for her morning meditation, feeling the need to cleanse herself of the clouds caused by the previous day's imbibing.

Fifteen minutes later, contented and refreshed, Kitty opened her eyes. Directly in front of her, but on the other side of the small park, an Asian woman was moving gracefully, like a ballet dancer in slow motion. She was slithering her arms and legs in arcs around her perfectly-balanced body. It was a continuous motion that flowed with a quiet and confident power.

Finally, the movements stopped and the women stood motionless for several seconds. Kitty's curiosity was piqued, so she decided to go satisfy it. She approached the Asian woman, who had begun to walk the perimeter of the garden. The woman stopped and bowed. Kitty judged her to be in her mid-thirties. Her clothes were loose fitting, gray/black and simple. She was tiny. Her black hair was as fine as spider silk.

"I hope I'm not bothering you," Kitty began. "I couldn't help but admire the way you were dancing over there a minute ago. What do you call it?"

The woman's brown eyes contrasted with the ice-blue in Kitty's. With a slightly clipped Asian accent, her petite voice said, "It is called T'ai Chi (Tie-Chee). It is how I begin each morning."

"It's beautiful," Kitty said. "How did you learn it?"

"My grandmother taught me when I was very small. In China, many people do T'ai Chi to get their mind and body in harmony. It is both an exercise and meditation." She paused for the right words. "You must first find your own center...and then you can know the world around you."

This sounded like some sort of proverb to Kitty. "My name is Kitty

O'Riley. I live in Kansas City but I'm out here visiting my grandson who is attending school at Stanford."

The Asian woman bowed respectfully and said, "I am Lee Mae." She bowed again and said nothing more.

Eager to continue the conversation, Kitty said, "I'm staying at the Fairmont across the street. Do you live in San Francisco?"

"I live a few blocks from here with my uncle and my daughter, Lee Ping. My uncle works at the fish market down on the wharf."

"I'd like to talk to you a little more about T'ai Chi. Do you have a few minutes?"

With the slightest nod of her head, Lee Mae closed her eyes and opened them again, which Kitty interpreted as consent. They talked for nearly an hour, including a demonstration of several of the movements. "*Chi* is a spiritual energy running through your body that connects you to the earth," she explained, looking into Kitty's eyes, looking for understanding.

Kitty returned her gaze for a moment and was silent. Finally, she asked, "Would you teach me how to do that?"

Lee Mae's shy smile turned into a crooked-toothed grin. "It is something that takes some time...Mrs. O'Riley."

The topic of conversation changed and Kitty learned that Lee Mae had fled to America because her husband, disgusted that he had not been given a son, intended to abandon their infant daughter. Apparently, it was not uncommon in China, but it was the first Kitty had heard of it. Lee Mae had served as a cabin boy for passage on the ship. For the last fifteen years, she had been working as a maid during the day, cleaning and cooking for her uncle the rest of the time

Lee Mae had to be coaxed into talking about herself and was too shy to ask Kitty any questions. Kitty offered that she, too, had fled to America, but across a different ocean. They gradually became comfortable in each other's presence, and that's when Kitty learned something else, something disturbing.

"There is little money, and what there is, is spent on booze or lost in gambling at the fish market. My uncle told me last night that Lee Ping must quit school and go to work. He said we need the money and what was the use for a girl to go to school anyway. He said she is young and pretty and there is a way for her to make money in San Francisco. He didn't say it, but I knew what he had in mind for my daughter. I slept little last night, trying to think of what I could do. My uncle has been good to us, taking us into his home, and it is his right. I was hoping to find the answer when I came to the park this morning."

A shiver ran through Kitty's body, unable to conceive how a man could order his own niece's fifteen-year-old daughter to work street-corners. Kitty reached over and took Lee Mae's hands in hers. She had always made quick decisions but what she was about to do felt a little impulsive even to her. "How would you like to come to Kansas City to live with me? Lee Ping can go to high school there and you can teach me T'ai Chi, plus help around the house. You can also teach me how to read, write and speak Chinese. I haven't tried to learn a new language in a long time. The challenge would be fun."

Chapter 34

June 2, 1974
Mission Hills, Kansas

Joe drove his Volvo through the open gate and parked it in front of the house. He had spent the last five days driving home from school, including three nights in Reno raising a little hell. After completing his finals, he felt like celebrating, and that's what he and Brady had done. Both their wallets were considerably lighter when they pulled out of Reno, but their bloodshot eyes were evidence of a well-earned good time.

Joe got out from behind the wheel and stretched, having driven the last leg from Denver that day. He had stayed at Brady's folks the night before and headed out after an early breakfast. "Ahhh, summer vacation." he said. He grabbed a satchel, made of old blue jeans, from the back seat and headed up the steps to the front door.

As usual, the door was not locked. He pushed it open and walked in, throwing the satchel on the French, antique love seat in the foyer. "Hellloooo!!!" he yelled as he passed beneath the chandelier hanging from the high vaulted ceiling. Immediately, he heard footsteps somewhere upstairs, signaling the success of his hail. Stepping back to improve his view of the landing at the top of the winding staircase, he smiled, knowing who belonged to the scampering feet.

Through the archway, a figure burst into view and a girlish squeal filled the air as Lee Ping ran to meet him. Her bare, agile feet fluttered down the stairs, perilously close to a headlong sprawl. She was wearing a pair of blue-jean cutoffs and a t-shirt with the words LANCER above and SENIORS below a big "74". Joe spread his arms to catch the ninety-eight-pound human projectile, which had just launched itself two steps before reaching the Italian tile floor.

Joe was big, but Lee Ping's momentum made him take a step backward to maintain his balance as he swallowed her in his arms. "How ya doing, Jump?" he asked, as she threw her long, black hair out of the way and kissed his cheek. He squeezed her hard, till she gasped for breath, and then set her down.

"Doin' great, meathead," she said with a huge smile. "I'm glad you're home. I was hoping you'd get here for my graduation. Finally, out of high school!"

"Where's the Cat?" Joe asked. That's what he irreverently called his grandmother, contending she was too old to be a Kitty.

"She's still at work, I think." Lee Ping reached up and grabbed a hand full of Joe's long, wavy hair that was resting on his shoulder. "Your hair is going to be as long as mine pretty soon," she said, giving it a tug.

He clutched her wrist, forcing her to release his hair, and spun her around. "Yeah, sure. That stringy stuff of yours is all the way down to your ass," he said with mock disgust. Lee Ping's hair was actually fine and silky smooth. Joe knew it was her pride and joy, and therefore, usually said something derogatory about it.

She shot back, "One of us is *supposed* to look like a girl, and unless your tits start growing pretty soon, I guess it's gonna have to be me."

He swatted her on the butt, and then turned to go out to start carrying his stuff in from the car. "Where's your mom?" he asked over his shoulder.

"She was in the laundry room doing some ironing. She probably didn't hear you come in because of the dryer."

Lee Ping followed Joe out the door to help him carry in his things. She adored him. The crush began two-and-a-half years ago when he drove them all to the San Francisco airport. It was the first time she had set eyes on him, the start of a new life for her and her mother, and the luckiest day ever. But it would be luckier still if she could get him to notice her as more than just a little girl.

He had always made fun of her name. Once he found out that Lee was their family name and Ping was her first name, he no longer called her Lee Ping. It was either Ping Pong or Jump. Other people called her Ping Pong, too, but *Jump* was Joe's exclusive nick-name for her. The name was derived, cleverly, Joe thought, from *Lee Ping* to *Leaping* to *Jump*.

Lee Ping hopped on the hood as Joe got into his car to drive it around to the garage where the back stairwell led to the basement. Five months ago, during Christmas break, Joe had fixed up a room down there for a little privacy, relinquishing the upstairs to the three females of the house. The basement also had a fireplace, century-old pool table and wet bar.

Joe set his coffee mug down on the counter, opened the refrigerator, and grabbed a gallon-bottle of milk. Just as he was reaching into the cabinet for a bowl, Lee Ping walked into the kitchen in a large night shirt that read STANFORD ATHLETIC DEPARTMENT. "Cereal?" he asked. "I was wondering what happened to that t-shirt."

Scratching her side, a sleepy smile and hair in total disarray, Lee Ping said, "You gave it to me. You just didn't know it yet. And no, I don't want any cereal. I'm going to have some orange juice and wake up first."

"Your hair looks great," he said sarcastically. "You ought to wear it like that all the time."

She gave him the finger, softening the message with a smile.

Joe sliced half a banana into his Corn Flakes and walked out to the back patio with the Sunday funnies.

The only furniture remaining in the billiard room, now simply referred to as *the room*, was a couple of low writing tables and several large pillows. Lee Ping had taught Joe how to do T'ai Chi, and at times, the four of them would do it together in *the room*. Joe preferred to do T'ai Chi outside, alone. It made him feel one with nature, healthy, balanced. In addition to T'ai Chi, *the room* served as a place for meditation and language lessons.

Kitty had become fluent, from a conversing standpoint, in the Mandarin dialect that Lee Mae and Lee Ping used. She still had a long way to go with reading and writing. The three of them spoke only Chinese to each other on Tuesdays and Thursdays. It had been Kitty's idea; the notion getting its inspiration from the vacations she and Joe had taken when they spoke only French or Russian. Kitty was currently teaching both Lee Ping and Lee Mae how to speak French.

Joe slammed his car door and stomped across the driveway, entering the house through the back door. He had driven home from work with his windows down in the ninety-five degree heat. The cool air-conditioning in the house hit him with a force. However, it did little to simmer the fire he had burning inside. Still wearing his hard hat, he marched directly over to the refrigerator, grabbed a cold beer and popped the top. Downing half the Budweiser without moving his feet, he finally reached up, pulled off his yellow hard hat, and let his long ponytail fall down his back. He set the hat on the counter and lifted the can again to his lips.

He was pissed. He'd been working for R & R Browning Development this summer to get some experience in building large structures. His grandmother knew Randolph Browning, Sr., which made it simple to get on the Crown Center Project. It was simply a matter of her asking Randolph Sr. to call the current president, Randolph Jr., and it was done. The reason Joe was pissed had to do with the fact that there was also a Randolph III.

The heir apparent was a second-year engineering student, preparing to move into the family tradition. Joe had no problem with that, except in this case, three was not a charm. *Three* was an asshole. Around his grandmother, Joe called him *trois*, the French word for three. Around everyone else, Joe referred to Randolph Browning III as *Twat*.

Every time the Project Boss had an interesting job that needed a young engineer's level of expertise, Twat claimed family rights. Even that wouldn't be so bad except that today, Twat began critiquing Joe's work on a part of the project that was unrelated to the heir apparent's own efforts. Joe had merely said, "F—— you," and walked off the job.

He threw the empty beer can into the garbage beneath the sink, opened the refrigerator and grabbed another. He walked out of the kitchen thinking, R & R Browning's in trouble if that moron is going to be in charge some day.

The house was quiet. It was still early afternoon, so The Cat would be at work. Joe walked through the house, allowing the air conditioning to cool him down as he sipped on his beer. As he passed *the room*, he noticed Lee Mae lying on a mat; her body contorted in an unnatural yet relaxed position. "Mae Mae, how do you get your legs to do that?"

The Chinese woman slowly uncoiled her body, like a snake unwinding itself from a tree branch. Joe picked up a mat, spread it out next to hers and sat down to unlace his work boots. "You're home early," she said. Her calm demeanor immediately began to defuse Joe's frustration and tension.

"Yeah...things didn't go so well at work today." He tossed his boots and socks aside, curling his muscular legs into a half-lotus position... stiffly. He straightened up his back and sighed, his body remembering how comfortable the position was. They sat together in silence for a little while. Joe started going over his recent confrontation with Randy in his mind, which rekindled his aggravation.

"I'm not learning a damned thing at Browning. I took the job to get some experience, but all the good stuff goes to the boss's son." Joe reached behind his head, pulled the rubber band out of his hair, and let his long locks fall freely over his shoulders. "I'm wasting my time with that jerk around. If I'm not going to learn anything, I might as well quit. I might already have."

Lee Mae just sat quietly and calmly, letting Joe talk out his frustration. Finally, after it appeared that he was finished, she slowly moved her left hand behind her back, raising her right palm in front of Joe's face. She turned it this way and that, letting it swivel on her wrist. Her slender fingers, the petite back of her hand, the cupped palm, all combined to resemble the head of a snake.

Joe's eyes followed the graceful movements and gradually a smile creased his face. "OK, it's a hand, a very sleek one. What are you trying to tell me, Mae Mae?"

A smile touched her eyes and mouth. "So far, I'm just trying to capture your attention and bring it into this room." She pulled the hand down, slid it behind her back and brought the other one out, resting it on her crossed legs in front of her. She said, "I want you to think about *one hand clapping*."

Joe sat there for a second, waiting for her to continue. When she just stared back at him, he frowned and said, "What? Is that it? What are you talking about?"

"I want you to think about *one hand clapping*," she repeated.

"It doesn't make any sense."

"That's the point." Lee Mae studied his face. "When you achieve silence, the loudest silence there is...it is where nothing and everything meet. It is something to strive for, yet one cannot strive for it."

Joe shook his head slowly, trying to grasp her meaning. Lee Mae frequently said things that were nonsensical, at least to him. He sighed. "I still don't understand."

"You can only understand what you are ready to understand. I am merely trying to point the way."

Chapter 35

A faint light was beginning to appear through the window high above her head. She couldn't see the snow, but the wind whistling through the window well gave evidence of the cold, blustery weather outside. Lee Ping was home for Christmas break after her first semester at the University of Kansas in Lawrence. It was toasty warm under the covers in the chilly basement bedroom. She peered out of her cocoon, as the room gradually took form in the dim but growing light.

She sighed contentedly before slipping out the side of the bed, careful not to wake Joe, who was breathing softly next to her. It was just light enough to find her Stanford sweatshirt, which she quickly pulled over her head. Her red KU sweatpants were another matter. She remembered that last night Joe had been whirling them around his head, but she couldn't recall in which direction they had taken flight. She tiptoed around, naked from the waist down, trying to find them in the semi-dark room. She bumped into a table, jostling several beer cans, which caused Joe to stir restlessly, but did not wake him.

Lee Ping glanced at the grayish window, anxious that time was running out on any attempt to get upstairs unnoticed. She tugged on the bottom of the sweatshirt, stretching it down to her upper thigh, thus covering the essentials. She gently grasped the knob to the door, slipped out like a wisp of smoke and closed it quietly behind her. Turning, she was glad she could make out the shape of the pool table enough to avoid running into it on her way to the stairs.

A shiver ran through Lee Ping's body as she tiptoed across the cold tile floor of the kitchen. She pushed through the swinging kitchen door and found no lights burning in the main part of the house. She made her way toward the big spiral staircase, but as she passed *the room*, a soft but firm voice cut through the silence.

"Lee Ping, would you please come here for a moment?"

Lee Ping jumped in surprise, her heart suddenly pounding in her chest. A defensive reflex action caused Lee Ping's hands to release her grip on her sweatshirt and clutch her throat, her arms protecting her abdomen. The silhouetted figure of a statue, which turned out to be Kitty, doing her T'ai Chi, began to move toward her through the shadows.

Even in the half-light, the state of Lee Ping's undress became clearly evident as Kitty approached her. Lee Ping quickly yanked her sweatshirt back down, covering herself. "Come in and sit with me for a little while." Kitty stretched out her arm, inviting Lee Ping to join her in *the room*. "I'll get you an afghan so you don't freeze your bottom."

It was close to noon before Joe made an appearance upstairs. He rarely slept in like that, but the cold outside and warmth under his blankets lured him to a life of lazy decadence. His hair was still wet from his shower when he found Lee Mae making turkey sandwiches in the kitchen. "Mae Mae, are we having turkey again? This will be three days in a row," he complained.

Without turning from her task, she said, "You're free to make whatever you'd like. Your grandmother and I decided to finish the turkey off so we could be done with it. You know how we never throw anything away."

Joe shrugged, "I think I'll just have some cereal and yogurt."

"Suit yourself. By the way, your presence is requested in your grandmother's study; that is, if you're not going back to bed."

"What's she want? Did she say?"

"I'm just the messenger, dear. You'll have to go up and find out for yourself. Why don't you take a cup of coffee with you and I'll fix your cereal and yogurt? Do you want a sliced banana or strawberries on your cereal?"

"You choose, thanks," he said.

When he rapped a knuckle against the door, announcing his arrival, Kitty looked up from a stack of papers she was working on but did not smile...a bad sign. In Russian she said, "I'd like to talk to you about something, Joseph. Please shut the door and sit down."

Joe didn't know what this was about, but he did not like the way it was starting out. One thing he did know was that when his grandmother addressed him in Russian or French, she expected him to respond in the same language.

He shut the door, turned back to face her and said in flawless Russian,

"What's wrong? You are obviously not happy about something."

"Sit down," she said firmly, "please."

He walked over to a beautiful French antique chair, sat down gently and rested his elbows on the chair's ornately carved arms. Facing his grandmother, he raised his eyebrows as a signal that he was ready for whatever she intended to deliver; still not looking forward to it, but ready.

Continuing in Russian, Kitty said matter-of-factly, "I had an interesting discussion with Lee Ping early this morning. Very early, I might add." She stopped to give Joe a chance to respond.

Joe gave her a noncommittal expression, raising his eyebrows again with a hint of a thin-lipped grin.

"And, since she left your bed hours before you did, I've had some time to think about all that she told me."

So that's it, Joe thought to himself. "We knew you wouldn't understand, so we decided not to advertise it," he stated. "We were just playing around."

Taking off her reading glasses, Kitty stood up from behind her desk. She was wearing a beautifully hand-painted kimono, which she straightened unconsciously while she fought to control her voice. "You may have been fooling around," she said calmly, "but I think Lee Ping is in love with you. At least she thinks she is. Why don't you tell me your side of the story." Kitty eased herself back into the chair, determined to keep this conversation on an adult-to-adult basis.

"You want to hear about last night?" Joe asked, his Russian accent coming as easily as the words.

"Why don't you start with the Ozarks last summer," she offered. "I thought you were going to run the boat and provide some mature judgment."

Joe explained how his role as chaperon for a bunch of soon-to-be college coeds, including Lee Ping, had taken an unexpected left turn. Ten minutes later, finishing with how the girls had decided to go skinny-dipping about two in the morning, he said, "And that's about all I'm going to say about that night except that Lee Ping was still in my bed when the sun came up and we hadn't spent much of the time sleeping."

Kitty stared out the window from her chair, flashing back to a riverbank when she was twenty years old. She had given herself to Billy. She remembered that it had been wonderful, but she had been scared, at first. Billy had been gentle...and strong...and her body had responded. Oh, how it had responded. Suddenly, a sadness and loneliness swept over her. *Now, she had only Little Joe left. No, she had Lee Mae and Lee Ping, too.* This thought brought Kitty back to the present. She shifted her gaze to Joe's face and saw him watching her. She had been drifting down memory lane. Her grandson had respectfully, patiently, let her indulge. *He is a good boy,* she thought to herself.

Kitty placed her elbows on the desk; hands clasped together, resting her chin on her interlocked fingers. She took a long, deep breath, letting it out slowly. "Lee Ping's description of that trip was much briefer, but she admitted making the first move. She also mentioned several, let's call them, episodes, since then."

"Lee Ping and I are good friends. We have fun together. And the sex thing...it's not hurting anybody. You know, Cat, that's the way the world is these days. Hell, we may piss off the Russians and all be dead tomorrow."

The casual use of her nickname, and his flippant attitude, irritated Kitty, but she didn't let it show. "I'll say this one more time. You may think it's just playing around, but I'm concerned about Lee Ping. You two live in the same house, for Christ's sake! Try to use that head of yours for something more than a place to put your hat. Now get out of here and let me work." She smiled as she uttered these final words, wanting to keep their relationship and communication channels open.

"We only live in the same house during the summer and on breaks," said Joe, his voice trailing off as he meandered down the hall, glancing at family pictures that had hung there since he could remember.

Kitty looked down at the papers on the desk in front of her, not seeing them. Having had her say on the matter, she sighed, dismissing the subject of Joe and Lee Ping. Her mind flipped back to a comment her grandson had made moments earlier; *...Piss off the Russians and we'll all be dead tomorrow.* She had fled her own country over fifty years ago. She had found a new life, made a new life, one of great accomplishment and satisfaction. When she thought about the Bolsheviks, it stirred her insides. She was sad for the Russian people, living as Communists.

Kitty asked herself, *How much longer can I wait?*

Chapter 36

June 23, 1978
Kansas City, Missouri

Kitty sat at the head table, two chairs over from the podium where the mayor of Kansas City was about to speak. She had just finished a small slice of Sophina, the cornerstone of America's largest dessert-producing empire, Kitty's Kakes. The Latvian cheesecake was an appropriate, and obvious, choice for the retirement celebration of the founder, though Kitty could no longer enjoy the dessert due to utter saturation.

The mayor's role was Master of Ceremonies, so after making a few preliminary statements of welcome, and some general tongue-wagging, he proceeded to introduce the first speaker. Other than the guest of honor and her partner, none had a more distinguished career with the company than the former president of Kitty's Kakes, Wray Brady. He had started with the company in 1920, when he was only eighteen. He was Kitty's junior by a little more than a year.

About half of the three-hundred-plus guests were current or former employees of Kitty's Kakes, which meant that Wray was known personally, or by reputation, by most of those present. Wray had played an instrumental role in the growth years of the bakery company and had retired a rich man at age sixty-seven. That had been nine years ago. James, Kitty's partner, had died shortly after Wray's retirement, causing Kitty to re-establish herself at the helm of daily operations. She had maintained that responsibility, as well as being chairman of the board until this day.

Wray's edge had lost its sharpness. He rambled through his speech, covering decades of Kitty's accomplishments and victories for the company. He retold the story of how he had first gotten his chance as a driver, in 1921, because the co-founder had broken his arm, trying to crank-start their Model-T Ford delivery truck. The story was legend at Kitty's Kakes but was received patiently and graciously by the crowd.

Joe, sitting next to his grandmother, placed his hand on hers. He wanted to comfort her because he knew the effect the mention of James had on her. She looked at him and smiled, knowing that he knew made her feel better. Wray sat down to a thunder of applause.

The mayor got up to introduce the next speaker, the Kansas State Governor. Kitty and Governor Anthony had been business associates for years before he had run for governor. He was from Wichita but had grain elevators strung across Nebraska and South Dakota as well as Kansas. His mills in Omaha and Kansas City supplied the majority of Kitty's Kakes' flour. Kitty's railroad connections and shipping division provided his company with an economical means to transport his grain, making the relationship mutually beneficial.

Kitty had avoided politics as much as possible her entire life. However, when her friend, Gary Anthony, decided to run for governor of their state, she had gotten behind his campaign effort, contributing enormous amounts of manpower and whatever financial backing was legally acceptable. Thereafter, she would accept no preferential treatment for Kitty's Kakes or any of her other ventures, which was a relief for Governor Anthony, politically, and had cemented his already high opinion of her. The fact was *Kitty and Her Kakes*, which is what he called the company, didn't need any help.

He, too, expounded on Kitty's tremendous achievements, beginning with the well-known fact of her roots as a poor Russian immigrant. He even suggested that the motivation for starting the huge conglomerate was basically to earn enough money to buy a horse. This produced a roar of laughter from the crowd as Kitty's eyes got moist, remembering her beloved Majesty. Most of the audience was well aware of the reputation of the O'Riley horse-breeding operation, so, few people doubted the truth of the governor's statement.

Governor Anthony concluded his comments with a little surprise. He pulled a small envelope out of his breast pocket, unfolding the hand-written note it contained. He apologized as he fumbled briefly with his reading glasses, making the expected comment about his advancing age. He read the note aloud:

Dear Kitty,

It is with great pleasure that I have been given the opportunity to offer my profound congratulations on your illustrious career, as well as my best wishes for your planned retirement. We have both watched America grow up this century, and I feel none have played a more significant role in the business community than you have.

Please accept my regret at not being able to participate in your celebration in person. You know that any time you are in the neighborhood, you're invited to stay with Rosalyn and me.

Very truly yours,
Jimmy Carter

Governor Anthony folded the note, written on the President of the United State's personal stationery, and held it out to Kitty. He prompted her to stand by lifting on her elbow with one hand and pulling her chair back out of the way with the other. Escorting her to the podium, which was only about three steps, he leaned up to the microphone. "I give you, Mrs. O'Riley."

The room exploded with applause. Every person rose to their feet, displaying the genuine respect and affection this woman instilled in people. They rejected the normal tendency to quiet down after the appropriate tribute. Becoming slightly embarrassed, Kitty said "Thank you" a couple of times, hoping they would regain their seats so she could begin. Finally, with a smile and a hint of exasperation in her voice, she said, "I'm leaving if you all don't shut up."

The comment interjected laughter into the applause, but also had the desired effect of getting the crowd to take their seats. Most of those attending were used to taking orders from this seventy-seven-year-old woman. When it became quiet, it was total. She said nothing, just looked out at the faces turned up to where she stood. The absolute silence lasted about ten seconds, but it seemed like minutes.

"Thank you, Governor Anthony," she began, "Wray," nodding toward each. "My name is Xenia, Catrina, Milanov, Vyikzonoskia, Wixon, O'Riley; but everybody calls me Kitty." A rumble of laughter rolled through the crowd. "I remember in the twenties I was called *She Boss* behind my back.

As Wray and a few of the rest of you know, James Monroe, my dear sidekick, was called *He Boss*."

Kitty had to swallow hard to get rid of the growing lump in her throat before she could continue. "James and I started Kitty's Kakes a long time ago, and since we don't want people to think our governor is a liar, it *was* started so I could buy back a horse that was stolen from me when I came to America from Russia. You've heard Wray Brady expound on the history of good luck and successes our company has had over the years, so I won't go into all of that again. I would just like to say that we all did it together, and none of it would have been possible anywhere but America.

"Now, I'm not going to start waving the flag, but I want to thank someone for my being here today; David Rowland Francis. I was very young when he was the American Ambassador to Russia in 1917. He told me a lot of amazing things about this country, about all the automobiles in the streets, and well...I decided that America was where I wanted to be. At the time, I was running away from what Russia was becoming, has become. He helped me get here. I am very fortunate that he did, and I try not to forget that it could easily have been otherwise. David has been dead a long time now." Digressing, Kitty said, "Actually, he was the Governor of Missouri at one time in the 1800's."

Kitty paused but there was utter silence. No chairs scraped the floor, no one coughed...quiet. Finally she said, "Now it's time for me to move on again. And I'm going to go by ship, like in 1917. I'm not sure if it's a small ship or a big boat, but it's going to have my name on it. I've decided to travel around the world by sea. It should take about a year, and I'm leaving as soon as we can get the *Catrina* outfitted."

There was another pause as Kitty scanned the familiar faces of those seated at the nearest tables. "My grandson, Joseph, will continue to sit on the board of directors of Kitty's Kakes, as he has for the last two years. The chairmanship, however, will be turned over to Logan Sweeney. As you all know, he is very capable and I have no reservations about his ability to lead this company." Smiling, she added, "Being Irish didn't hurt." The crowd chuckled again, knowing that O'Riley was not her heritage but the blarney was in her heart, if not her blood.

വ

Joe and Kitty strolled through the stables while they talked. As they passed each horse, Kitty made comments regarding the animal's needs in terms of care, and, or, training. Joe was re-acquainting himself with the various duties and aspects of running the house, stables and surrounding land. They still employed a foreman and ranch hands, of course, but the owner had to know what was going on, just the same.

They had finished their review of the animals and were out leaning against the rails of the exercise corral when Joe finally asked the question that had been bothering him ever since his grandmother had decided to retire. "So, what if Logan talks the board into making some drastic move that will affect the future of the entire company? I mean, you still own seventy-percent of the stock of Kitty's Kakes."

Kitty looked at her grandson's concerned face and smiled. She pinched his cheek affectionately and said, "I've already told you, you let the board make the decisions. I'm retired and they're in charge. That's why you only have one vote. You don't want all that responsibility either. You're there mainly so the thousands of employees don't think we've abandoned them."

Kitty took his hand as they started back toward the house. "If something happens to me while I'm gone, I've left papers and authorizations in the vault of Ernie Mitts' bank in Chicago. As you know, Daniel, Ernie's son, took over as president when his father died. He has instructions to execute those papers and deliver them to the board of Kitty's Kakes, in the event I haven't returned one year from now."

Chapter 37

Baltimore, Maryland

Kitty stood on the pier, looking across the ten-yard expanse of water that separated her from a very large yacht. Next to her was a man wearing an expensive suit, collar unbuttoned, tie loosened. The pier happened to be part of the Baltimore shipyards, and the yacht was in the process of becoming the *Catrina*. They watched a man hanging over the stern in a type of swing. The man was hand-painting the name on the boat and was just finishing up the –T- as Kitty asked, "What time am I supposed to talk to the director?"

The man in the expensive suit shifted his eyes from the painter to Kitty's face. "Actually, your appointment is with the deputy director, and he can see you at one o'clock. My driver is waiting over there." He tilted his head indicating the parking lot. "He'll run us down to D.C. as soon as you're done here."

Kitty had flown in to Baltimore the night before and checked into the Hyatt so she could be at the shipyard early this morning. She had already spent an hour with the man in charge of refitting the *Catrina*. The boat was a vintage, one-hundred-and-ten-foot-long ketch, with two masts and huge diesel engines. The price tag amounted to millions. Once completed, there would be few, if any, sailing vessels like it in the world.

On the drive down to Washington, the senator from Illinois was trying to appease his passenger, with little success. "Mrs. O'Riley, it is very difficult to get in to see the Director of the CIA, particularly when you're not willing to tell him what you want to talk about. It was like pulling teeth to get an appointment with the deputy director. I think the fact that he was curious to meet the woman who built Kitty's Kakes was the key to getting you in, more than anything I did."

Kitty laid her hand softly on the young senator's arm and said, "Nolan, I know you tried and I appreciate it. It's just that I prefer to speak to the person making the decisions. It's so much more efficient. That's the way I've always done business, but I understand that government doesn't always work like Main Street."

The young senator from Illinois tried to decide if he detected a condescending tinge to that last remark. Finally, accepting the truth in the statement, he gave up trying to figure out what this intriguing woman thought about his chosen profession. They dropped the subject and rode the rest of the way in silence, except for a brief discussion about how business was doing in his home state. Kitty had extensive investments and two bakeries in the Chicago area, which is why he was trying to do this favor for her in the first place.

After entering the building, passing through a metal detector, and showing ID's to the security guard at the desk, they took the elevator to the fourth floor. The door slid open, exposing a large, plush foyer area with a receptionist's desk. Kitty suspected this to be another security checkpoint. Nolan politely slipped his hand around Kitty's elbow as they approached the stunning young brunette sitting behind the desk.

Having been forewarned of their arrival by the lobby security man, the woman flashed a brilliant smile at Kitty and the senator, saying, "The Deputy Director is just finishing something up, but he is expecting you. Please have a seat for a moment. May I get you a cup of coffee or something?"

Afternoon coffee had never appealed to Kitty, but the senator took the receptionist up on her offer. "Just black, please," he said. The young woman stood up to get it, her fashionable red dress and high heels completing the picture of a statuesque model.

Kitty watched Nolan watch the woman as the red dress disappeared through the hidden door behind a plant. Kitty thought to herself, *He is thinking she's a great-looking airhead secretary who probably can't even type.* Whispering, Kitty said confidentially, "I'd say 36-24-36, maybe five-foot-ten; how about you?"

The comment surprised the senator to the point of catching him with his mouth open, dumbfounded.

Kitty smiled broadly, then, continuing to whisper, said, "She's probably got her Masters in Criminology or Political Science and is a black belt in Karate to boot."

The senator could still think of nothing appropriate to say. He just looked into the cool, blue eyes that seemed to be sparkling back at him.

The receptionist emerged with a porcelain coffee cup that sported an American flag, steam rising above the lip. "If you would follow me, please, the Deputy Director will see you now. I'll carry your coffee for you, Senator. She led the pair down a paneled corridor, her sleek red dress and matching heels accentuating her considerable height. At the end of the hall, the woman knocked politely at the open door of a corner office and stepped aside for Kitty and her escort to enter. She handed Nolan his coffee as he passed.

A man in his early forties closed a file he had been reading and rose to greet his visitors. As he stepped around the edge of his desk, he grabbed his jacket from a side chair as if to put it on, and then with a smile said, "We don't need these, do we Senator?" He laid the jacket back on the chair, then reached out his hand, saying, "It's good to see you again, Nolan."

Nolan clasped his hand firmly and said, "Frank, I want you to meet Kitty O'Riley. Mrs. O'Riley, this is Frank Bishop, the Deputy Director of CIA Operations."

Again, Frank stretched out his hand, but less aggressively this time. "Mrs. O'Riley, I've been looking forward to this part of my schedule all day," he said graciously.

Kitty smiled cordially and returned his handshake with equal pressure. "It was kind of you to accommodate my request, Mr. Bishop. Hopefully, I won't take up too much of your time." Kitty turned to the senator and said, "I can't tell you how much I appreciate your help, Nolan. Thank you."

The senator's eyebrows went up at the obvious dismissal. He had intended to remain present during the discussion. What did a woman who had retired with over a hundred million dollars want with the CIA? Reluctantly, Nolan asked Kitty, "Would you like my driver to come back for you and give you a ride to the airport?"

"Thank you, Senator. Maybe you could ask him to leave my bag with the security man downstairs. I'm sure it will be no trouble to catch a cab when the time comes. But thank you again for everything, and keep those Illinois state taxes down if you can."

Kitty maintained the warm smile on her face, but this last comment was clearly the end of their conversation.

"Good-bye then," he said. "Thanks, Frank." He turned and left the office.

Just outside the door the gorgeous brunette, who had remained discretely out of sight in case she was needed, greeted him. "I'll see you out, Senator." She stepped into the office far enough to gently pull the door shut, then latched on to the senator's arm and marched him back down the paneled hallway to the foyer.

With his arm being drawn provocatively against her ample bosom, Nolan enjoyed his consolation prize. Coffee slopped over the side of the cup onto his shoes, unnoticed.

With the door closed behind her, Kitty took the offered seat across the desk from Frank Bishop. She had a rather slim leather brief case on her lap that doubled for a purse. She slipped a manila file out of the case, laid it ceremoniously on the desk in front of her, and said, "Shall I begin, Deputy?"

Startled by her directness, Frank blinked, thinking...this should be interesting. He said, "By all means, Mrs. O'Riley. I am anxious to hear how our operation can be of service to such an outstanding business leader such as yourself. And please, call me Frank. May I call you Kitty?"

Kitty nodded her head, just perceptibly, took a deep breath and plunged in. "You know, Frank, I had hoped to be able to meet with the Director." She held up her hand to soften the blow, "Nothing against you, you understand. It's just that, what I have to say probably needs to be said to him face-to-face and, I simply don't want to waste your time or mine." Before Frank could interject, Kitty continued. "With that in mind, I would like you to give him a message for me." She laid her hand softly on the manila file in front of her, saying, "Tell him I have some interesting information about *Ignace* and would like to meet with him."

Frank looked at her, expecting her to continue. She returned his gaze but said nothing more. "And?" he asked.

"That's it," Kitty replied. "Just tell him I would like to speak to him about *Ignace*. I'm sure he'll understand."

Frank Bishop was not used to being a messenger boy. Being dismissed, much like the senator was moments ago, also did not sit well with him. "I'm sorry, Mrs. O'Riley, but I'm afraid you'll have to settle for me. The Director is really quite busy at the moment."

Their eyes locked, neither wanting to stare the other down, but both unwilling to be the first to break contact.

Kitty decided to take another tack. She smiled, conceding the battle in order to win the war. With a *carefully* friendly voice, she said, "You know, Frank, you're right. There's really no reason why I have to speak to Director Polk right now. A friend of mine named Jimmy and his wife, Rosalyn, have invited me to stay with them tonight. So maybe between now and tomorrow there will be some break-through with your boss's scheduling priorities and, who knows, maybe I'll get lucky." Kitty stood up, the meeting concluded. She slipped the manila file back into her smooth leather case before looking back at the Deputy Director.

Frank had not moved. He sat back in his chair, observing the unusually confident woman standing before him. He was pondering the *Jimmy and Roselyn* comment, trying to decide if it was a bluff or not. His options were, # 1 —call his boss to find out if this *Ignace* thing is a hot button. # 2 —call her bluff and let her walk. The latter action would result in one of two scenarios. She would either stay at the White House tonight and meet with Director Polk tomorrow, by presidential order, or she would find another way to contact the Director and use the *Ignace* thing anyway.

The decision was easy. He would simply deliver the message to Director Polk, as she had asked. If *Ignace* was a hot button, he might as well push it himself and avoid the possible disfavor of the President. If *Ignace* meant nothing to Nathanial W. Polk, Director of CIA Operations, he was home free. He had done what the woman had asked, and she could sleep with Carter's dog for all he cared. He'd be in the clear.

The expression on Frank Bishop's face showed that he had made his decision. It had only taken a couple of seconds. Kitty had been observing him nonchalantly as the wheels turned behind the official's blank stare. Without a word, she sat down again.

Knowing she could read his thoughts, but no longer caring, Frank picked up his phone and pressed one of about twenty buttons located on the face panel. Immediately, he heard the familiar click of the scrambling device and, a microsecond later, the buzz of the Director's private line. It made no difference where Director Polk happened to be at any given moment in time. That button put Frank straight through to his boss anywhere in the world.

As it turned out, the Director was in an Agency helicopter on his way to a meeting, his golf clubs stashed in the cargo bay. Director Polk put down the black leather *Foot Joy* golf shoe he was about to put on, and took the phone from his aide. "Polk here," he said above the muffled whirring of the rotary blades.

"Nathan, this is Frank. Sorry to bother you, but I've got a woman here by the name of Kitty O'Riley who says she wants to talk to you about *Ignace*."

It took about a second-and-a-half for the word to register with the Director of the CIA. "Frank, would you say that again, please?"

The Deputy Director repeated the statement.

"OK, Frank. I heard you that time. Kitty O'Riley...do I know her? Is she sitting there with you right now?"

"Yes, she is, boss. You probably know of her as the CEO of Kitty's Kakes, the big bakery firm."

The blood began draining from Nathanial Polk's face. The good humor he had been in moments ago left him just as quickly. There would be no golf today. There was a fire to put out.

Kitty saw a glint of surprise in Frank Bishop's eyes just before he set the receiver down.

"He'll be here in a few minutes," Frank said, a little awkwardly. He stood up and forced a smile to his lips, which did not reach his eyes, and added, "Since it doesn't seem like there is anything further I can do for you, Mrs. O'Riley, I'll take you back to the lobby where you'll be more comfortable until Director Polk arrives."

As they entered the foyer, Frank said, "Miss Dreher, Mrs. O'Riley will be meeting with Director Polk in a few minutes. Would you please make her feel at home while she waits?" All thought of referring to Kitty by her first name was long gone.

Kitty, however, was a gracious winner. "Mr. Bishop, I am extremely grateful for your time. And believe me when I say that it was necessary for me to talk with Mr. Polk in person."

The Deputy Director nodded politely, turned on his heel and strode up the paneled hallway to his office. Kitty heard him say something to his secretary just before the door to his office slammed shut. She turned back to the receptionist and raised her eyebrows as if to say, *I think he's mad, but I couldn't help it.*

Miss Dreher's warm brown eyes smiled back at Kitty, admiringly. She had not often witnessed Frank Bishop at a disadvantage, and certainly never when it involved a woman at least fifteen years his senior. "Please sit down and make yourself comfortable, Mrs. O'Riley. I'm sure Frank...I Mean, Mr. Bishop, will get over whatever it is. Have you changed your mind about something to drink while you wait?"

Kitty warmed up to the genuine friendliness of the young woman. "Please call me Kitty, and yes, I would appreciate a small glass of ice water if you have it."

The receptionist slipped back through the door behind the plant. A couple of seconds later she returned with a crystal tumbler of water, the ice tinkling against the glass as she walked. "There you go, Mrs...I mean, Kitty." She grinned, her eyes glistening with life. "Isn't it a lot of trouble? You know, trying to decide whether to use a person's first name or last, or Miss or Mrs. or Ms. What a waste of energy."

Kitty accepted the water with two hands. "Thank you." She paused to take a sip. "I agree about the name thing. What shall I call you?"

"My name is Barbara Dreher, but my friends and family call me *Brownie*. She cocked her head to the side, took a handful of her long brown hair and yanked on it. "I got the name when I was a kid. My older brothers are both blond and..." she shrugged, "I guess it stuck."

Kitty patted the chair next to her, inviting Brownie to sit. While talking about Washington, Brownie revealed that she had attended Georgetown University. Kitty decided to test the prediction she had made to the Senator from Illinois upon their arrival. "So, tell me; what was your major?"

Brownie replied, "Philosophy, but I'm working on my Master's in International Government. This job has been great because I can get most of my reading done while I'm at work, and I really need the money for tuition and to pay my rent."

Kitty smiled, inwardly lost in thought for a moment. "How much of the world have you seen so far?" she asked.

Brownie shook her head. "Not much. I'd like to travel once I've finished my thesis, though. Haven't exactly figured out how I'm going to pay for it. I was kind of hoping to meet a congressman or senator or somebody, who needs a government assistant for foreign affairs...or something." Her last statement trailed off lamely as she fell silent.

Kitty reached for her glass of water, took a sip and said, "Keep at it. You never know when something unexpected will turn up. Who knows, maybe I'll have an opportunity for you myself; once I've talked to Director Polk, that is."

Chapter 38

Nathanial William Polk sat at his desk, unconsciously straightening his hair, which was in disarray. He had just entered the building from the roof, the chopper blades still winding down above his head. His golf shirt and casual pants felt slightly foreign in this setting. He was disinclined to change clothes for this unexpected and unwelcome visitor.

Once again, Miss Dreher escorted Kitty down the paneled hallway of the executive floor for CIA Operations. This time, they walked past Frank Bishop's closed office door, ignored the inquiring eyes of his secretary, and proceeded to the office of Director Polk. When they entered the office, Miss Dreher merely said, "This is Mrs. O'Riley, Sir," and left, closing the door behind her.

The Director did not stand and offer his hand. He pointed to a chair with his eyes, instructing her to sit. When Kitty was seated, he said, "I don't know you, but I know who you are. So let's get down to it. What do you want from me, Mrs. O'Riley?" He looked Kitty straight in the eyes, demanding an answer.

Kitty had spent her life in meetings where confrontation and intimidation were part of the setting. She knew when to threaten, when to be cordial, and when to be matter-of-fact. *Ignace* was the threat, and she had already used it to get this audience. It was too late for cordial, so Kitty decided to move on to matter-of-fact.

She began, "I want you to know that I only intended to use *Ignace* as a means to see you. The insider-trading scheme that vaulted you into a position of power and politics doesn't need to be exposed. If you hear me out, *Ignace* can remain a small Indian village in Montana and nothing more.

"Oh, and the same goes for my mention of the White House to Mr. Bishop. I do not want to bring the President into this, but I had to use his name to get Frank to even contact you. Frank knows nothing about *Ignace*. At least, I said nothing to him about it other than to relay the name to you."

Polk repeated, "So, what do you want from me?"

"I want something that is in your power to give, and you may be the only person who can give it to me. I want to go to Russia."

The Director of the CIA looked at the woman sitting across the desk from him. "Would you like to repeat that, please? And this time, how about filling in some of the gaps. You know, embellish it a little."

His sarcastic tone almost made Kitty smile. "I don't mean I want to go over and visit for a couple of weeks. And I don't want to defect. At least, I don't intend to be a Communist, give up American secrets or anything like that. I want to live in Russia for a while as a Russian citizen, and I don't want anyone to know I'm doing it."

Nathanial Polk leaned back in his leather chair, stared at the ceiling and wondered why this woman had intentionally messed up his one chance this month to play golf. He thought about the elk hunting trip with his buddies near Ignace, and how he had weighed the risks and rewards of acting on a tip. A corporate secret, offered to cover a rather large wager on jacks-over-sevens. He sat forward in his chair, scratching his ear. "Is that it?" he asked. "And you want the Agency to help you? You know, millions of people are trying to get out of the Soviet Union but can't."

Kitty could see that Nathanial Polk was annoyed. She set her leather briefcase on the floor, sat back a little to relax, and said, "You see, I was born in Russia some time ago. When I was a teenager, my parents were killed, so I came to America to start a new life. I have always promised myself to go back some day."

"And since you're rich and think you've found a skeleton in my distant past, you think our government should jump to satisfy you're slightest whim."

It was Kitty's turn to be annoyed. "It's not a whim. I might not be able to make the Bolsheviks pay for killing my family, but I'm getting old and I at least have to go back." Her voice took on the sharpness of a knife as she continued. "The Bolsheviks started killing anyone who had money and property and..."

"Whoooaaa!!!" Nathanial Polk raised both hands for her to stop. "What year are we talking about?"

"1917."

Polk did the simple math. "That means you're over seventy years old! Come on, Mrs. O'Riley. I don't have time for this nonsense. You're trying to tell me that your parents were killed in the Russian revolution and you were a teenager at the time?" He was now bearing down on his desk with both hands, halfway out of his chair, making himself as imposing a figure as possible.

Kitty sat sweetly, yet defiantly, not flinching in the least. She smiled at Polk's glaring face and said, "I'll accept that as a compliment regarding my youthful appearance. But you are quite right. I am seventy-seven years old at the moment. In fact, that is why I want to go back to Russia, now. I doubt I'll live forever, so it's now or never. Please, sit down and let me fill you in on a few things. I truly have no wish to take up any more of your time than is necessary. In fact, you may get in that golf game yet. In a minute I'm going to tell you something interesting about Brezhnev."

The mention of the Soviet Premier's name upped the ante several chips. Nathanial Polk sat back in his chair, prepared to hear a story that might be worth hearing more than once. He flipped on the private-recorder switch with his foot.

Having regained the Director's attention, Kitty said, "First of all, as to my age, I started Kitty's Kakes in 1919 in Kansas City, and you can easily check that. It's a matter of record. As I was saying before, my parents, Dmitri and Sara Milanov, were wealthy. We owned a huge estate and a very large house not far from Smolensk. Part of what I have to tell you has to do with the house. My father was best friends with Tsar Nicholas Romanov. In fact, to me, the Tsar was Uncle Nicholas. My mother was best friends with Nicholas's sister, Xenia, and I happen to be named after her."

Kitty could see on Polk's face that this was starting to sound like a fairy tale to him. She reached for her leather case. With a slight sigh of resignation, Kitty produced a small velvet purse. "This will go a lot faster if you would just believe me." She unsnapped the tiny purse and pulled out two sapphire-and-diamond earrings. "These were given to my mother by the Tsar's sister." Kitty laid them on the desk so that Polk could see them. But before he could say anything, she produced a gold ring with a huge green emerald, and placed it next to the earrings. "And this was given to Uncle Nicholas by my father."

Kitty made a peculiar face. "I suppose I could have purchased this jewelry. Still, before leaving home I felt they would help convince you of the authenticity of my story," she shrugged.

Polk had a difficult time taking his eyes off the jewels. He turned one of the earrings around and around in his fingers. The precious gems were shimmering with sparkles, bringing them alive. Even he could tell the settings were old. He handed all three pieces back to Kitty, who returned them reverently to the velvet purse.

Kitty continued in a subdued voice, "I was there when my parents were killed by the Bolsheviks. My older brother had gone to fight the Germans in the war, but I watched as the murderers raped my mother and then killed both her and my father." Kitty had learned over the years how to block out the scene pretty well. However, at times, this being one of them, the vivid details swarmed over her, causing her heart to start beating faster. She could feel the blood rushing to her head and for a moment was afraid she would black out, just as she had that day so many years ago.

Polk hit a button on his phone, "Ms. Malone, would you bring us two glasses of water, please?" To Kitty, he said, "Relax for a minute. That must have been a horrible experience. Would you like something stronger? I could use a drink myself," he said graciously.

Kitty shook her head. "It's a little early for me."

Ms. Malone, Polk's middle-aged, black secretary, brought the glasses of water in, setting Kitty's on a coaster on the large, dark-wood desk, and handing the other to her boss. "Thank you," he said, as she turned and left without a word. Marty Malone was very bright and had a TOP SECRET government clearance. She fetched water for her boss because she wanted to, and because they were a team, not because it was in her job description.

Kitty took a sip of water, which made her feel better, so she took another one. "I escaped to Latvia where I stayed with Sophie's parents. Sophie was our cook and her husband, Morso, was our stablemaster. It's a long story and I won't get into it now, but I made my way to America, as I said before. But I never gave up on the idea of returning some day. Actually, I did make it back in '37 to see if I could find my brother, Joseph, but it was no use." Looking down at the glass in her hands, Kitty said, "At least I've found out he survived that war and the next. But now..." she shrugged her shoulders again.

Nathanial Polk listened attentively to Kitty's words. "You were going to tell me something about a house?" He prompted her gently.

Kitty looked up as if from a dream, her memories obviously carrying her back to another time, another place. "Yes, yes. I'm kind of drifting; I'm sorry." She paused to order her thoughts. "We lived in a very big house with lots of land." Kitty made kind of a swirling motion with her hand to indicate she was back on track now. She sat up, the topic invigorating her as she regained her presence and vitality. "That's the key," she said, pointing her index finger at Polk, "The house; the Milanov family estate. Several years ago I saw my house on the news. Brezhnev was staying there on vacation. It's one of his dachas. It was probably a rare clip, I suppose, but it was our house. I know that for a fact."

Nathanial W. Polk stared blankly at the woman sitting before him, his mind clicking along at an enormous rate; Brezhnev, vacation...early 70's. The possibilities of what had just fallen into his lap were intriguing. He reached for his phone, hit the button that read *Deputy Director*, and said into the speaker, "Frank? ...Nathan. Get your coat and meet me on the roof in five minutes. We're going to Langley."

Chapter 39

July 17, 1978
Langley, Virginia

Kitty sat at an ornately-inlaid conference table in a wood-paneled room with plush carpeting. The walls were adorned with tasteful pieces of original art. On the helicopter ride to the CIA facility, Kitty had been impressed by the cutting-edge technology and quality of the vehicle. It was evident that the chopper had been wired to communicate with the world.

During their transport, Nathanial W. Polk had explained that several members of the agency would have to be brought in on the operation if Kitty hoped to have her request granted. Recognizing that Frank Bishop was one of them, Kitty quickly set about smoothing his ruffled feathers. The two were chatting amiably when the skids touched down at Langley's landing pad.

Now, alone in the conference room, Kitty mentally inventoried the remaining tasks required to outfit the *Catrina*. During their morning meeting at the shipyard, the contractor had predicted the job would be done in ten days, if he and his crew worked through the weekend. Kitty hoped the CIA could do their part in the same time frame. She was anxious to get this show on the road, but she was prepared to be patient. At least, she kept telling herself that. Patience was not one of her strong suits.

The door at the far end of the room opened. Kitty looked up to see a woman and two men walk in, shutting the door behind them. Nathanial Polk, still wearing his golf apparel, sat down at the table next to Kitty and waved the other two toward the seats across from them. The conference table would accommodate twelve to fourteen. Kitty could only speculate on what topics had been debated within these paneled walls.

Before introductions were made, a man Kitty had never seen before, said, "Excuse me, but if you do not pass this first test, we will waste no more time." The man spoke Russian like a native, and Kitty intuitively felt he had a *city accent*, probably Moscow. Continuing to speak quite rapidly, he said, "You and I are going to discuss anything you wish for the next five minutes, and then I will give the Director my opinion of your command of the language, or the lack of it." He nodded his head to Kitty, putting the ball in her court.

Speaking conversationally, as if Russian was still her first language, Kitty began, "When I was a little girl, my mother said that unless I learned to speak French, I would never amount to much."

The man acknowledged her fluency with a smile. "Your Russian is quite good, Mrs. O'Riley. So tell me, did you learn to speak French?"

Kitty switched to French, saying, "Of course. I was a very obedient child." She smiled at the man, then switched back to Russian. "Actually, I wasn't all that obedient, but languages are something I've always been good at. If you want to know the truth, I don't think I'll have any problem blending in verbally with my Russian comrades, except for one thing...or two. I don't know the slang, and I'm sure my accent has *melted* over the years. I've never lost my ability to speak the language of my childhood, but there have been so few opportunities to pick up the street talk. There aren't a lot of Russian tourists running around America."

Kitty had chosen a practical subject rather than simply talking about the weather. If she could get some updating on current phrases and nuances of the language, it might come in very handy down the road.

The man winked at Kitty, then turned to Director Polk. Reverting to English, he said, "Mrs. O'Riley will have no problem blending in, as she puts it. That is, if she gets a little renewed exposure to our comrade's accent. In fact, her grammar and diction may be too good. I think I can give her some help so she sounds like a good communist."

Polk nodded his head. "Thanks, Sergei. I'll get back to you."

The man stood up, turned back to Kitty and said in French, "My name is Sergei Borgdonovich. It was very nice to meet you, Mrs. O'Riley." He stuck out his hand and when Kitty accepted it, he clasped his other hand around hers. You know, Russia is not a soft and comfortable place these days. I hope you know what you are doing. I'll help you if I can, though."

"*Merci*" was all Kitty said, but their eyes met and she could see the concern the man felt.

As Sergei left the room, Kitty turned to the middle-aged woman across the table from her and then back to Nathanial Polk, who said, "Mrs. O'Riley, this is Mary Cicha. She is going to talk to you about your family's Russian estate." Ms. Cicha opened a folder that contained about fifty 8 1/2" x 11" sheets of paper. The top sheet was a map, which she turned and pushed across the table toward Kitty. "Can you tell us where the house is?"

Kitty pulled the map directly in front of her, making it square with the table's edge, and scanned its features. It was an everyday, run-of-the-mill, *Rand McNally type* map of the western third of the Soviet Union. Kitty smiled inwardly, *This is a real sophisticated group—a road map*. Over the years, Kitty had gazed countless times at just such a map while reminiscing about her family and childhood. She could locate the Milanov estate as easily as she could identify Dallas or Chicago on a map of the United States. With her index finger, she pointed to the spot and said, "It's on the eastern shore of Kaspl'a Lake, right here."

Nathanial Polk, standing behind Kitty, looking over her shoulder, nodded his head knowingly but glanced at his analyst for confirmation. Mary said, "Got that one right. At least we're talking about the same place. She took the next three pieces of paper from the pile, slid them across the table and said, "OK, Mrs. O'Riley, which one of these structures looks like the house you grew up in?"

Kitty looked down at the photographs. They were all views from above, presumably from a spy plane or maybe a satellite. The pictures reminded Kitty of the shots of a football game from the Goodyear blimp. She recognized the Milanov estate immediately, but continued to study the pictures of all three. She was impressed with the sharpness and clarity of the photography. Kitty heard Polk shuffle his feet behind her, looked up and noticed the uncomfortable expression on Ms. Cicha's face. "Sorry," Kitty said with a smile. "I was just admiring the pictures. Here's the house." She picked up the one on the right and handed it over her shoulder to Polk, without turning around.

Kitty looked at Mary just in time to catch the barely perceptive nod, which told the Director they were still in business.

They spent the next hour-and-a-half going over the rest of the contents of the folder. Some of the pictures were still-shots taken from the clip she'd seen on television. Others were fuzzy and looked like they'd been taken at a distance by a child with a box camera. She could see people in a few of them but they were blurry. Most of the photographs were aerial views of the house and grounds. Some of the images of the house had been altered, where an artist had removed the roof, then used his imagination to create what the inside floor plan might be. Kitty nudged her memory into recalling minute details of the huge three-story mansion. She redrew the simulated floor plans with some type of special pen. It wasn't lead or ink. It seemed more like a fine-tipped wax pencil.

Kitty also noted with interest that the stables were still there. At least, one of several out-buildings was located where the stables used to be. She flashed back to the day her parents had been killed, and re-lived the fire raging in the stables where Mouka and Majesty had been boarded.

The rustling of paper broke into Kitty's reverie as Mary began putting the pictures and drawings back into the folder. Nathanial Polk, now seated at the near end of the table, said, "Thank you, Mary. That's all for now."

He waited for Mary to close the door behind her before turning to Kitty. "So, let's talk a little about what you have in mind. If I'm going to help you get into Russia, you have to tell me what you're planning to do when you get there."

Kitty looked at him for a moment. "You know, I'm not exactly sure." She held up her hand to stop his protest. "What I mean is; I'm not sure how I'm going to do it. I want to see if I can get our house and estate back." She looked at Polk for a reaction; got none. "And I'd like to cause the government a little pain somehow, for murdering my parents...a lot of pain would be better." She looked at him again; still nothing. "And, if I could find out something about my brother; that would really be the most important thing."

Kitty raised her eyebrows, indicating she was finished. The Director of the CIA gave her a withered look, rather than laughing in her face. "How in the name of Jesus do you intend to do any of that? ...I know, you're not exactly sure," he mocked, unable to restrain himself. "You're kidding yourself if you think you can march into the enemy's backyard and re-claim the leader's dacha as your own. I don't think we can help you."

Kitty's clear blue eyes became cold. She spat the words. "I'm going Mr. Polk. Your involvement is one of expediency. And Nathanial, let me remind you, your entire future depends on your cooperation."

Kitty sat back for a moment to let him reflect on her words, but their eyes remained locked. Kitty had used the threat again, and now it had become a power struggle. "You know, Mr. Polk, I didn't know how I was going to start my new life in America sixty years ago. But, as you see, things have worked out very well. What would you have me do with my remaining time? Sit on the porch and watch cars go by?"

"How about spending these good years traveling to fun, safe places? What's this I heard you and Frank talking about in the helicopter? You're outfitting an ocean-going yacht, or something? I don't get it."

Kitty smiled kind of sheepishly. "It's my cover for the folks at home, a diversion. My grandson would never go along with my traveling to Russia on my own. He'd want to go along, and he's too young to be trapped there if something goes wrong. I won't risk that. Plus, for reasons I'm sure you understand, the last thing I need is for the papers to start writing: MILLIONAIRE BUSINESS LEADER RETIRES TO AVENGE PARENTS' 1917 MURDER IN SOVIET UNION."

Polk nodded. "You intend to *officially* sail off into the sunset. But what's really going to happen; the CIA is going to slip you into Russia, instead, so you can play commando."

Kitty's eyes narrowed at Polk's snide comment.

"Sorry," he said, smiling. "You know, that part of the plan's not bad, the *diversion* as you put it. I still think it's a harebrained idea to go to Russia with three near-impossible objectives and no course of action." Polk paused. "Let's just play this out for a moment. Assuming the CIA is willing to help you. It seems to me that it would make sense for you to actually be on the yacht for a while. You could make a big splash in the Mediterranean somewhere. You know, whoop it up at Monte Carlo or a Greek Island maybe. We could make sure the story gets spilled to the papers in the States. Then, the press will have had their day, and you will just be another rich, retired American, blah blah blah blah blah... At which point, we can smuggle you into Russia. I like it...I think."

Chapter 40

Soviet Union

Shahlo walked through the door of the tavern, looking immediately toward the table in the corner by the window. Joseph, sitting alone, waved to her and pointed at the bar. Shahlo saw there was neither bottle nor glass on his table, smiled at him and turned away. When she approached the table she was carrying two empty glasses, a full bottle of vodka and a plate of sprats with lemon wedges.

"I waited for you," he said as she set the things on the table and took the seat across from him.

"I can see that, thank you. Didn't want beer, did you?"

"This is good." Joseph poured a couple of inches of vodka in both glasses, raised his and said, "Life." He tossed down the clear liquor, set his glass down heartily and popped one of the small fish in his mouth.

"You didn't give me a chance to squeeze the lemon yet." To which, Joseph just shrugged. "How did you know I was going to stop here?" she continued.

He looked at her as if it were a stupid question, which it was. "Who else would have parked that car out front?" He looked out the window at the bright red Ferrari at the curb.

Shahlo squinted her sand-colored eyes at him, playfully, then leaned her head back and emptied her glass. "I give up," she said, "why'd you drive that car into town?"

"I replaced the front struts today and took it out on the highway to see how they felt. Decided to make a pit stop to lubricate the driver," he added with a smile.

"If you get drunk and wreck that car, they'll send you back to the Gulag," she whispered.

Joseph nodded his head once, refilled their glasses. "We're only going to have three." He chose another herring, licked the dripping lemon juice and oil from its tail, and sucked it into his mouth. He smacked his lips and chased the tiny fish with his second shot of vodka.

The tavern's door swung open. Two men covered with mud and dust walked in, their boots making tracks across the worn linoleum floor. The second man yelled to Joseph, "Nice car, Peter!"

Joseph waved at him. "It was a birthday present." He winked at Shahlo and popped another fish into his mouth. During the ten years Joseph had spent in the Stalingrad tractor factory, he'd developed into a master-mechanic. Given the right tools, Joseph could fix anything and everyone in town and the surrounding area knew it.

For years in the Gulag, the only respite he had from the back-breaking work in the mines was when they needed him to work on disabled trucks and mining machinery that had broken down. To Joseph, it was like a holiday to be working on machines, though he complained about it for appearance's sake.

Shahlo downed her second drink and pushed back from the table. "Two is enough for me," she said. "The girls are going to be home from school soon. You'll be home for dinner?" It was a question that wasn't really so much a question as a strong suggestion.

Chapter 41

Coast of Portugal

There were beads of sweat forming on Kitty's arms as they moved slowly, gracefully, deliberately. Her bronze skin glistened in mid-morning sunlight from above and reflecting off the water. A sporadic, soft breeze cooled her as she lifted her foot from the gently rolling deck and placed it down again. Her body and mind were absorbed with the practiced T'ai Chi movements.

She had sprayed the beautiful teakwood deck with salt water to cool it off before she started her moving meditation exercise. The sun and breeze were drying the smooth planks rapidly, allowing Kitty just another ten minutes or so before the deck would be too hot to tolerate with bare feet. Normally, she did her T'ai Chi in the early dawn before the sun had much strength, but today she had decided to sleep in, a concession to the numerous bottles of excellent Portuguese wine they had consumed the night before.

When she finished, she raised her eyes to take in the rock cliffs towering above the masts of the anchored ketch. The brilliant blue sky and emerald water framed the black coastline in a spectacular contrast of color. Kitty took a deep breath, loving the clean sea air, slipped into her canvas boat shoes and made her way forward.

Barbara Dreher's white bikini bottoms accentuated the deep brown tan she had nurtured since leaving Chesapeake Bay three weeks ago.

Hearing Kitty's footsteps, Brownie clutched the skimpy piece of material that served as her top, made a half-hearted attempt to conceal her breasts and rolled onto her back. "Good morning," she said. "Does your head hurt as much as mine does?"

Kitty laughed, "Sleeping till nine-thirty helped considerably. Two aspirin and my T'ai Chi did the rest. I feel pretty good now. That was some party. I wonder how Sergei feels this morning."

In a hushed voice, almost a whisper, Brownie said conspiratorially, "Don't worry; those CIA guys are trained for that sort of thing." And then in her normal voice, "I'm kind of sorry he's not going farther with us. He's a lot of fun."

Kitty chuckled, "He sure was last night. What a dancer. I think he's going to miss your sunbathing sessions the most." She gave Brownie a maternal smile, acknowledging the fact that the younger woman had no tan lines above her waist. *What the hell, this is Europe.*

Sergei Borgdonovich had accompanied the ladies on the *Catrina* for the sail across the Atlantic. He had posed as an old friend of the Dreher family, but had spent most of his time schooling Kitty on her Russian accent, street talk and current events. Yesterday Kitty and Brownie had gone ashore with him and his gear for a farewell dinner.

With Sergei gone, Brownie was the only one on board that was aware of Kitty's *Russian objective.* The skipper, Captain Jarvis, had been hired for a yearlong excursion, although Kitty had told him that she might disembark discreetly somewhere along the way, to take up residence where no one could locate her or bother her with worldly affairs. He assumed she would become a recluse in Switzerland or a South Pacific Island or something.

Certainly the crew, consisting of four men and a female cook, knew nothing of Kitty's real destination. The men had the job of sailing and maintaining the one-hundred-and-ten-foot vessel, and they reported to the captain. The cook, whose name was Kate, reported to Brownie. In addition to the culinary duties, Kate was responsible for cleaning the staterooms for Kitty, Brownie and Captain Jarvis.

Brownie fastened the clasp of her bikini top, spun it around and pulled it into place. She poked a little flesh here and there, adjusting the fit and stood up. "How about some coffee and a little breakfast?"

"Sounds good to me," said Kitty. They locked arms, walking side by side toward the after cabin where they ate most of their meals. "Captain Jarvis said we'd be ready to weigh anchor at six bells. I think a little food will help my sea legs considerably."

Kitty and Brownie both enjoyed the nautical jargon and were attempting to incorporate this new language into their regular dialogue. "Open the hatch, matey," Kitty said with a laugh. They went below into air-conditioned luxury that few sailors ever experience.

❧

As Joe sat down to breakfast, he scanned the headlines of the *Kansas City Star*. Opening the paper, he noticed a picture in the bottom left-hand corner of a woman wearing a Spanish matador's hat, her long skirts whirling in the air. Joe began reading the accompanying article titled: *AREA DESSERT QUEEN KICKS UP HER HEELS*. The byline was from Barcelona, Spain. He read the article quickly, studied the picture more closely, and read the caption: *Mrs. Kitty O'Riley defies Father Time, and appears to be making the most of her recent retirement. The seventy-seven-year-old matriarch of Kansas City-based Kitty's Kakes is shown here, taking part in the Dance of the Bulls.*

Joe shook his head, smiling with admiration for his grandmother's lust for life. At the same time, he was kicking himself for not being there with her. His watch told him he was running late for his morning meeting, so he gulped down his orange juice and inhaled his toast. He left the front page on the table where Lee Mae would be sure to see Kitty's picture, stuffed the rest of the paper under his arm and grabbed his coffee. On his way to the door, he snatched a banana from the fruit bowl and began thinking about how he was going to persuade the City Planning Commission to bless his project.

❧

Kitty sat at the desk in her stateroom. Her quarters were in the stern of the *Catrina* and would more accurately be described as a large suite or even an apartment. But since it were located on a boat, "stateroom" was the term she used.

The vessel rocked gently back and forth, at anchor in Naples' well protected harbor. A refreshing breeze blew through the open ports. Kitty was busy writing postcards. So far, she had dutifully mailed postcards back to Joseph, Lee Mae and Lee Ping at each port-of-call. The task she was focused on now had to do with the postcards she was supposed to be sending for the remainder of the year. She flipped through the stack of cards that Frank Bishop had supplied for her before their departure: Palermo, Athens, Istanbul, Bombay, Singapore... Kitty sighed, wishing she had been doing a few every day so the work would be mostly done by now.

Manila, Hong Kong, Osaka...

A knock on her door signaled a welcome reprieve from her card writing. Kitty put an exclamation point at the end of *Wish you were here!* and threw the pen down on the table. "Come in."

Brownie entered with two large glasses of orange juice that contained swizzle sticks, ice and a suspicious looking red swirl running through the juice. "Thought you might need a little refreshment," she said, walking over to Kitty and offering one of the drinks.

Kitty smiled as she held the drink up to her face to inspect the red streak running through it. "This looks like it might taste better than plain old orange juice. Does it have a name?" She sniffed the drink and then took a sip.

Brownie replied, "We girls used to drink something at a bar near Georgetown called *screaming orgasms*. I was always kind of fond of that name. How about if we call this...," she paused, pondering the question, took a sip, looked into the glass and then..., "how about if we call this a *moaning mermaid*? Gives it kind of a maritime flavor, don't you think?"

Kitty laughed, held up her glass in salute, drank. With the back of her hand, she wiped a few droplets from the corners of her mouth. "Not bad. You know, if we really want a maritime flavor, we could mix in a little salt water. Captain Jarvis would probably think it's great. We could call it *Naples' Nipple*. You know, sort of the milk of the sea."

Brownie burst into laughter, causing her to nearly spill her drink. She couldn't get over the quick wit of this seventy-seven-year-old woman, particularly when the drift was innuendo or sarcasm. It was like they were just a couple of pals...coeds or something.

After picking up the postcards, Kitty moved from behind the desk and headed for the breakfast/card table. "Pull up a chair, my dear. You can help me think of things to say on these cards that need to be sent back home." She plopped the stack of cards and her *moaning mermaid* down on the glass table, settling into one of the four white-wicker chairs. "If you would, bring the pencils, pens and pad of paper from the desk before you sit down. Unfortunately, they all have to be in my handwriting, but it will speed things up if you write some of the messages so I can copy them. I'm afraid they'll start sounding pretty stale after about thirty...*I wish you were here's*."

Knowing that this was their last day and night together began to bring Brownie's spirits down. She had agreed to be part of Kitty's cover, continuing on around the world after Kitty's departure to Russia. What an opportunity; an all-expense-paid cruise around the world, on a magnificent luxury yacht, no less. She would have all the time she needed to work on her final International Government thesis. Plus, Kitty insisted that she move into this stateroom suite.

She could invite guests from home to join her or, if she met someone along the way, she could offer them a ride, so to speak. Still, she had become tremendously fond of this personable older woman. Brownie smiled to herself. She just couldn't think of Kitty in those terms. There was still too much life and vigor flowing through those veins to think of her as old. Prolonged middle-age, maybe.

They each had two more *moaning mermaids* as they worked on the postcards. Kitty talked about her experiences as a child in Russia. She was beginning to get excited about her impending quest but started to question the wisdom of her decision to make a go of it alone. *How comforting it would be to have a companion to share the dangers with, to know there was at least one person she could count on.*

Brownie recognized the far-away look in Kitty's eyes and said, "I'm going to miss you. Are these cards the last thing you have to do before tomorrow?"

Kitty snapped back to the present, no longer speculating on what the next leg of her travels might bring. She said, "Come on. Let's go on deck and I'll give you one last T'ai Chi lesson. You keep getting stuck in that one spot and forget what you're doing. I'll finish these cards before I go to bed."

They stood up and both realized the *moaning mermaids* were going to make balancing a challenge. Kitty giggled as Brownie stumbled into the wall by the door. "Screw the T'ai Chi," Kitty said, laughing. "We can't stand up straight, much less concentrate on our centers of energy. You'll just have to remember what I've taught you as best you can. Let's go ashore and have some dinner and maybe a bottle of Chianti. I need to get to bed early tonight so I can wake up sober and be ready to hit the road."

Chapter 42

September 13, 1978
Sheremetyevo International Airport
Moscow, USSR

Despondent and nearly numb from exhaustion, Kitty sat in her window seat as the rude man next to her kept bumping against her leg. He was attempting to retrieve his oversized canvas satchel from beneath the seat in front of them. The antiquated plane was not only full, it was bursting at the seams. Every seat was occupied long before the door had been closed for take-off. In disbelief, Kitty had watched people, standing in the aisles, grab hold of seatbacks to balance themselves as the jet took off. More than a few mothers had a child...or children, sitting in their laps. The flight gave her a new appreciation for the phrase, *standing room only*. The good news was that they had landed safely, and presumably, this *cattle-car with wings* would soon be part of her past.

She had boarded this particular Aeroflot aircraft four hours ago in Kiev. And before that, a Turkish airliner had flown her from Istanbul to Kiev. The last time she had been exposed to civilized air travel was the Air France leg, transporting her from Naples to Istanbul. *Was that only yesterday morning?* Kitty thought to herself. The flights had been tolerable if she looked at each one individually; although calling this last one tolerable would be generous. Taken as a whole, piling the flights up one on top of the other, then, adding all the delays in the airports and on the runways... It was a travel experience Kitty would not soon forget. Nor was she likely to attempt it again.

However, there had been some good fortune along the way. The one issue Kitty had been most apprehensive about was now behind her...passing through customs in the airport at Kiev. Although tedious and slow, it had gone without a hitch.

As she deplaned in Istanbul, a woman about fifty years old had met Kitty. She had never seen the woman before, but the woman had obviously studied pictures of Kitty, walking right up to her and giving her a big hug. They had walked together to the women's restroom, taken adjoining stalls, and simply exchanged clothes. After washing their hands at the basin, each took the other's suitcase and purse, walked out of the restroom and headed in opposite directions.

The plain, drab garments Kitty was now wearing were ugly, yet functional and clean. She had left her passport and all other identifying information in her purse. She was no longer Mrs. Kitty O'Riley. She had found a bench with some room, sat down and unzipped her purse...her new *old* purse. It was kind of like Little Joe looking into his Christmas stocking when he was a kid. The name on her papers read, *Nataliya Svetlana Pushkin*. The papers were worn but not quite tattered. To Kitty, they looked like authentic documents. Apparently, the customs official had thought so, too.

Finally in Moscow, waiting for the plane to empty from the exit door up front, Kitty pulled the purse from under her elbow and unzipped it. There would be no customs this time, only the ordeal of locating her bag at the luggage counter. She pulled the claim-check stub out of the purse, squeezing it in her palm. She stuck her clutched fist into the pocket of the coarse brown coat she was wearing, feeling grateful for the security of this dark warm refuge, if only for her hand.

Kitty closed her eyes. Soon she was strolling along a path that led through a meadow full of wild flowers. She recognized the scene and quickened her pace toward the pond where several horses were grazing nearby. Majesty raised his head as she approached, whinnied and trotted up to welcome her. She lifted her hand to pat his soft nose affectionately...

Suddenly, the dream vaporized as Kitty felt her body being shaken. She opened her eyes to see a man leaning over her with his hand on her shoulder. He was not being rough, but certainly persistent in his effort to rouse her. She looked around, noting the interior of the plane as the last few passengers streamed by toward the exit door. A wave of depression flooded in on her. In an instant, she had been transported from a beautiful sunny meadow in Kansas, to...to the ugly reality of this dirty, cramped plane. The disappointment on her face was evident to the man looming over her. He smiled warmly, his kindly face chasing Kitty's troubles away. "I must have dozed off," she said, a little embarrassed.

The man responded by offering Kitty his hand to help her slide out of the row of seats. "You must speak Russian, my dear. Come, it is time for us to get off the plane. We've been on here long enough, don't you think?" The man's voice was friendly yet firm, the Russian words flowing naturally.

It dawned on Kitty that she had awakened unexpectedly, and the first words out her mouth had been spoken in English. Anxiety touched her face as she looked at the man questioningly. In Russian, she asked, "Do you know me?"

The man half pulled her out of her seat to get her moving. In a near whisper he said, "I'm keeping an eye on you for a little while to make sure you get off on the right foot. My name is Viktor. But your name is no longer O'Riley and you no longer speak English, correct?"

Kitty uttered the word "*Da*," and allowed herself to be ushered up the aisle to the exit door. Kitty shuddered slightly when she realized there was no attendant, no pilot, no copilot, or anyone standing up front to say, *Thank you; good bye; have a nice day* as in America; just an empty aisle with an empty doorway, leading to the open air and the unprotected walk to the terminal building. She was in the Soviet Union now.

Chapter 43

Kitty stood silently in the cool, misty air of dawn. It was mid-October and she had no illusions about what to expect of the sun's heat that day. She hoped the sun would make an appearance, more for the cheerfulness of its light, than the warmth of its rays. She pulled the coarse brown coat closer to her neck and moved her feet across the cold, barren bricks of Red Square.

Upon arrival in Moscow six weeks ago, she had, with Viktor's help, found a room in a common boarding house. It was shelter, but no more than that. Her first twenty-four hours in her new/former country were spent in bed, trying to overcome the exhaustion from the lengthy trip. In truth, there had been no *trying* involved. She merely collapsed on the mattress, wrapped herself in the blanket that came with the room, and said good-bye to the world for a solid eighteen hours. When Kitty woke, she shuffled down the hall for her first experience with the communal bathroom.

Then, there was another eight hours of mattress time, but not to sleep. It was basically a time of soul searching, fitful dozing, and agenda planning. Finally, Kitty decided that eating was a necessity of life, so she got up to see what could be done about it.

Kitty spent several days getting acclimated to her new environment. She talked with people in the shops and on the streets, but made no attempt to develop any relationships. Her goal was to settle in to the mind-set and lifestyle of a *good communist*. At least, she wanted to be able to present the appearance of an everyday citizen...comrade.

Part of the orientation was getting used to the currency. She had plenty of rubles, compliments of the un-named woman in the Istanbul airport. It didn't take Kitty long, however, to discover that little could be bought in the shops, even if one had the money. After about a week, she decided to investigate the whereabouts of the black market, which turned out to be a pretty viable segment of the economy. She acquired several items of need, although decent food wasn't among them. It took her a while longer to solve that problem.

Before parting company that first night, Kitty and Viktor had made arrangements to meet exactly one month later. After two weeks of exploring Moscow, getting a feel for the attitudes of the rank and file, Kitty decided to take a train to Leningrad. She would spend the two remaining weeks before the rendezvous with Viktor, re-acquainting herself with the historic capital of Peter the Great.

She had many fond childhood memories of that splendid city. Accompanied by her parents, she had marveled at the beautiful sights of a proud and prosperous Russian culture. She remembered attending the ballet and sitting in the Tsar's private box. Kitty had felt very special and mature when the dancers had all bowed graciously in their direction, paying tribute to the sovereign and his entourage.

But times had changed. The luster was gone. The vibrant activity and life had turned dismal and grey. The magnificence she had seen in her youthful innocence and naiveté was covered over by dirt and grime. She could tell the greatness was still there, painfully waiting to be liberated.

Before she left the city, which had been named *Petrograd* in her day, she visited the harbor. She saw the very place where she had boarded a ship to flee the country in 1917. The dull water stank and was ugly with pollution. The scourge that had pulled her world from beneath her when she was a child still had its grip firmly around the country's throat. With perfect clarity, Kitty remembered the relief she had felt, over sixty years ago, when she had escaped this pall that still hung over the land.

Kitty returned to Moscow, a dark shadow dampening her spirit. She met Viktor at the predetermined place, a park rather than her room. He felt it unwise to be seen together again by the tenants of her building. "This is the Soviet Union," he had explained. They talked and drank coffee for several hours in a small cafe, while he smoked cigarette after cigarette. By the time they were through, it had been decided that Kitty would go to Smolensk as soon as arrangements could be made. The arrangements amounted to Viktor finding a suitable place for her to live and work.

Kitty had received word from him two weeks later and was now packed and ready to go. At ten o'clock the train for Smolensk would pull out of the station with Nataliya Svetlana Pushkin on board. She had three more hours to ponder her future before the train was to leave. She stumbled on one of the bricks that lined Red Square and wondered how many Soviet tanks and soldiers had paraded over that same spot.

She sighed, the moisture in her breath visible in the cold as it joined the foggy mist around her. *Six weeks*, she thought to herself. *I'm here; I'm alive. Now let's see what the next six weeks brings.* Kitty turned in the direction of her boarding house. It was a two-mile walk. She had to pick up her bag, take the subway to Yaroslavl Station. Soon, she would be one step closer to home.

Chapter 44

February 20, 1979
Smolensk, USSR

Bundled up in every warm thing she owned, Kitty trudged through shifting drifts of snow the half mile from the factory to her apartment. It was already dark at just after five o'clock. The temperature was ten degrees below zero, not unusual for February, the wind blowing with biting teeth. Icy barbs tried to penetrate her clothing, searching for exposed skin.

Kitty's clear blue eyes looked out from the small space between her hat and wool muffler. Yellow light, pouring from the double windows up ahead, was a welcome sight. She crossed the snow-packed street and, with a mitten-clad hand, fought the door open against the formidable wind. The wind was an adversary to be reckoned with, seemingly every day. Its force slammed the door shut behind Kitty as she stepped into the Soviet state-operated store.

The large, oil-burning stove provided the only heat in the single-room building. Kitty moved over to the corner where the ancient, cast-iron stove was being *worshipped* by a man and a woman. They sat in straight-backed, unmatching wooden chairs that looked as if they might collapse at any moment. Their proximity to the stove was such that they could get the maximum benefit from the precious oil being consumed without being consumed themselves.

Kitty stamped her boots on the wooden floor, tugged off her mittens, her fox-fur hat, and unwrapped the woolen muffler from around her neck. The tantalizing heat formed an aura around the stove. She rubbed her palms together a couple of times before unbuttoning her long, winter coat. The coat was Siberian mountain goat. Its purchase, probably the best decision she had made since arriving last fall in this ice station called Smolensk.

"Good evening," Kitty said to the couple huddled by the stove. "This heat feels good to an old woman's bones. Do you mind if I warm up for a minute before buying my groceries?" She pulled a used paper sack from a pocket of her coat.

The man's stained teeth were crooked and broken but the smile on his grizzled face conveyed unguarded honesty. He stood up and said, "Please, Comrade Pushkin...here, sit down for a moment next to my wife. I will gather up whatever you need." He held the back of the rickety old chair until Kitty was seated, snatching the folded bag from her hand. "What is it that I can get for you? We have some mutton, but...it is not so good. Maybe you would like some fish. I still have some trout that has been frozen solid since it was caught last November."

"That would be very nice, Comrade Borkov. And some cheese if you have any."

The storekeeper shuffled back to the rear of the building to a small door leading to the ice locker. During six months of the year it was not necessary to waste rubles on artificial refrigeration. The ice locker was merely an enclosed concrete space the size of a single-car garage, with generous outside ventilation in the form of open widows covered with steel bars, designed to protect the food from hungry animals; *the four and two legged variety.*

When Comrade Borkov reappeared through the door, he was carrying a brown paper package covered with frost and ice crystals, proving the effectiveness of his natural freezer space. He laid the package on the counter, wiped the frost and ice crystals off with a towel and set it aside.

He walked over to the glass-covered cabinet and selected a hunk of cheese from his meager perishable stores. He set the cheese on the counter, picked up a large black-handled knife, and sliced a wedge off with a forceful down-stroke. The piece was about an eighth of the whole, and looked like a piece of rubberized pie. Borkov wrapped Kitty's cheese in some brown paper, returned the remainder to the glass cabinet and said, "Is there anything else, Comrade Pushkin?"

Kitty had been chatting quietly about the lousy weather with Ruda Borkov while soaking in the warmth of the fire. She stood up and moved toward the counter, "Actually, Comrade, I would take a liter of Vodka if you have any today. I know it is hard to keep a supply with the weather these days but...well, it's my birthday and I thought it might help to warm up the atmosphere in my apartment tonight."

The storekeeper broke into another smile, stained teeth and all. "Ah!!! Your birthday you say. Well, Comrade, vodka it is." He took out a key from his pocket to unlock a heavy wooden cabinet behind the counter. "You know, it's about the only thing those goat...I mean, the Politburo has been able to produce. I hear that pretty soon there may be restrictions on vodka, too." Borkov slipped a peek at his wife who was glaring at him, unbeknownst to Kitty.

Ruda had warned him many times about his tongue. Goat-turds, he had almost called them. *Even with the reforms and changes, the Party could still squash you like a bug, Ivan,* she had told him. This woman, Comrade Pushkin, seemed safe enough, but you never know. She had just moved to Smolensk a few months ago and one had to be careful.

"So it's your birthday, Comrade Pushkin!" Borkov set a liter bottle of common vodka on the counter for Kitty. He also pulled a half-empty bottle of Stolichnaya and three small glasses from beneath the counter. "I think that calls for a drink of the good stuff. Ruda, come on over here a minute." He filled all three glasses to the brim, handed the first one to his wife, then Kitty, and then raised his own with a solid, "Budem zdorovy!" (Let's stay healthy)

They all threw their heads back, draining the glasses in a single motion. Almost simultaneously, the sturdy glasses were slammed down on the counter in the traditional manner, followed by wiping the corners of their mouths with fingers or sleeve.

Smiling broadly, Ruda held up a single finger. "Ivan, you did not do that right. Fill them up again."

Without hesitation, the storekeeper topped off the three glasses for a second go-around.

Ruda held her glass a little higher than the others, signifying that she was going to lead this toast. She looked at Kitty jovially, "By the way, Comrade Pushkin, what is your first name?"

Kitty returned her smile, saying, "Nataliya, but you can call me *Natty.*"

Still holding their drinks in the air, Ruda asked, "Well, Natty, how many birthdays is this?"

With a barely perceptible hesitation, Kitty said, "I am sixty-two today." She realized bringing up her birthday was a careless mistake. Nataliya Svetlana Pushkin's birthday was in October. Kitty recovered the smile that had briefly left her face. Looking into Ruda's eyes, Kitty saw the woman's acceptance and breathed a little easier.

"Natty, Pazdravlyaju s dnjom razhdenija!" (Congratulations on your birthday). Ruda clinked her glass against Kitty's and her husband's then threw down the second shot of vodka. Ivan and Kitty did the same and again all three glasses were on the counter.

"You're right, Ruda. That was better." Borkov picked up the bottle, ready to pour a third drink.

Kitty quickly slipped a hand over the top of her glass. "I think that is enough for me until I get home. You are both very kind to help me celebrate my birthday, but I do not want to lose my balance and fall in this cold weather." Kitty laughed good-naturedly. "You might find me in the morning still lying there, stiff as a board. I think I'd better be on my way." Turning, Kitty said over her shoulder, "How much do I owe you, Comrade Borkov, for the fish, cheese and vodka?" She walked over to the stove and began putting her warm clothes back on.

Ivan Borkov was a very sensible and honest man, but he did not care much about the exact price of things, or even when he got paid. He got out a pencil and wrote down the amount for each item, rounding generously in Kitty's favor. He circled the total, set the pencil down and unlocked a drawer beneath the counter. Kitty approached the counter with her mittens tucked under her arm, counting out rubles as she walked.

From the drawer, Borkov had taken a Hershey bar with almonds and set it next to Kitty's other groceries.

Surprised by the familiar wrapper, Kitty's head jerked up, eyes searching the storekeeper's face for a sign that he was aware of her American background. She saw only the huge, friendly smile of a man eager to share a treasure. He looked like a little boy with a hand full of dandelions, his expectant face waiting for his mother's delighted approval, as if he were giving her a dozen roses. Kitty realized the magnitude of this gesture, and tears sprang to her eyes as she reached out and placed a gentle hand on his stubbly-whiskered face.

Obviously pleased by Kitty's reaction, he said, "Happy birthday, Natty." And for his wife's benefit, "Do not tell anyone where you got the American chocolate."

"It is a great gift, Comrade Borkov, but you must keep the chocolate. It is so difficult to get."

"Oh! I have several more," he lied. "Enjoy your birthday."

Kitty looked down at the total written in pencil on the brown paper, counting out the amount but secretly increasing the number of rubles to more than double the sum. "Ivan, you and Ruda have made this a very special birthday for me." She put the rubles on the counter in a wad so that Borkov could not count them. She pulled on her mittens, wrapped the woolen muffler around her neck and across her face. She tugged her hat down so only her eyes were exposed.

Ivan lifted the bag of groceries, walked with her to the door, opening it with one hand and passing the bag into Kitty's arms with the other. "Be careful, Comrade Pushkin, and do not slip on the ice. Do you want me to walk with you to your apartment?"

"No thank you, Comrade, and please shut the door. You're heating all of Russia." Kitty lowered her head, plunging back into the frigid night, the sack in her arms and the wind whipping at her clothes. As she plodded along, the vodka warmed her stomach, the Hershey bar warmed her heart, the winter sought to freeze the rest.

Chapter 45

Kansas City

Joe stared at the familiar handwriting on the postcard from Wake Island; yet another card with no date written on it except the postmark. The concern was etched in his face. He turned the card over and gazed at the palm trees in silhouette against the beautiful sunset. The fact that his grandmother had been good to her word, by not calling even once, had not really surprised him. *"I will call if I am in trouble and need your help. If you do not get a call, it means I am doing fine."*

Joe could still hear her uttering those words before she left, over nine months ago. That is the way they had always dealt with each other on trips. Kitty had always looked at it positively, expecting things to go perfectly well. She had told him when he began to travel on his own, *"I'm not going to sit around the phone waiting for you to call. I'll start worrying when I get a call from the police. And I want you to do the same."*

Joe had been a little surprised when he didn't get a call at Christmas time, but *that's Grandma*, he decided. But the card from Hong Kong had not commented on the typhoon, which they must have narrowly missed. And the card from Osaka had said nothing of the earthquake, which must have hit while they were ashore in Japan. Each omission was not in itself significant, but added together, they formed an alarming pattern.

And now this, a trivial thing, but it really bothered him. The postcard in his hands was postmarked April 21, 1979. His birthday was April 22nd, and yet, she had made no mention of it. Not a *Happy Birthday*, no present, no nothing. He had just called Lee Ping in Boston, where she was cutting her journalistic teeth at the Boston Globe City Newspaper. Since Kitty was sending postcards to both of them, they kept each other updated on the *Catrina's* progress. Lee Ping maintained a travel log by marking a globe of the earth with pins and a magic marker.

But when Joe brought up the issue of Kitty's lack of acknowledging his birthday, his fears were confirmed. Several seconds of silence on the other end of the line told Joe that Lee Ping was stunned as well. They had always made a big deal about birthdays. It had always been that person's day in the sun. It was like the old TV show, QUEEN FOR A DAY. He couldn't believe his grandmother was so preoccupied that it didn't even occur to her to wish him a happy birthday. Something was wrong. He hated to think about what it might be, but something was definitely wrong.

Chapter 46

Kitty had been working in the kitchens of the textile factory for over six months. It was hard work, but she was lucky that Viktor had found something that she could do. Baking bread and cooking for the workers' noon meal was right up her alley. She arrived at six o'clock every morning, began heating up the ovens, then started mixing the ingredients for whatever variety of bread she was making that day. At first, it was always the same; plain, wheat-flour, everyday bread. But as she got to know her supervisor better, Kitty began asking about adding other types of grain. Then, she gradually began to try other things like molasses or brown sugar.

She found out that there was always an abundance of something in the area, as long as she wasn't too particular what it was. It reminded Kitty of an episode of M*A*S*H she had seen. *Hawkeye had needed morphine for his patients in the worst way, but the army delivered a whole truckload of tongue depressors.* As long as Kitty adapted to whatever was available she was *in business.* The feedback from the workers was so positive that her supervisor began asking Kitty what she wanted in advance, if there was a choice.

After the bread was in the ovens, Kitty began working on the other parts of the meal. The factory supported about twelve hundred workers, so there was lots of food to prepare every day. Kitty was one of five cooks, although she had started out as more of a helper, which meant grunt work. Officially, there were two cooks and three helpers. The helpers were called assistants, whose job it was to open the cans and boxes, do the carrying, most of the chopping, and any of the other tasks the real cooks needed done.

Kitty had been an assistant for only about three weeks when it became apparent that her talents were being wasted. The young cook, Akilina, to whom she was assigned to help, was clearly over her head. Inevitably, Kitty began assuming more and more of the cooking duties while Akilina volunteered to do some of the grunt work, watching and learning in the process.

Springtime does not come early to Smolensk. Finally, by the first week of May, wild and planted flowers were popping out of the ground. The trees were turning pale green with buds bursting through their protective husks, eager to become leaves. The blossoms on the flowering trees not only reminded Kitty of her home in Kansas City, they brought back memories of the thick forested hills of the Milanov estate on Lake Kaspl'a.

Kitty had not lost sight of her ultimate goal, not for one second. She would return to her childhood home, the one taken away from her family so many years ago. First, she had to establish a base. Her cover, provided by the CIA, involved the history of a woman from Odessa. However, Viktor had convinced Kitty that before risking exposure to government officials, she needed a residence she knew. A track record she could feel; a place, where people knew *her* as Nataliya Svetlana Pushkin, *Natty*. She needed to feel part of the country, the culture. Not to mention, winter in this part of the world is no time to be out exploring the countryside.

But now it was spring. Kitty's thoughts were focused on her next step, which was to somehow penetrate the Soviet Premier's vacation estate. She felt like she was about to make a pilgrimage to the Holy Land. She had not set foot on the hallowed soil since having to flee an almost certain death as a teenager. Visions of her mother's rape and murder always accompanied her thoughts of returning home. As did the nightmare of her own narrow escape, being forced to kill in order stay alive. Kitty pushed these scenes back into the closely guarded corner of her mind. However, the memories made her ambition all the more resolute.

May 9th was *Victory Day*, a day to celebrate defeating the Germans in World War II. Kitty decided to take advantage of her day off. The factory would be closed, the schools, most businesses. She borrowed a small overnight bag from the woman in the apartment next door, packed it, and walked to the train station.

Chapter 47

Joe O'Riley sat across the desk from the president of The Chicago First National Bank. Daniel Mitts had known Joe all of Joe's life. Daniel's dad, Ernie, used to say, *Kitty O'Riley is the shrewdest business tycoon you'll ever hope to meet. If she wants to develop a business, or has some project in mind, you just ask her how much the Bank can invest.*

Daniel's conservatively dressed secretary knocked lightly on the door, entering his office without waiting for her boss's response. Ms. Sutton had worked for him long enough to know when he could be interrupted and when she needed his consent to enter. "Good Morning, Joe" she said, brightly.

"Hi, Vicki; how's it going?"

"Great!" she exclaimed, "So, where's your grandmother now?"

Joe hesitated before answering. "She should be arriving in Hawaii soon," he muttered.

"Is something wrong?"

"Actually," Joe relented, "I'm afraid something may have happened to her. That's why I'm here." He nodded at the files of paper that Vicki still held in her hands. "I want to take a look at those records and see if anything looks funny."

"My lord," Vicki gasped, as she quick-stepped it over to a round table in the corner of the large office, spreading the files out. "Here, it will be easier for you to go through these if you have a little room. She pushed back one of the four expensively-upholstered leather chairs for Joe to sit in. "Is there anything else I can do for you?" she asked, full of genuine concern. At the bank, Kitty was not only a legend in a business sense, she was also a very popular human being. She bordered on celebrity status in the mind of the bank president's secretary.

"Thank you very much, Vicki. There's probably nothing to it." Joe opened the first file and started poring through the payroll records of the crew on the *Catrina*. Payment was made by wire, every two weeks, to a local bank in whichever port they happened to be at the time. All authorized by Brownie Dreher.

He reviewed maintenance records, minor ship's repairs, general expenses and petty cash. Joe scanned through the other files relating to Kitty's business investments handled by the Chicago First National Bank. An hour and a half later, he closed the last file, stood up and stretched. Everything seemed to be in order.

Daniel looked up from his desk, where he had been going over some work of his own. "Well, did you find anything?"

"Everything looks clean as a whistle." Joe shook his head, surprised he hadn't found something. "Before I came up here, I checked with Logan Sweeney and he says there haven't been any requests for funds through Kitty's Kakes. He said they would have to be authorized by him, so he would know if there had been. ...Damn! If it's not money, what is it? I can't get over this feeling that something's not as it should be."

Joe walked over to shake the bank president's hand. "I don't suppose you could let me have a look at that stuff she stashed for the year she'd be gone, could you?"

"You know I can't do that, Joe. I haven't seen it. In fact, nobody has seen it except her. The instructions were explicit. No one is to open that lock-box for one year from the date she left, which was August. I'll bet Logan would like to see what's in that box, too. Anyway, I can't help you there...sorry."

Joe nodded his head, absently. His eyes glazed over, his mind somewhere in the Pacific. "Can you have your driver give me a lift to O'Hare? I think I'll just fly to Hawaii and see for myself. That's supposed to be her next stop and I miss that old smiling face of hers so much. I'd like nothing better than to have her laugh at my foolishness."

Daniel pressed a button on his phone.

"Yes, Mr. Mitts?"

"Have Jerry pull my car 'round front. Joe needs a ride to Midway. And, Vicki, call Sam and tell him the Lear's going to need enough fuel on board to get to San Francisco and to submit a flight-plan all the way Honolulu. Thanks."

Joe stuck out his hand, clasping the older man's knuckles firmly, affectionately. "Thank you, Sir. I'll call you from the islands."

☙

Joe peered out at the palm trees through the small oval windows of the Lear Jet. He thanked Sam and the co-pilot for the smooth flight out and hopped down the three retractable steps to the pavement. In the terminal, he found a little clothing shop and picked out a brightly colored Hawaiian shirt, some white shorts, and a pair of flip-flops with a rainbow on the side. "Do you have a dressing room?" he asked the lady. They didn't, so he opted for the airport restroom.

Joe went through his pockets, transferring everything to his new shorts, and pondered what to do with his clothes. He had already left his windbreaker in the jet. He decided to leave them hanging on the hook. He did grab his two-hundred-and-fifty dollar shoes, however, sticking them into the bag with the clean boxers he'd bought before heading back out to the concourse.

Joe was hoping this little escapade would turn out to be a vacation. Hell, he might even ride back to the States on the *Catrina* with his grandmother. Unfortunately, the nagging feeling of trouble still ate at him.

It took Joe the rest of the day, and three marinas, to find out any information about the *Catrina's* expected landfall. It was well past dark when he handed the keys of his rental car to the doorman at the Moana Hotel. By noon tomorrow he'd know if he was just being silly, or not.

Chapter 48

May 9, 1979
Ol'sa, USSR

Twenty miles down the track from the Smolensk Station, the train pulled into a little farming community named Ol'sa. Through her window, Kitty watched lines of people marching in the streets. There were banners and red flags everywhere. It was just the second whistle stop from where she started. She stepped down to the depot platform and walked into the building, hoping to find a map of the area on the wall.

The dirty white walls of the main room looked like they hadn't been painted in decades. Discovering no map, Kitty turned to the clerk that was staring at her from behind a counter. She stepped up, thought better of it, and asked for the restroom. After washing her hands, she nodded toward the clerk on her way out, wiping her hands on her coat, for lack of towels or toilet paper.

Standing in the sunshine on the depot's platform, Kitty could hear a band playing in the distance toward the center of town. She watched a couple of train cars being unloaded. Crates of live chickens were coming off one car, and cloth sacks full of grain or seed or something, were coming off another. An old flatbed truck was backed up to the crates of squawking birds. A woman was lifting the crates and passing them to two teenage girls standing in the back of the truck.

"Can I ask you a question, comrade?" said Kitty as she approached.

The woman turned and smiled. "The first question is free, after that..."

Kitty hesitated, startled by the woman's tan-colored eyes. The woman's smile grew wider, evidently accustomed to just such a reaction. "I was born with them," the woman said, blinking twice to give Kitty a chance to recover.

"I'm sorry. I wanted to ask you where I can find the road that goes north." Remaining cautious, Kitty was intentionally vague about where she was going.

"Two choices." The woman stretched out her arm, pointing over Kitty's shoulder. "One, the east edge of town; the other, a couple miles to the west of here. If you want a ride, we're going north in about an hour.'

"Thank you. Nice morning for a walk." As Kitty pulled a blue scarf out of her bag to cover her head, the woman returned to her task. Kitty walked through town, watching the people march in the streets. Others were milling around or standing in small groups talking, laughing. She looked in the windows of the stores and other buildings, though most were locked and dark inside. There was a lot of color in the streets to go along with the music, but Kitty suspected the town was usually drab and gray; *lipstick on a pig*. Victory day, one day of frivolity in an otherwise dismal existence.

On the outskirts of town, Kitty lifted the bag's strap over her head so it was across her chest, left the pavement and headed north on what would have been a hard-packed dirt road. Instead, last night's rain had turned the road's surface into mud. Kitty's ankle-high work shoes had globs of mud clinging to them almost immediately, weighing her down.

She slogged over to the side of the road and began looking for a stick or something to scrape the mud from her shoes. Having done that, she looked back at the mucky mess called a road, cursed the Soviet transportation department, if there was one, and decided to walk in the ditch where the grass and weeds prevented the mud from swallowing her feet. She made better time on the side, although her feet were thoroughly soaked from the wet grass before she had covered a mile.

Fortunately, the sun was out and would dry up the road before too long. Kitty's spirits began to rise, knowing she was so close to home. The birds were singing cheerfully, cattle grazing in the fields, and wild flowers were growing everywhere. As Kitty topped a knoll, she could see that the fields turned into forested hills up ahead. A burst of excitement filled her as she envisioned just beyond those bluffs, the pure, blue water of Lake Kaspl'a. She had been waiting sixty years for this. Her pace quickened a little, her pounding heart reminded her to maintain a sensible, steady pace.

Chapter 49

Joseph's head bumped against the window, waking him up. Shahlo spun the steering wheel to the right, swerving back to the center of the road. "Sorry," she said.

Joseph rubbed the side of his head and looked around to get his bearings. "Do you want me to drive?" he asked. His hangover was still creating a dull fog in his head. He looked out the back window. The girls were braced against the chicken crates, apparently enjoying the wild ride.

"I'm fine," said Shahlo. "This road is even worse than the other one." Earlier that morning, they had driven south to Ol'sa on the west road.

"It was worth a try," Joseph said. "Just keep it moving and stay out of the ditch."

"If we go in the ditch it won't be my fault. There's no tread on the tires."

"Just keep it moving and stay out of the ditch."

Shahlo gave Joseph a withered look. She hated it when he repeated his statements, like she wasn't smart enough to get it the first time.

He smiled at her. "Don't like it when I do that, do you?"

"Just bein' old doesn't make you wise," she said, smiling back at him.

Joseph saw something in the distance through the windshield and squinted his eyes, straining to focus on it. "Is that an animal or a person up there?"

Shahlo glanced up to see what he was looking at, felt the truck start to swerve, and jerked the wheel over to correct it. "I'm trying to concentrate. Tell me if it gets in the road. If it stays in the ditch, don't worry about it...I was told not to go in the ditch." She turned her head just far enough to stick her tongue out at him, keeping her eyes pointed forward.

The dull, unmistakable sound of a motor gradually penetrated the noise made by Kitty's trudging feet. She turned around and saw an ancient truck clear the rise and come into view. The deep-throated sound of the engine got steadily louder. Kitty decided it must be the truck she saw at the train depot and continued her march. As it approached she moved a little farther from the road, just in case.

The girls in the back waved as the beat-up, old truck passed her, going up a slight incline at about ten miles an hour. One of the front fenders was missing, but ironically, the engine purred like it was brand new. At the top of the hill, the truck stopped; one brake-light shining red, the other dark. The driver's door opened and a woman climbed out.

"You change your mind about a ride?" she yelled, walking toward Kitty to meet her halfway.

Kitty stepped onto the road next to Shahlo. The girls leaned against the sideboards of the truck, chicken crates alive with clucking and scratching sounds. "It's pretty muddy," said Kitty, "but I don't have much farther to go."

Shahlo looked around, and seeing no likely destination, looked back at Kitty. "Are you sure you know where you are?"

Kitty realized she should have planned ahead for this obvious question. Movement in the rear window of the truck caught her eye. The grisly face of an old man was peering at her through the small, oblong window. "Is that their grandfather?"

Shahlo smiled. "He's their father."

Kitty raised her eyebrows in surprise before she could stop herself; *you are very attractive - exotic even, mid forties. He must be eighty.* She touched Shahlo's arm, an apology passed between them, blue eyes to tan.

"Peter saved my life a long time ago," said Shahlo, "and we fell in love." She shrugged. "He's lived through some hard times. ...Yesterday, he got fired."

Side-stepping this topic, Kitty said. "Your daughters are very pretty." She looked up at the girls but was drawn back to the old man's face. An ugly scar gave the man a ghoulish look. "Well, I'll be on my way. Thank you for stopping, comrade."

As Kitty returned to the grassy roadside, she heard Shahlo call after her. "That forest up the road is a government compound. It could be dangerous for you if you are caught trespassing."

Kitty lifted a hand, acknowledging the warning, and continued her trek.

Chapter 50

A man wearing a white dress-shirt, red tie, and well-tailored dark wool slacks sat in front of a console full of television monitors. His hair was brown and wavy, with streaks of gray at the temples. He was concentrating on some paperwork and his ears were covered by a set of headphones. Every few seconds he would raise his head to scan the half dozen monitors.

Another man stood by the open, second story window, watching the tree branches sway in the light breeze. He had close-cropped blond hair and was dressed similarly to the man at the console, except that he was wearing a shoulder holster. The leather straps crisscrossed his muscular upper body. He had his revolver in his hands and was pointing it out the window.

Suddenly, a loud, crisp *SNAP* caused the man at the console to jerk his head up to see what had happened. He pulled the earphones off his head. "Stop that!" he shouted. "Goddammit, Gludic! I'm trying to get something done here! Put that gun away and shut the f——ing window! It smells like horseshit in here!" He replaced the earphones on his head before resuming his paperwork.

Glancing up, he saw that Gludic was taking aim at another target, most likely a menacing tree. He pulled the earphones off again, anger edging his voice. "You shoot that gun once more and it's your ass! Go make a visual security check of the grounds... NOW!" he ordered.

Gludic returned his revolver to its holster below his left arm, his own temper beginning to rise. "Commander, what the f—— are all these monitors for if we got to go out and physically check the f——ing grounds all the time? Plus, it's almost lunchti..."

This time the voice of the man at the console was low and calm, cutting him off. "The General Secretary will be here tomorrow, as you know. It is important that we make sure there are no intruders within the restricted area. I have given you a direct order and if you do not do as I say immediately, I will have you shot. In fact, I will shoot you myself. Take the electric crawler; I want you to circle the entire lake."

Gludic Bovich could tell by looking into his superior's eyes, and by the tone of his voice, that discretion was important to his future right now. He didn't think Comrade Kurslov would actually shoot him, but...*he might*.

He put on his jacket, picked up his two-way radio and started for the door.

"The window!"

Gludic moved quickly to the window, closed it, locked it, and slipped out the door. He was biting on his lip as he descended the stairs, blood rising to his face.

Once outside he felt better, more independent, away from *f——ing commanders*. He turned to the right, opening the first stall where the electric crawler was stored. He yanked on the large cables, unplugging the vehicle's batteries from the recharger, and got in behind the wheel. The Crawler was about twice the size of an American golf cart with a *half-track* in back. It also had power to oversized knobby-tired wheels in front. It was built low to the ground for stability and could handle about anything as a terrain vehicle, short of climbing trees.

Crawler was really a misnomer because the machine could do thirty miles-per-hour over rough ground. It had huge batteries, but at peak performance the vehicle was only good for a few hours. At golf course speed it would go all day.

Gludic turned it on and drove out of the stall. The building, which housed the crawler, as well as the security office upstairs, was actually a stable for riding and jumping horses. However, General Secretary Brezhnev had converted the structure into a garage, housing a dozen vintage cars from Europe and the United States, plus a brand new, orange Lamborghini.

Gludic nearly stopped to re-close the stall doors but changed his mind, stuck his middle finger out in Commander Kurslov's general direction and stepped on the accelerator. The crawler sped silently past the huge old mansion, skirting the immaculate grounds immediately surrounding the house.

Except for the road, leading through the woods to the outside world, no pavement could be found in the compound. During the 30's, flagstones had been laid in the vicinity of the house, including the courtyard. The rest of the land within the security area remained grass, or dirt trails, as an accommodation for the horses.

Gludic took a left, leaving the stone surface, and headed down the hill on the dirt trail to the lake. The rain had made the trail slippery, but in the crawler it wasn't even an issue. As he neared the fork in the road, he backed off on his speed while he decided which way around the lake he wanted to go. It really didn't matter. He would end up right back here either way. He smiled to himself, thinking this might be the extent of the important decisions he would face today. Then he remembered that keeping his mouth shut and not getting shot was definitely the most important decision he'd make.

Mentally, he tossed a coin - *right*. He turned the crawler in that direction, pressed the pedal to the floor, and took off like a bat out of hell. With the wind blowing through his hair, he soon had to slow down to negotiate the curves of the hilly trail. He sat back in his seat, deciding to relax and enjoy the ride. This was actually much better than sitting cooped up in a room with all those monitors. "Up yours, Kurslov."

Kitty stood looking up at the heavy-duty chain-link fence. It was eight feet high, with coiled razor-wire on top of that. It was buried in the ground, and a space of six feet on either side had been cleared of undergrowth and virtually all living plant life. It was obvious that chemicals had been used to achieve this degree of desolation in the middle of a forest. She presumed the perimeter was guarded, *probably with dogs. Camp David is likely to be isolated and protected the same way. Who can blame them?*

The bag suddenly became heavy on her shoulder, her legs tired. Kitty started to get a sinking feeling in her stomach as she looked up at the formidable barrier. *Who do I think I am, James Bond?*

She decided to follow the fence for a while to see if an opportunity presented itself. "I didn't come all this way and go to all this trouble to get within a half-mile of home, and then quit." Talking out loud alone in the woods seemed natural. And yet, somehow it was strange. There were certainly no other man-made noises to be heard around her. Only the chirping of birds, rustling squirrels and wind in the trees broke the utter silence of the forest. It was splendid and lonely at the same time.

As Kitty walked along the cleared path on her side of the fence, she thought maybe an overhanging branch...or something. After about a quarter of a mile, she accepted the fact that whoever was in charge of security had already thought to trim back the branches, precisely for the reason she was looking for one.

Starting to get frustrated, Kitty began looking for something to mash down the razor wire on top of the fence so she could simply climb over it. This idea began to sound so good, so elementary, that she started to suspect there must be sensors in the wire somehow. Convinced this must be the case, she stepped up to within a couple inches of the fence, inspecting it. She also considered whether the darn thing might electrocute her. She was careful not to touch it, somewhat surprised she hadn't already done so. It was hard not giving it the *wet-paint-touch-test*. And then she saw a tiny, hair-thin wire interwoven throughout the chain-link. *You sneaky bastards.*

Beginning to run out of options, Kitty decided to follow the fence a little while longer and, if nothing turned up, begin working on plan B, which was *talking her way through the gate*. She kept hoping for some sort of lucky break, and just when she thought she'd better return to the road, Kitty saw an answer to her dilemma. In a low area ahead, runoff water had washed away the soil beneath the fence.

Kitty pulled the overnight bag off her shoulder, and sinking to her knees, pushed it through the opening. Then, wriggling on her stomach, she worked her way underneath the fence, being careful not to touch it. With a triumphant smile on her face and clothes covered with mud, Kitty looked up at the fence from the other side. "So there!" she chortled.

What Kitty didn't know was that a tiny green light had blinked when she pushed her bag under the fence. The green light had blinked much longer when she went through herself. The rest of what she didn't know involved a red signal-light that was now flashing on the console right in front of Security Commander Gregor Kurslov.

Oblivious to the silent warning she had triggered, Kitty got to her feet. She decided to wait until the mud dried to brush it off her clothes, picked up her bag and began climbing the rest of the way up the hill.

Kurslov already had his two-way radio microphone to his lips. "Gludic, we have a possible infiltration of the perimeter fence. In fact, I have a double violation of a light sensor in the gamma quadrant. Acknowledge, and advise current position."

Gludic's voice responded through the speakers built into the console. "Commander, message received. I am currently on the opposite side of the lake from gamma. It's probably just another pair of raccoons or a couple of stray dogs. I take it you don't have a visual."

"The cameras do not sweep that particular area. And Gludic, let me remind you that Brezhnev's personal security staff will be arriving first thing in the morning. We do not want to be caught with our pants down by having some derelict with a gun running around loose, now do we? Investigate immediately and report back to me what you find. If you're right, I'll settle for Lassie's carcass. The violation was checkpoint G-L-6."

Gludic reached for the laminated map of the security layout. Every camera and sensor was located on the map, designated by an alpha-numeric code. He quickly found *gamma, light sensor #6*, identified *spur #23* as the nearest connecting route, and stuffed the map back into the small compartment. He withdrew the revolver from his shoulder holster, noted that only one round was missing from the eighteen-round clip, and returned the gun to its concealed position. He twisted around to lift the cover of what looked like a long toolbox. He removed the AK-47 assault-rifle; again making sure it was loaded. He set the rifle in the boot in front of the passenger's seat of the crawler.

That was it. Gludic was ready. He pressed hard on the accelerator, spurring the crawler to life. The beauty of the vehicle for this type of operation was that the electrical motor was absolutely silent. The only sound was from the tires and half-track, zipping across the soft earth. Gludic figured it was about four miles to spur #23, at which point he would leave the lake shore trail and cut over to the perimeter fence. The distance from the lake to the perimeter varied, but was generally about two-thirds of a mile. Quickly doing the math in his head, Gludic calculated he would be at 'G-L-6' in about twelve minutes if he averaged twenty-five miles an hour. No simple feat on these winding trails.

Cresting the long, sloping hill, Kitty was disappointed at not being able to see the deep blue waters of the lake she knew to be there. Even with only buds on the trees, it was still too thick for her to get an actual view of the dream she had carried for so many years. The evergreens that were inter-mixed with the budding trees on the hillside caused much of the difficulty. She pressed on, plowing her way through the wet leaves, which were several inches deep. Areas that were predominantly pine, made for much easier walking due to the smooth carpet of needles beneath her feet.

She began heading down the slope, her pace quickening as it had on the road a couple of hours ago. But this time she did not keep herself in check. Her legs should have been tired with all she had put them through that day, but the adrenaline was carrying her forward. Unable to wait for the real thing, her mind retrieved childhood memories of what Kaspl'a would look like. The sunlight filtering through the trees was brighter just ahead. The terrain was becoming rocky, causing the trees to be more sparse. Finally, Kitty detoured around a particularly large outcropping of boulders and was rewarded with a breath-taking scene that made her halt in her tracks.

The sky was now clear, sunshine pouring down on Kitty's face as she gazed out over the treetops to the deep blue water below. The impact of the total panorama overwhelmed her, bringing tears to her eyes. She worked her way out to the edge of the rocky point, set her bag down, and spread her arms as if they were wings. Her heart fluttered with emotion, remembering, longing for the life that had been snatched away from her... she was back home.

Kurslov's voice exploded over the two-way radio. "Gludic! I have a visual! Gludic! Acknowledge ...what is your present location?"

There were twenty-four video cameras spread across the compound, scanning the area incessantly. They were mounted on top of poles extending above the trees. Functioning individually, each camera was displayed on an alternating basis on one of three monitors in the security office. The sweeping mechanism on each camera-mount could be overridden by the security officer, allowing him to direct the field of view.

Gludic stepped firmly on the crawler's anti-lock brakes, bringing the vehicle to a halt in a matter of a few feet. From the first time he had been in the crawler, its acceleration and stopping power had been impressive. "Bovich here," Gludic responded, "what have you got, Commander?"

"Bovich, I said what is your present location?"

"I have just turned off of Spur #23 and am headed down the perimeter fence to G-L-6. What do you see, Commander?" he repeated.

"The intruder is stationary on the western slope. He is on a ledge in plain sight. It looks like he is trying to get his bearings. I would say... directly between you and the lake. Advise taking spur #24 back toward the lake trail to intercept."

"Is there just one intruder, Commander?" Gludic asked over the radio.

"That's all the cameras have picked up so far, Bovich. He has a bag that might contain either weapons or explosives. He's wearing a blue hood. The distance and angle are preventing me from seeing his face. Do not allow him to elude you. Now go!"

Kurslov unconsciously rubbed his hands together, his eyes glued to the three monitors. Most of the time when the sensors had detected a breach in the perimeter, it had been a deer or some other animal...or they had never figured out what it was. This time it was clearly human, and with the General Secretary arriving tomorrow...he didn't believe in coincidences.

Kitty decided to move down to the lake's shore. She wanted to feel the cool water on her skin, touch it, drink it. She was feeling light and carefree, like a child again. She started to lean down to pick up her bag.

Something hit her from behind. It felt like a baseball bat wrapped in a towel. The force knocked her off her feet, off her rocky perch, through the air...down.

Gludic smiled. *One shot from seventy-five yards; not bad.* He put the pistol back into his shoulder holster. Being rated First- Marksman with a handgun at his training academy was a constant source of satisfaction for Gludic Bovich. He trotted over to the base of the rock shelf where he judged the body would be. As expected, the perpetrator was sprawled in the underbrush. He turned the body over. *A woman.* He pulled the two-way radio from his belt and switched it on. "Commander Kurslov," he said calmly into the radio. "I have apprehended the intruder and eliminated the threat."

There were several seconds of silence. He was about to repeat the message when he heard the click, indicating a response.

"Comrade Bovich? What does eliminate mean? Did you shoot him?"

"Yes sir."

"Is he dead?"

"Don't know yet. There's lots of blood and she's not moving." Gludic looked up. "I'd say she fell about..."

"Did you say it is a female?"

Gludic looked down dispassionately at the lifeless body. "Yes, sir, sort of an older one. I'm going to go up and see what was in the bag."

"Bovich, get the bag, put the body in your vehicle and get back here immediately."

"Yes sir, commander."

Chapter 51

Kailua, Hawaii

Joe started his day with a walk along the beach, followed by breakfast by the pool of the Moana Hotel. The table's umbrella shaded him from the sun while he tried to read the morning paper. He was too anxious to pay much attention to the news.

When he arrived at the prestigious Kailua Yacht Club, he identified himself to the man in the little gatehouse at the main entrance. The man, wearing a starched white uniform, had confirmed the expected arrival of the *Catrina* and requested his relationship to the vessel before opening the electrically locked gate to the grounds.

After waiting in the parking lot for the morning rain-shower to finish cleansing the island of yesterday's dust, Joe followed the walkway around a corner of the club that turned into a winding stone path through lush gardens. A sign at a fork in the trail gave him a choice; *Marina to the right, Terrace / Grill to the left.*

He chose left, emerged through a trellis brimming with flowers, and was confronted by a dark-skinned young woman with flowers in her hair, grass-skirt, smooth brown belly, and a smile that looked genuine. Joe returned her smile and raised a finger, indicating he was alone.

The terraced patio was built into the lava rock. She led him to one of several sets of small tables with chairs, arranged so that members could sip *mai tai's*, while watching the sleek sailboats and powerful cruisers come and go. A waiter arrived immediately with a menu. "Just water, please," said Joe, and settled in to wait.

Half an hour passed with nothing to do except envy the seagulls, floating on the wind, and watch maintenance activities on several of the club members' boats. It was a natural harbor, enhanced by a man-made jetty to help protect the vessels from the Pacific's powerful waves.

Like an actor making an entrance on stage, a ship under full sail rounded the point and came into view. Her white sails and superb lines were stunning against the blue water, blue sky and black rock.

Joe's eyes welled with tears at the sight; powerful, beautiful, carrying the only family he had, the person who raised him, had taken care of him all of his life. He pushed back his chair and headed for the path to the marina.

Captain Jarvis had just requested instructions over the boat's radio, hoping to be allowed to bring her in under sail.

"Engines are required, Captain," the pier attendant replied. "A pilot will be out to you in a launch to lead you in."

The *Catrina* was still a mile out to sea when Joe arrived at the end of the pier. "My name is Joe O'Riley," he said to the attendant. "My grandmother is the owner, and I'd like to ride out with the pilot if that's alright."

The white cap with gold braid on the brim gave the middle-aged man an air of authority. He sized Joe up with cautious dignity, befitting the position. Dropping the pretense, he smiled, slapped Joe on the shoulder and yelled to the pilot. "Kana, you got a mate!"

The sixteen-year-old boy looked up at his father from the deck of the launch. He was in the process of stowing some gear in one of the holds. Over the deep-throated rumble of two diesel engines, he yelled to Joe, "Come aboard." It was the boy's job to guide any skippers that were unfamiliar with the harbor, to their appropriate spot. He had been in, on, or near the water every day of his life, which was not only typical of the islands, it was unavoidable.

Joe climbed into the boat and sat in the stern. He could feel the powerful engines vibrate through the cushion of his seat. "Throw the lines over, Pop!" Kana yelled. He inched the throttles forward and held it slow and steady in the *no-wake* zone. Once past the buoy, he opened it up, and they were off.

On deck, the *Catrina's* crew was trimming and hauling down the sails. Brownie stood by the rail, having learned when and where to get out of the way as the men plied their craft. She strained her eyes in the direction of the pilot's boat coming out to meet them, noting there was someone sitting aft. As the launch drew along side, Brownie thought the face of the guy in back looked familiar but she couldn't place it.

"Where's my grandmother?" Joe yelled over the engines.

"Oh shit!" Brownie muttered to herself.

Fifteen hours later, Joe and Brownie were standing in front of a clerk at the Hay Adams Hotel in Washington D.C. It was 11:00 in the morning, Washington time. *Before leaving the yacht club, Brownie had initiated a wire for the crew's payroll to the nearest Honolulu bank. At the executive airport, while Joe arranged to charter a jet, Brownie had placed a call and left a message for her former boss, the Director of CIA Operations. Including an hour stop in L.A. for refueling, it had been a ten hour flight.*

"Sorry, we're all full," the clerk said. "There's a big music and art festival going on and I think you'll find that all the hotels in the capital, decent or otherwise, are booked solid. We've turned quite a few people away already. I'm sorry."

Joe reached for his wallet, pulled out two fifties and said, "Are you sure you don't have anything? We've come all the way from Hawaii and we're beat."

The man let his eyes wander between Joe's Hawaiian shirt and Brownies swimsuit cover-up, snagged the bills from Joe's fingers and picked up a house phone. "I'll see what I can do." He dialed a two-digit number. "Do you have any of the rooms cleaned yet?" .... "Thank you." The clerk turned his back, scanning rows of cubbyholes where the room keys were kept. He pulled a key out of one of the slots. Lowering his voice, he said, "This room is already confirmed for this evening. If in fact, nothing opens up, you may be asked to relinquish it." He looked at his watch. "You are likely to be able get some sleep in the meantime. And with some luck, keep the room for the night."

"We'll take it," said Joe

"Does it have two beds?" asked Brownie.

The clerk gave her a side-wards glance. "Where is your luggage?" he asked, ignoring her question.

Joe took the key and held up the shopping bag, containing his boxers and a pair of shoes. Brownie had a make-up case and single dress on a hanger covered with plastic. "We were in a hurry," said Joe.

The clerk grimaced. "Well then, nighty-night."

Chapter 52

Gludic Bovich drove the crawler into the courtyard behind the big stone house. Kurslov was standing there waiting for him, his arms crossed, a scowl on his face. Gludic was still pleased with himself, having apprehended the intruder and single-handedly removed the risk to the General Secretary. He might even get a medal for this.

Gludic brought the crawler to a stop a few feet from the Commander of Security. The limp, disheveled body was dumped in the back like lawn trash.

Staring into Gludic's eyes, Kurslov walked around to the back of the crawler and looked down at the bloody mess. "So this was the threat to our national security," he said sarcastically. "Did it ever occur to you that we might want to talk to this person, interrogate her, *torture* her for the truth? Or maybe this woman just happened on the compound by mistake. Did you ever think of that? No, you killed her!"

Kurslov moved the black bag that Bovich had thrown on top of the body. He then pulled the bloody sky-blue scarf away from the woman's face so he could get a better look. He realized the woman's still handsome face had once been beautiful. Disgusted, he muttered, "And you shot her in the back." He raised her shoulder to examine the fatal wound. The movement caused a moaning sound to escape the depths of Kitty's throat. She was still alive.

Kitty lay unconscious in one of the upstairs bedrooms. The room was painted light blue. The curtains were white and the carpet, gray. When she was a child, this room had been occupied by the French tutor, Mademoiselle Beaubien. An antique, canopy bed stood against one wall. Its bedspread was white with blue turned-down sheets that matched the walls.

A door opened quietly as a woman and three men walked in. One of the men was Soviet General Secretary, Leonid Brezhnev. "If what you say is true, there is no reason to risk moving her to a hospital. She is certainly not disturbing me, Dr. Galinski. This is an extra room and I will only be here three days. Take care of her, doctor...whoever she is." Brezhnev departed, tugging Commander Kurslov on the arm, indicating he should follow.

In the hallway Brezhnev turned to the security chief. "Commander, the zeal with which your man shot an old woman disturbs me."

Kurslov opened his mouth to apologize but was stopped short by a raised palm, ordering silence. "It is how things were done in the old days. But, Commander, we are not like that anymore."

"General Secretary, it was..."

"I could understand if your man was being threatened and he was saving himself," Brezhnev continued, "or hopefully protecting his General Secretary. However, Bovich you said his name was?" Kurslov nodded. "But to Bovich, this was target practice. He used his revolver, for god's sake. If this was really a security situation, the man would have used an appropriate weapon."

"The man has been reprimanded...severely...sir." Kurslov knew the General Secretary opposed the Stalin mentality.

"I'm sure you have handled it satisfactorily, Commander. I would be interested in knowing who the woman is, but let's use some discretion. Be sure to make that clear to the doctor from the village before he goes. Dr. Galinski will take over, at least while I am here. She has assured me that the medical facilities we have here are adequate."

Standing beside their patient, the General Secretary's private physician and the doctor from the village conferred privately. "Dr. Galinski, you now know as much about her condition as I do." The amount of blood lost and potential infection were the primary concerns, since the bullet had not pierced any vital organs. "It is fortunate that unless something unusual happens, the woman will recover. But I have something else to tell you. Last night, this woman was delirious. The calm you see now only began at dawn."

The highly trained Dr. Galinski nodded her head knowingly, trying not to seem impatient. In reality, she felt Dr. Yakovlev was no more than a horse doctor, relegated to treating the common ailments of the workers within this sector. "Yes, Doctor, oftentimes patients will calm down at daybreak. It is a very curious phenomenon," she said, patronizing him.

"That is not the point I wish to make, Doctor." Dr. Yakovlev ignored the insult, acting as though it had gone over his head. "Myself, I speak only Russian. But I am sure that this woman, in her delirium, spoke English words over and over again. I understood none of it, of course, but I thought you should know. But that is not all. She seemed to speak in French and what sounded like Chinese. It was very strange, Dr. Galinski. I just thought you should know," he repeated.

Dr. Galinski didn't know what to make of that, but dismissed it as the delusions of a country bumpkin. "Very good, Doctor. Is there anything else?"

"There is one more thing. You..." As Dr. Galinski rolled her eyes impatiently, Dr. Yakovlev fell silent in mid-sentence. "No, nothing else, sorry," he muttered.

"Good!" she said. "I will take it from here. If you are able to keep silent about all matters you have seen in this house, I think there may be reason for you to look forward to some extra privileges. However, if you..."

"I understand, Dr. Galinski. Thank you." He picked up his bag and left the room without another word.

The General Secretary's private physician looked down at her patient, who was resting peacefully. "It is too bad they did not just let you die, my dear; a suitable end to a meaningless life."

Chapter 53

Sitting behind his desk looking tired, Nathanial Polk said, "Send them in, Marty."

Joe stood to the side, allowing Brownie to enter first. They both shook the CIA Director's hand and took the two seats across from his desk. Several balloons hovered above the director's credenza: *-IT'S A GIRL-*

Brownie smiled, "Congratulations, Nathanial! What did you name her?"

"Amy Lee," he said, making no attempt to hide the pleasure on his face when he thought about his daughter.

"That's two of each, isn't it?" Brownie asked. "How's Helen Marie doing?"

"Oh, they're both fine. Thank you for asking. The good news is she's nursing, so I don't have to get up. The bad news is I wake up anyway, so we're all a little tired. Amilee, as she is called so far, was born May 1st, so it's only been a week; seems longer. After seventeen years, we're starting to remember how the routine goes. You know, Dottie is a junior in high school and the boys are in college." Polk shrugged. "Helen Marie misses her glass of wine more than anything. Nine months is a long time. She'll be glad when she's no longer nursing. I think she intends to get plastered."

A serious expression replaced the smile on the CIA Director's face as he shifted his gaze from Brownie to Joe. "So, young man, I suppose you want to hear about your grandmother. ...Let me start out by saying that she took on this idea of going to the Soviet Union completely on her own. I think you will agree that she goes after what she wants pretty aggressively."

Joe couldn't help but smile. "I'd say that's a fair way of putting it."

"Anyway, in this case, Mrs. O'Riley used a certain amount of coercion to...to have her way with me, let us say." Innuendo, when referring to a seventy-eight-year-old woman, would normally seem strange, but they both let it slide. "The truth is she wanted one last chance at finding out what happened to her brother. Plus, she has ambitions of somehow getting back the family estate, and I haven't got a clue as to how that's going to work. It was clear there is a certain amount of vengeance involved for what they did to her parents."

Joe couldn't argue with that analysis one bit. He had come to terms with why his grandmother had not told him of her plans. He definitely would have insisted on going with her, regardless of the danger...or because of it.

"So when was the last time you received word about her well-being? I mean, do you even know if she is alive...or in a prison somewhere in Siberia?"

Polk hesitated for a moment before speaking. "I'm sure you can understand why I can't say anything specific." He paused again, choosing his words carefully. "I have reason to believe, as of last month, that your grandmother has found a job and is living satisfactorily, if not comfortably, in an apartment in southwestern Russia. And that is all I am going to say."

Joe looked into the Director's eyes. Honesty and sincerity stared back at him. There was finality there, too. Joe had heard all he was going to. "I want you to get me in the same way you did my grandmother. I speak Russian just as well as she does, and I'm going to help her do whatever it is she wants to do. I owe her more than you can imagine."

To this, Polk sat back in his chair, sighed heavily and stared at the ceiling for several seconds. Finally, his eyes returned to Joe's face. "If your grandmother is linked with the CIA, she could be shot. A prison in Siberia, as you put it, would also be a possibility. So far, she...we have managed to avoid suspicion by *the Comrades*. But if you go stumbling in there too, who knows what kind of danger you will be putting her in. I won't do it."

Joe could see that he had little hope of changing the CIA Director's mind on this one. He thought about it, pressed his mind for an argument to convince him, but came up with nothing.

And then Brownie, having kept quiet the entire time, spoke a single word; "*Ignace.*"

Chapter 54

Dr. Daldma Yakovlev sat at a small table in the dimly lit, smoky tavern, staring at a shot glass full of vodka. Also on the table within arm's reach was a string of eight empty shot glasses and three full ones all lined up. As he gazed at the clear liquid, which filled the ninth glass to the brim, he was thinking about an old woman lying in bed a few miles away. He had extracted the bullet, cleaned and bandaged the wound. The bump on her head probably indicated a concussion, though since she was unconscious, he couldn't be sure. The KGB agent had said she fell about twelve feet when she was hit.

But it wasn't the woman's condition that bothered him. He was pretty sure she would recover. It was the strange gibberish that flowed from the woman's mouth. It was like she was possessed. And inside her mouth, the teeth, the dental work. He had started to tell Dr. Galinski about the dental work, but the hag was too important to listen. He reached for the glass of vodka and downed it with a single gulp.

As he meticulously lined up the ninth glass in its proper position, a man stood over him, looking down. "Well, Doctor, I see you are working on a problem. I was doing the same thing two nights ago. Have you found a solution?"

"No, Peter," Dr. Yakovlev muttered, "I am neither drinking to the solution nor drowning my sorrows, yet. I am still working on the problem." His speech was slow, tainted with vodka.

There was a tradition at the tavern in the little town of Kaspl'a. When people had a difficult problem to work out, they would line up twelve glasses of vodka on a table. The glasses were about the size of a small juice glass. While thinking about a solution for their problem, they drank the first six glasses of vodka. After the sixth glass, they either had their solution or they didn't. If they had their solution, they drank the other six glasses, rejoicing in the fact that they had figured it out. Otherwise, they decided there was no solution and would carry on as best they could without one; but first, drank the other six glasses to get drunk, deadening the pain from having not been able to solve the problem. It was not a terribly effective system, but one that was very popular among the men of the town.

Joseph sat down at the table across from his friend. "Maybe if you told me about it, I could help." he offered.

At the far end of the tavern a group of teenagers were making music with instruments they had brought with them. Besides music, they were producing plenty of boisterous laughter and shouting. Several of the young women, wearing American-made blue jeans, were trying to get their boyfriends to dance.

"I can't talk about it, Peter. It's about *the compound*," he said, lowering his voice, slurring his words.

Joseph held up his hand, turned in his chair to see if he could get the attention of one of his daughters, hoping to get them to hold the noise down a little. He turned back to the doctor, knowing it was no use. His hearing loss was annoying. He leaned forward in his chair to make up for it.

"My problem also has to do with *the compound*," Joseph whispered conspiratorially.

"I heard you were fired," the doctor said.

"I wrecked Brezhnev's favorite car."

"I saw the '59 Cadillac on the back of a truck as I was leaving today. Unfortunate."

Joseph nodded. "Now tell me. What is your problem?"

❧

It was twenty-four hours, from the time Kitty was shot, before she was fully alert. Her body hurt all over, a dull ache muffled by some sort of pain medication. The medication made her a little hazy when she was awake and allowed her to drop off to sleep with no effort at all. In addition to the pain medication, through the IV stuck in her arm, she had a central venous line below her collar bone that provided fluids, nutrition and antibiotics. By the second day after she was shot, she was ready to sit up, eat regular food and start planning her next move.

Based on her surroundings, Kitty assumed she was in her old house, though she didn't recognize anything and hadn't been allowed to get up to look out the window. The nurse had told her she'd been shot and that was all. A female doctor had looked in on her twice that she was aware of, but answered no questions. To say the doctor was *aloof* would be close, *disinterested*...even closer.

"I'd like to go outside," Kitty said to the nurse on her third day of internment. The IV's were gone and she was tired of lying in bed. She was anxious to have a look around for reasons the nurse couldn't possibly realize.

"I'm going to change your bandage this morning. After that, we'll see."

An hour later, Dr. Galinski examined the wound with little more than a passing glance. Speaking to the nurse, she said, "If the woman wants to get some air, and you are willing to take her, I do not object."

Kitty was tempted to reach out and pinch the woman for her rudeness. Pinch her hard enough to make it bleed. Instead, she said, "Thank you, Doctor."

Without even acknowledging that Kitty had spoken, the doctor added, "Commander Kurslov will speak to her first. Re-bandage the wound and then wait in the hall until he is finished."

Kitty had answered dozens of questions about who she was and why she was trespassing in a restricted area. Today, the KGB Commander, standing at the foot of her bed, asked all the same questions over again to see if her answers were consistent. Her story was that she needed a break from the factory work and had heard there was a beautiful unspoiled lake amongst the trees. She just told the truth about going under the fence. The inquisition had finally stopped, ending with Kurslov's, *Thank you, comrade*, and his departure.

The nurse draped a blue blanket over Kitty's lap and around her legs, pushed the wheelchair slowly out the bedroom door and down the hallway. "The General Secretary is gone. Would you like to see part of the house before we go outside? There are a couple of rooms that are forbidden but I can show you the rest. It is good that Premier Khrushchev put in an elevator."

"That would be very nice."

Kitty was both delighted and agonized at every turn. She gasped in surprise at the up-to-date kitchen. She sighed in disappointment at the absence of her favorite chandeliers in the huge dining room. "What happened to the chandeliers?" she asked.

"I don't know what you mean, Natty."

"Never mind," Kitty mumbled.

The granite fireplace in the billiard room was just how she remembered it. She could recall spying on her father, Uncle Nicholas (the Tsar), and the other hunters while they drank and played billiards after the annual fox hunt. Her brother had only ridden in one hunt before going off to war. Riding in the fox hunt had been her burning desire when she was a child. A dream denied by her father and left unfulfilled. This thought led to the memory of her mother's rape and her parent's death at the hands of the Bolsheviks. It stirred embers in Kitty's soul, anger that had been smoldering for a lifetime.

"Let's go back to my room, Toma. I've seen enough."

"What is the matter, Natty?"

"I said I've seen enough!" Kitty snapped.

"Very well, you probably just need some rest."

"I need more than that. I need to find out who stole the chandeliers!" Kitty realized she needed to calm down. "Don't pay any attention to this old woman, Toma. Thank you for showing me the house. Can we still go outside for a little while?"

The sun was shining, the birds were singing and flitting around, and Kitty's spirits lifted as they strolled the beautiful grounds surrounding the house. Her nose caught a scent and she pointed. "Can we go see the horses?"

"Yes," Toma replied, "but that is where the General Secretary keeps his automobile collection. The stables are a little farther." The nurse directed the wheelchair toward a path leading through the trees. "Are you fond of horses, Natty?"

"Since I was old enough to walk," said Kitty. "Can we go a little faster?" she urged. "In fact, I'll bet I could just walk and save you the trouble."

"Not yet. Dr. Galinski doesn't want you jostling that wound of yours, and you lost so much blood."

Kitty almost responded with what she thought of the doctor, caught herself and said, "I'm not a very good patient, am I? Thank you for showing me around."

The stables and a split-rail fence appeared through the trees. Kitty could see about fifteen horses grazing at the far end of the clearing. The dense forest continued up the hill beyond. It was as beautiful as anything Kitty had ever seen. They spent about ten minutes in silence watching through the fence while the horses milled around.

"It's peaceful out here, isn't it?" said Toma.

"Yes it is. Look at those two colts playing with each other."

"There's nothing like a little sunshine to help heal one's body." The man's voice surprised both nurse and patient. Toma turned the wheelchair so she and Kitty could face the newcomer.

"Good afternoon comrade. It's a pretty day and the doctor recommended that Comrade Pushkin get some air."

The man bowed his head slightly as if to say *see, the doctor agrees with me.* He smiled and said, "My name is Mikhail. Do you mind if I join you?" Kitty's eyes were drawn to the deep-red birthmark above his forehead. He stepped forward and rested his elbows on the chest-high rail fence. "Moscow does not offer scenes such as this. I am from the farmlands in the south and miss this sort of thing." He was wearing a tan windbreaker, casual slacks and brown shoes.

"Do you ride much when you're home?" Kitty asked, poking for some common ground.

The man turned and leaned his back against the fence. "Not recently, no." He hesitated a moment, then asked, "Who are you and where do you come from?"

Kitty was disturbed by the directness of the man's question. She blurted, "Are these more questions from the KGB?"

"Just a little friendly conversation, comrade." As he turned back to watch the horses, he asked, "Are you in trouble with the KGB?"

"No, but I have been interrogated like a criminal, not to mention being shot. And all I did was wander onto this...this piece of land by mistake."

"You need to be more careful, comrade." The man's voice was calm and warm.

"So, if you're not with the security men, what are you doing here?" Kitty ventured. She felt Toma's hand squeeze her right shoulder...a warning.

Still facing the pasture, Mikhail said, "I am here because the General Secretary requested that I accompany comrade Andropov. Now, the others have gone back to the Kremlin for a meeting this afternoon about the trouble with Afghanistan. But since I am the Secretary of Agriculture, it was not necessary for me to attend."

Toma could not believe this official was openly discussing matters of state with a peasant woman and her nurse. "Natty, would you like to see the stalls where the horses are kept? I'm sure the Secretary of Agriculture has problems he needs to consider." She turned the wheelchair to go.

"Wait, I have not yet learned your names. I am Mikhail Sergeevich Gorbachev." He looked at Toma, expectantly.

"Tamara Dostrenko. I am on Dr. Galinski's staff."

Mikhail's gaze fell upon Kitty. "And you are Natty? There must be more than that." He smiled at Kitty to encourage her.

"My name is Nataliya Svetlana Pushkin, and my home is in Smolensk, where I work at the textile factory."

"Thank you, Natty. I hope you recover quickly from that unfortunate accident. I'm staying a couple of more days. Maybe we will see each other again." He nodded to Toma, releasing them.

As Toma pushed the wheelchair toward the stable, she whispered, "He is so young to be a Secretary. Most of the others have one foot in the grave."

Toma opened one side of the large double-doors to the stable. At the far end, both doors were open wide to the pasture and, she could see the silhouette of a man and a horse against the bright sunlight. The man was stooped over, near the horse's front legs. "May we come inside," she shouted.

"Just shut the door behind you," he responded, concentrating on his task.

Toma pushed Kitty's wheelchair across the hard-pack dirt floor of the stable. The smell inside the building was so familiar and reminiscent to Kitty that she could barely contain herself. Her expert eye scanned the stalls, the tack hanging from hooks on the walls, the tidiness of the stable itself. As they got nearer, her attention switched to the powerful white stallion with his right foreleg raised in the farrier's grasp. She blinked, noting the peculiar saddle on his back.

Toma stopped about ten feet short of them. "That is a magnificent animal," Kitty remarked. Her voice was low and soothing, sensitive to the intensity exuding from the horse.

The man raised his head to see who was addressing him. "Thank you, comrade. He threw a shoe this morning. I'm just about done." The man pounded a small spike through the bottom of the iron horseshoe, into the horse's hoof. He then pulled some pliers from his belt and bent the tip of the spike over so it would hold the shoe in place. "There, that should do it." He released the horse's leg, stood up and ran his hand down the strong white neck of the stallion. "Good boy." He turned to his visitors while stretching his back, stiff from the awkward stooping position.

Kitty judged the man to be in his early twenties. "Toma, please help me out of this chair."

The nurse started to protest, but seeing that Kitty was already getting out of the wheelchair, helped her stand up."

"Thank you, Toma," Kitty said as she steadied her balance. She looked at the young man and smiled. "I have not seen a horse like this in a long time."

"You have probably never seen a horse like this, comrade. That's close enough," he added as Kitty took a step toward them. "He is anxious to be out with his mares." As if to prove this statement, the white stallion began to prance around nervously, pulling on his lead rope that was tied to a post.

Kitty ignored the man's warning and the horse's skittish manner. With her hand outstretched, palm up, she approached. "There now, big fella. I'm not going to hurt you," she said smoothly. "I just want to say hello." The stallion's nervousness began to subside, though his eyes remained wide, ears pricked high...alert. "There now, that's better," Kitty cooed. "I wish I had a treat for you." Her hand was now below the horse's head, letting him make the next move. The stallion sniffed at her fingers, then nuzzled her palm, as if looking for the treat Kitty had mentioned.

The man stepped away, deciding to let her continue. Kitty began to run her hand along the stallion's neck and shoulder. She patted him gently yet firmly. Hesitating for a moment to look at the unusual saddle, she made her way down one side, up the other and back again, patting the stallion on the rear as she past behind. Toma was tense as her patient exposed herself to a dangerous kick.

The man knew he was in the presence of a woman who knew horses, a peer. "What do you think, comrade, was I right? You have never seen a horse like this."

Kitty looked at the man, tears welling in her eyes. "You would be surprised at the horses I've seen, but the saddle...and no stirrups?"

The man smiled at Kitty. "That is how I learned to ride as a little boy, on reindeer."

Kitty raised her eyebrows, looking at him more closely to see if he was kidding her.

He shrugged in response. "It's true. My father made the saddle for me a long time ago."

"I'd like to hear more about that. My name is Natty. Would you ask the stablemaster if I can ride him in a couple of days when I'm a little stronger?" She reached out her hand, winced in pain when he took it.

He quickly released his grip. "I am the stablemaster. My name is Bek." He looked at Toma who shook her head ever so slightly. "It was nice to meet you, Natty," he said. Maybe we can go for a ride in a few days if it is approved." The stallion started getting antsy to get back to his harem. "I need to turn him out now."

Chapter 55

Shahlo walked into the kitchen of their apartment and put a package in the refrigerator. Joseph, who was sitting at the table cleaning his rifle, said, "What did you bring home for dinner?"

"Chicken. There was an extra one from the dinner the other night, and well, he was already dead, so..." Shahlo stepped over and pecked Joseph on the cheek. "Why are you cleaning your gun?"

"Something to do," he said, setting the oily rag on the table.

"Would you not do that?" She snatched the rag off the table and held it to the side with her thumb and forefinger like it was a dead rat. "Are you going hunting?"

"I was just thinking about getting fired...and it made me want to clean my rifle." Joseph smiled at his wife.

Shahlo made a fist and shook it at him, accompanied by a stern look that ended with a smile. "No point in shooting that *old rabbit* (Brezhnev), he's going to die any day now. Which reminds me; that person that was supposedly shot the other day, it was the woman we saw at the train depot and later on the road. The nurse was pushing her around in a wheelchair and they came into the kitchen. It was like she was getting a tour."

They heard the front door of the apartment open, and then slam shut. "We're in the kitchen," Shahlo yelled down the hallway. When their son walked into the kitchen and Shahlo looked down at his boots, her mouth dropped open. No sound came out. None was needed. Otabek raised his eyebrows – *message received* – and backed out of the kitchen, turned and retreated back out the front door where he removed his boots that were crusted with mud and horse dung.

He returned in his stocking feet. "That better, mom?"

"Better, now go take a shower. You smell like a horse."

"You know, somebody really did get shot the other day. The nurse was

238

pushing a woman around in a wheelchair. They came out to the stable."

"We were just talking about that," said Joseph. "Be careful, it could be something else. The *bears* (KGB) might be looking for..."

"Come on, pop. How likely is it they'd use an old woman to..."

"It's very likely. *Up north* (Gulag labor camps) it was usually a *worker* (fellow prisoner), but sometimes it was women, children; *anyone could come up with a story* (informers)."

"That was *Uncle Joe* (Stalin)."

"I said, be careful. That's all."

Otabek rolled his eyes, looked at his mother and walked out of the kitchen. "I'm going to take a shower before the girls get home from school."

The next morning Kitty was up and ready to go out to the stables when Toma entered her room with a breakfast tray. "Well, you're looking refreshed after a night's sleep," the nurse said cheerfully.

"I feel stronger, too. Can we go for a morning walk? I need to get my blood moving. You don't have to push me around in that damn wheelchair."

Toma, chuckled at her patient's exuberance. "Actually, Dr. Galinski told me to finish the annual medical exams on the dacha's staff this morning; maybe this afternoon."

"But..." Kitty began.

"Now, eat your breakfast. You need the food and juice to rebuild your tissue and the blood you lost." Toma set the tray down on the table near the window. "I'll be back this afternoon. ...And by the way, Dr. Galinski is sending you home, tomorrow. That's why I have to do the exams this morning. I'm leaving tomorrow too, back to Moscow." She shut the door behind her.

The unexpected announcement of her imminent departure took the wind right out of Kitty's sails. She sat down on the edge of her bed, numb. *Back to the factory job; back to her dingy apartment.* Kitty pounded her fist against the mattress, angry, helpless. She did not like being told what to do and when to do it. She gulped down the fruit juice, grabbed a piece of toast from the tray and walked out the door into the hallway.

Kitty descended the back stairs into the kitchen. There was a cook working at one of the sinks with her back turned. Hoping to slip by undetected, Kitty walked as quietly as she could toward the door leading outside. The woman heard her and turned around. Kitty's guilty smile turned to incredulity when she recognized the woman with the astonishing tan-colored eyes. "It is a small world, comrade," said Kitty.

"Yes comrade, it is a small world." Shahlo stood with her hands on her hips, content to let Kitty explain what she was doing there. Shahlo only shared a small portion of Joseph's paranoia. She had accepted that their apartment was probably bugged with electronic surveillance. But she was skeptical about his theory that this old woman they'd met at the train depot was a KGB informant. Still, the woman was sneaking around, literally behind her back...

Kitty's eyes wandered around the kitchen. After a few moments of indecision, she settled on telling the truth. "The nurse is busy and I just want to go outside for a little while." Without waiting for Shahlo's response, Kitty opened the back door and let herself out.

Unfortunately, Commander Kurslov was standing about fifty feet away, studying some papers he held in his hand. He looked up, started to walk toward her. "Is there a reason you are outside, alone?"

"Well, I'm..."

"That's alright, commander. I'll keep an eye on her." The voice of authority came from behind Kitty's shoulder. "Would you like to see the rose garden, Comrade Pushkin?" The Secretary of Agriculture put down the newspaper he was reading and pushed his chair back from the patio table where he was sitting. He extended his arm to Kitty.

"That would be very nice," she replied, taking his elbow in her hand. "Lead the way." Kitty had almost turned toward the garden when she realized how vigilant she would have to be to maintain her cover, acting as if she knew nothing about her surroundings. The security chief nodded his head as Mikhail Gorbachev and Nataliya Pushkin strolled past.

"I couldn't stand to be cooped up on a day like this," Kitty confided when they were out of earshot. "I fear it is too early in the season for the roses to be in bloom, but I would love to see the garden, anyway."

The two sat on a bench near the fountain. The fountain was at the center of a wide ring of trellises, swallowed by climbing rose vines. Carefully designed patches of smaller rose bushes were evenly spaced among the trellises. Kitty remembered that her mother, and the gardeners, had maintained over a thousand bushes.

After chatting for about fifteen minutes, Mikhail patted Kitty on the knee. "I have to go back inside. Maybe you should come along. I'd hate to see them put you in shackles," he joked, getting to his feet.

Kitty accepted his hand and stood up. "You are a young man, Mikhail Gorbachev, and I expect you'll do great things some day. Toma has told me that I am to go back to Smolensk tomorrow. So this may be our last visit."

They began to walk back to the house. "Are you looking forward to getting back home, Comrade Pushkin?" Mikhail could tell by Kitty's tone that she was not excited about the prospect.

"I do not enjoy feeling like a prisoner." Kitty gestured toward the upstairs bedroom, *her cell*, with the tilt of her head. "And I have a good job at the factory." She paused to scan the surroundings, her family's home, her home. She sighed. "But I am fond of living in the country, if only there were a way."

The thinly veiled plea was not lost on the Secretary of Agriculture. "Living in the country would be my choice as well," he said.

Toma was good to her word. By mid-afternoon her medical exams were done and she and her patient were back at their position by the split-rail fence, watching the horses move about. Kitty was seated in her wheelchair once again, choosing not to divulge her clandestine stroll to the rose garden. Toma sat on a bench next to her.

"Look, there's the white stallion coming out of the trees," said Toma, pointing to the right.

"What a beautiful animal." The admiration in Kitty's voice was real, her eyes glued to the white horse. "I forgot the stableman's name. He looked so young."

"His name is Bek...something or other. I understand his father was stablemaster for years. The boy was always following him around like a shadow, helping. So when the father got too old to manage the horses, Bek took over. His father's name is Peter and he's also an excellent mechanic, at least that's what I heard. I know nothing about cars. He took care of the General Secretary's automobiles, up until last week." A smile of pity crossed her lips. "He crashed one of Comrade Brezhnev's cars. That was it for the old guy." As if on cue, the stableman appeared from behind the building, leading a horse that was favoring a back leg, wrapped in a bandage.

Kitty grimaced. The mare was obviously pregnant, which would make whatever the problem was, trickier, maybe fatal.

Toma's medical training and sensitivities did not extend to horses.

Nodding toward Bek but ignoring the lame horse, she said, "For that matter, his mother works in the...is the head cook, I think. She has extraordinary eyes." Toma watched Kitty closely for a reaction.

"What's so unusual about them?" Kitty asked, once again choosing not to acknowledge her morning escapade.

"Natty, Commander Kurslov told me he saw you come out the door of the kitchen this morning. Do you deny it?"

"I'm just a harmless old woman, comrade. I just wanted to go for a walk. I didn't mean to get you into trouble."

"Well Natty, thank you for your concern. But if you break the rules, it is you that will be in trouble."

Kitty nodded, acknowledging the warning.

"Natty, something has changed. You are not going home tomorrow after all. The foreman at your factory is anxious to have you return to work, but Dr. Galinski does not think you can handle the duties in the factory's kitchen yet. So you will stay here for a few more days while you recover. I will speak to the cook about you helping out with the meals for the staff, starting tomorrow."

Shortly after breakfast a black government car waited with its engine running, the driver standing by the door, bored. Dr. Galinski's nurse, stood talking to the security chief, Commander Kurslov. Toma gestured for the driver to come get her bag. The conversation halted when he approached and continued once he was some distance away, something he was quite used to.

"Commander, I do not know what interest Secretary Gorbachev has in this woman. It is probably nothing, yet he did make the call. You're absolutely sure everything checked out with her papers and background?" Toma's eyes bore into the Commander, demanding that he knew he was accountable.

"Yes Colonel Dostrenko, we traced her back more than twenty years, all the way to Odessa. There was nothing out of place. What did you tell Secretary Gorbachev?"

"Nothing. He knows me only to be a nurse on Dr. Galinski's staff. For that matter, Dr. Galinski does not know of my other duties. Other than being a very good doctor, she is an arrogant moron. There is no reason for either of them to be told more."

"Yes Comrade Colonel. And what orders do you have for me?"

Toma looked at him, deadly serious. "Be alert, comrade. There is something odd about Nataliya Pushkin. I have not figured it out, yet. But I can't be away from the General Secretary any longer. It is better that she remain here where you can watch her. That is why I agreed to Comrade Gorbachev's request. Call me once a day to report. If she does something suspicious, call me immediately. The doctor from town will come tomorrow to check her wound and change the bandage. Good bye Commander. I of course will be back next week with the General Secretary." Toma turned on her heel, walked briskly to the car and got into the back seat.

As the car sped away, the security chief sighed with relief. *The bitch is finally gone.* Kurslov noticed the cook staring at him out the kitchen window. He smiled and almost waved. *Careful,* he thought to himself.

Shahlo knew exactly what the commander was thinking. She forced a wide grin. *After several days of peace, later today or tomorrow he is going to be all over me.*

Chapter 56

It only took a few days for Kitty to fall into her new routine. She was allowed to sleep as late as she wanted. Rest was an important factor to help her body heal. However, not being a late sleeper, she was up, sharing coffee and juice with Secretary Gorbachev each morning. They chatted about a variety of things until he had to get to work on the presentation he would make the following week.

After helping Shahlo with lunch preparations for the staff, and eating lunch herself, Kitty was supposed to take a nap; doctor's orders. In the afternoon she split her time out by the stables and helping Shahlo with dinner preparations.

During Kitty's time in the kitchen, she was struck by the number of times the security man, Kurslov, came in to check on her. She thought it was comical that he thought she posed such a threat. It didn't take long before Kitty realized this was only an excuse for Kurslov to flirt with the cook.

Based on the interaction between the two, it was clear to Kitty that the cook had an agenda of her own. It was less clear what that agenda might be. On two occasions they left the kitchen together and she returned alone; once with a button of her uniform undone. Kitty decided that Shahlo was playing a dangerous game.

Joseph was in a dense forest, his environment of choice since he was a boy. He leaned his rifle against a tree and pulled a large branch from a pile of brush, dragging it away. He removed more limbs and sticks off the pile, one after another until he had uncovered several old wooden planks lying flat against the hillside. When he finished clearing the rest of the debris, he grabbed a stick, dug it beneath one of the planks and pried it loose. He made a crack big enough to get his fingers through and pulled the board free. It left a gap that looked like a missing tooth. The black space behind it was just that, black space.

It took Joseph another twenty minutes to remove all the planks. When he was done there was a hole in the hillside that looked like the mouth of a cave. Unlike a cave, it had ancient timbers supporting the dirt and rock; a mine. A silver mine, dug on the Milanov estate at the beginning of the century. This opening on the backside of the hill had served as an escape route for the miners in case of a cave-in. The tunnel had been dug just large enough for a man to pass through, stooped over. It connected with the main shaft, deep in the bowels of the rock where the vein of silver was mined.

Joseph lit the kerosene lamp he had brought with him, grabbed his rifle and entered the tunnel. It was about a quarter of a mile to the main entrance of the mine on the other side of the mountain. The bluff wasn't really big enough to be considered a mountain but that's what they called it when they were little. He had only journeyed from one end to the other twice; once when he was fifteen, with his best friend, Peter Sharikov, and twelve years ago when he had returned to the family estate.

Joseph didn't have a plan. He had a lantern, and he had a rifle. The first thing he needed to do was to prove he could get into the compound undetected. After that, it would be time make a plan.

Shahlo opened the apartment door and shut it behind her. The place was quiet, except for the rumble of their old refrigerator. She walked down the hall, into the kitchen and hit the side of the refrigerator with the back of her elbow to stop the noise. She opened its door, set a package inside and started to unbutton her uniform as she headed for the bedroom.

Joseph was lying on the bed, asleep. His clothes were filthy and torn, scratches on his hands and face. Shahlo stopped short, wondering what he'd been up to. She finished with the buttons and let the uniform slip to the floor, deciding to take a shower before disturbing him to find out. "At least you took your boots off," she said softly, his rhythmic snoring peaceful to her ears.

She turned on the shower, and while waiting for the water to warm up, looked in the mirror and noticed a mark that Commander Kurslov had made on one of her breasts. She closed her eyes and sighed, relaxing her shoulders to release the tension.

Chapter 57

"You should probably be careful about making too much of the record harvest last year; a small pat on your back, maybe. The bar is already set high enough."

Gorbachev tilted his head, looking over his coffee cup and the rims of his reading glasses. "Natty, you are just full of these tidbits of wisdom."

Kitty sat on the patio with the Secretary of Agriculture, discussing the presentation he was to make to Leonid Brezhnev and eight other leaders of the Party. It was to be an update for agricultural production in the Soviet Union. They were at the mid-way point of the five-year plan that began in 1976, the tenth plan in succession since Stalin initiated the framework in the 1920s. Sergei had covered the major points of the plan for Kitty on their voyage across the Atlantic, part of her indoctrination as a good Communist Party member.

Gorbachev set his coffee cup down. "Since the General Secretary labeled the Plan, *Efficiency and Quality*, I will emphasize those aspects of our results, rather than quantity." He looked at Kitty with a twinkle in his eyes. Kitty nodded her head in approval.

Suddenly the twinkle was gone and the face of the Secretary of Agriculture became serious. "Natty, I think it's time to tell me who you really are."

Kitty's eyes fluttered. "I...I don't know what you mean."

Gorbachev sat back in his chair, waiting.

Kitty struggled to recover, her mind racing for a direction, an escape. "I am only interested in helping you if I can."

"Comrade Andropov is behind this, is he not? You are a university professor or something, not a cook in a factory. I never really believed you had been shot."

Kitty tried not to show the relief his answer gave her. There was hope.

If she could only conceal the truth long enough to gain his trust, an ally as a human being. Kitty had been drawn into the intellectual stimulation of their conversations. Over the last several days, they had discussed transportation issues and solutions, balancing supply and demand, concepts about worker incentives, knowledge she had developed over a lifetime as a CEO in the most powerful economy in history. In the back of her mind, there was always the need to be careful. She had obviously let him see too much.

"I have not always been a cook," she conceded.

Gorbachev smiled, accepting her answer as confirmation that he had been right. He and Yuri Andropov were from the same hometown, Stavropol. Andropov was Chairman of the KGB and his influence had helped Gorbachev soar through the party ranks. And Andropov would be attending the presentation in a few days with the other leaders. The balding man with a birthmark on his forehead reached out and gently placed his hand on Kitty's. "Thank you for your advice, comrade."

Shahlo walked into the kitchen, straightening her uniform. She tied an apron around her waist. "Are you almost done, Natty? We're running a little behind."

Kitty looked up, a large knife in her hand, half of the fresh vegetables on the cutting board already chopped, half to go. Kitty gave the younger woman a rather insubordinate glance, and said, "If you would spend more time in the kitchen, things would go more smoothly."

"There was something I had to take care of. Now it's done."

"You are married and have three children," said Kitty, scraping a mound of chopped vegetables into a stainless steel bowl with her knife.

Shahlo turned, her mouth open. A bit of fire in her tan eyes made her look almost feline. "It is because of my husband that I do what I do, comrade." Shahlo immediately regretted her words. She had promised Joseph she would be careful around her new assistant. He had warned her that Comrade Pushkin might trick her into saying things that could be dangerous. Joseph also knew that it would be prudent for his wife to be friendly with the chief of security; to what degree was left unsaid. Regaining her composure, Shahlo added, "I have four children, not three. Our oldest girl, Shirin, is at the University of Moscow." She walked over, took the half-filled bowl of chopped vegetables and said, "Just do your job, comrade."

Kitty grasped Shahlo's wrist, stopping her. "You are right, comrade. It is none of my business. I'm sorry."

Shahlo walked down the hall of their apartment and found Otabek washing a dish in the kitchen sink. "We're going to have dinner in less than an hour," she said. "What did you just eat that's going to spoil your appetite?"

"I was hungry. Found a piece of pie, or something, in the refrigerator and it was great; did you make it?"

"That cheesecake was for your father, young man. No, I didn't make it. My new helper did. Did she come out to the stable again today?"

"She comes every day. Natty knows a lot about horses. She even helped me make a different kind of splint for Muffin. Said it would help support the extra weight because she's so pregnant. That mare's as big as a house."

"You talking about Muffin?" Joseph asked, leading the two girls into the kitchen, now full of people. Marla and Darla both set their books on the counter and headed straight for the refrigerator. The twins were like shadows of each other, their movements nearly synchronized.

"Yeah, Natty helped me make a splint for her today. Sorry I ate your pie."

"What pie?"

"It was cheesecake. I wanted you to try it, dear," said Shahlo, giving Joseph a peck on the cheek. "It was quite good. How was school, girls?"

"Fine," they answered in unison. "Bek, did you eat it all?" asked Darla.

"It was only a little piece. I'm going to take a shower." He wanted to beat his sisters to what might be the last of the hot water.

Shahlo watched her son depart, and then smiled at Joseph and the twins. She opened the refrigerator, pushed aside several things on a lower shelf, reached behind them and pulled out a covered plate. "The nurse told me that Comrade Pushkin is an expert at baking. At least, according to the factory manager where Natty works. So I asked her if she could handle desert for the formal dinner, which is in two days. Natty made this cheesecake with chocolate in it. Maksim will have to approve, but it is so good, even the General Secretary's chef will be impressed."

Shahlo set the plate and three forks on the table. "I had a feeling that it would all be gone if Bek got home first."

"Just cut it in two," said Joseph. "Let the girls eat it. I think I'll have a drink instead." He reached for a bottle of Vodka from one cabinet, and a glass from another.

Shahlo watched her husband and shook her head. "You told me how good the cheesecake was that your cook used to make. I just wanted you to try this to see what you think. It's very good." She stabbed a corner of the creamy chocolate with one of the forks and stepped over to Joseph, who had filled a water glass nearly to the brim. It looked like water but it wasn't. She stuck the fork in his face and said, "Try it."

"It won't compare to Sophie's," he said. He stood up and walked into the living room with his glass of vodka.

Chapter 58

Smolensk, Soviet Union

Joe O'Riley followed Viktor up three steps and through the main door of an apartment building. Inside, there was a stairwell to the right and a long empty hallway in front of them, doors to three units on either side. Each block of apartments had thirty-six units; six floors, six per floor.

Viktor had never been to this building. His meetings with Kitty took place every two months, in a public setting with lots of people around. Their next meeting wasn't scheduled for another three weeks. He was not happy about being here. He was also not happy about being saddled with this young American. *Granted, the kid could speak Russian very well, but he knew nothing, no training. It was dangerous.*

The building's mailboxes, including apartment number and tenant's last name, were built into the wall opposite the stairwell. Joe saw Pushkin above the number 4c, and was excited about seeing his grandmother, though it was hard for him to accept that she was a resident in this dingy place.

The elevator had a two-by-four nailed across the opening, its door gaping half-open, dark inside. They turned to the stairwell and started to climb. Joe outpaced Viktor to the end of the hall and rapped on the door that displayed the number 4c. Kitty's shift at the factory ended an hour ago, so they expected her to be home. There was no response. Joe knocked again, louder this time. He was so anxious to see her that he was gritting his teeth and nearly hopping from one foot to the other.

A door behind them opened and a middle-aged woman stepped into the hallway. "She's not home." When Viktor and Joe glared at her, she added, "Haven't seen her for over a week."

Viktor grabbed Joe's arm and squeezed it hard, a warning not to say anything. His mind quickly ran through the likely scenarios that would explain Kitty's absence. None of them were good. "We're old friends of hers. Do you know where she is?"

"She borrowed an overnight bag of mine and said she was going to visit some old friends. Guess that wasn't you," she said with a smile. "I thought she was only going to be gone for a day."

Joe's agitation was about to boil over. He'd spent a long two days flying to Finland. He waited another three days in a CIA safe-house before crossing the border into the Soviet Union in a truck. Three grueling days later, making deliveries on the way, he made contact with Viktor in Moscow. The day after that, today, he was standing in a rundown apartment building, exhausted, deflated and angry. "Is that all you can tell us?" he blurted.

The woman nearly took a step backward. "Natty said she was taking the train to Ol'sa." The woman raised her hands in resignation. "The apartment supervisor is in the next building, first floor." She tilted her head to the left to indicate which way, and went back into her apartment, quickly shutting the door.

Chapter 59

"Are you ready for tomorrow, comrade?"

The Secretary of Agriculture set his coffee cup down and looked at Kitty, his eyes steady. "Comrade Andropov has advised me that my presentation is being postponed." He raised his eyebrows, questioning Kitty as to whether she was not already aware of this. He was still working under the theory that she had been planted there to help him make a favorable impression with his report.

"Did he say why?" asked Kitty, her face expressionless.

"There are other, more pressing matters to discuss. I am returning to Moscow this afternoon."

"But the shelves in the stores are empty. What could be more pressing than feeding our people?"

"Comrade Pushkin, I do not tell the General Secretary what to include in his agenda."

Kitty wanted to say, *Maybe you should.* "Forgive me, Mikhail. It would have been a big opportunity for you...and your message."

Gorbachev softened his tone. "It was Comrade Andropov that requested we postpone the update on the five-year plan. He wants to use the time to debate the problems in Afghanistan. The United States is meddling in it now. And there is the nuclear arms treaty. Comrade Brezhnev is meeting with President Carter next month."

Kitty shook her head slowly. "The world is a complicated place. It's too bad we fight with the Americans every step of the way."

"Natty, if you and I were in charge, maybe things would be different."

"Wouldn't that be something?" She sipped her coffee, made a face because it had turned cold, and set it down. Kitty's mind was being tickled. "That really would be something." She blinked a couple of times and pinched her earlobe with her finger-tips. "Do you have time to go out to watch the horses for a little while? I want to think about what you just said."

They sat on the bench together in silence, watching the horses graze in the pasture. After about ten minutes, Kitty took a deep breath and let it out slowly. She patted him on the knee, requesting his attention.

"Yes, Natty?"

"Comrade Secretary," she began, "I have decided to take a chance, a big chance. Several days ago you asked me to tell you who I really am. I was not sent to you by Andropov as you suggested. I came on my own."

Gorbachev turned his shoulders toward her, attentive and wary. Their eyes met and held.

"If you asked me if I am Russian, I would say, yes. If you asked me if I am an American, I would say, yes. My Russian name is Catrina Milanov. My American name is Kitty O'Riley." Gorbachev's eyes had grown larger, more intense. He remained silent, but looked as if he might be getting ready to call security.

Kitty read his body language, pressed her palms together and said, "Give me fifteen minutes. Then decide." She pleaded with her eyes and he nodded his head, barely.

She told him her story, the whole story, beginning with growing up in this very house. Bolsheviks murdering her parents, escaping to America. She told him about knowing the Tsar, the brother she lost, Kitty's Kakes. She explained how she had set out on a cruise around the world so she could slip into the Soviet Union, working in a factory in Smolensk, how she came here to see her family home, and was shot.

When she was done, she added, "I am telling you all this because I want to make you a proposal. Before I do, you can ask me anything you want except specific details of how I became Nataliya Pushkin. The United States has agents, the Soviets have agents. Let me just say that I am not one."

Mikhail Gorbachev looked at Kitty, considering his options, astounded at her revelation. "I agree that you are taking a big chance. I can't imagine what sort of proposal you can make that will prevent me from telling Commander Kurslov to arrest you. But let's hear it."

Kitty accepted his response as about as fair as she had a right to expect. "First, if we are successful in what I am about to propose, this property will be returned to me as rightful owner." She looked him in the eye, letting that soak in for a moment. "I'm going to help you become General Secretary."

Chapter 60

By the time the staff's lunch had been prepared, eaten, and kitchen cleaned, Secretary Gorbachev was well on his way back to Moscow.

The Chief of Security picked up the phone on the second ring. "Kurslov," he barked.

"Your guest, Comrade Pushkin, had two visitors at her apartment last evening. Is your printer on?"

"Yes, Comrade Colonel." The hum and clicking sound of the printer immediately filled the security office above the garage. The stylus swept back and forth across the page. Soon, a black and white picture emerged of two faces in a narrow hallway.

"...Yes, commander, that is exactly what I want you to do," said Toma Dostrenko. She hung up the phone and opened the unmarked door of her private office in the Kremlin.

Kitty sat on the passenger's side of the truck next to Shahlo, who was driving. The road was rough, ruts caused by the rain last week, jostling them inside the cab. They were going to town for supplies, including the market to choose fresh produce for the upcoming meals for those attending the meetings. Commander Kurslov had *suggested* to Shahlo that Natty accompany her on this errand. Gludic Bovich was also headed to Ol'sa, though he was driving a black sedan on the road several miles west of them. Kitty gazed out the window, a lot on her mind.

After providing some sketchy details to the Secretary of Agriculture about her plan to make him one of the two most powerful men in the world, she had gotten little more than a shake of his head. "That's ridiculous," he scoffed. He stood up and looked down at her. "I am nothing more than a flea on the Bear's back." He left her to sit on the bench alone. Smiling inwardly, Kitty decided that since she was not yet in handcuffs and shackles, he must at least be thinking about it.

"Are you surprised the chef agreed to the cheesecake without tasting it first?" Kitty asked Shahlo.

Shahlo hesitated. It was Kurslov that had told her to go ahead and get enough ingredients while they were in town. She looked at her assistant and said, "I never know what to expect in this job." Shahlo could tell that the security chief was up to something. But what...?

Joe and Viktor had been wandering around Ol'sa all morning, following the lead from Kitty's neighbor in the hallway of the apartment building. Viktor had declined to speak to the apartment supervisor; too dangerous for everyone involved. So far this morning, they had turned up absolutely nothing in the way of information about Natty Pushkin.

For the last half hour, Joe and Viktor had been sitting on a bench in a small park. The park was across the road from the train depot. There was a large lot adjoining the tracks, used for loading and unloading trucks and train-cars. The state-run grocery store was adjacent to the lot, a very efficient arrangement. If people in the area needed something, this was where they came. Joe and Viktor had discovered that it was literally the only action in town.

There were several open-air stands scattered around the lot outside the store. For goods that were scarce, which was nearly everything, it made little sense to stock the shelves inside the store, just to have them stripped clean a couple of hours later. Joe continuously scanned the people pressing in one line or another for whatever was available. The train had pulled out an hour ago, signaling an upsurge in the crowd. The people arrived in vehicles or on foot from various directions, carrying baskets or empty sacks under their arms. It was too early in the season for local produce, so anything fresh was from the Ukraine and other points south near the Black Sea.

"If nothing happens by the time the market closes, we'll drive back to Smolensk," said Viktor. "I don't like the idea of contacting her factory manager, but..." he shrugged.

Joe marveled at the cars and trucks. They all looked the same, drab and plain. Many were models unfamiliar to him. He watched an old truck, missing one front fender, back into a vacant spot and park. A middle aged woman got out on the driver's side. She limped the first couple of steps, rubbed the stiffness out of her thigh, and then entered the store along with someone that had gotten out on the passenger's side.

Joe was anxious and bored at the same time. He wanted to do something, find his grandmother. He could sense Kitty was in some sort of trouble by how Viktor, a trained agent, was acting. "I'm going to walk around," he said.

Viktor nodded, continuing to scrutinize the crowd without looking like he was interested in the least. By the time Joe had crossed the road and was out of view, Viktor had spotted something that got his attention. It was a man, leaning against a pole, doing exactly the same thing he himself was doing: searching the crowd without appearing to be searching the crowd.

When the man's head locked onto something, Viktor stood up. He meandered across the road, watching the man with his peripheral vision while trying to locate who had prompted the sudden interest. The man's line of sight led Viktor to Natty Pushkin, standing with another woman near one of the stands. At the same time, Viktor saw Joe moving toward his grandmother, grinning like a boy with a new puppy. Years of experience allowed Viktor to hurry through the crowd without being noticed. He intercepted Joe about ten feet from Kitty and slipped his hand over his mouth, an iron grip on his elbow propelling him in the opposite direction.

Viktor stood in line, waiting for his turn. He had an empty sack he'd bought for a couple of rubles from the man next to him. He was keeping an eye on Kitty and Shahlo, who were in another line about thirty feet away. Viktor had sent Joe back to the bench in the park across the street, with instructions to keep his face hidden with a newspaper they had recovered from the trash. The man watching Natty Pushkin was taking care not to be seen by her or her companion as he moved around in the crowd. He also appeared to be looking for someone else. He had pulled a piece of paper from his pocket on two occasions, looked at it and then looked at someone in the crowd. It was obvious to Viktor that it was a picture of a person he was looking for.

Shahlo said, "When we're done here, we'll go back inside and get the things we need for your cheesecake." Most of what they needed was being loaded onto their truck by the storekeeper. Although he didn't know who would be eating the food, he was well aware of the level of authority requesting it. Shahlo and Kitty were standing in line to get some zucchini for Shahlo's family.

Premium vodka, caviar and many other essentials would be coming from Moscow with the General Secretary's chef. Cuban cigars were part of that cargo. Fidel Castro was useful for more than just being an annoyance to the Americans.

Viktor and Joe sat in their car and waited. As Gludic Bovich's black sedan turned the corner, Viktor started the engine, put it in gear and joined the convoy. Kitty and Shahlo led the way north in the old truck. The amount of space between vehicles made it seem that each had the country road to themselves.

"Why do you keep rubbing your leg?" asked Kitty.

Shahlo looked down as her hand massaged the muscle of her right thigh. "I'm not even aware I'm doing it anymore. I broke my leg when I was young. Standing in line, or driving, makes it ache; the changing weather, too. It bothers me more in the spring and fall, but I'm used to it now."

"How'd you break it?"

"I fell. I don't actually remember it. It was pretty bad. We were in the middle of nowhere and Peter saved me. I barely knew him then."

"It's too bad he lost his job." Kitty rolled down her window to let in the warm spring air. "You know, I don't think I even know your last name."

"Sharikov." Shahlo heard a gasp and glanced at Natty, who was staring at her with eyes wide.

Kitty's jaw hung open while her mind raced. She had almost cried, *My brother's best friend was named Peter Sharikov!*

"What's wrong?" asked Shahlo, surprised by the strong reaction.

"I used to know a family named Sharikov when I was a girl, that's all."

"But you grew up in Odessa, right? My husband's family lived not far from here."

Kitty patted her chest just below her throat, calming herself. "I didn't tell Commander Kurslov, but I used to live around here too. A really long time ago. Do we have time to go to Kaspl'a? I'd like to meet your husband to see if we knew some of the same people."

This time it was Shahlo's turn to stare. She tore her eyes from Natty, knowing she had probably said too much already. Joseph had decided to bury the name Milanov over a dozen years ago when they arrived in the area. Since that time, not one single person had ever claimed to have known the Sharikovs...until now.

"We can only stay a minute. If that cream spoils or the melons get too hot..." Shahlo parked the truck in front of the apartment building.

Kitty had been relentless about wanting to meet Shahlo's husband. She had seen his face from a distance that first day through the small rear window of the truck. But after sixty years, the scar, and it was only a glance. *Could this really be the same Peter Sharikov?* Kitty was excited as she followed Shahlo up the walk.

Shahlo was wondering how she had gotten herself into this predicament. "We really need to get back and start dinner." She opened the door. "Peter!"

...No answer. The quiet was deafening to Kitty. The living room was clearly empty. She looked down the hallway toward the kitchen.

"Maybe he's taking a nap," said Shahlo. "I'll go see." For once, she was hoping her husband was at the tavern.

Kitty was one step behind Shahlo as they passed through the kitchen and down the hall to the bedroom. His back was to them when they entered. "Peter, are you asleep?" Shahlo whispered. Kitty was peeking around Shahlo's shoulder, unable to restrain herself. Joseph rolled over.

"Oh...! Oh my god!" Kitty pushed past Shahlo, hands on her cheeks, her eyes riveted on her brother's face. She burst into tears. "Joseph, oh Joseph, I can't believe it." Kitty slid on top of him and started kissing his face, sobbing, caressing him. "It's Trina, it's me, Trina."

Joseph was bewildered, still hazy from sleep. "Shahlo, what's going on? Who is this?"

Shahlo just stood there, watching. She had heard Natty call her husband, Joseph. Nobody had called him that in more than a decade, not even her. "Natty, what are you doing?"

They heard a knock at the front door. Just seconds later, there was another knock, louder, more demanding. "Go see who that is," said Joseph, totally disoriented. Eighty years old, still half asleep, a crazy woman laying on top of him, crying, kissing him, his wife standing there looking down at him. "Who are you?" he demanded, pushing Kitty away so he could focus on her face.

Another knock, louder still, got Shahlo moving. She trotted through the apartment and opened the front door. Gludic Bovich stood there, a stern look on his face, his hand inside his jacket, ready to pull his gun from its shoulder holster. "Where is Nataliya Pushkin!?"

Chapter 61

Viktor and Joe watched as the women emerged from the apartment building. The KBG agent followed them out and pulled the door shut. Concealed behind a row of bushes, Viktor tried to judge the women's status. *Were they being arrested?* They were not cuffed, but there was something odd about their body language. They got into the truck. The agent got back into his black sedan, following the truck down the street as it drove off.

"I wonder what that was all about." said Viktor.

"I think we should follow them," said Joe. "If we lose her now we may never find her again."

"I'm pretty sure where they're going. The dacha is only three miles from here, but I agree. We better follow them...just in case."

They kept their distance, at the edge of sight. When the truck made the turn into the compound, Viktor stopped and turned the car around. "I wish your grandmother was wearing a wire. It would help to be listening in on this."

"Now what?" asked Joe.

"We go back to the apartment in Kaspl'a and see if anyone is still there. If not, we break in."

In the truck on the way back to the compound, Kitty explained who she was. In the short time they had, Shahlo's ears were bombarded with several dozen, rapid-fire sentences that laid out six decades of Catrina Milanov's life. As they were waved through the perimeter check point of the compound, Kitty said, "Tell me everything you can about my brother."

Shahlo drove as slowly as she dared. She began with how she and Joseph had fled the Gulag, breaking her leg, being saved and then living with reindeer herders in Siberia for six years... An impatient honk interrupted her. In her side mirror, Gludic's black sedan was nearly touching the truck's rear bumper. "Up yours," she muttered. She turned to Kitty. "It's not safe to talk inside, and I'll be going home after dinner. Try not to act any differently toward me." She parked the truck at the back entrance leading to the kitchen.

℘

Two hours after dawn, Joseph led the way through the woods. Viktor followed, staying ten feet behind to avoid catching a branch in the face as they maneuvered through the brush. Joe picked up the rear, carrying a flashlight and the kerosene lantern. It took them half an hour to reach their destination. Joseph leaned his rifle against a tree and started to pull branches from a pile lying on the forest floor.

Viktor placed the water bottle and flashlight he was carrying next to Joseph's rifle, and added the semi-automatic weapon he had strapped over his shoulder. Joe followed suit, and within ten minutes, the brush and wooden planks were gone, exposing a black, gaping hole in the ground.

Joseph lit the lamp, grabbed his rifle and said, "I'll go first." He bent over and disappeared into the hole.

Viktor looked at Joe and said, "You go next."

Joe flipped on his flashlight and looked doubtfully at the tunnel. They were about to plunge a quarter of a mile into the side of a hill, beneath millions of tons of rock. He stepped toward the entrance, hesitated, fear building inside him. He turned toward Viktor. "I don't even like crowded elevators," he said. "I'm not sure I can do this."

"You stay here. Keep out of sight," said Viktor, preferring not to have the young American along, anyway. He clutched his rifle, clicked on his flashlight and stepped toward the hole.

"Wait, it's my grandmother. I've got to go, too." Joe stooped down and entered the tunnel before he had a chance to change his mind. The initial thirty feet of the tunnel was straight, descending gradually. His flashlight showed the rough walls and floor of the narrow passage, carved out of the earth with pick and shovel at the turn of the last century. Glimpses of dim, yellow light from Joseph's lantern provided a glow in front of him. The air was cool, damp and musty.

Joe heard Viktor covering the entrance with some branches, and a moment later, the butt of Viktor's gun scrape the wall. Joe was twenty feet inside the mountain, trapped.

Up ahead, Joseph passed the first bend, snuffing out most of the lantern's light. Joe hit his head on a jagged rock and dropped his flashlight. It clattered down next to his feet and went out. Terror seized him in the darkness, the panic of being buried alive. He started to gasp for breath. He tried to turn around, hit his head again and got wedged in his crouching position. "Viktor, get out of the way," he cried, and started to crawl backwards, mindless of the pain to his hands and knees.

"It's OK, Joe, keep coming. I'll help you out."

Kitty's sleepless night left her feeling like a zombie as she began to prepare breakfast. Seeing her brother for the first time in sixty years, and then, having to leave him again minutes later; it was traumatizing and wonderful at the same time. When the KGB agent had stomped down the hallway of the apartment, into the bedroom, Joseph turned back into Peter Sharikov; Kitty into Natty Pushkin.

Shahlo recovered quickly enough to feign outrage at the intrusion. Somehow they had pulled it off. Gludic seemed disappointed and ordered them to return to the compound to unload the truck. He had reported the unscheduled stop to Commander Kurslov, but that no one had attempted to contact Comrade Pushkin there or at the market.

Kitty had the biscuits in the oven and slices of ham in the cast iron skillet when Shahlo entered the kitchen through the back door. A quick glance from the tan-colored eyes, a warning, reminded Comrade Pushkin of the danger of this place. Shahlo tied an apron around her waist and said, "Natty, will you help me take this garbage outside?"

Two minutes later, alone, Shahlo said, "Listen carefully. As soon as the kitchen is cleaned up after breakfast, go out to the stables. Otabek will be waiting for you. Your brother wants you to meet him at *Ivan's Dream*. Peter said you would know what that means; do you?"

Kitty nodded, "Yes, of course. It's the old silver mine. It was our hiding place when we were kids."

"Can you still find it?"

Kitty nodded again.

"Otabek will have a horse for you to ride. If someone sees you, just tell him the stablemaster got tired of you pestering him, so he finally let you go for a ride. By the way, Commander Kurslov has approved it, unofficially.

Understand?"

Kitty understood that *unofficial approval* probably meant that *sins-of-the-flesh, Shahlo's flesh,* were part of the bargain.

Shahlo saw some of the staff walking toward the kitchen. "Come on, it's almost time for breakfast." They closed the trash bin and quickly headed back to the kitchen. "One more thing," Shahlo said in a low voice. "Your grandson will be there too...and a man named Viktor."

"Joe's here?" Kitty stopped abruptly. A barrage of thoughts, fighting for attention, swept through her mind. "How...how can that be?"

"No time now," said Shahlo, tugging on her arm. "Breakfast is late."

Chapter 62

Kitty saw the white stallion in the corral through an opening in the trees. He was looking distressed about being separated from the mares. She entered the stable from one end just as Otabek was leaving from the other. He had a rope in one hand and a canvas bucket in the other. He turned when he heard the door creak. "It's going to take a few minutes to catch one of the mares, sorry."

"Wait!" Kitty moved hastily to join him. She saw the anxiety on his face melt as a broad smile took its place.

"Aunt Trina," he said softly. "I never thought I would ever get to say those words." He tilted his head down and kissed her cheek. "Bovich stopped me on my way here to ask me some questions. I'll hurry, though." He raised the bucket of oats to show her that he had the proper enticement.

Kitty said, "The stallion is already in the corral. I'll just ride him."

Otabek looked at her apprehensively. "My dad told me stories about how you used to be able to ride as good as him, but..."

"I could ride better than him. Probably still can. And I'm not as old as he is."

Otabek smiled at the fire in her voice, the confidence. He could tell they were brother and sister. He shook his head, still not convinced.

They walked outside. Beyond the corral, they heard the sound of motors through the trees, early arrivals for tomorrow's meetings that would begin with a formal dinner tonight.

"Let's see how he reacts to you," Otabek said, opening the gate to the corral. He's pretty nervous right now and those cars aren't going to help."

"I'll do it." Kitty reached her hand into the bucket and came out with a fistful of oats. "What's his name?"

"Majesty."

Kitty's head snapped around in surprise. She hesitated as tears formed in her eyes. "That settles it then," her voice heavy with emotion. She started to glide across the corral, a smooth stream of words easing the tension with every step. The stallion's ears, which were pricked high in full alert, started to soften. Otabek saw in her manner a powerful gentleness that worked like magic on the volatile stallion. Kitty let him sniff, and then eat, the oats in her hand while she rubbed his muscular neck. After a long minute of gaining his trust, Kitty said, "Give me a leg-up."

Amazed at what he had just witnessed, Otabek said, "I'll go get a saddle and blanket."

"Don't need 'em. Just give me a boost."

Otabek did as he was told, impressed at how she slid onto the stallion's back so easily. He started to drape the rope around the stallion's neck...

"I don't need the rope either. When we get to where we're going, I'll let him go. I'm sure he'll come back to the mares." Kitty patted the horse on the neck, grabbed a fistful of mane and walked him out of the corral, into the pasture.

Otabek started to trot off toward the trees.

"Where are you going?" Kitty asked.

"I'm going to open the pasture gate for you."

Kitty smiled at her newfound nephew. "Don't bother. My brother would never give the name, *Majesty,* to a horse that couldn't jump."

Otabek cringed at the thought of his newfound aunt going airborne with no bridle, no saddle...just *riding* bareback was challenging enough.

Kitty clicked her tongue and the stallion broke into a high-stepping trot, nearly prancing, as they got the feel of each other. Kitty made a wide circle, back to where Otabek was standing, and said, "Changed my mind, Bek, go get the gate. Maybe twenty years ago, when I was still a kid..." She smiled and shrugged. "No reason to show off."

As Otabek headed for the gate, Kitty turned the stallion in the opposite direction, leaned forward, and gave him her heels. They galloped along the perimeter of the pasture with Kitty hugging tightly with her legs, flowing with the motion of the powerful animal. She blew Otabek a kiss as she passed and he closed the gate, watching them ride down the trail until they were out of sight.

Commander Kurslov, focusing on a monitor in his office, rubbed his chin as the white hindquarters of the stallion disappeared into the trees. His misgivings about approving the ride ratcheted up several notches by the display of horsemanship. He began to fumble with knobs to align proper surveillance cameras to various monitors on his console. He had expected Comrade Pushkin to be cautiously walking one of the mares along a riding trail, enjoying the sunshine. Instead, it looked like he might have allowed his prisoner to escape...on the day the General Secretary was to arrive. Not to mention, a dozen other top leaders, and his boss, Colonel Toma Dostrenko.

Kitty rode along the trail, choosing one fork and then another, maintaining the general direction she needed to go. With more than a mile to cover, she relaxed and reminisced about rides just like this in her childhood. She tried to guess what was around each bend, but couldn't. However, when presented with the view, it was immediately familiar. On a long, straight stretch Kitty urged Majesty to pick up the pace. The stallion was more than willing, lengthening his stride, flying past the trees. It was the most exhilarating ride she'd had in years.

When they crested a hill, Kitty recognized the spot immediately. She slowed them to a trot, a walk, and then patted his neck. "This is it." Kitty slid off his back in one smooth motion, slapped the white stallion on the rear, and said, "Go back to your girlfriends."

She stepped off the trail and waded into the dense trees and underbrush. Working her way up a draw, she soon reached the mouth of the old silver mine. The foliage had grown unimpeded for so many years a person could easily walk within thirty feet of the entrance without knowing it was there.

Joseph stood in the shadows with his rifle cradled in the nook of his arm. Viktor stood next to him, his AK-47 semi-automatic hanging from its strap over his right shoulder. As Kitty entered the mine she couldn't see anything until her eyes started to adjust from the glare of the sunshine outside. Gradually, like ghosts emerging through the stone walls, the shapes of two men became apparent. They were dirty, disheveled, and grinning like schoolboys.

Kitty rushed forward to embrace her brother. Joseph had just enough time to hand his rifle to Viktor before the impact. "I was hoping you could remember how to find this place," he said, as they squeezed the breath out of each other.

Kitty cried tears of joy, holding on, feeling every inch where their bodies touched. She looked at Viktor through blurry eyes. "Hello Viktor."

"I'm glad you're alright, Natty. I was worried about you." The agent was scolding her without showing his fangs. "Do you think you were followed?"

"Not unless the KGB has grown wings. That white stallion is a lot of horse." She loosened her grip on Joseph and stepped back. "Shahlo said my grandson was with you. Is Joe in the Soviet Union?" She looked down the mine shaft into black nothingness and then back at Viktor. "Is he here?"

"He's guarding the entrance at the other end, waiting for us. Here's a flashlight. Are you ready?"

"Ready for what?"

"To leave. We came to get you out of here. The other entrance is outside the perimeter fence. The sooner we go the better."

Kitty looked at Joseph, who nodded. He knelt down to re-light the kerosene lantern for their trek back through the mountain. "Wait a minute," she said. "We need to talk about this first."

Viktor handed Joseph's rifle back to him. "You're sure this mine is in a blind-spot for the surveillance cameras?" He stepped over to the entrance and peered out.

"I'm sure they were able to watch Trina part of the time on her way here but there are lots of gaps. This area is one of them."

"Good, but I still don't like it. By now, they've probably seen the horse without a rider. We should at least get farther into the mine. How about that room?"

"Ivan's Dream," said Joseph. "Follow me." He picked up the lantern and led the way.

Kitty followed her older brother into the mine, just like she had a thousand times when they were kids. She was looking forward to seeing their old hiding place, though her mind was focused on their plan to escape...or not. They had to crawl the last twenty feet when they entered the side-tunnel.

Joseph set the lantern in the center of the space that was like a small room, the solid rock ceiling about five feet high. Kitty investigated the far end of the room where her father and Ivan, the mine foreman, had created a cave-in to hide the rich vein of silver. She could tell it had not been disturbed in all these years. The silver was still there.

"We don't have much time," said Viktor. "Natty, what is there to talk about? The KGB are not stupid. When they discover who you are and that the CIA helped you, you're going to prison. Or shot as a spy. This may be our last good chance."

"I've already told them who I am," Kitty said defiantly. "At least, one of them. And he knows I had help getting into the Soviet Union." It struck Kitty that she had probably put Viktor in more danger than she previously realized. She softened her eyes and her tone. "I didn't give him anything specific...and he isn't KGB."

"Natty, there is no way for you to know who is or who isn't KGB. Believe me. And they have ways to make you talk." Viktor was already doing an analysis on the chances his cover had been blown, and the implications.

Joseph looked at his sister and said, "It wasn't the nurse, was it? Toma? Shahlo thinks she is KGB because of things Kurslov has said, and the way he acts around her."

Kitty stared at him in disbelief. "Toma?" Kitty started to feel the walls closing in on her. Her naivety was going to get them all killed. "It wasn't the nurse. It was the Secretary of Agriculture, Mikhail Gorbachev."

It was Viktor's turn to stare. "He is a member of the Supreme Council. Did you know that?"

"I don't even know what that is," Kitty admitted. "I just know he's different. We've talked a lot...about a lot of things."

Viktor shook his head. "We have to go. It might already be too late."

As Viktor started to rise, Joseph held up his hand to stop him. "Trina, why did you tell him who you are? You must have had a reason."

Kitty knew how it was going to sound before she said it. She said it anyway. "We talked about how things could change in the Soviet Union, how it could be better. I told him I wanted to help make him General Secretary."

The silence that followed was total. Viktor and Joseph looked at Kitty to see if she was serious. They looked at each other. They looked back at Kitty.

Viktor closed his eyes. When he opened them, he said, "I'm leaving. You should come too. We can get you another alias, get you settled somewhere else. It is not safe here."

"Viktor, I'm sorry if I have put you in danger. This is something I want to do...am going to do." Kitty looked at her brother. "Joseph, we might not live here as Milanov's, but we are home and we are together. If this works out, who knows...?"

Viktor waved his hand, as if swatting at flies. "This is lunacy, Natty, suicide. Mikhail Gorbachev has some support from Yuri Andropov, but he is too young. Most people don't even know who he is. He is never going to be General Secretary, and you are never going to change the Soviet Union; believe me. If I could carry you out, I would."

"Thank you, Viktor, for the help you have given me. I have cheesecake to make. There is a big dinner tonight."

Epilogue

A month later, Joe received a letter, delivered by government courier to his Kansas City home. Separate copies of the letter were also delivered to Logan Sweeney, CEO of Kitty's Kakes, and Daniel Mitts, President of the First National Bank of Chicago. It spelled out how they were to create capital from Kitty O'Riley's various holdings. The funds were to be wired to a specific account in Langley, Virginia. Daniel Mitts received a second letter, stipulating that a certain file, labeled *Ignace*, be relinquished, unopened, to Nathanial Polk, Director of the Central Intelligence Agency.

After a year with no further word whatsoever from his grandmother, a knock on Joe's front door interrupted his train of thought. He was standing at a table in his office, making final revisions to construction drawings for a new shopping mall. Without lifting his eyes from the plans, and slightly agitated, he said, "Would you get that dear?"

Brownie Dreher O'Riley closed the dishwasher and dried her hands on a kitchen towel. She peered through the small window in the door before opening it. The man on the front step wore a serious expression. The blood drained from Brownie's face as she flung the door open. "Mr. Bishop, what is it!?" The Deputy Director of the CIA looked surprised, and then smiled. Brownie began to breathe again.

"Mrs. O'Riley, may I come in?"

"Of course, I'm sorry." She stepped aside and turned. "Joe!" she yelled toward the back of the house.

The urgency in her voice brought her husband to the foyer at a trot. When Joe saw Frank Bishop he stopped abruptly, mouth open, no words. When Frank smiled at him he reacted exactly as his wife had. He began to breathe again.

A few minutes later, the three of them were seated in the living room.

The Deputy Director set his glass of ice tea on the table next to him and said to Brownie, "Congratulations."

Her eyes twinkled as she placed her hand on her belly. "Does it show already? I'm only three months."

Frank raised his eyebrows. He pointed at her left hand that sported a diamond ring. "I meant getting married." His face reddened a little. "And now you've given away your secret. Well, congratulations again."

Joe was quickly becoming impatient to hear the purpose of this unexpected visit. "Thank you, sir, we're very excited. Now, tell us what's up."

The Deputy Director produced a single sheet of paper from his breast pocket, unfolded it, and handed it to Joe. "This is an accounting of the funds we have been managing for your grandmother for the last year. At this time, we intend to return the full amount to you...as soon as you tell us where you would like to have it deposited."

Joe looked at the figure at the bottom of the column of numbers. It was slightly more than twenty million dollars. He met the Deputy Director's eyes, expecting an explanation.

"Your grandmother is doing a service for this country. We have been monitoring her activities and have concluded that if she is successful the impact could be significant to our national security. There is, however, considerable personal risk involved. Director Polk has decided to provide funding and whatever support is necessary to assist her effort."

"Are you saying that my grandmother is now working for the CIA?"

"I suppose that would be a reasonable way to describe it, with two exceptions. She is neither receiving a salary nor taking orders from *The Agency*."

Leonid Brezhnev died on November 10, 1982. Shortly thereafter, the first block of Natty Pushkin's plan was put in place. Mikhail Gorbachev's mentor, Yuri Andropov, was made General Secretary of the Soviet Union.